Dear Readers,

Since we first started advertising *Scarlet* books we've had a lot of positive feedback about our covers, so I thought you might like to hear how we decide which cover best fits each *Scarlet* title. Well, when we've chosen a manuscript which will make an exciting addition to our publications, photo shoots are arranged and a selection of the best pictures are sent back to us by our designers.

The whole *Scarlet* team then gets together to decide which photograph will catch the reader's eyes and (most importantly!) sell the book. The comments made during our meetings are often intriguing: 'Why,' asked one of our team recently, 'can't the hero have even more buttons undone!' When we settle on the ideal cover, all the elements that make up the 'look' of a *Scarlet* book are added: the lips logo, the back cover blurb, the title lettering is picked out in foil . . . and yet another stunning cover is ready to wrap around a brand new and exciting *Scarlet* novel.

Till next month,
Best wishes,

Sally Cooper

SALLY COOPER,
Editor-in-Chief – *Scarlet*

PS I'm always delighted to hear from readers. Why not complete the questionnaire at the back of the book and let me know what *you* think of *Scarlet*!

About the Author

One of **Barbara Stewart's** earliest memories is of living next to a library and opposite the swimming baths – was she the first swimming bookworm? When she grew up, she dreamed of being a librarian, but money was scarce, so she went to work as a secretary.

In her cherished spare time she loved the theatre, jazz, countryside and the sea, but found time to marry and raise two wonderful sons.

Then Barbara decided to enrol in a writing course . . . but the tutor told her there was little he could teach her. 'So,' says Barbara, 'I made my own course. I read everything I could get my hands on. I studied good writing. I wrote all the time and I subscribed to writers' magazines. Writing is craft and practice. You teach yourself as you go along.' In 1992, Barbara's first novel was published and she hasn't looked back since.

*Other **Scarlet** titles available this month:*

SUMMER OF FIRE by Jill Sheldon
DEVLIN'S DESIRE by Margaret Callaghan
STARSTRUCK by Lianne Conway

BARBARA STEWART

INTOXICATING LADY

SCARLET

Enquiries to:
Robinson Publishing Ltd
7 Kensington Church Court
London W8 4SP

First published in the UK by Scarlet, 1996

A copy of the British Library Cataloguing in
Publication data is available from the British Library

ISBN 1-85487-707-0

Printed and bound in the EC

10 9 8 7 6 5 4 3 2 1

To my sons, Keith and Stephen,
with love

CHAPTER 1

Don't panic. They've made a mistake, that's all.

Reading the letter a second time, Danielle tried to ignore the sinking sensation in her stomach. *It's the computer – yes . . . the computer. Someone will probably say.*

Of course.

Forcing herself to take a calming breath, she almost laughed.

Almost . . .

The letter that could blow her world apart fell from her fingers on to a nest of bills. With an air of 'when things need doing, do 'em' the telephone was in her hand and she was punching out a number. At the same time her eyes went to the window facing her desk.

From where she sat, straight-backed, leaning on her elbows with the receiver to her ear, listening to the ringing tone and humming a shaky song, she could take comfort from the sight of row upon row of fruit-laden vines.

Rooks wheeled and cawed overhead, drawing her

attention to a sky as thick as a beige carpet – a sinking sky, not far from the thinning treetops. It was one of those end-of-the-world days – a day like a visitor who hadn't wanted to come and was determined to remain gloomy.

Not good. Bad weather, especially wet, could do a lot of damage during harvest-time. She sighed inwardly. Not to mention birds and rabbits. She could have done without shocks like this letter, that was for sure.

Nonetheless, her voice was steady and she even widened her mouth into a smile, for that was her way. 'Piers Lamont, please.'

The reply in her anxious ear, however, caught her unawares, being neither jocular nor charming enough to be Piers – unless she had interrupted one of the hangovers to which he was apparently – and proudly – prone.

'Piers Lamont's office – Kingsley Hunter here,' announced a voice, stone-cold sober and indifferent. 'Who is speaking?'

Her smile died. 'Danielle Summerfield. It's urgent. When do you expect Piers – ?'

'Aha . . . Miss Summerfield.'

Something in the voice sent prickles down her spine. She pushed a strand of dark hair from her face with cold fingers. And something else . . . intuition if you like . . . told her that she had played into this man's hands by ringing.

'You can forget about talking to Piers for quite a

while.' The words shot down the line in a way that made her cheeks sting.

Who does he think he is? She rustled through papers and envelopes. Where was that letter? Pouncing on it, she noticed for the first time that the letter was not signed by Piers; the signature was godawful . . . She peered closer in the gloom. The frowning, black looped scrawl without a doubt, she thought with irony, belonged to the owner of *that* voice catapulting into her ear now.

'Have you a problem, Miss Summerfield?'

Have I a problem? Try bankruptcy for size! Scanning the printed title beneath his name, she pulled a resigned face. All right . . . so he was Lamont's sales and property director!

She waved the headed notepaper like a white flag. 'This letter I've received from you . . .'

'Well?'

She bit her lip. It was as if a heavy hand had come down on her shoulder with a message. *Remember . . . remember who he is.* He sounded just as you would expect the director of a countrywide chain of wine shops to sound. Yet Piers, the top boss, was a lamb – with a sense of humour. He hadn't mentioned that he was going away; the trip must have been unexpected. She felt a flood of relief. Of course. Mistakes happened when the boss went away, didn't they?

Easing her voice back to its natural warm, low pitch, she said happily, 'I believe there's been a

3

mistake. The letter says you'll have to call and negotiate the contract for next year, but – '

'I know what it says. I read everything I sign.'

'Yes, but . . .' She gave a most un-Danielle-like croak of a laugh. 'Piers said the contract was already prepared and would be automatically renewed, so – '

The voice smashed down like a butcher's cleaver. 'Did he? Well, well. From where I sit I see nothing in writing. So,' he snapped, I must carry out the proper procedure and negotiate.'

Her stomach lurched. 'Piers is quite satisfied with my wines and my prices,' she told him stiffly, slapping the letter down on the desk.

'When did he tell you this?'

'Just a few days ago.'

'He visits you regularly, I understand?'

There was an insinuation in the tone of voice and choice of words that she didn't grasp right away; she only knew that he got her back up. Yet a voice in her head was reminding her, most insistently, that this was no way to behave to a customer. You might almost say, to *the* customer. She groaned silently. *So cool it.*

With an almighty effort, she smiled into the telephone. 'Look, as I said, this is a mistake . . . if I can just talk to Piers – '

'We'll discuss it tomorrow,' he interrupted icily.

'Tomorrow?'

'I see from the diary that he is in the . . . er . . . habit of seeing you every Tuesday. My, you're

4

honoured, aren't you? For Piers Lamont himself to make an hour's drive from London to visit our smallest wine supplier . . .'

She sucked in her breath and answered curtly. 'Piers happens to be a family friend.'

There was a brief and stony pause, followed by words just as curt. 'Nevertheless, I'll come in Piers's place. Tomorrow at . . . five o'clock, isn't it? Rather late for a business discussion, but maybe he comes for something else too. Tea or a glass of your wine. Whatever . . . I trust I'll be offered the same hospitality.'

You'll be lucky, she thought truculently, smarting at his tone. It was most unfair; she had never spoken to the man before and he had no reason to attack her this way.

'Really, Mr Hunter, I don't . . .' It had been on the tip of her tongue to say that there was no reason why she should do business with someone as repulsive as he, but she was stopped just in time by the warning flash of red from the window envelopes scattered on her desk.

He might almost have guessed her unspoken words, for he bade her a brief goodbye and rang off with a deadly click. For a moment her heart responded, and sank to her green wellies. When the buzzing in her ear changed to an anxious wail, she fumbled to replace the receiver, wiping her damp hands against her tense, denim-clad thighs.

Her wide apart eyes were unusually sombre, with an anxious frown between them. Tomorrow she would have to meet Kingsley Hunter in the flesh. Ugh! She wrapped comforting arms around herself, as if cold, rocking slightly. To think that only this morning she had felt that the tide had turned and her smile, when she had greeted the day, had been real, not forced.

Then Griff had delivered her mail, and then she had made a telephone call and spoken to an odious man who, she was sure, never smiled. She heaved a despondent sigh. Kingsley Hunter would be a flushed, puffy, under-exercised sufferer of high blood pressure and over-indulgence – which gave him his *charming* temperament, she decided, with unaccustomed sarcasm.

Longing for a breath of air, she jumped up, walked around the desk – a great monstrosity which had been her grandfather's delight – crossed the room to the door, and stepped out of the wooden hut.

As she pulled the door closed behind her a sickly sun pushed the frowning clouds apart and looked down.

Delighted, she raised her face, allowing the calming warmth to drape her shoulders and relieve the tension. Somewhat restored, she let her gaze wander contentedly among the grizzled trees of the orchard over on the right then return to rest on the most satisfying sight of all.

Stretching as far ahead as she could see, and as far to the left, as if the world began and ended there, were her vines, marching up the slopes like a massive green-clothed army.

She mentally registered the hum of machinery coming from the winery behind her office, gave a satisfied nod and trudged in the opposite direction, tucking her hair inside a man's shabby tweed cap as she went.

She headed for the sloping ground where the vines grew; rows of skinny bent trunks crucified upon lateral wires, holding up precious clusters of grapes.

Then she was amongst them, smelling them, touching them, tasting sweet juice on her tongue and feeling that special, spine-tingling joy. Her generous mouth widened in a gratified smile as she plodded along dappled sunlit corridors, where vines stretched overhead and grass grew long – for every effort was concentrated upon harvesting.

In four weeks the harvest would mostly be finished – apart from the Chasselas grape, which wouldn't ripen until mid-November; time enough then to get the grass cut . . . and there were other jobs piling up. She ducked to avoid dangling fruit: plump, mouthwatering and, after months of work, tremendously exciting to see.

Then she heard it. A sound that chilled her blood. She stopped in her tracks, stomach churning.

Wind. Hissing through the orchard below. Then it came puffing and blowing up the slope, rustling the vines so that the hand-shaped leaves threw dancing shadows on the soil, wiped her face with the vinegary scent of grape – a scent that it seemed to her had been with her always. The thin voices of pickers, a dog's

bark, twittering birds – all were muffled by the
louder voice of the bullying wind. She shivered
with the old fear.

She had no desire to return to the office and the
nightmare echo of Kingsley Hunter's voice, so there
was nothing for it but to grit her teeth and make her
way up through the dithering shadows towards the
pickers, concentrating upon telling herself what a
fool she had been to let that man rile her. Hadn't
Grandfather always make a big thing about being
nice to customers?

A door in her memory clicked open. She closed it.

Her, 'Morning, girls,' was cheerful. Pulling cutters
from a pocket of her dungarees, she reached up and
clipped through a stalk. The heavy cluster of fruit fell
into the palm of her hand, the grapes as cold and firm
as green marbles. Humming to herself, determined to
ignore the wind, she placed it in the bin with others.

Working alongside the down-to-earth girls had the
desired effect. With her feet firmly astride, she
breathed in the sweet smell of trodden down reddish
earth, peppery weeds and grapes. Her mouth widened
with laughter and mischief set her pixie-like face alight
beneath the cap which bundled her dark hair out of the
way – something else that needed cutting, she supposed, but not to worry . . . after the harvest . . .

The picture she had drawn in her mind of Kingsley Hunter made her dark eyes dance as she picked.
She could see him now; tight mouth, piggy eyes . . .

Damn him for spoiling my day.

CHAPTER 2

The day had begun like any other for most of the people living in and around the village of Hidden.

Cherie Smart, widow, who ran the post-office-cum-general stores, placed a mug of tea amongst the bubble gum and cheap chews on the counter in front of Griff and requested the latest gossip.

Griff, to whom this was a daily ritual – his red Royal Mail van could be seen parked innocently outside the shop every weekday morning at nine – merely smiled knowingly and gulped his tea.

He greedily eyed the glass dome which protected a selection of cakes. 'I'll have one of those,' he said. 'Something that won't make a mess; that Bath bun will do.' Paula had used to cook him a nice breakfast; she had got up at five, especially. Now fat was out and roughage was in. Whitewash milk and branflakes were no company.

'Much more to do?' Cherie enquired, lifting out the cake with tongs and using a white paper bag for a plate.

Griff set down his mug, thanked her and took the

9

cake. 'Just the village. I dropped off a load at the vineyard.'

'Oh?' Cherie perked up. She was a tall woman, in her late fifties. Her hair was rigidly waved, the colour of builders' sand, and her expression was usually curious or half-knowing – occasionally confused. Sharp blue eyes observed life magnified by imagination and thick-lensed glasses. Her angular body seemed back to front, for while her back curved in her stomach ballooned, and she had developed the habit of resting her arms on it when standing. As she was doing now.

Swallowing cake, Griff remarked, 'Still can't get used to seeing the post addressed to her now – instead of the old man, like.'

'I'll tell you something else,' Cherie said through tightened dark red lips. 'People still talk about the way Danielle and old Mrs Summerfield acted at the funeral. Still warm in his grave, he was, when that girl went back to work.' Her mouth settled into a thin line of distaste.

'She carries a lot on her shoulders,' Griff countered, in his taut, stubborn way. 'She gave my girl a job, and lots of others around here are grateful to the yard for work.' He picked up his mug, washed down the last of the cake with a mouthful of tea and wished he dared light a cigarette. But if he did the news would get back to his wife faster than the speed of light.

'Lack of respect, if you ask me.' Cherie sniffed and turned her head towards the window, her eyes seeing something other than the red van, the green, the church and the school. 'Daniel Summerfield,' Griff heard her say, 'was a wonderful man. Not everyone,' she announced importantly, 'knew him as I did.'

The door opened, setting the bell jangling in its own peculiar way. It was a nagging, bellyaching bell that got on everyone's nerves.

Griff looked round with a guilty expression.

'Morning, Postman.' The door jangled closed.

'Just talking about your boss, Joanna,' said Cherie, standing erect and looking down her powdered nose, which was in its sniffy 'incomers' mode.

'Lucky Danielle,' Joanna drawled huskily, drawing deeply on her cigarette.

Cherie took in the woman's dark, windblown cropped hair, ruddy complexion and stocky body. She had a strong, square face with an uptilted nose, hard blue don't-mess-me-about eyes and – so they said – a sharp tongue. Cherie decided to say nothing about the 'No Smoking' sign.

Joanna smiled knowingly and dug into the pocket of the old jeans she was wearing. 'Half a pound of cheddar, please. I forgot to get it at the supermarket.'

While Cherie plunged wire murderously through a slab of cheese Griff gulped the last of his tea. 'When you get to the vineyard, would you remind my kid, Suzie, it's early dinner tonight?'

'Will do,' Joanna answered, glancing at her watch.

'She sometimes calls at a mate's house after work,' he added fondly.

Joanna gave him a long look, went to speak –

11

didn't. An air of 'laugh and the world kicks you in the teeth' wove around her with the smoke from the cigarette she still held in one of her long-fingered, pale and unexpectedly soft red-tipped hands.

Griff quickly placed his cap on his head. 'We go to the supermarket every Monday evening,' he fussed. 'It's quieter then, like.'

Cherie slapped the greaseproof-papered cheese down on the counter. Griff opened the door; teasing smoke followed him out.

Joanna coughed. 'Put this in the window, will you?'

She held out a postcard.

Cherie took the card and read it. Her nose wrinkled. 'Oh!' she exclaimed, looking up. 'Oh, dear – you're going to – '

Joanna's cherry-red sweater loomed across the counter. 'Am I? Well, well.' With a sweet smile, she whispered, 'Don't tell anyone, will you?'

And, while Cherie looked at her in confusion, the door clanged open and in burst a cheerful chatter of relieved-to-be-free mothers.

He came in like the wind.

One minute Danielle was alone, the next the office door burst open and she looked up from her paper-strewn desk with a start.

He was as tall and lean as her conifers, and expensively suntanned, with silver hair groomed to shine like a crown on a regally held head.

What disturbed her most was that while she had

12

pulled her gaping mouth almost immediately into a smile, he was regarding her grimly. It was like holding out a welcoming hand and being rebuffed as he swept forward, inspecting her the way he might a maggot in his healthy salad at his no doubt exclusive restaurant.

He didn't offer his hand, so neither did Danielle. She was too busy trying to hide the fact that she felt intimidated.

It was for all the world as if a wild animal had burst through the door, and her immediate reaction was the primitive one: instant flight. The feeling was followed by a niggle of annoyance with herself – and with him.

The curl to his lips might have been a smile or a snarl, for his voice mangled the niceties, perhaps deliberately. 'Afternoon. You're the boss, I take it?'

The aggression on his face – Slavic in shape, with well-defined cheekbones – said plainly that she had no right to be any such thing.

Her skin tingled a warning. Tilting her chin, she crashed straight into a stare coloured the blue-grey of wet slate.

'Pleased to meet you, Mr Hunter,' she lied. 'Take a seat.'

She watched him drop his no doubt vitamin-filled body, with a sinuous grace for his size, not into the chair she had indicated across the no-man's land of her leather-topped desk, but directly beside her, with the air of someone deliberately trying to annoy.

Feeling at a disadvantage, she swivelled to face him. The high-backed chair gave a series of miserable squeals.

She sat on its edge, brown leather boots pressing down on the green carpet tiles, trying to keep the chair still, as if a squeaking chair let her down in some way.

She had faced bullies before. Even convent school had not been without its bullying element. As a result, she had learned the hard way that you stand up to them, that you never, ever let them see you're afraid. It made you tough, being short.

He flicked back green shirt-cuffs. Danielle, who was prone to flashes of insight, recognized a more refined version of rolling up sleeves and inviting a fight. Her body tensed.

I have no reason to be, but I'm afraid of him.

All he said was, 'Well! Surprise, surprise.' His voice and the way he looked her over were slow and deliberate, with unconcealed hostility. 'Danielle . . . I imagined a Danielle to be a tall, slim, sophisticated blonde.'

Being the dead opposite, a typical endomorph, she coloured, retaliating sharply, 'Sorry to disappoint, but my appearance has nothing to do with business.' Her preference to be friends with everyone made her add an uncertain, 'I'm known as Danny.'

'Of course,' he nodded, knowing-eyed.

Danielle moved uncomfortably. The chair objected. What was happening here?

It was strange, her reaction to him . . . unlike

14

anything she had known before. If asked to describe how she felt, she would have said, like swimming in a dark sea with a shark somewhere nearby.

She disliked the way he was studying her – curious yet indifferent at the same time, if that were possible. And she was irritated by his insolent tone as he went on.

'Danny suits you better. Rounder, smaller – the playful puppy type, who maybe sometimes bites off more than she can chew.'

She clicked her tongue, sighed. 'You can call me Danielle.'

With that, she crossed one leg over the other and rested her hands on the frayed armrests of her chair, trying to look cool.

She had a heart-sinking impression that everything wanting in the office – and there was a lot – was crying out for his attention.

And not only the office. To her annoyance, she felt a faint heat burning her skin at the way he was inspecting the ginger trouser suit and knotted cream shawl which she had slung on in a hurry to replace her working clothes. He might have been examining a bottle of wine, the way he studied her shape; she felt almost lifted up and held to the light. What was he searching for?

'Voluptuous, spicy – but not to my taste. Too vinegary,' was his slick verdict.

She made herself count to ten. *I'll be pleasant to him if it kills me!* And with enormous will she made her tone of voice teasingly friendly.

'Your taste might change when you grow up. Can we get on with business, Mr Hunter?' She flashed him one of her really brilliant smiles.

His disapproving expression made mincemeat of her smile, but he flicked open a black leather brief-case. Her imagination whirled . . . flickering celluloid images . . . black cases . . . pistols at dawn.

Idiot! Pull yourself together.

She watched him drawing out a plastic file of papers, holding them in a hand which had quite obviously been recently holding a Tequila Sunrise at a beach bar, while he replaced the case on the floor.

She put on a polite face as he discussed prices and quantities. Not for a moment would she let him see how his emphatic purr was turning her inside out with worry.

He didn't waste words. Having already put her on the defensive, he was now placing her in the invidious position of having to fight for her business – having to sell herself cheap if he had his way. And he looked like the type who always did have his way.

When the talking stopped, a silence, weighing heavily with hopelessness, took over.

He sprawled back in his chair, with one gleaming black shoe across the other knee, irritatingly relaxed and sure of himself. She saw the look he gave her – a look that said plainly, You've no chance.

She folded her price list in two, fingers smoothing the edge, visualizing Piers sitting here in the office last week, facing her with those enormous, latching-

16

onto-you dark eyes which dominated his small face. Dear, familiar, safe Piers, with his thunderous brows and lightning smiles and terrible lavender shirts.

As clear as if he were here now, she could hear him assuring her that Lamont's profits, despite ominous rumblings from the City, had remained steady; she could hear the rise and fall of his mellifluous voice, the affectionate tone of sincerity, as he dismissed her fears that Lamont's might order less wine from her. What had happened to that contract?

And what was going on now? It seemed as if Kingsley Hunter was taking advantage of the situation; maybe it was kudos he was after, in Piers' absence?

What would Grandfather have done in my place?

What Kingsley Hunter did was to raise his brows and hold out his hands, palms up, in a most insolent indication that he was waiting.

It hurt her to say quietly, 'I'll freeze my prices for a year. That's as far as I can go.' It was, she told herself firmly, a question of principle – as well as the fact that she would find it difficult to survive if she reduced her prices. On the other hand, if she lost Lamont's order, survival was even less certain.

Her tongue nervously flicked her lips as she stared down unseeingly at the razor-edged paper in her hand.

'Where *is* Piers?'

'Piers? Preparing for a long holiday.' Watching her head shoot up, seeing her disappointment, he

17

narrowed his eyes and added coldly, 'Meanwhile, I'm in charge.'

Her heart sank, for unconsciously she had been hanging onto the thought of Piers and the powerful, leave-everything-to-me aura that his small stature oozed.

Her bottom lip jutted out. 'I'd like to speak to Piers before he goes.' But then her heart gave an anxious flutter, for Kingsley Hunter's quarter-smile had triumph and something spiteful in it.

He had a habit of slowly shaking his head in a knowing way. He did it now. 'I'm sure you would. But no go. You deal with me from now on.'

Glancing out of the window behind her, which overlooked the winery, he added something which knocked the stuffing out of her.

'You never know. My company might make you an offer for that.'

She was momentarily speechless. 'The vineyard's not for sale.' The words came out like a cry of pain. 'Whatever gave you that idea?'

'My enquiries told me – and I've very reliable sources – that things here are a bit dicey.'

'Rubbish,' she snapped, resenting the sensation she had of being stalked and edged into a corner.

'I've done my homework. It seems that your grandfather believed in putting most of his eggs in one basket – my company being the basket.' Get out of that, his expression said.

Her glance flickered to the tweed cap on her desk

18

and she fought to hide her panic, for in truth she couldn't deny what he said. But the reasons were obvious. Lamont's was the biggest wine shop chain in the country, and she still had a vague memory of being introduced to Piers as a child, of her grandfather's delighted face shedding years of lines, of his excitement about a contract and her impression that Piers was a kind of Father Christmas. He and her grandfather had been friends ever since – a fact which seemed to irritate Kingsley Hunter.

He smiled – sort of. 'That's the way it is,' he said softly, 'and you damn well know it. Without our contract, you're finished.'

Danielle felt like someone who had been leaning against a fence when it suddenly fell down.

It was hard to breathe all of a sudden.

Her heart banged against her ribs, in tune with the machines in the winery next door.

To give herself time to recover, she sought comfort from the familiarity of her territory: the three walls taken up with windows, the north wall filled with charts, calendars, graphs, notices and photographs. She even registered the sounds, like the sore-throated scream of the crows, a distant tractor, the trundle of fork-lift trucks from the cobbled yard. Familiar things in a suddenly unreal world.

Her stricken eyes moved back to the photographs. A silly move because there he was – dour yet so stalwart, so dear – and she still missed him, even though he had been gone almost a year. She felt a

19

knife-like thrust of pain, and the child in her raged at him for leaving her alone, even, at this moment, for leaving her the vineyard.

Kingsley Hunter, meanwhile, with a satisfied twist to his lips, was watching her closely. Could he, she wondered, be pushing me because I'm a woman? Her lips tightened. She was unprepared for the primitive sensations that being cornered aroused, the scratch of her nerves as spite clawed inside her like an animal seeking release. For the second time in her life she wanted to hurt someone.

For the second time in her life . . . she could do nothing. The vineyard came first. Just like then, she was powerless.

She hated him for bringing it all back.

There was a small explosion in her head – so real she almost jumped.

Her hostile glare took in a face that was younger than she had first supposed, tanned skin almost unlined, hair a shade lighter than his grey hand-tailored suit, and black shoes – the sort sold by those little shops in Bond Street which only catered for expensive feet. Everything about him touched a raw nerve.

A scene unrolled in her memory . . . Grandfather, with his weary clothes, exhaustion set in his face like concrete – a stern face that Grandmother could light up like the matches he put to his cigarettes . . . There were overheard promises: one day you'll have a holiday, my love; I'll take you back to Italy.

Returning her thoughts to Kingsley Hunter, there was no doubt in Danielle's mind that he could afford to buy a vineyard himself, if he wanted one; she couldn't help feeling resentful.

For the man who had everything . . . one vineyard!

'Why . . .?' Her voice came out hoarse. She cleared her razor-filled throat and began again. 'Why would your company want to buy a vineyard which, according to you, is in difficulties, Mr Hunter?'

'Because we have sufficient funds to put in more modern equipment, and my business sense is clearly far superior to yours.' His voice lowered to a self-satisfied, irritating purr. 'The place has potential, in the right hands.'

He might just as well have said, 'in a man's hands.' She bridled, responding in a stinging tone. 'Especially at a bargain price, right? I can't believe this. If I don't cut my prices you'll withhold the contract, force me out of business and come in with a rescue package. Charming!'

Despite her contemptuous outburst, he remained impassive. He merely shook his head, as if at a foolish child. 'We're free to order from whichever supplier we can get the best deal from. They call it business. As for buying the vineyard – ' a mocking note entered his voice ' – think what you could do with the money. A nice little home somewhere, no worries . . .'

She made her eyes hate him. 'Don't make me laugh!' Worried sick, she added, 'I'll let you have

21

the discount, and I'll manage – because I've plans you know nothing of. And as far as selling is concerned . . . no deal.'

Her mouth crashed closed.

Their glances collided and held, reflecting deep, dark, stubborn anger and blue-grey surprise.

She knew by the feeling like a sinking brick in her stomach that she had gone too far. This wasn't the way a business meeting should go. Was it her fault? How come there was an undercurrent of tension and the peculiar feeling that they were not discussing business at all? It was, of course, possible for two people to meet and feel an instant dislike, to rub each other up the wrong way; it happened all the time. If only it weren't happening with this man.

'There's just one more thing . . .' he said, rising to his feet, addressing the top of her seething head.

'Surprise me, Mr Hunter.'

Expecting the worst, she watched him gather up his papers and slide them into the plastic folder.

My life disappearing into a body bag.

'Before I consider the contract any further,' he said, slipping the file into the briefcase, 'I want to spend a week here looking into the way things are run, and your . . . er . . . association with my company.' Two loud reports, like gunshots, locked the briefcase. Her insides reacted with a frightened quiver.

'I'm not with you.' She frowned, watching his nonchalant stroll over to the wall. 'Everything is perfectly above board here. Why?'

He stood with his back to her, studying photographs of the vineyard, from when Daniel Summerfield had first started it in the 1950s up to last year. He moved on to a framed sampler and, with his legs planted apart, hands clasped behind his back, read the words aloud. ' "The Wine of Life keeps oozing drop by drop, The Leaves of Life keep falling one by one".' Words which, quite naturally, had wrung her heart over the last few months, and she felt her nerves tighten.

It was as he stood there, so sure of himself, flaunting his power, with his finger on the destruct button of her life, that she was shaken by the weird sensation that this man had come to hunt her down.

You're imagining things, she told herself, watching his unconcerned tour of her office . . . past the fridge, her mud-caked wellington boots by the door, the wine rack, the kettle and coffee things on top of the filing cabinet with half a bottle of milk, a Mars bar . . .

'What do you mean, Mr Hunter?'

He stopped short, his eye caught by something on the hospitality table – her latest idea. He appeared displeased.

There were bottles, glasses, a biscuit tin, corkscrew and a copper bowl of roses . . . late summer roses, dripping scarlet petals over a plain white cloth.

Reaching out, his brown fingers grasped a bottle by its long green neck; he lifted it and read the label.

When he turned to face her, it was as if his features were carved in stone.

'I'm hoping, Danielle Summerfield, you'll invite me to stay in that charming Tudor cottage of yours.'

She caught her breath at the unexpectedness of it. For a moment she could only stare at him. Finally, she gave an indignant cry. 'That's blackmail – it's . . . it's unfair.'

'Unfair?' He strode towards her, thumped the bottle down on the desk and rested his hands on her bills. 'Life is unfair,' he stated. 'More so to some people than to others. In order to secure your . . . er . . . co-operation, the contract will be handed to you on the day I leave.'

She knew she would never forget this moment: his face, gaunt with irritation, thrust close to hers, a hint of throat-catching aftershave and, above all, the accusing slate eyes that splintered her bones . . .

She found herself recoiling. 'You can't . . . I live alone and . . . and you know what villages are for gossip . . .' Her voice trailed away; it sounded pathetic, even if true.

He laughed – a laugh that made her blood run cold. 'I should imagine that your reputation keeps the bush telegraph busy.'

She heard the breath whistle in through her teeth. 'Hold on!' She hurled the words angrily into his face. 'The only reputation I have around here is for hard work.'

He straightened up to well over six feet, towering

over her, oozing contempt. 'Missed something, then, haven't they?'

'Damn cheek!' She jumped up, leaving the chair swinging and shrieking. 'You come here, threaten to cancel your order, make slanderous accusations and suggest buying not only my business – ' she eyed him wildly ' – but me too. Well, neither is for sale . . . You can go jump – '

'Buying you?' he cut in, eyebrows arched. 'I don't want *you*.' The corners of his mouth twisted. 'Good God, girl! Let me tell you my taste in both wine and women is impeccable. Separate rooms will do nicely, thank you.'

'Separate rooms?' She stood with hands clenched, her eyes dark pools of doubt and suspicion and dismay.

He smiled. 'Don't look so disappointed.'

Never had she felt such hatred. 'I don't take paying guests.'

'Then perhaps you should.' He pointed a finger at his head. 'Business sense!'

Seeing a 'got you' – type gleam in his eyes, her urge to slap that complacent face was becoming un-controllable! He had deliberately misled her in order to humiliate her and, what was more, somehow he had made her defensive outburst seem like the temper tantrum of a child.

Her fingers grasped for and closed around the cold neck of the bottle . . .

Looking amused, he snatched up his briefcase.

25

'Am I invited?' he asked, swinging across the room to the door, 'Or . . .' he pulled the door open '. . . first thing in the morning do I cancel the order on the grounds that the business is not efficiently run?'

Seeing her face, he added, 'I'll move in right away – the sooner the better; my gear's in the car. What time's dinner?'

'The chef's just walked out.'

'In that case . . . I believe I saw a pub in the village. I'll be back.'

The door snapped closed.

She heard his smart shoes crunching gravel, and when that faded she found herself still gripping the bottle with a picture of her vineyard on its label. She pulled it up to her chest and held on tight, battening down, as she had learned to do, the part of her that she knew subconsciously was wilder than it should be.

A car engine sprang healthily to life. Beyond the window behind her desk the winery building hid all but a corner of the new car park from her view, but from there the self-satisfied nose of a Mercedes appeared, the same colour as his hair, its body as long and sleek, purring contentment. Spurting gravel, it turned and bounced away down the track until she could no longer see it, could only imagine its journey past her cottage and out through the gate beneath the sign, 'INTOXICATING LADY' meaning 'woman who enjoys life'.

She pictured him turning into the lane. He would

speed along the straight part, between the shipsmast pine woods, would hopefully lose himself in the twisty, dead-leaved lanes, where great oaks met overhead . . . But no . . . just her luck . . . he would end up in the aptly named village of Hidden, and with no trouble – the village being merely a green circled by houses, church, school and shop – would find his way into the car park of The Pilgrim's Rest.

Oh, God, if only he would carry on to the motorway and not come back, she cried to herself, as the full impact of her situation hit her. He had her by the throat. She was helpless and he knew it.

In fact, he knew an awful lot about her. The humiliation of being in his power cut her deep; she had seen by the look in his eyes that he was aware of it and was enjoying her helplessness.

Blinking back tears, she pushed her price lists to one side, picked up Lamont's letter, crushed the ice-white paper and hurled it across the room.

CHAPTER 3

Danielle lay in bed, in the beamed room she had slept in as a child – the room she had continued to use after Grandfather died and Grandmother Francesca moved away.

In the larger bedroom across the hall floorboards creaked, a resisting drawer squealed and grated shut, curtains rattled along the tiny windows close to the sloping floor.

The horror of it. Her adored home, her retreat, her privacy. Invaded. Her face on the pillow was sulky and, to be honest, she felt unusually sorry for herself.

Kingsley Hunter had returned from the pub within an hour. She was crouched at the pine kitchen table, trying to force herself to eat, when a cannon-like boom echoed along the passage as the outraged lion's head knocker smashed against stout oak in an insistent, bone-splintering summons. Her slippers whispered reluctantly across chilly stone to answer it.

She had been trying to pretend it was all a nightmare, and it certainly was unreal enough to be. But the noise he was making was hardly her imagination.

Wrenching open the door, she stood back, fervently wishing she could refuse to let him in. With a curt nod, he stepped into the hall, accompanied by a coolness smelling of languishing bonfires and night-scented creepers. Closing the door, she panicked quietly and calmly pointed to the stairs.

'Up there, first right.' *I can be abrupt, without being rude*, she decided.

His cold eyes rested on her briefly before travelling up the carved stair-rail and polished wooden stairs to the stained glass window on the landing and the table before it. There was a vase on the table, a tall vase of willow-green crystal, in which she had arranged bronze and cream chrysanthemums, and beside it a copper bowl filled with the spicy orange and ginger pot-pourri she made herself. With the night shut out the hall seemed to be gently breathing a warm, intimate welcome.

He sniffed. 'Mmm! What's up the other flight of stairs, to the left?' he asked, resting a glossy leather weekend case on the floor.

'My bedroom, a bathroom and a spare room at the end of the passage. Your room was once two – it stretches from front to back and has the benefit of three windows overlooking the front of the vineyard – ' she took a deep breath ' – and the woods and hills.'

She might have been a landlady receiving a guest, which was how she had decided to play it. It was

29

annoying, therefore, to see his lips twitch as if he found her speech amusing. 'You've a shower and toilet,' she added huffily, turning pointedly towards the kitchen. 'So you won't have to use the bathroom at my side of the house.'

'I might prefer baths to showers.'

'Tough!'

With her good resolution gone by the board, she flung herself back into the kitchen. There was a way of closing a door that said, Stay out . . .

Her thoughts whirled. Thank goodness she had persuaded Grandy to have the *en-suite* bathroom installed in his bedroom; he had begrudged the expense, but she had cajoled him into it for Francesca's sake. After he'd died, Francesca had moved out after a row over the vineyard. She had wanted Danielle to sell.

Just as well, Danielle reflected, that she had not moved then from her own bedroom, which meant that the big one, with its king-sized four-poster bed, was still empty of possessions.

Call it sentiment, but she had not wanted to use their bedroom somehow; there was something reassuring about her childhood room, even if she had only used it during the school holidays. Perhaps because of that. For, hating boarding-school as she had done, her room during the holidays had been nothing less than a haven. From the window-seat she could see the vines and she could almost touch the limbs of a great beech tree, her silent guardian and friend and receiver of confidences for as long as she could remember.

Her omelette was cold, and as she chewed she was reminded of chewing an eraser – a disgusting habit which had become the rage at school once. She swallowed and it dropped into the chaos that had once been her stomach. If only she could wipe out the fear she felt, this extraordinary fear. He made her feel different in a way she didn't like.

A sound at the door seemed to rattle her bones. She glanced around and then pointedly back at her plate.

He sauntered inside. 'Just exploring.'

'This is the kitchen,' she said with sarcasm.

His aftershave filled the room with something like ferns and damp moss and sun-warmed tree-bark; he had removed his jacket and tie and his shirt, in the palest of pale greens, looked as if it might feel like velvet to the touch and exposed his tanned throat.

Just look at him. Who does he think he is?

He prowled, inspecting the rack of drying flowers and herbs above their heads, her array of copper and brass – not as polished as they might be – the blue-patterned china on the pine dresser, books on cookery, wine and aromatherapy, teddy bear magnets on the fridge and a newspaper-covered table by the window crowded with geraniums she had brought in for the winter and had not got around to repotting and which had now shown their disgust by growing long and spindly in an effort to reach the window and escape.

'That won't make you grow up to be a big girl,' he remarked, inspecting the remains of the omelette.

Her knife and fork clattered down onto the plate. 'I suggest,' she said with grim politeness, 'that seeing as you have for devious reasons of your own landed yourself here, you allow me to live my life as I'm entitled to. This is not a police state; I can eat what I like, go where I like and live how I like.

'If you don't allow me the courtesy of that, then I shall purchase a tent and put it up in the car park and live there – and to hell what people think.' She took a deep breath. 'Or I could even,' she said with relish, 'ask Francesca, my grandmother, to come and stay; believe me, she'll have your life history off you before you can say blackmail.'

She saw Kingsley Hunter raise his brows; she saw surprise in his slow smile.

'You know,' he said, placing his hands on slim hips, 'you're quite a cat – you hiss, hiss . . . scratch, scratch!' A quizzical gleam lit his eyes. 'What's your playful mood like, darling? Do you purr-rr?'

With an exaggerated sigh, she jumped up and stalked to the sink, filling a bowl with water, squirting washing up liquid with a vengeance. 'I suggest we spend as little time together as possible,' she told him, scraping the remains of the omelette into a bin and crashing her china and cutlery in the water.

She glared through the small window which framed a view of the yard, downcast washing dangling from a line, an old shed, a backdrop of hills. She had dreamed of turning the shed into a shop, maybe serving teas. *Dreams!*

'There's a portable television in the corner over there; you can put it in your room. I hope,' she said, snatching up a teatowel and a plate, 'to keep the sitting-room to myself.' She pressed a switch and coffee began to filter into a jug, mouthwateringly fragrant. 'I'm making coffee,' she announced unnecessarily. 'Help yourself to some.'

The machine made a rude gargle. After drying her hands, she thrust the teatowel on a hook with such force that the hook, being the adhesive type, fell off the wall. Sighing, she poured her own coffee, added sugar and milk, and, feeling she had settled the domestic arrangements with the right amount of aloofness, she carried her mug out of the kitchen across the hall into the sitting room and slammed the door closed with her foot. Not before noting however, the surprise on his face.

It gave her some satisfaction to think that he had probably expected her to run around after him, entertain him, lick his expensive shoes!

Nevertheless, she stood for a moment with her back to the door, eyes closed, hearing the creak of the stairs. Maybe she should not have reacted the way she had; maybe she should be kowtowing to him because of who he was. But she couldn't . . . she just couldn't.

Pulling herself together, she stood her mug on the bureau and crossed the room to the French doors.

Pushing them open, she stepped out onto a walled area which the sun-loving Francesca had planned to make into a patio, with flowerpots and garden furniture.

Danielle had little time for such indulgences. She breathed deeply, drawing in the comforting, invisible presence of the hills, calmed by the peace of it. Light suddenly plopped down from the upstairs room, splashing onto the concrete, removing the shadows from her eyes. She stepped back inside, drew the heavy chintz curtains and switched on brass table-lamps.

At the other end of the room – this room had probably also been two small ones in the last century – she swished the curtains closed against the sight of his car in the car park, gleaming in the dark like a grey slug.

Back at the bureau, she bent her head into the rose-pink pool of light from the lamp. Her face was grave as she checked receipts and bills, jabbed at a calculator, nibbled her pen and sipped coffee.

At last she sighed, sat back, massaged the back of her neck, stretched and, with a groan, flung down her pen.

Okay, you're trapped. Accept it, she told herself firmly. She went through various points one by one. Kingsley Hunter disliked her for some reason, yet he wanted to stay here. Why? There was something fishy about his explanation. As well, there was a mystery somewhere. Had it anything to do with

Piers' sudden holiday? And why the antagonism? Had she taken it too personally?

She acknowledged a weakness in her character, an inability to cope with being disliked, which as a child had made her feel physically ill enough to vomit. *Surely*, she asked herself, *I've outgrown this? I'm mature and confident enough now not to yearn to be liked by everyone. What does it matter whether Mr Hunter likes me or not?*

On the other hand, maybe he just disliked women. He could be enjoying a sense of power. It took all sorts!

After two hours she was no nearer the answer, and it bugged her. A problem was one thing; you saw what needed doing and sought the solution. But, in this case, parts of the problem were like muddy water; how did you cope with what you couldn't see?

Only one thing was clear. She was – damn it – dependent upon him for the contract. Which meant she had to accept his conditions. *Remember that*, she warned herself, yawning. *Try to behave and not get his back up.*

Curb that tongue of yours, the silver-framed photograph on the bureau of a white-haired, tomato-faced stern man seemed to be saying. Be good.

It was always 'Be good'. Euphemistically speaking . . . Don't disturb the more important things there are to do.

A week isn't much to give up, she told him silently,

yawning again, rubbing her gritty eyes. It's not for ever.

In the end she'd slammed the accounts book shut and gone to bed early with a wine growers' magazine.

Unable to concentrate, she lay sleepless, listening to the gentle hoot of an owl, the scream of an animal, the creaking of old timbers inside the house and living boughs rustling outside. Sounds that were familiar.

But some were alien. When her uninvited guest used the shower, the plumbing rumbled through the house like an express train, and she imagined him standing beneath the jets. The thought made her flesh tingle.

Restlessly she burrowed her face in the calm white pillow, wishing the great rumbling tummy of the cottage would settle down so she could get some sleep. The cottage sounded as upset as herself. 'What have I done to deserve him?' she groaned aloud, dreading the morning.

CHAPTER 4

Danielle gave Kingsley Hunter an angelic smile and swirled milk from a blue and white jug onto Shredded Wheat.

He had just made her day by telling her that he would be going to his office each morning.

She hid her relief behind a mask of indifference and an exaggerated sniff. 'Your toast's burning.'

Over by the electric oven a knife scraped toast, setting her teeth on edge, and acrid smoke wafted towards her; she was really put out of her routine, she decided, coughing. She normally slopped around in her dressing gown before throwing on clothes, going down the track to do her rounds and then into her office. Once Griff had dropped by with the mail and she had sorted through it, she joined the pickers – the best time of the day.

'I'll be back by three,' he told her. With a crash, the pan returned beneath the grill; the pedal bin's gaping mouth received the blackened toast and thumped closed.

'I don't care what time you return,' she told him,

pouring milk into her coffee. The coffee turned pale and she sighed, for she was supposed to be pleasant, wasn't she? Not to crawl – she couldn't do that, not for anybody – but hadn't she decided last night, to . . .? 'I mean,' she added, 'you're a guest. Come and go as you like.'

Sliding the grill pan out again, he cursed. 'This handle's hot.'

She couldn't help laughing. 'Gets like that.'

His expression said that an efficient household would own a toaster. And his glare was an open message that she was far from being the wine of the month. It seemed to include her hair, her jeans and the fawn sweater which had been made for a longer body than hers. As most clothes had.

Pushing back her hair, which for some reason Francesca had described as a barbed wire entanglement – she never joked about appearances – Danielle watched him spread his toast with butter. *No point in wearing anything decent with the work I have to do. Just because he's clingfilm wrapped and untouched by human hand . . .*

While he ate he paraded around the kitchen, stopping before the calendar. It was a watercolour print of Victorians enjoying a picnic; a cloth was spread with a carafe of wine, a loaf of bread, china and a spray of roses. There was a verse beneath.

Taking a gold pen from his jacket pocket, he circled a date, replaced the pen, washed his plate and teddy bear coffee-mug and stalked from the

38

room. The scent of aftershave and soap remained, to mingle with charred toast and coffee and resentment.

'If you need anything from my company, you speak to me,' he ordered her grimly, head skimming the top of the door as he turned. 'Piers is unavailable, so don't try to contact him. His mail will be opened by either a secretary or myself.'

So what? She frowned, hearing the stairs squeak beneath his tread. No more than a minute later he was bouncing back down, passing the open kitchen door carrying his briefcase. She saw his disdainful glance at her wellies in the hall, heard the front door slam, his shining shoes crunching down the path and . . . Damn!

The gate had fallen from its hinges at last and was leaning against the wall, she remembered; she imagined his expression and mockingly put a finger to her nose and pushed it up in the air.

Blowing out her relief, she jumped up and went to the calendar. The date he had marked was the following Monday; thank goodness, his last day. Remembering his restless pacing, she didn't feel that he was keen on being with her either. Then why was he here? She frowned to herself, sighing for her normal, peaceful breakfast-time.

The day had started badly, and didn't improve.

She had her head stuck in the ice-cream cabinet, searching for her favourite consolation – chocolate

Cornetto – when Cherie called out, 'Heard about Joanna?'

'What about Jo?' If only Cherie would restock her ice-creams more often. 'Aha!' Danielle cried, like a detective in a murder case. She held up her frozen hand in triumph. 'Got it!'

'Joanna's taking in ironing,' Cherie said, with a challenging look.

'Is she?' Danielle wondered about biscuits, but probably Mr Hunter didn't eat things like that.

Cherie was intent upon pursuing her subject. 'Don't know where she gets the time from. I mean, she has her job with you, she plays with the band and teaches music at the school, now the ironing. I never have a minute to myself,' she said importantly.

'Some people are like that,' Danielle murmured, absorbed in peeling just the right amount of wrapper from the ice-cream, as you would a banana. 'Always have time, some people.'

Cherie went on the attack. 'Seems you aren't paying her enough, if she needs the ironing.'

'I pay the going rate,' Danielle retorted, prodding an indignant tongue into her ice-cream. Swallowing, she added, 'Anyway, her job isn't full-time, you know.'

Cherie glanced from the window. 'There's another one no better than she should be.'

'Who?' mumbled Danielle, from a cold, chocolate-filled mouth.

'That Annette – always with boys. She'll get herself into trouble, that one. 'Course, she came from London. It's a weird set-up, if you ask me.'

The chocolate ran warm down her throat now. 'I'll have half a pound of butter, Cherie.'

Cherie took the butter from the fridge and slid it into a bag, saying, 'There's Joanna's first husband still living in the village, in the house *they* built together, with his second wife and her daughter, and Joanna living just down the road.' She gave a disapproving sniff. 'Like something you read about in the papers.'

Danielle placed a packet of spaghetti on the counter and caught icy drips from the cornet with her tongue. 'Jo doesn't live in the village exactly; she needn't come here if she doesn't want to.'

'We never wanted that house to be built,' Cherie confided. 'We had a petition about it, if you remember.'

Danielle crunched the cornet and swallowed, shaking her head. 'I was probably away at school. Anyway, it's a nice house. And Annette gets on well with Jo.'

'Goes to visit her,' Cherie confided, clasped hands resting on her stomach, thumbs moving together in a kind of dance. 'Weird, if you ask me,' she said excitedly.

Danielle tossed the ice-cream wrapping in a bin and wiped her hands down her jeans. 'Know what I think?' she asked, pulling a purse from her shoulder-bag.

41

Cherie's thumbs became still. 'What?'

'Bread,' stated Danielle. 'I think I'd better take some bread, too. A toaster, please, and one of those ready-to-bake French loaves. I'm too tied up to go to the supermarket this week.'

Watching Danielle go, Cherie sourly wondered why she was smiling so grimly to herself.

Danielle had dealt with quite a few problems – not least being machines which thought they had reached retirement age – by the time Kingsley Hunter's Mercedes slithered into the car park. He came to find her straight away.

She was standing outside the winery talking, and she swore under her breath when she saw him loping towards her with an easy, graceful stride. 'Let's keep our fingers crossed that it works, Tom,' she said with a quick smile, and walked away. Better if Mr Hunter didn't know about her troublesome machines.

'Trouble?' he asked, coming up to her. She could have hit him.

They exchanged venomous glances across a pallet piled with plump purple grapes. The sweet and sticky air was loud with the moaning of hovering flies and wasps. He moved lightly to one side to allow a fork-lift driver to pick up the pallet and rattle away with it inside the shed. Almost immediately another fork-lift whined across the yard to pick up the next.

She waved her arms. 'Everything's fine.' Leading him away, she kept her ears pricked for the blessedly normal rumble coming from inside the massive shed.

'Are the grapes picked and processed on the same day?' he asked, crunching along beside her.

'Naturally.' She threw an impatient glance up at his set face. 'And how was your . . . er . . . half-day? How do you manage to do Piers' work as well as your own?'

'By being well organized, by delegating and by preparing in advance,' he answered, in his sleek way. 'Besides, maybe Piers didn't have a great deal to do – apart from visiting vineyards and wine-tastings.'

His voice hardened whenever he mentioned Piers, she noticed curiously, and did she imagine the sarcasm? Certainly he didn't seem to like Piers – which was odd, she thought, picturing the elegant man with a riveting presence of whom she was terribly fond.

They were heading towards the vines, and as Danielle glanced anxiously up at the moody sky all thoughts of Piers went from her mind.

After a while, the man stalking beside her announced, 'I telephoned Piers this morning. I told him I'll be spending some time here looking into the business. He didn't seem particularly pleased, but no doubt once he begins his holiday all thoughts of work and its . . . problems . . . will disappear.'

Murmuring an absent-minded, 'How nice,' she stepped off the path, crushing tough weeds and grass underfoot.

A sudden grip on her arm prevented her from

walking, and she paused, looking up questioningly into accusing eyes. 'Did you hear what I said?'

She pulled away, shocked to feel the imprint of his fingers stinging her skin beneath the sweater. 'I heard. Whatever are you so touchy for? Piers is going on holiday – so what?' She lifted her arms and let them slap her thighs. 'Maybe I'm not in the mood for conversation, I have other things to worry about, like rain and mildew. Okay?' She found herself almost shouting.

'You're an unfeeling bitch. Or is it sour grapes because he didn't tell you himself? No pun intended.'

'Piers didn't talk much about himself,' she objected, feeling confused.

'Of course not. Men like that are weavers of spells,' he retorted. 'They need mystery.'

With that, he stalked away between the vines, setting overhead grapes swinging and leaving Danielle staring after him, rubbing the back of her neck with the air of one desperately puzzled and trying to make sense of things.

After a moment, with an exasperated 'Damn you' addressed to his disappearing back, she flung herself the other away.

It wasn't long, though, before her steps slowed and she strolled up the slope, trying to retrieve her contentment. It was good here alone, with the leaves throwing shadows on the sweet-smelling earth, and just birdsong, the thud of rubber boots and the swish

44

of long grass in her ears. Nevertheless, his spiteful words rankled . . .

Reaching the pickers, she cheerfully called out greetings and started to help load up a bin, listening to their conversation.

'Hey, Jo, who's that bloke?'

'Don't know, Suzie. But he's got a sexy walk, whoever he is, and I adore tall, distinguished-looking men.'

Danielle, picking steadily, refused to look round.

She heard shrieks of laughter.

'He's more my type, Jo . . . sophisticated – y' know what I mean?'

'Lay off. You're still wet behind the ears. Look at that posh suit . . . that tan. Wouldn't look twice at you.'

'No,' came the retort. 'Because once would slay him!'

'Ha! Ha!'

An imaginative description of the muscle, skin and bone beneath the suit brought more laughter, and Danielle's lips tightened. Ignoring them, she carried on with her work.

'Good afternoon, ladies.'

Danielle, without turning round, called out in a warning voice, 'This is Mr Hunter, girls. He's . . . er . . . going to be around for a few days, learning about the vineyard business.'

Stretching, she snipped and lovingly cradled the cold bunches in her square, tanned and stained hands.

45

'Can I help?' he drawled, coming up beside her.

Placing the grapes on top of the pile, she threw him a pitying glance. 'In those clothes?'

'As I'm here to learn,' he persisted, 'how many acres do you have?'

Popping a grape in her mouth, she rolled it on her tongue, nicking the silky skin with her teeth so that the juice burst into her throat. The flesh had just the right squelch to it.

Come off it, she wanted to say, you must have read up on my vineyard. But with the girls' ears flapping, she could only swallow and tell him sulkily, 'Twenty.' Unable to keep the pride from her voice, she added, 'Grandfather started with six.'

'It's a dicey business – with the English climate, I mean,' he suggested.

'Not really. At the moment my main worry is rain – could cause rotting. As long as grapes get adequate days in the summer above twelve degrees, they cope.' She reached up and snipped. 'People don't realize vines can withstand cold winters; late spring frost is the problem.' She carefully placed the grapes in the bin.

As she worked she sang softly to herself, refusing to allow him to see that she was embarrassed by the fact that whenever she glanced his way he was watching her. Occasionally, though, she saw his eyes flicker up and down the bodies of the other girls, and there was an animal tensing in him that she resented.

46

She found herself studying him, seeing through the girls' eyes the skin, muscle and bone which the good cut of the suit accentuated and which they apparently found so exciting and irresistible – although he wasn't handsome in the accepted sense. She looked for the virility they had shivered over, she looked for this animal magnetism which would apparently have women drooling at his feet. She wrapped her fingers gently around the grapes, loving the firm, waxy texture of them, thinking, *Spoilt rotten, he is, I'll bet.*

Suddenly he was turning back to her. 'How many staff do you have?'

Fuming at his interrogation, she carried on snipping. 'Ten for planting, nursery work, pruning, training, weed control, spraying, leaf-cutting, mowing – and wine-making, of course. Tom, my manager, deals with machinery and things. Two in the office, plus Suzie, who does a bit out here as well. Casuals for harvesting.' She spoke like a deadpan guide.

I'll be polite, but I'll bore him to death this week.

She moved along the row. He was right beside her. 'I see the vines are planted on a north-facing slope.'

Sighing, she answered, 'North or south suits. A belt of trees protects them from the south-west wind. They're my neighbour's trees actually – the elms and oaks. Grandfather planted screens of poplars and alders, as you see, here and there; there's a screen of cherry trees further down, and the orchard runs the whole length of the north side – a natural wind-break.' She paused in her work to glance down the hill.

After a long moment, he asked, in the manner of one searching for something to say, 'What's the soil?'

'Mmm?' She turned her head. A small, curious frown darted between her dark eyes. 'Oh, sand and clay.' She studied him from beneath the peak of her cap, wondering about his hair. He couldn't be more than thirty-five.

He was watching her. She saw amusement creep into his eyes. 'Go on,' he said in a reasonable tone of voice. 'This is fascinating.'

'This ground once belonged . . . to . . . er . . . monks of the Augustinian order. Wine was made in monasteries in medieval times. They say the climate was milder then . . . more favourable for . . . viticulture.'

Hearing Suzie giggle, she brushed her sticky hands down her jeans and strode away, thrusting her cutters into her pocket, swinging downhill between the arches of grapes until she reached the gravel path and turned along the track, past her office and the winery, and on towards the waiting cottage.

She had the nightmarish sensation of needing to hurry, to run inside as she had done once before . . .

The door slammed in her head.

A sudden shiver ran through her; she put her arms around herself.

Gravel crunched behind her. 'You look cold.'

'I'm a cold person; I love the sun,' she answered shortly, not looking round, marching through the gap where the gate should be. Another job to do.

'Cold? That's not what I've heard.'

His voice was ugly again, and she felt vulnerable enough to hurt. 'Why do you twist everything I say?'

'Do I?'

The sweet smell of honeysuckle met her at the door like a blow, for the cottage was no longer the haven it had once been. That was why she rounded on him, pulling off the cap so her hair tumbled to her shoulders. 'Whatever I am is no business of yours. Only the vineyard is.'

There was the trapped sensation again, and, hating his power over her, she spun round, pushed open the door and stepped inside, calling over her shoulder, 'I'm not going to tell you to make yourself at home; I don't give a damn what you do.' Tugging off her boots, full of hurt, she added over the thump of rubber on flagstones, 'I suggest you eat at the pub.' So much for her good intention to be polite. Oh, what the hell!

He followed her to the foot of the stairs. 'What are you going to do?'

She turned. 'What is this? Are you my keeper or something? I'm going to wash, if you must know, then tour the winery and do a bit more in the office. With your permission, I might go outside the gate – with a late pass, of course – to visit the pub. Or is it out of bounds?'

On the fifth stair, her dirt-stained hand gripping the banister, she glared down into those slanting eyes.

He was smiling slightly, as if she amused him. He looked wholesome, one hand in his jacket pocket, the other by his side, easy, confident, hair silky as fox fur.

She was angrier. Running fingers through her hair, she made it nearly stand on end. Looking down, she saw that earthy marks streaked her jeans. Turning, she hurried away.

It took her longer than usual, for she found it necessary to change her clothes too. Might as well get ready for the evening now, she decided. Save coming back to the house. Blast the man; it wasn't like home any more.

She reminded herself, however. No contract . . . no home!

Francesca would have her way.

She flung on the first thing she came across in the wardrobe; the trouser suit with the long, loose jacket she had worn yesterday. She wore a cream camisole underneath, pulled tan leather boots onto her feet. Her lips were naturally red, and as plump as her grapes. She looked a picture of health, with even white teeth, bright eyes and skin that glowed warm peach from the outdoors – and which would have to remain bare.

More important things to worry about than make-up, she decided, standing up and pushing back the dressing table stool. Like how she was going to endure Kingsley Hunter for a week. *I can't even be nice to him for five minutes.*

Meeting her guilty-looking, woebegone self in the mirror, she crinkled her face into a smile. That was better. Time would pass, eventually, and she would get the cheque which would enable the business to carry on for another year – just about. She could make some cutbacks, and she had a few ideas brewing. Grandy, bless him, was . . . had been . . . unreceptive to new ideas. If she had the money she could expand, buy some more ground.

Hadn't she read somewhere that setbacks sometimes meant an exciting change of direction? No point in being depressed, she must just make the best of things. Better to be happy than miserable. She shrugged and, humming, albeit a little shakily, picked up her shoulder-bag and swept from the room.

He appeared at the bottom of the stairs. 'You sing a lot, don't you?'

'Life's a song,' she said, with a pleasant smile, and swept past him to the front door, ignoring his scowl.

Stalking up the track, she sensed that her happy-go-lucky nature irritated the man striding beside her. She couldn't help wanting to sing and laugh; she had always been that way. You might think he *wanted* her to be miserable, had deliberately set out to upset her, but she dismissed the thought as absurd. It was nothing personal – purely his way of doing business, that was all.

'Tom,' she called to the stocky man in blue over-alls. 'I'm going around now.' She lightly made the introductions. 'This is my manager,' she informed Kingsley Hunter, who studied with interest the taut, unsmiling face of the dark-haired man who said little and gave the impression of a tightly wound spring.

After the men had shaken hands, she walked between them into the winery – a great barn-like place, with whitewashed walls and side doors open to the sky.

Just inside, she pointed out a blue scale, and beside that the filter.

'The small plate filter removes the presses of yeast, and the wine passes through fibrous filter sheets.'

Their footsteps rang on the recently washed stone floor as they crossed the shed, sidestepping drain-cover gratings and puddles. There was a strong smell of disinfectant. With Kingsley Hunter beside her, she strolled along the line of machinery. 'A bottle-washer and dryer, a bottle-labeller, and there – ' she pointed ' – you see the capper applying metal screw-type caps.'

He drew closer to her, frowning at the noise from the bottle-sterilizer.

'Music to our ears, isn't it, Tom?' She flashed a defiant smile over her shoulder at the man closely following them. He half smiled. Understanding passed between them, a look that spoke of deep friendship; it made her feel a lot better.

Fluorescent light glowed on stainless steel tanks

52

and a fork-lift was loading grapes into an upper hopper for crushing. Above the machinery, near the roof, an iron walkway ran around the shed, reached by an iron ladder.

'I won't go up tonight, Tom. Everything okay?'

'All shipshape. The chute's fine now, Danny.'

'Had trouble?' asked Kingsley, rubbing his chin, looking keenly from one to the other.

'Nothing we couldn't handle,' she replied, her voice as sharp as the pine they breathed. Pointing towards the roof, she added, 'That chute brings the cartons down to this level.' She heard the ring of pride in her voice. And why not?

She felt his eyes on her – penetrating her, in fact.

'Is there something you don't understand, Mr Hunter?' she challenged, flushing slightly.

He rubbed the side of his nose and looked away. 'No, no. I'm fine.'

'I'll be in the office for a while if anyone wants me,' she told Tom.

'Right you are. Going to the pub later, Danny?'

She nodded, eyes warm and crinkly. 'See you there.' It seemed to her that she had someone to protect her. Not that she was sure from what, and not that she couldn't look after herself, but . . .

Tom, a quiet man some described as withdrawn, had been a rock over the last few months.

Outside the shed, she paused. Evening shadows were gathering among the orchard trees, drawing a purple curtain around the view which always caught at her throat, especially at dusk . . . a patchwork of green and brown, distant woodlands and oast-houses, pointed as ships' sails, darkening hills which circled the valley they were in . . .

Evening always brought to mind the hymn, Grandfather's favourite, they had sung at the funeral. 'The day thou gavest Lord is ended.' Tears crammed the back of her eyes, for somehow twilight was the loneliest time of the day.

Kingsley Hunter's sneer broke into her reverie. 'Do all your staff treat you so familiarly, or is he special?'

She hurried away across the yard. Hating him, she waited until she could trust herself to speak and said, 'Most of the staff have known me since I was a child; it would be silly to start expecting them to call me Miss Summerfield just because my grandfather is . . .' her heart smote her '. . . no longer here.'

Sweeping past two wooden prefabricated buildings which housed her office staff and a small laboratory, she made for her office. 'In any case,' she called over her shoulder, 'I prefer working with friends . . . you can't beat it. I'm lucky to have so many people who care. That's important to me. The staff, and friends – Tom and Piers.'

'Piers cares, does he?'

Hating his sarcastic tone, she said coldly, 'Piers is a very caring person, *Mr Hunter*.'

He reached the door first, holding it open, and as she slipped past his probing gaze she was uncomfortably aware of just how often he unsettled her with such intense scrutiny. As if he were, indeed, far more interested in herself than in the vineyard. But that couldn't be so, could it? He had already said that she wasn't his type.

She crossed the room to her desk. That searching look caused a mini earthquake in the pit of her stomach. She might hide it from him, but she couldn't hide it from her stomach, this fear, the way she felt as if all the strength had left her body when she imagined losing the vineyard and her beloved home.

'What are you afraid of?' Following her in, he closed the door with a snap and stood with his back to it, watching her sit on the squealing chair which swamped her. 'As you said, you have nothing to hide.'

'You know what I'm afraid of,' she told him impulsively. 'I'm terrified of losing my vineyard. Does that make you feel better?' He seemed surprised, and she went on, 'Apart from that, you're making me a prisoner in my own home. And you're prying into my private life.' When he remained silent, she shrugged and began to go through some papers on her desk, making notes on a pad.

He started his usual pacing around the room.

After a while, he began to question her about the winery. She answered absent-mindedly, until something . . . maybe genuine interest in his voice . . . made her look up.

He was standing with the fading light of the window behind him, hands in his pockets, eyes slits.

He really was interested, she saw, laying down her pen. And her anger died a little as she spoke about her work – warily at first, but the questions he asked soon sent her words tumbling over themselves to explain, accompanied by her ever moving hands.

'Your eyes are sparkling,' he suddenly drawled.

She merely said, in a small voice, as if he had scolded her, 'I just love my home and my work.' She hadn't meant the pleading to show in her voice.

Again, she received a searching stare.

Frowning, he walked over and let his long body drop into the chair beside her desk, stretching with obvious enjoyment. 'I can understand that.'

'Can you?'

'You look so doubtful,' he said with a smile. 'But I'd much rather work with a natural product than push paper. It must be nice to love your job.'

'I'd like to see you give up your soft job to slave out in the fields seven days a week,' she scoffed. 'I don't spend long in this office, you know.'

'A labour of love,' he murmured, allowing those slanting eyes, more softly lit than usual, to linger with open curiosity on her expressive face.

She found herself lost for words, with a throat as dry as a bone. 'Er . . . would you like to sample a glass of my Pinot Noir?'

He looked her over. 'Why not?'

Thankfully, she rose and went over to the table.

Why, she wondered, picking up a bottle, *does he rile me, even when he's being reasonable? I know we got off on the wrong foot, but . . . it was his fault.*

'Allow me.' He was beside her, wielding the bottle-opener, pulling the cork so smoothly that only a faint plop disturbed the silence.

She upturned one glass and he upturned another, tilting the bottle. The wine streamed down with a satisfying gurgle, tinting the crystal glasses rose-pink.

'A new wine?'

She nodded, raising her glass to make a critical inspection. 'We planted nought point two hectares.'

He picked up a card from beside the bottle, reading out loud. ' "Unique character, fine and lively, expresses joy of life".'

Replacing the card, he raised his glass and slowly drank, savouring each mouthful before he swallowed. 'I'll drink to that,' he said after a moment. 'You're certainly a unique character, Danielle Summerfield, with the most expressive, lively eyes I've ever seen – eyes as dark and shiny as chestnuts.'

She felt herself blush, quite unsure how to take this. There was no reply to make, and she drank to hide her embarrassment.

He clicked his glass down on the table and turned to face the west window. The sun was falling like a red balloon into a field of grapes, and he said, with some irony, 'Wine is a perfect balance between man and nature. Everything in harmony. It's . . . nice here, with time to watch the sunset. Quite pleasant.'

There was tiredness in his voice, a slope to his shoulders, which made the spongy bit inside her which ached for people soften. She swallowed her drink once more.

He kept his face hidden. 'I'm going to be here for a week. We might as well co-operate with each other.'

Co-operate! She felt like one of those ducks in a fairground, which people shot at so that they fell down and then sprang back up again. *One minute he wants to make friends, the next he's being hateful,* she puzzled. One minute she was down, the next up. Hadn't he been the one, she thought indignantly, who'd been abominably rude from the start? Maybe she was uptight herself, with the contract being so crucial, but she hadn't imagined his rudeness.

The spongy bit inside her hardened.

Her empty glass landed on the table with a thud. 'How do I know you'll keep your word about the contract?'

He turned. The sky behind him burst into flame. His hair, she saw, was warmed with rose, like the wine. 'Is that what kept you awake last night, Danielle?' The mocking note had returned to his voice. 'I heard you tossing and turning.'

The amusement in his eyes touched a raw nerve. It had been reassurance she wanted, dammit. She hated herself for needing it – hated him for having put her in such a vulnerable position. The blood rushed to her face, and she hated that too. Picking up her shoulder-bag, she stalked around the desk and made for the door. 'I'm off,' she called, a hand on the doorhandle. 'Impossible to do any work here. I hope I don't see you until morning.'

She slammed the door behind her and the walls moved.

The office – her domain – was really quite fragile.

CHAPTER 5

Suzie exploded with a dramatic, 'Hell!'

The four boys and girl with her at the bar glanced round and saw Danielle striding into the pub, closely followed by Tom.

'Have to watch yourself now,' Iris Standing taunted from behind the bar, with bored, resentful eyes. 'Four lagers, two vodkas and . . . 'She placed a glass of shandy before Suzie with a deliberate movement.

Suzie exchanged eyebrow-raised silent messages with Annette . . . *Iris can't bear anyone to have fun if she can't. Bet she's had another row with her old man.*

Furtively sliding one of the vodkas closer to Suzie, Annette said aloud, 'You've got to be pathetic to work for sixty quid a week, Suze.'

'It's a job,' said Suzie, looking sheepish.

Annette lowered her voice. 'Liven up, Suze. If you do as I say you'll get more. In London . . . '

The door opened. Iris's face lit up. She moved along the bar as if joined by a length of string to the new arrival. He settled himself on a stool like an athlete about to vault, hands at his crotch, legs swinging each side. He was a fair, pony-tailed man, self-satisfied, in his thirties, wearing a black sweater over jeans which, like himself, had a newly washed and pressed look.

'Evening, Robin. Usual?'

'Usual, Iris,' he answered pleasantly.

She studied him as he glanced around the pub to see who was there. She could have drawn from memory his intelligent, hollow-cheeked face, the soft brown eyes and sensitive mouth.

'I've joined the Institute for Beginners Art,' she told him eagerly, flushing a little, tugging the jacket of her new red suit down over her hips.

He turned back to her. 'Good.' He smiled, and waited while she drew his lager. 'Where's Ron?'

'Down in the cellar,' she said shortly.

Half standing, he delved into his hip pocket. She took his body-warm coins and turned to the cash register.

'I like the hairdo,' he told her appeasingly.

Glancing in the mirrored wall, she checked her gleaming auburn blunt-cut bob. He always took an interest in a woman's appearance.

She turned with a relieved smile. 'I went into Canterbury to have it done. Your pictures are up,' she added, as a reward.

'Ah!' He eyed the walls as he drank. After a moment, he left his drink, wandered about, then paused before a painting and spoke to Annette.

When he returned to the bar, Iris saw he was smiling. 'What's the joke?'

Still grinning, he said, 'Tony Reagan's new stepdaughter, Annette, saw the price ticket and said she wouldn't pay eighty pounds for it. I told her I was the artist and she said she still wouldn't. Outspoken girl. Beautiful too,' he said, greedy-eyed.

He'd been commissioned to do a range of nostalgic-type birthday cards. What would she say if she asked her to sit for him? That wonderful hair, the long face and nose, hooded eyes . . .

'Iris!' called an exasperated, thirsty customer. 'Are you with us, love?'

Despite her watching out for Kingsley Hunter, he didn't appear. Danielle was able to retrieve her good humour and enjoy a laugh and a joke over chilli con carne in the reassuring company of people she had known since she was a child.

They moved eventually from the larger room kept for diners, functions and live music sessions, and Tom quickly went to claim the only vacant church pew seats in the lounge bar. She was still pushing through the crowd, stopping to greet people she knew, enjoying the scent of chips and beer, the atmosphere of conviviality. Conviviality apart from one man.

Seeing him, Danielle made her way towards the bar counter, where he stood alone, brooding into his Guiness.

She touched his worn tweed shoulder and smiled

62

into the face that sprang round, teeth bared, to see who it was. It was a weather-warped, I-hate-the-world scowler, his face, with thin lips and jutting chin. But by the time she had joked with him, teased him, treated him as if he were the same as any other friend, there was a sort of gratitude to be seen in his watery old eyes if anyone had looked.

When she at last reached the table, Tom started to speak and she leaned close. What with music, voices, laughter, encouraging bellows, the thud of darts and the clicking of billiard balls it was difficult to hear . . . 'I didn't hear . . . Sorry.'

'Only you, Danny, would try to chat up old Hutchinson,' he repeated in his dry way.

'I know.' She grinned. 'That's why I do. He's a challenge. Besides, the old love's lonely.'

'You're a nutcase,' he said, eyeing her fondly. 'By the way, they're saying that chap, Mr Hunter, is staying at your place.'

'Who's saying?' She picked up her drink and sipped.

He fidgeted, his strong hand closing around the handle of a beer tankard as he answered, 'The staff.'

'For once,' she giggled, 'the gossip's right.'

Gulping down his beer, he wiped his hand across his mouth. 'Do you think . . . er . . .?'

'What?' Holding her glass up to the light, she squinted through the clear golden liquid at the pained, distorted expression on Tom's wind-burned face.

'Well, it's not right really, is it?'

Her glass clicked down on the table. 'Don't be an idiot, Tom. This is the nineteen-nineties, you know. He's here on business. His company merged a few years ago with another one – it's one of the biggest in the country.'

'Sure, but . . . if he needed digs he could stay with me.' Tom rented a cottage in one of Hidden's back alleys, near the church – a most peculiar cottage – and where he would put a visitor, she didn't know.

She waved her hands in the air. 'Come on, I have an empty *en suite* bedroom – and besides, it wouldn't be a bad idea to take paying guests. Everyone's doing it.' She grinned. 'We'll put a sign on the gate. "B and B".'

Tom looked at her through sea-grey slits. He could get intense at times over things that bothered him.

Her attention wandered to the inglenook fireplace, where flames curled and crackled around logs, sending sparks shooting up the chimney. The scent of applewood was strong and sweet, and she was close enough to feel warmth on her cheeks. Brassware displayed in the grate and on the mantelpiece danced with brilliant reflections.

Summer's over, she realized sadly, glancing around the blackened, brick-walled room, at the oak beams decorated with dried hops, the cosy-looking red wall-lights softly glowing on glasses above the bar counter. It was then that she saw Kingsley Hunter.

A log fell. Sparks glowed in her eyes. ''Scuse me, Tom.'

Squeezing her way to the bar, she came up beside him. 'Having a nice evening, Mr Hunter? I'd like to introduce you to someone. This is Mr Hutchinson – he owns the farm next to the vineyard. I think you two could be great friends, and it will be someone to talk to, won't it?'

Returning to Tom, she plonked herself down and laughed into her wine.

'You didn't introduce Mr Hunter to old misery-guts, did you?'

She nodded, beaming. 'They're two of a kind.'

He studied her. 'Nice to see you back,' he said gruffly.

Danielle's smile went out like a candle.

'I mean you . . . the girl with the laughing eyes.'

'I know what you mean. It's just . . .'

'You feel guilty?'

She nodded, surprised at his understanding. 'I do – just a bit.'

She grinned again, the warm, infectious smile Tom knew so well, and he felt the time was right to take her hand and squeeze it.

'You helped,' she told him, a little embarrassed.

Her grateful eyes shone at him for a moment, and then characteristically swept away, searching the crowd with those ever moving eyes.

He watched the laughter in her face, the alertness

of her. What did her eyes seek? he wondered. She looked out on the world with good humour, yet she had a don't-touch-me dignity that didn't go with her blood-filled lips. She was like an audience of one. She watched more than joined. Sought entertainment, yet never got on the stage. Some, mostly olduns and youngsters, said she had a smile that dried tears.

Where did she go when the show was over?

When her eyes rested on him, she made him feel as if he wanted to hold his hopeful breath and remain still until her eyes flew away again, maybe in search of more interesting, fun people.

Nothing, apart from the yard, went deep. She could seem flighty, but she was a worker. She had the interest of the yard at heart and he did too. They were a good team and he was sure she knew it. All he had to do was be patient.

He had seen the way she cut down any man who tried it on. She had had a protected childhood, he supposed. There was an old-world air about her, while he himself had been around. Now he wanted to settle, and this, being a long, long way from his Bermondsey childhood, was an ideal place in which to do so.

He would bide his time. But he would be watching to make sure no one else got the prize.

They were called over then to play darts, and he went reluctantly. Danielle wasn't keen, but was too good-natured to refuse when they were two short for

66

the team. He saw that Kingsley Hunter and Mr Hutchinson had gone.

And Danielle burned bright again, for her friends.

Danielle was about to aim her dart when someone caught her arm. She turned. Suzie, with her fleshy, damp, childlike mouth, innocent blue eyes and chalky-pale baby face was looking anxious and pious. 'Don't tell Dad I'm here,' she pleaded in her bell-like voice.

'Nothing to do with me,' Danielle told her, throwing the dart at the board.

Griff's tight, firm voice rang in her ears. 'My kid's always in by ten. Goes to the youth club or a friend's house. No trouble.' The dart hit the wire and fell to the floor.

With a pleased, crafty sort of laugh, Suzie returned to her friends. She was a tall, slim, unmade bed of a girl, who drew the boys like moths to a flame and who had given up her dream of being a vet because it had meant college, and life was a much more exciting prospect. Or so she had told Danielle, with the air of someone about to sit down at a a banquet and gorge.

Remembering what Cherie had told her in the shop, Danielle watched Suzie whisper in Annette's ear and giggle. Annette wore skin-tight black trousers and a short leather jacket, her thin bare feet were stuffed into high heels. It was the girl's hair that caught most people's attention. It was the colour of

Weetabix, and fell to her waist in light-catching waves.

She had a friendly but raucous voice, which seemed now to be fascinating the youngsters with an account of her life in London. Her actions were over-dramatized, excited, almost hyperactive. Her friends responded with baying, empty laughter.

Danielle felt a pang of disquiet. But it was none of her business who Suzie saw in her own time.

She had stayed later than she had intended, and when Tom said he was supping up, she left with him. 'I'll walk with you,' he insisted. She didn't argue.

The noise from the pub faded, leaving a companionable silence. Only their feet made soft, shuffling noises over damp leaves and the occasional car swished past. The scent of pine from the woods was familiar and heady; in places the giant oaks hid the moon. They turned in through the wide gates beneath the 'INTOXICATING LADY' sign, and approached the cottage.

The night was clogged with the autumn scent of dying undergrowth; drifting smoke from dying bonfires blew through her mind with memories.

With a shiver, she looked up at brittle stars crowding a glacial sky and asked, 'Did you see the wonderful sunset tonight, Tom?'

'Can't say I did. They were two-a-penny at sea.'

She sighed. There was something about the night that made her not want it to end, and Tom hovered at the front door as if he, too, felt the same. She was tempted, for she had fallen back a lot on Tom for company and consolation these last few months. Something quiet and compassionate about him had bandaged her sore moments.

In the end, she used work as an excuse for not inviting him in for coffee.

'You work too hard,' he said awkwardly.

'And you're repeating yourself,' she retorted, laughing softly. 'I like to do my accounts at night.'

'Other people,' he grunted, 'go to bed with a good book, or a good . . .'

'Night, Tom.'

His sigh was a caught-back groan. 'G'night, Danny.'

Letting herself into the cottage, she snapped the door closed and stood listening. The grandfather clock ticked loudly, but there was no other sound. With a puff of relief, she went into the sitting room and switched on the lamp on the bureau, but she decided against music. If he was asleep, best not arouse him. Like arousing the devil. She grinned wickedly.

It was gone twelve before she groped her way upstairs, rubbing her eyes. And then she couldn't sleep. Why did money problems turn into spectres during the night? She groaned to herself. Bills and final demands flew around the bedroom like bats!

At last she could stand it no longer. Thrusting her legs from the bed, she reached for slippers, couldn't find them, and on bare feet crept out of her room onto the landing. Why should I have to creep around

69

my own home? she wondered crossly, smelling the orange and ginger pot-pourri and feeling for the stairs.

The stairs creaked, every one, but at last she reached the kitchen, pushed the door almost closed with a sigh of relief and clicked on the light. Blinking, she crossed to the Aga, shivering as cold air came up through the stone flags and gripped her feet like frozen socks. She reached for a saucepan, took milk from the fridge and stood close to the oven's ever warm body.

She spooned Horlicks into a mug, stirred boiling milk into it without crashing the spoon as she usually did, and, turning back to the door, very nearly dropped the mug, such was her shock.

CHAPTER 6

Danielle could only stare, trying to ignore the fact that her stomach was being uncomfortably disarranged. Kingsley Hunter, meanwhile, resplendent in a navy and red silk dressing gown, completely unperturbed, pushed himself away from the door where he had been leaning.

Warily, she watched him cross the room towards her, not liking the impatience written clearly on his face.

His arms reached out for her.

Before she could protest, he lifted her as if she weighed nothing and sat her on the great pine table upon which she could remember sitting as a toddler, pretending she was on a ship sailing away to France, where she had been told her father lived.

She didn't spill a drop of her drink either, but it was utterly galling.

'What the hell . . .?' And what an idiot she felt, perched there like a child, in her cream cotton pyjamas, curling her cold pink toes.

'You'll catch your death on that floor,' was his

71

explanation, scornful more than concerned. 'Where are your slippers?'

She just wasn't used to such fuss, and to hide her burning face she lifted the mug to her lips. 'Upstairs somewhere; I couldn't find them. It's warm in here, with the Aga,' she protested between sips.

'Nonsense,' he threw over his shoulder, striding away.

By the time he returned downstairs she had scalded her throat with the drink and slipped from the table, finding herself some way below his shoulder when he came up to her, holding out her slippers. 'Here.'

This was ridiculous – he was making her feel guilty for being a nuisance. And there was something about the look on his face . . . 'Have you been in my room?' she demanded crossly, easing her feet into red fluffy mules.

'Why not? You weren't there.'

She flushed, not certain what he meant.

He eyed her keenly. 'I see you collect teddy bears.'

'What do you collect . . . vineyards?' She stared up at him defiantly, but instead of receiving the expected scathing comment, she felt something happen to her which had something to do with their locked eyes.

After what seemed ages, she turned away, crossed over to the sink, washed the saucepan and her mug and moved to leave the room with as much dignity as she could muster in pyjamas. As she padded past him, he caught hold of her arm.

72

'Wait.'

It was a command and, feeling the warm grip of his fingers through the flimsy material, she couldn't help thinking how strange it was that she had never been close to an undressed man before in the middle of the night. He smelled of newly baked bread, and his night-time body had a musky intimacy.

'Well?' she asked, tossing the hair from her eyes.

He did a strange thing. Lifting his hand from her arm, he helpfully pushed a stray curl back behind her ear; the gesture was oddly fussy, and so gentle that the pads of his fingers merely skimmed the skin on her brow, making her feel childish and quite thrown.

His hand fell, but his eyes remained on her hair. 'Like dark chocolate . . . so lush,' he murmured, in the tone of one thinking aloud. 'I had a dog that colour once.'

'I had a dog once, called Kit,' she blurted awkwardly. Memory raced back. A memory she kept hidden . . . in normal circumstances.

It had happened a long time ago, so long ago that she could keep the door closed on it. Except, that was, on rare occasions when something reminded her . . . like autumn, the barking of a dog . . .

She shuddered and backed away. Some horror in her eyes made his face crease with irritation, or it might have been disappointment. In any case, he wasn't pleased.

His voice, though, was making an effort to be

pleasant. 'I'm surprised you have no dog now; I'd have thought living alone . . .'

She shook her head. 'No dog.'

'You don't like dogs?'

'It's not that.' Her heart hammered, and from the disturbed memories she pulled a reason. 'You love them too much, don't you? And then they die . . .'

She glanced at the bland face of the pine wall-clock. Her voice was clipped, emotionless. 'It's late. I feel I've kept you up, Mr Hunter.'

'You'll be exhausted in the morning yourself,' he told her.

'Yes, well . . . I couldn't sleep.'

'No.' He hesitated, then turned away.

Watching him wander around the kitchen, unsure whether she should go or stay, she couldn't believe her ears when he asked, with a tetchy frown, 'Would you like me to make you another drink?'

She pulled her dropped mouth into shape. – 'No. Why should you?'

He shrugged. 'I just thought . . .' In front of the calendar, he asked abruptly, 'Did you have many picnics as a child?'

'No.' Heaving a resigned sigh, Danielle pulled out a chair, perching uncomfortably, feeling its hard edge through her pyjamas. 'Everyone was busy. Er . . . did you?'

'Lots.' In a quiet voice, he read the verse beneath the picture. 'Here with a Loaf of Bread beneath the Bough, A Flask of Wine, a Book of Verse – and Thou

74

Beside me singing in the Wilderness – And Wilderness is Paradise enow'.

Dead silence . . .

Until the fridge suddenly jumped, as if someone had kicked it, rattling bottles, humming loudly as fridges past their prime do.

She watched him warily as he pulled a chair out from the table and settled opposite her, face set.

'You shouldn't fight your demons at night,' he said in the tone she hated, as if he spoke to a child. 'And work problems should be left at work,' he added.

She lifted her chin. 'I live on the job,' she reminded him. 'Besides, I don't usually. It's just . . .'

His brows quirked. 'Me? Or . . .?'

'Well, it's a bit of a . . . It's unsettling, having you here.' She felt quite proud of herself for having put it so politely.

He looked satisfied. 'Might do you good to talk about it, then go to bed with a clear head.'

She shrugged, eying his smug look with distaste, and felt a late-night sort of resignation. With a pout, hands spread palms up, she asked, 'What's there to talk about?'

He regarded her with a level stare, saying, 'I think you're dangerously under-capitalized.'

'You know what the problems are, Mr Hunter.'

'Kingsley, for God's sake.'

Despite his sharp tone, she couldn't help smiling. Formality was completely out of place at the present time, that was for sure.

75

His eyes lingered on the dimple below her left cheek. 'What's funny?'

'Us, having a business conference, like this.' She gave one of her giggles that tended to end in a hiccup, and his frown made it all the funnier.

'I was trying to help, Danielle.'

'Oh,' she said with exaggerated disgust. 'Naughty me.' Seeing the ice return to his eyes, and wondering why he brought out the devil in her, she added seriously, 'Increasing duty means we can't afford a good promotion, then there's interest on plant investment. Grandy – that was my grandfather – said that when the Chancellor increased excise duty in the 1974 budget, sales fell by thirty-five per cent.' She threw her hands in the air. 'Can you believe that?'

As she spoke Danielle saw by his intent gaze that he followed every word. It was disconcerting. 'Duty going up sent prices up – ' she shrugged ' – causing further consumer resistance. By the end of that year, profit was halved. In the 1975 budget, apparently duty went through the roof . . . one hundred and three percent.' On a note of anger, she ended, 'You seem to blame Grandy, but, you see, it's a fight from start to finish.'

'But if you mounted a sales drive backed up by a major advertising company . . .'

She spread her hands. 'I've just told you why I can't do that,' she said, a trifle impatiently. 'The cashflow problem . . . the damn duty.'

I must be tired, she thought discontentedly. She

usually enjoyed discussing business. After all, Grandy had humoured her, Francesca had disliked any mention of the vineyard, and she couldn't talk this way with her staff. There had really only been Piers. Yet at this moment she was struck with a listlessness that surprised her. Until she remembered that it was the middle of the night. She was obviously not like the night owl she could hear hooting beyond the window.

As was her way, she tried to make a joke of it. Getting to her feet, she gave him a brilliant smile, causing him to look at her warily. 'I think we should go to bed now,' she told him gaily. And with a dramatic come-hither look, she executed a sexy glide towards the door.

It happened suddenly.

Hard fingers clutched her arm, swinging her round. Blue-grey hating eyes fell to her upturned face, from which she felt the blood draining.

'You cheap little . . .'

She struggled to free herself. 'What?'

'Why do you have no sense of responsibility? Why are you such a sybarite? Can you never be serious?' he demanded, releasing her.

She caught hold of the door to steady herself. 'What the hell's the matter with you?' she yelled.

Kingsley's eyes swept downwards, and following them she saw that her pyjama jacket had come undone. She had meant to tighten the buttonholes but had never got around to it. But what made her reel was the shock in his eyes as they fastened on to her half-exposed breasts.

She quickly did up the buttons. 'I think *you*, Kingsley, have a problem. Not me.'

He looked furious. 'Is that how you see yourself,' he sneered, 'as a solver of sexual problems?'

She could have hit him! Turning, she avoided temptation by hurrying up the stairs and into her room, unable to believe the seesaw effect he had on her.

'I do keep trying to be nice, don't I?' she heatedly asked a teddy bear.

Yet deep down inside lurked the suspicion that she had had an effect upon Kingsley too. Somehow, the thought pleased her. She was tired and muzzy – temper gone, but at the back of her mind an idea that up until now she had felt entirely in his power, and tonight there had been a slight shift.

Though he must see many more attractive sights than a plump girl in an old pair of pyjamas with her hair tumbling all over the place. She held her hair up on top of her head and put on a model-girl pose, moistening her lips and pouting at her reflection.

But there was only a bear on the dressing table to see her, and he looked most unimpressed. She sighed and, kicking off her slippers, climbed between cold sheets.

She had finished her afternoon rounds of the winery, and was wondering what had happened to him when he appeared, outlined against the sky, in the open side of the shed. She couldn't miss his silver-fox head, nor the lurch of fear in the pit of her stomach.

He was wearing blue overalls, with jeans showing beneath. 'Will I do?'

'Depends,' answered Danielle crisply, 'upon what you want to do.' She raised her voice. 'Tom, I'm going down to the cellars.'

'Right you are.'

She wasn't at all surprised, when she descended the stone steps in the corner of the winery, to hear footsteps padding behind her.

'Where did you find the overalls?' she asked, keys jangling as she unlocked the door at the bottom.

'In my wardrobe. Hope you don't mind.'

They had been Grandy's, of course. He, too, had been a tall man. 'I'm surprised you asked,' she said huskily, as his hand appeared over her shoulder to push open the heavy door. 'You seem to be taking over here.'

His harsh laugh followed her inside and down the stone stairs.

The open door brought in the only light apart from the red glow from electric meters on the wall, giving the upside-down bottles a green tinge. White walls glistened eerily in the gloom; the sweet air struck chilly. 'Mind the hosepipe,' she warned him, stepping over the black snake. 'And don't touch any bottles – they're likely to explode.'

79

In a voice hushed, almost reverent, he reminded her, 'I am in the wine business, remember.'

'Spooky, isn't it? Full of spirits,' she quipped.

Kingsley didn't even smile, instead she saw him glance at the oak casks.

'Two hundred and fifty pounds each, they cost,' she told him ruefully, wondering if he had any sense of humour at all. It seemed the more she smiled, the longer his face grew. People like that were a challenge – she couldn't resist trying all the more to make them smile. It was a devil in her, Grandy used to say.

'How long do the casks last?' he asked.

'About ten years.' Pointing to a rack, she said, 'Brandy. Takes eight bottles of wine to make one bottle. Hence the cost to you.'

He followed her through a folded-back plastic door and they walked further into a darker, crypt-like atmosphere. Her voice floated towards the walls and bounced back. 'This is where the wine's fermented.'

Kingsley went over to inspect one of the green tanks which almost touched the ceiling.

'We fill the tanks as much as possible,' she told him, noticing how his hair was luminous in the dim light of a wall-lamp. 'You'll see a line of sediment at the bottom. If the wine sits with sediment for a while, the flavour improves.'

'Wonder if that applies to people too?' he commented, padding away on very expensive trainers and disappearing between a row of tanks.

Unable to think of a reply, she silently followed him, her rubber boots making soft thuds on the stone floor. Only faint light reached this isolated area. And no sound other than a hum of machinery.

Kingsley turned to face her; the humming was in her ears and she moved closer in order to hear, looking up at him, waiting with a teasing, next-question-please smile.

And for some reason her heart leapt into her throat; she began to tremble.

He reached for her and it was like someone wrenching back curtains and letting sunshine pour in. From inside her something unexpected and un-stoppable surged to meet him, and she found herself sucked into the pulse-racing magnetic force that she had known from the beginning was there.

Drawing her closer, his hold was light on her arms, yet a sea of urgent tides controlled her, and sent her plunging into a place of no time, thought or reason.

Only sensations.

The warm strength of his arms, the flat of his hands as they moved to the nape of her neck and the small of her back. Gasping for sweet air, she instead breathed his warm breath as he covered her face with kisses like splashes of molten velvet.

His lips became urgent, pushing aside her sweater to seek sensitive hollows in her neck and throat; lips so frantic that her body caught their excitement and, with mounting desire, she moved her face round, chasing the mouth that wouldn't place itself on hers.

When she found his lips, arrested them, her own seemed to explode on contact.

His kiss was long, hard – almost a punishment – shocking her so that she raised her arms to push him away.

Instead, she, herself, was urgently rejected.

Her 'No' came at the same time, and she meant it as a warning for him to stop. But Kingsley had already pushed past her and padded away; his face, as he turned towards light, was taut with anger. What had she done now?

She rested a shaking hand against her burning face, remembering his insinuations. Did he think that because she had responded – God, why *had* she? – she was easy? Had it only confirmed his opinion of her?

Above her head, on top of the wine vats, oxygen bubbled through glass tubes because that was the natural way of it. Her nose, as always in here, felt cold and started to run. All the heat in her body drained away and the bubbles went flat.

But she was different.

She found him in the outer area, inspecting a rack of bottles with indented bottoms. 'Sparkling wine?'

'Yes,' she replied, making an effort to keep her voice normal and stop her body trembling. 'They must have a quarter turn each day . . . the . . . the sediment moves down into the neck of the bottle.'

Avoiding her eyes, he pointed to a machine. 'French, isn't it?'

She groped in her pocket for a tissue, and blew her nose. 'Mmm. Each bottle is held into the plastic hood and the cap is removed. The mushroom shape of the cork is . . . is caused by the force of the bottle. But you know that.'

'Of course. Just as I know that in wine cellars things are . . . likely to explode.'

'Sometimes caused by rough handling,' she said resentfully. 'And not being treated with proper respect.' She sniffed.

Without a word, Kingsley hurried up the stairs, holding the door open as if it was a distasteful chore.

She followed more slowly, back into the world she had forgotten existed, where unreal daylight, like bitter lemons, intruded from the open side of the shed.

'Going to the office, Danny?'

Thrusting the keys back into her pocket, she blinked. For a second she wondered what Tom was doing there, suspicious eyes darting between her and Kingsley.

'I usually do, don't I?' She smiled to soften her abrupt tone.

'Red said she's got those figures you wanted,' he said, in his tense, throat-knotted voice.

'Great.' She hurried out of the winery, apparently not caring less whether Kingsley followed or not.

With his footsteps padding behind her, she dodged fork-lifts and made her way towards the smaller of the wooden offices.

Pushing open the door, she stepped inside. Kingsley followed her in, his eyes sweeping the small laboratory, passing then swivelling back to the filing cabinet.

A girl in white overalls stood there. A girl with a wide, white forehead and red curls showing beneath a white cap. Seeing Danielle, she hurriedly dabbed out a cigarette.

Nevertheless, her small twisted mouth gave her a stubborn look, and her green eyes narrowed, as if she thought that Danielle's obsession against smoking, since forty-a-day Daniel Summerfield had died of a massive coronary, was an infringement upon her liberty.

Danielle's sharp voice made her feelings about the cigarette known. 'Can I have the figures, Red?'

The girl, without a word, held out a file.

Taking it, Danielle made swift introductions, throwing Kingsley a look of contempt – which he didn't notice, for he seemed mesmerized.

Turning on her heel, Danielle swept around the small room, almost wanting to find something to pick fault with and hating herself. The room, however, was spotless, and she called Kingsley's attention to the list of figures she was holding. He'd said he was here to check out the place, and she intended not only to give him indigestion but to make him swallow his words. Which she hoped would choke him!

'Red takes daily samples from the press house, checks the sugar content, the acidity of the juice and

84

its clarity. You might have noticed a number on each vat.'

Kingsley smiled politely and glanced at the figures – and then glanced back at the figure he was obviously more interested in, she thought sourly. Not that much of the slender Red could be seen beneath her white overall, but he obviously found what was on show good enough to go on.

He was asking Red about herself. Her real name was Daisy, she was telling him. He was obviously impressed . . . by her qualifications too. 'A microbiologist?' He whistled.

Danielle glanced at the clock. 'Five o'clock. Time you went home, Red, you look tired. I'll send Suzzie in to help you for a bit tomorrow.' In an effort to be friendly, she pointed to a notice on the wall. 'Are you going to the harvest dance?'

The girl shrugged. 'Maybe.'

'Bye, then.' Danielle swept away, allowing Kingsley to pull the door closed after them.

He whistled again, and she threw him a withering glance. 'I'm going to do some picking. Perhaps,' she suggested hopefully, 'you'd like to go somewhere else.'

He threw up his arms and slapped them down on his thighs. 'I'm dressed for work, and work I shall.'

The man who had kissed her had disappeared, almost as if she had imagined him. 'If you go into the office,' she said tartly, 'and charm Suzie's mum, Paula, you might get a pair of cutting shears; they're

85

safer for inexperienced people. Wouldn't like you to chop off a finger.' Glancing at his hands, she suppressed a shiver.

She had reached the slopes before she casually glanced round to see if he was coming. He wasn't. And, to her annoyance, she found it difficult to keep her mind on the job, because her eyes kept wandering along those juicy lanes, in and out of the shadows, back towards the distant office building, and, catching a glimpse of a silver head beside a red one, she felt a savage thrust of irritation.

She was well aware of the wall that she put up whenever a man made a pass – not that there had been many; she had been too busy here.

There was Tom, of course . . . Over the last year he had become a sort of anchor. For death made the world an alien place; familiar territory and even people took on the guise of strangeness, you might be stranded on the bleak moon, so lonely and strange did life feel. In that enormous black void which had stretched seemingly without end Tom had reached out, and she had held his hand. But there was still that barrier between herself and any man who became affectionate.

And now Kingsley had kissed her. Without affection.

Why? Did having her in his power excite him? She might have grown up in a convent, but the girls had escaped for holidays and returned moody or elated, panting to tell of their sexual exploits, true or false.

86

Power over a woman was apparently what men craved. Was it possible that Kingsley had deliberately exerted pressure in order to give him a hold over her?

She dismissed the idea as too over the top. And yet there was her feeling that he was hunting her down, that there was something personal in it. It wasn't possible, was it, that . . .? A wave of horror hit her. Supposing he hoped to have an affair with her, and get the vineyard that way. With her money troubles adding to the pressure, he probably thought she would be an easy target.

She snipped the stalks on the bunches of grapes as if they were the veins in his throat.

Maybe, though, he had another interest now. Red, for example. Red wouldn't give him a vineyard, but by all accounts she would give him – Well . . . you couldn't go by gossip.

In fact Red had often said that she wasn't interested in a relationship for years yet, that her career was the most important thing. As soon as the opportunity arose for her to join a large, important company, she would do so. She had been honest about that.

Danielle's mind went blank, for there he was, swinging along the rows, leaving the grapes bouncing in his wake. And, yes, he did have a sexy walk, as a giggle further along the row of pickers suggested. He stalked along like a lion, a beast prowling the jungle, and she felt again the now familiar shiver . . .

CHAPTER 7

'Another week.' Danielle, using the kitchen telephone, glanced at the calendar. 'Another week,' she told her grandmother, 'and the harvest will be half over.' She listened for a while, and smiled a tired smile. 'I *am* actually . . . exhausted. We've been at it from dawn to dusk, and the men are working until nearly midnight.' She gave one of her giggles. 'All for a drop of wine. Anyway, see you Sunday. Bye.'

She didn't really have the time to spare, she supposed, hanging the phone on the hook, but Francesca appeared to look forward to her visits, although they had never been close. In fact, Danielle was irritated by her.

She had no sooner replaced the receiver when Kingsley swept in on a breeze of shower gel, having changed into trousers and a sweater, asking, 'Who was on the phone?'

She drew herself up. 'I beg your pardon?'

'I wondered if it was for me,' he answered, rubbing the side of his nose with a suggestion of awkwardness.

'Well, it wasn't,' she answered shortly. 'Are you expecting a call? I mean, did you leave a forwarding number with your girlfriends?' She waited, with a high degree of tension, for his reply; almost certainly he wouldn't say he was married.

His face relaxed into one of his half-smiles. 'What makes you think they're in the plural?'

'You look the type who likes to play the field.'

'Why not? There's safety in numbers, as you yourself know. Actually, I left this number with my secretary, as I'm here in the afternoons.'

She closed her burning eyes, feeling exhaustion clutch her body like a vice. This was awful. Whenever she was with Kingsley she felt as if her skin had been peeled back, leaving her raw. And at the moment she didn't feel able to cope with it.

Fingers closed around her wrist. 'Come and sit down,' a stranger's gentle voice ordered.

When her aching bones had collapsed on a chair, he said brusquely, 'I'm not going to apologize for what happened today, in the cellar.'

'Why should you? I suspect it would be completely out of character,' she said grumpily. And for good measure flashed him a tired glower of dislike.

'I know,' Kingsley added with a hint of pique, 'that you're involved elsewhere.'

She hardly heard him, for it occurred to her suddenly that maybe he was missing his girlfriends – he was sexually frustrated, and that was why he had made a pass at her.

'You do?' she snapped, pushing away a mental picture of Kingsley Hunter with a woman.

'I can't help wishing you weren't,' he said, eyeing her pained expression with the first uncertainty she had seen in him.

She opened her mouth . . .

'No, don't bother with explanations.' Turning away, he began to pace the floor. 'I've come to the conclusion that you're wasted on him, that's all. I hate to see you ruin your life – not to mention another's.'

'Another's?'

He stopped pacing. 'His wife's.'

'Whose wife?'

Voice heavy with sarcasm, he said, 'Come on, now . . . Piers didn't pretend to be unmarried, surely.'

'Ah. Piers.' The penny dropped! Kingsley's barbed words, his insinuations . . . She put her hand to her mouth, not knowing whether to laugh or cry.

His face closed up and he spoke once more with that detached coldness. 'As I said . . . an unfeeling bitch. Obviously his wife's feelings are of no account. And your own predicament doesn't seem to bother you. Life's one long joke, I suppose.'

'As you said,' she replied wearily.

Their eyes met across the room, and she was so stunned by the cold hatred directed her way that when he strode towards her she jumped to her feet, appalled.

90

Reaching out, his hands gripped her shoulders and he scowled down into her face. 'Why struggle? You know you can't escape until you've heard me out.'

From the past it swept back . . . skin-shrinking terror as she remembered . . . like an animal . . . trapped . . . unable to move. What sort of a man had she allowed into her home? 'Okay,' she managed to say through a thick throat. 'You're a strong guy, so say your piece.'

He did. 'Why can't you keep to your own man?'

There was a grim silence.

Something he saw in her face made him release her suddenly, but his voice stormed on. 'And why is it that whenever I come near you, you look frightened?'

Danielle, gripping the table for support, couldn't believe her ears. 'What do you expect?' she cried. 'When you've blackmailed me, taken over my home and made a pass at me? You said the arrangement would be business only; you've gone back on your word.' Unhappily, she ended, 'I should have known that a man can't be trusted.'

Drooping with tiredness, she turned to go, missing his frown, the slow, almost begrudging softening of his sharp features.

'Wait.' He touched her shoulder, gently this time. When she turned, they regarded each other without speaking. After a minute, he shook his head slowly. 'Danielle . . .' Something seemed to catch in his throat; clearing it, he offered, 'Like me to cook you a meal?'

She shook her head, too tired to be surprised.

'I can cook, you know,' he said gently.

She met a rare smile which somehow, she felt, held an apology. 'I don't mean that. I'm just . . . I can't understand your moods. I can't keep up with them.'

His right brow quirked. 'You're a mystery too. I came here expecting . . .' He shrugged. 'Never mind. What is there to cook?'

She stretched, yawned and oh, she hated arguments – so she gave in. 'Spaghetti, tomatoes, mince.'

'And I noticed herbs in your garden. Are you suggesting . . .?'

She nodded.

'Spaghetti Bolognese,' they said together.

Startled by his natural, unaffected laugh, she said doubtfully, 'Do you mean we have something in common?'

With a businesslike air, he stepped up to the sink, and she stared as he filled a saucepan with water and set it on the Aga, saying, 'I think we've discovered a mutual attraction. Dinner in an hour?'

'Oh . . . er . . . right. I'll be there.' She made for the stairs, thinking that she would never climb them, she was so weary.

What a difference a bath made. With her damp hair pulled back behind a black velvet band, she discarded her old dressing gown and descended the stairs smelling of oranges, wearing a rose-red housecoat that Francesca had given her for Christmas, done right up to the neck.

Kingsley expertly poured rosé wine and allowed her to sip and nod approvingly before filling the glass to the brim. The kitchen was filled with the satisfying smell of garlic, tomatoes and basil, and the steaming French bread she saw him take from the oven.

The nightmare returned to the past, where it belonged.

Homely things could be so soothing . . .

She watched butter melt and stain the bread gold, before she placed a crisp piece in her mouth and crunched with a sigh of pleasure.

'I worry about you,' he told her, setting a heaped plate before her, dribbling olive oil over the spaghetti.

She grated parmesan over the meat sauce. 'Why?'

'I don't know.' He took a mouthful. 'Good?'

She ate, and licked her lips. 'Ten out of ten.'

'I don't want to,' he told her, sipping his wine.

'I'm sure you don't,' she said seriously, helping herself to salad. 'But we sometimes can't help ourselves.'

'Is that how it is with Piers?'

She thought for a moment. This was getting too cosy. He was obviously playing a game, and the prize would be the vineyard. Look how much at home he'd made himself in her cottage. Plus the fact, of course, that she knew full well that men used sex as a weapon. Piers was Kingsley's boss. As Piers' mistress, well

. . . she might be able to take advantage of her position.

Smiling at her thoughts, she put down her knife and fork, reached for her wine glass. 'That's the way it is.'

Tipping her head, feeling the wine slip down her throat, she closed her eyes in momentary, if rather mixed-up bliss.

'Thanks for the dinner,' she said, because she had been brought up that way.

He was watching her, and his answer was unexpected. 'I enjoyed cooking for you. It's the first time I've cooked for anyone else. Made a change not to have someone fussing over me.'

Which left her even more confused.

'I'm not going to tell anyone yet, Griff,' warned Cherie, with a little frown.

He put down his mug and almost stood to attention. 'I can keep a secret, you know.'

She nodded absently and ran her eyes around the empty shop. She glanced longingly from the window and turned back to him with a pleased smile. 'Guess who's coming across the green. Our latest incomer . . . Dottie Trout.'

'Who?'

'Dorothea Trutt, really. You know – took over old Fred Pike's cottage.' Cherie looked indignant. 'She's a mystery, that one. Round the twist, if you ask me. Looks like . . . you know.'

Griff, used to Cherie, said nothing.

'You know . . . from that old film.'

'Mmm.'

'That old film. What was it called?' She drummed her fingers on her stomach. '*Sunset Boulevard* – that's it. But the woman . . . what was her name?'

The bell clanged as the door opened, letting in Dorothea Trutt, shrivelled brown leaves and a gust of wind. She slammed the door and turned, posing in her yellow fluffy jacket and orange dress, head encased in a black turban. Her lined face was thickly made up – wide mouth a slash of crimson and eyes, which must have been lovely once, being almond-shaped, heavily mascaraed.

Accepting their stares with a gratified smile, she tottered over to the off-licence section. 'I ran out of necessities.' Her voice was wobbly, cultured, actressy, and seemed to add silently. Or I wouldn't be in here. A strong smell of spirits came from her, mingling with cheese, disinfectant, firelighters and newsprint.

Returning to where Griff and Cherie were trying not to laugh, she placed her bottle on the counter and fumbled for money in a pouch-type purse – the sort often seen at antique fairs in the big hotel on the Canterbury road.

When the door had clanged shut behind her, Cherie fanned the air and said in a self-important voice, 'Draws the pension, you know.'

'Comes to us all,' shrugged Griff, putting down his mug and strolling to the door.

As the door opened, Cherie called, 'Norma Desmond.'

Griff halted. 'Eh?'

'*Sunset Boulevard.*'

'Oh!' Griff waved and went out, slamming the door behind him.

Before he climbed into the van he stood for a moment, looking around, feeling put out by Cherie's news. He loved this hill-hugged village lost in woodlands. The road to the vineyard was lined with great oaks which knitted overhead and had stood for centuries. He liked that. He liked their permanence. He didn't like change.

Danielle was wearily climbing down from the forklift, when for a stomach-churning moment she felt her foot miss the step.

Immediately a pair of arms circled her and set her back on her feet. Gratefully, she turned.

'Thanks, Tom.'

'My pleasure.'

Returning his smile, she thought, as she often did, how nice he was to have around, and what a good choice her grandfather had made taking him on.

He had been an astute reader of character in his own opinion. And perhaps, she thought now, as Tom's watchful eyes checked her as if she were one of his machines, Grandy had been right.

She wondered if Grandy had ever met Kingsley. His name had never been mentioned between them.

As if on cue, he appeared around the corner from the direction of the track – or the laboratory, she thought sourly, taking a step back from Tom's encircling arm.

Kingsley's face looked as if it didn't like what it saw, and even Tom watched him approach with displeasure.

Kingsley's 'Evening' was curt enough to discourage further conversation.

'Evening. I'll be here until ten, if you want me, Danny,' said Tom, tight-lipped and stubborn. His bushy brows were raised in an arc that she knew was a question. Was she going to ask him to call into the cottage on his way home, for a nightcap?

With a grateful smile, she said, 'I'm going home for a break, then I'll come back.'

Straightening her cap, she watched him walk away. 'You weren't very nice to him,' she told Kingsley.

'But you were,' Kingsley said nastily as they walked across the yard and turned onto the track, making for the cottage. Then he added, 'Are you limping?'

She glanced up at him. 'Just a little. I slipped off the fork-lift and Tom had to save me from a nasty fall. He was slightly too late, but better late than never.'

Seeing his shamed expression, she laughed, and Kingsley had the grace to admit, 'I know it's none of my business, but I worry about you.'

That's a turn up for the books, she thought, hiding

a smile. 'Everyone seems to worry about me lately. I'm not used to it.'

They had reached the cottage and he opened the door, letting her brush past him. 'You know,' he said, following her inside, 'when you're alone, I hear you sing. When you're with your friends you sparkle.' He moved behind her along the passage. 'When you're with me, you're aloof.'

They reached the kitchen and she strode inside without answering, switching on the coffee-machine. A swift glance showed her his perplexed frown, and she understood immediately. He wasn't used to women holding back; he was used to having his own way. Huh! Not me, she told herself. He's not using me. She couldn't help, though, feeling bemused – and not altogether displeased – by the way the conversation was going.

His eyes followed her movements and rested briefly on the calendar.

'You fill up a room, Danielle; do you know that?'

Humming, she took a casserole dish from the fridge and placed it in the Aga, slammed the door and frivolously patted her stomach beneath her baggy sweater. 'Too much spaghetti, you mean?'

He caught her arm and glared down into her laughing eyes. 'You know I don't mean that. I mean, a man could get used to having you around.' He stared at her so intently that she felt herself turn on and heat up and deeply anticipate any movement he might make in her direction.

Instead, he spun round and hurried from the room. *Now what have I done?* she asked herself, and frowned.

Going to the bottom of the stairs she called after him. 'Dinner about eight?'

He shouted back what she thought was a yes, then she heard his door slam.

Sighing, she returned to the kitchen and thoughtfully stared at the calendar . . . at the overall hanging behind the gaping kitchen door . . . and, out in the hall, at his wellington boots standing beside hers.

Her mouth formed an O.

CHAPTER 8

Danielle pecked the old lady's blusher. 'I'm afraid this person forced his company on me.'

Francesca's eyes were a dark inquisition, down and up his long body. 'I can think of worse fates.'

Hiding a surprised smile at the discomfort on his face – a new face, polite and gentle . . . amazing how people changed according to the company they were with – Danielle made the introductions in an annoyed voice. 'My grandmother prefers to be called Francesca.'

Francesca laughed. 'Take a seat Mr Hunter, or – ' seeing his interested glance across to the photograph-laden antique sideboard, she nodded her coiffured head ' – browse around, stroll in the garden, feel free . . .'

Turning to Danielle, she said, 'Tch! You look tired. I must give you the name of a good face cream. Just like your grandfather – nothing exists but the yard.'

'Absolutely.' Danielle was resentfully aware that Francesca always deflated her – barbed criticism lurked in most of her remarks. 'I'll always put his dream first,' she added pointedly, letting her look say, At least he had me.

The meaningful glance she threw at Kingsley was wasted; he was holding a framed photograph, and with a pang she recognized herself as a child, with a dog.

She could barely keep the censure from her voice. 'The yard was your husband's life, Francesca, and – '

Francesca lifted an arthritic hand. 'Yes, I know . . . and it gave me a living. And, my dear, I've put in more than my share of back-breaking work.'

Danielle's brows arched, recalling the grand-mother of yesterday. Eyes impish, voice like warm toffee, that sometimes grew hard and cracked but mostly had a teasing sort of laughter in it. Smart, happy-natured, with a short attention span where Danielle was concerned. 'I can't cope with this,' Danielle could recall her saying. She must have been very young at the time – it was one of her first memories and she had been having a tantrum. Soon after that she had been sent to school. Being good, she had decided, kept her at home.

'Trouble with the young, Mr Hunter, is they forget that before they grew up life happened.' Francesca turned back to Danielle. 'Of course I worked . . . from dawn to dusk, seven days a week. Which is why I had to send you away to school. I would have loved to keep you at home; you were my delight.'

What a strange thing to say, reflected Danielle, staring doubtfully at the elegant, upright, still beautiful lady. Francesca had resented Danielle's closeness to Grandy and had preferred to be alone with her husband. At least, that was the way Danielle recalled it.

Her attention distracted by movement, Danielle turned her head and saw that Kingsley had slipped through the patio doors and was standing on the lawn, politely leaving them alone to talk. She watched him bend to inspect a bed of red foliage.

'I spent time with you during the holidays, do you remember?' The old lady's voice was urgent and Danielle, perched on the edge of a deep armchair, hands folded around her knees, turned to her, curious about the tremor in the normally buoyant voice.

'Yes, I remember.' There had been laughter, Danielle thought, but no love. And she couldn't pretend there was, even if that was what she wanted.

As if she read Danielle's eyes, Francesca went on slowly, 'The first time you came home for the holidays I met you at the station . . . I wanted to hug you, but you looked at me with such cold, accusing eyes, I . . .'

'We still had good times,' said Danielle, feeling a little sorry for her, but impatient too. In reality she had found the excursions, stately home tours and browsing around antique shops rather boring, preferring, instead, her solitary countryside rambles. Worst of all had been Francesca's impish pleasure

102

in planning surprises. Such as a welcome home party once . . . It still made Danielle shudder, remembering how she had walked into what she had thought was an empty room and found it full of village children she had never had time to get to know.

She heard Francesca say, 'Anyway, darling, when you left school I was glad I no longer needed to work in the vineyard so many hours; in a way I resented it for making us strangers. The vineyard is the boss, remember that.'

She dimpled across the room at Kingsley, in the flirtatious way she had with men; he had just slipped back inside. 'It gives life – the grape, Mr Hunter – but it exacts a toll, a life for a life. I watched it take your teenage years, Danny. You didn't have the fun, the boyfriends.' She clapped her hands in the dramatic way she had, setting bracelets rattling. 'I want no more of it.'

'He knew,' Danielle said, with feeling. 'That's why he left it to me.' She sighed to herself. She always vowed that she wouldn't argue with Francesca, but once here it happened.

Francesca's face clouded. Then she seemed to give herself the briefest of shakes, raising her chin in the air. She stood up slowly and, hardly leaning on her stick, crossed the room to the sideboard, reaching for a photograph of a girl with laughing dark eyes and a swarm of chocolate-coloured curls.

'Danny's mother – my daughter, Luiza,' she told Kingsley eagerly, searching his eyes for approval –

or, thought Danielle, watching guiltily, for a friend.

'She had the wanderlust, rather like me,' Francesca went on. 'She was in Paris, she met a French boy, they fell in love. They came back here to marry and Danny was born the following February.'

'What happened to Luiza?' asked Kingsley, studying the photograph of a proud, straight-backed girl, with a full figure and generous lips.

'Danny's the image of her mother, isn't she?' Francesca sighed. 'Shorter, though. Her father was small. What happened? The night Danny was born . . .' Her voice faded a little, as if reaching back into the past exhausted her. 'There was a terrible gale that night; Claude, Danny's father, went to meet the ambulance, it was taking so long. He found it in a ditch – a tree had smashed down on top of it. They sent out another, but by the time they got Luiza to the hospital complications had set in. She died . . . actually before Danny was born.'

Danielle rose and walked away through the patio doors, soothed by the life in the springy grass underfoot. She had heard the story before. *What's the point of dwelling on sadness?* she thought crossly.

There was an earthy scent of chrysanthemums and newly turned soil, you could smell dying, yet the tree-packed, well-behaved, lovingly tended garden blazed with copper, red and gold foliage.

'And Claude?' she heard Kingsley ask.

Danielle smiled at excited birds gathered around the birdhouse, squabbling over breadcrumbs, but, despite their clamour, she could still hear Francesca's reply.

'Claude? He went away . . . to the States. He had relatives there. Later he returned to France. We adopted Danielle, that's why she has our name.' There was a pause, and then she went on, 'It's very sad. Claude came back three years ago but, tragically, just over a year later he died. He knew he was dying; he wanted to see his child.'

His child! The child he had not wanted because she reminded him of his wife.

Danielle didn't want to hear any more. The year she had spent getting to know her father was seared in her memory, and that he had been taken from her so soon had been a bitter pill to swallow.

A shiny copper leaf slowly floated down and landed at her feet. She reached out and touched the rough trunk of a tree, then drew close enough to rest her cheek against it for a moment, closing her eyes, smelling the woody bark, letting its strength soak into her.

To some it might have seemed an odd gesture, but not to Danielle, who loved trees and indeed felt an affinity with them – they were almost human to her. As well as their shelter, and their cool, fragrant breath on a hot day, there was something majestic and permanent about their presence which gave her a sense of serenity and strength. They alone were always there for her.

A fat, worm-filled blackbird plopped heavily down

on to the birdhouse, sending the smaller birds flying off with distressed squawks. Danielle hurried inside, flinging out her arms. 'That's enough. Kingsley doesn't want to hear any more about my family. And don't you dare show him my baby photos,' she laughed, seeing Francesca's eyes dart across the sideboard with the greed of one who had hours to spend but was short of company.

'No, wait – I just wanted to show him your grandfather. Danielle adored him, Mr Hunter, followed him everywhere as a child. Here . . .' In her haste her swollen hands nearly dropped the heavy silver frame, and Kingsley caught it, holding in his clasp the face of an unsmiling, strong-willed man with deep-set, worried eyes beneath a tweed cap. Looking at it, you could see that he had been handsome once, and you felt he'd had no time for sentiment or weakness – in himself or others.

Francesca's face lit up. 'We met in Rome during the war.' A dimple appeared in her cheek. 'I was on the first train out of Naples after the war, carrying war brides,' she informed Kingsley importantly. 'We settled in Greenwich first – '

'That's a coincidence,' interrupted Kingsley. 'My mother lives in Greenwich.'

Francesca turned bright eyes on him. 'Do you live with her?'

'Not likely. I have a flat in Kensington.'

'Are you married?'

He shook his head and Francesca glanced slyly

across at Danielle, who, perched on a chair-arm, appeared to be more interested in tickling a self-satisfied, spoilt Persian cat who had settled on the cushion with the air of one who knew she could twist this person around her paw.

'Don't you want to marry, Mr Hunter?'

'No way.'

'Why ever not?'

'I don't want the responsibility, I suppose. If you don't mind my saying so, women can be . . . demanding, troublesome. Not a very original answer.' His smile was gentle, making him seem different from the man Danielle knew. He didn't seem at all put out, she saw, cringing.

'How do you manage, Mr Hunter – to look after yourself, I mean?'

He looked amused. 'I have a housekeeper, but I'm not a bad cook – am I Danielle?'

'You look well enough,' Francesca observed, when Danielle remained silent.

'I should be,' he told her. 'I have a mother who continually filled me with food and – ' he grimaced – ' everything that was good for me. I was very ill as a child and – ' he gave a rueful smile 'she made it her life's work to build me up.'

He met Danielle's surprised look for a long moment, until his inquisitor called his attention back.

'What was wrong with you?'

'In layman's language, my body couldn't absorb goodness from food,' he said, with that patient smile.

'I was fading away until doctors at Great Ormond Street, where I spent months of my childhood, found a cure.'

Francesca glanced at a flabbergasted Danielle and said to him warmly, 'Your mother did a good job.'

He nodded. 'She spent hours at hospitals, she nagged doctors, she refused to give in. Good food, exercise and fresh air were the order of the day. I still walk around London or jog around Greenwich Park when I'm there.'

Francesca looked him over. 'You're beautifully tanned. Have you been on holiday?'

'A working holiday.' He smiled. 'I travel to the south of France on business; we've made a lot of friends there whom we stay with. Only trouble is, our meetings tend to go on until the early hours.'

Ignoring Francesca's what-a-catch look in her direction, Danielle said quickly, 'I must go, there's work to do.'

'Isn't that the dress I bought you for your birthday, Danny?'

Glancing down at the barely worn blue chambray shirt-dress, she nodded, avoiding Kingsley's eyes. After all, he hadn't even commented.

'I'm pleased to see you wearing it instead of those dungarees – although I wish you hadn't covered it with that great floppy cardigan.' Francesca glanced curiously from one to the other.

Danielle sighed, recalling many such conversations. Clothes and appearances made Francesca's world, she thought scathingly, noting the impeccable make-up, the smart suit and polished shoes, the manicure and the delicate aura of Joy scent which always surrounded her.

Yet . . . it was so Francesca. Danielle felt a sudden lump in her throat. For the first time she recognized that there was something brave about the effort, which would be made however difficult it might be, or however trivial the occasion.

As they said goodbye Francesca squeezed Danielle's hand. 'Remember the saying they are not long, the days of wine and roses.' Her eyes sparkled. 'Go out and live. Be a friend of the grape, not a servant.'

'Sorry about that. You were good to her,' Danielle said honestly as she drove the truck back towards the vineyard. 'She can go on a bit, and she lives in the past. We've never been close – we're such opposites, I suppose. I apologise for the third degree and the boring family history.' She felt a little guilty; she always meant to be patient and less cross with Francesca . . . it was annoying that Kingsley had shown her up.

'No problem. I enjoyed her.'

She was surprised, and a glance showed her that he was taking a great deal of interest in the passing hopfields, which lay empty and forlorn at that time of year, harvest long over.

'Yes, well . . . good.' She swung her eyes back to concentrate on the winding lanes.

'I agree with her about the dress. Looks good.'

'I wore it to please her,' she replied, turning the wheel and feeling an odd kick in her stomach.

Watching her profile, he said slowly, 'I've noticed your need to please people.'

After a short silence she said quietly, 'Is that a bad thing?'

'No – unless it gets you into difficult situations.' His voice developed a sharp edge. 'Does it?'

'What?' she asked, confused.

'Wanting to please people; do you do things you otherwise wouldn't?'

She thought about it. 'Sometimes, I suppose. Why?'

'Oh, just trying to fathom you out.'

He waited while she negotiated a bend, and then went on, 'You must have sorely missed your grandfather when he died – you being so close to him, I mean?'

'Naturally.' They just about made it to the top of the hill and, staring ahead, she saw the church spire rising like King Arthur's sword from the tree-packed expanse of valley. Over the grumbling the engine was making, she heard him ask, 'What was your father like?'

She accelerated along a straight stretch of road with woodlands each side. Sunlight twined between stilt-man trunks, shadows fell onto the road as green puddles and the musky scent of raging bonfires came in through the open window with its own peculiar sadness.

'He was . . . um . . . small, big-eyed, serious; he smoked too many cigarettes,' she said, in a faraway voice, the smell of French tobacco blowing through her mind. 'He was musical – a pianist, he wrote songs as well. He had this . . .' Her voice faltered. After a bit, she went on, 'He had this glow of inner energy about him.' Not wanting to talk about the gradual dimming, his illness, she said, 'He was kind, sensitive, brave – everything,' she declared, with a break in her voice, 'that a man should be.'

Hating his probing questions, not being one to enjoy talking about herself, Danielle was thankful when the church came in sight, and on impulse she pulled over to the side of the road. 'I've one more call to make; it won't interest you. Wait here.' After pulling on the brake and switching off the engine, she opened the door and jumped down into the road.

She was standing at the graveside when she heard footsteps striking gravel behind her. But she felt no irritation, and somehow, in that place of such sepulchral silence, it seemed natural for him to place his arm across her shoulders.

'Your grandfather?'

Danielle nodded.

'Is your father here too?'

'He went to America for an operation. It failed.' She gazed down at the ground, remembering how hard she had prayed. 'He returned to France to die. He had a sad life,' Danielle told him. 'His father joined the French Resistance during the war and was

111

taken prisoner – his mother too; she was seven months pregnant. He was shot; she was rescued by her brother, a Resistance worker. She went home to her parents in the country to have the baby – my father, Claude – and then she left him there and returned to join the Resistance herself. She was shot only days before the war ended; Claude grew up with his grandparents.'

Danielle saw that Kingsley was digesting this and, like herself, finding it difficult to believe that people had lived such dangerous lives, that such atrocities had been committed, when around them lay the gentle English countryside.

Danielle recalled that blustery November day, just after the harvest last year, when she, or a shell of herself, had shivered here beside a smiling Francesca.

Today, her low, sing song voice read the inscription calmly, without tremor, without emotion, but almost with a trace of resentment. The words hung on the silence.

'There was a Door to which I found no Key,
There was a Veil past which I might not see.
Some little talk awhile of Me and Thee, there
    was –
And then no more of Thee and Me.'

Overhead, sweet, pure notes burst from the throat of a blackbird; Kingsley's hand was warm through the wool of her cardigan, and the surge of tragedy she had expected and dreaded to feel on this first impulsive visit to the grave wasn't there. There was only disbelief that Grandy had any connection with that mound of earth at all.

'Francesca loved him deeply,' Kingsley stated.

Danielle was silent. She had felt very jealous once. 'Francesca . . . well, she seemed to live for pleasure.'

'You take after her. Another "intoxicating lady".'

'Woman of joy,' she said softly. 'You know, having been disappointed over not having a son, Grandy apparently hoped for a grandson.' She grinned, gave an unknowingly vulnerable shake of her shoulders. 'My mother had apparently already chosen the name Daniel, after Grandy. But then I came along.' She gave a little laugh and turned to inspect his face. What she saw encouraged her to add, 'I used to think of a little boy Daniel as real – a sort of invisible twin. Silly . . .'

Looking down into her raised face, he felt vaguely angry and insisted, 'No, it isn't. Quite normal for an only child, an invisible playmate.'

She laughed and turned away, shrugging her shoulders. 'How would you know – ?' Confused, she broke off.

'I have a sister, Angie, who adores children; she runs a kindergarten in Kensington and if that isn't enough, she has two of her own.'

Danielle thought about that; she couldn't see him as an uncle – or even as a brother. But then she didn't know him at all really.

'You know, Francesca smiled at the funeral. All the way through it. She told me that he had named the vineyard after her because he said she had brought joy into his life . . . and so she wasn't going to cry at his funeral. So neither did I.'

Danielle turned eyes bright even in sadness on him. 'And then I found her one day, soon afterwards, clutching his overalls which used to hang on the back of the kitchen door and sobbing her heart out. I took them down and shoved them out of sight upstairs.'

The blackbird on a bough above their heads suddenly trilled again, and she raised her face, seeking him. 'If our bodies were like wine bottles we could see right down to the soul, but, as things are, we have to work out for ourselves that the widest smile can sparkle while sadness lurks in its depths.' Turning, she saw intensity in his gaze and gave a little shiver, embarrassed because she had spoken without thinking, and she hated talking of sadness.

As they started to walk away, he confided, 'My mother's a sad creature, you know.' Crunching beside her, back along the gravel path, he added, 'After Dad died, I looked after her as best I could . . . I was twenty-five before she remarried.'

Hearing the relief in his voice, she shot him an enquiring look. 'You liked your stepfather, then?'

His mouth twisted. 'He was good to me, but more importantly he was good to her – at first. It was a relief, I can tell you; she's one of those women who

114

turns everything into high drama and needs a shoulder to lean on. And,' he ended ruefully, 'she cried a lot.'

'Are they happy?'

He gave her a strange, sideways stare. 'She wants them to be. She's a great believer in happy families. Danielle . . .'

He came to a sudden stop, and she looked up, puzzled by his frown. He paused for such a long time that she thought he had forgotten what he wanted to say, as people sometimes do. 'She'd do anything to protect her family,' was what he finally said.

He had changed again – the morose look was back – and she smiled brightly to hide the ache in her heart that shouldn't have been there but was.

Happy families was a game she had never played, she reflected as they strolled on. Family life had always seemed something of a treat – like when she had been invited to spend holidays with school-friends. She had felt on the outside looking in, somehow, as if the family scene were a stage set, and she the audience.

Her thoughts and her steps came to a stop at the gate and, afraid of the wistfulness inside her, she said lightly, 'Family loyalties are not something with which I'm familiar.'

Walking through the gate, she turned to hold it open for him and found herself caught in a glare as he said accusingly, 'That's no excuse for breaking up marriages.'

'Oh, don't start again,' she sighed, stalking towards the truck. She often came away from Francesca's feeling drained by the constant harping back to the past and boring discussions on fashion and things which didn't interest her. She was in no mood for a continuation of the battle between Kingsley and herself either. Things had been so different today.

Pulling open the door, she clambered into the truck, slipped with a sigh into the driver's seat and turned, reaching out to close the door, only to find Kingsley holding it firmly open. 'And love?' he asked, with the old sneer. 'Love is unfamiliar to you?'

She started the engine. Looking down at his upturned face, seeing its curves and pronounced cheekbones once again settling into lines of hostility as he slammed the door, she wondered why he bore a grudge against her, even though she had never met him before last Tuesday.

She crashed the gears, which went well with her inner turbulence, as she watched his silver head pass the bonnet; with her lips pressed together, she waited as he climbed in and folded his long length into the seat beside her, feeling at that moment that she hated every inch of him with such ferocity she found herself gritting her teeth and gripping the wheel tensely.

She started singing beneath her breath, although she didn't know all the words, only the first line in fact. Something about days of wine and roses. She hummed the rest. Just to show that she was quite cheerful and not at all moved by his truculence. And because she knew it irritated him.

For some peculiar reason of his own, he couldn't bear to see her cheerful.

She drove around the green, past the pub; a few lunch-time drinkers were drifting out, heading for home. As did Danielle, with a sigh of relief.

Tom was in the pub, sitting beside the window, when he saw her pass by. He recognized her passenger.

'Last orders at the bar,' called Ron.

Tom went over, ordered a pint, delved into his pocket for money.

'Enjoy your lunch?' asked Ron in his anxious, friendly-puppy way.

'Great,' nodded Tom, who came in every Sunday for a roast beef dinner and often left shaking his head at how anyone as vague as Ron could be running a business. Good job he had Iris. She wore the trousers there.

But Tom had more on his mind today than Ron's shortcomings. His expression was morose and surly as he nursed the over-full glass back to his table.

He was remembering something the innocent-eyed Cherie had said when he'd called in for his Sunday paper.

She had put down her romance novel when the bell clanged, and with her usual unblinking air of frozen watchfulness had waited until he had chosen his paper.

117

Then, as if her mouth had been full of whipped cream, she'd asked, 'Who's that handsome man Danielle's going about with?'

'She's not going about with him. It's business,' he'd answered, slapping coins down on the counter and making for the door, glaring up at the belly-aching bell.

'You want to watch it,' she'd called after him.

He could have strangled her. For the first time he had his life all mapped out, now Cherie's knowing voice echoed, tearing at his dream.

He supped his beer, thinking about how it had all begun. His life.

Bermondsey. 1955. His mum had known Tommy Steele – a rock and roll star who'd grown up in the next street. Tom had been named after her idol and force-fed his music. He went to sea, just as Steele had done, only he never learned to play the guitar. His favourite music was engines – especially when they went wrong and he had to doctor them.

He left the Navy after ten years, living on his savings for a while, but then disliking the new-look Bermondsey even more than the old one, he'd bummed around Kent fruit-picking, helping out wherever he could. The gods must have been with him the day he'd walked beneath the sign, 'INTOXICATING LADY' for the first time.

He was street-wise, worldly-wise and wise to the ways of women. But not Danielle's type of woman. He was learning. He was patient. Distant horizons

118

were not new to him. Neither were storms.

Things couldn't have worked out better, with the old man dying. She depended upon him now. He saw himself as a star of his own little world, as Steele had been a star in his.

He had known Danielle since she was twelve. One minute she was a little kid – a bundle of mischief who sulked when she had to dress properly – the next there was something . . . different.

She had a sleepwalker's appearance, with haunted eyes, as if she knew about unbearable tragedies. There had been the trauma of the dog, of course. Or maybe it was just part of a girl's growing up.

Tom often wondered what had happened.

She had plump thighs, a bottom that made a man want to trace its shape. You knew by the bursting beneath those shapeless clothes that she would feel warm, soft and feminine in your arms, and there was something ridiculous about the fact that he could see a woman with a cleavage and little left to the imagination and be unmoved, but Danielle, with her belly a soft mound and her breasts bunched beneath old sweaters and a dungaree bib, was more erotic.

A bell clanged. He looked at his watch. Thinking of Danielle going past in the truck with that man, he felt a flood of white-hot anger. Why shouldn't he go and visit someone who always made him welcome? A Sunday afternoon of bed and mothering was what he needed . . .

* * *

119

When they got back, Danielle changed and hurried out to the slopes. Then, calmed by a couple of hours in the fresh air, she toured the winery and worked on papers in the office.

Kingsley, she assumed, was holed up in the cottage, for she saw no sign of him. Maybe he, too, did paperwork in his spare time.

She found concentrating difficult, partly because Kingsley intruded into her thoughts. He made her feel so emotional. She didn't like that. Or maybe she did.

Sucking a pen, Danielle stared at the door and went over the first time she'd seen him standing there, and her shock when he'd said he was staying with her for a week. And now the week was nearly over . . .

She crashed back to the present with a start.

Incredible that she had been too lost in thought to hear the wind rising, Now it was a prowling beast, rattling the windows and doors, trying to break in.

Idiot, she told herself, catching her trembling lip between her teeth. But no amount of talking to herself had ever eased the fear – the same old fear she had known as long as she could remember. What was more, Grandy had died on a day when the wind was prowling the house, whining, pawing at the door like the devil.

She rose, throat dry, fingers gripping the edge of the desk. While she told herself not to be stupid the whole building shook as if in wicked laughter; outside, loose objects were picked up by an invisible, vindictive hand and hurled aside. From the orchard, just beyond the room she was in, came a banshee howl.

At the same time the door flew open, and the blood drained from her face.

CHAPTER 9

'I've come to – What's wrong?' He bounded across the room and swung round to her side of the desk. 'Danielle?'

Before she could change her facial expression his hands were digging into her shoulders, and it seemed, as she shivered, that he was about to shake her. 'Tell me,' he ordered, in a voice that brooked no argument.

The fluttering of her heart slowed down and started up again, thumping with a different rhythm. She attempted a laugh. 'I'm being silly. I'm . . . I hate wind.'

He stepped back, the better to see her face. 'You're terrified,' he exclaimed, opening up his arms.

It was purely one human being comforting another. No more than that. She went inside his arms with a childlike confidence and naturalness. It wasn't until afterwards that she remembered . . . this had never happened before. No arms like this had ever held her – neither, she told herself quickly, had she needed them.

His chest throbbed in one ear and her other ear was covered by his warm, strong hand. The pressure of his arms was firm and gentle and never before, except maybe in the far country of her babyhood, could she remember feeling so protected. Becoming aware of this, she almost stopped breathing with surprise. And suddenly these moments seemed to dance.

How long did she stand there? She didn't know. Until she had to move in order to breathe. He stepped back, his arms fell away, and the wind once more hurled itself about, mangling her queasy stomach as always.

'Let's get back to the house,' he said with calm authority, to which she could only nod vehemently, glancing at the window, surprised to see the sky so dark. And she picked up her cap and tidied her papers. He locked the door behind them as they left.

Outside, as wild, cold hands went for her, she braced herself, her eyes trying to pierce the darkness. 'The vines will be fine. Come on,' he called, pulling her away from the side of the building and onto the path.

But she insisted upon stopping at the winery, knowing they would have had the sense to pull the great doors to.

He was as impatient as a stumping horse. Everything's safe, okay?' He kept a protective arm around her as they hurried up the track. 'If I don't hold on, you'll do a Mary Poppins and fly off,' he joked.

With her head bent against the wind, this was one

occasion when she could only smile weakly. Then there was the relief of fumbling with the door, Kingsley helping her, and pushing the door open, going quickly inside. And, as the door swung closed, muffled shrieks and a blessed stillness.

She stood for a blissful moment in a puddle of friendly light as Kingsley pressed switches. 'Wow!' she grinned weakly, sitting on a stair to pull off her boots. 'What a night!'

Meeting his concerned stare, she stood up. 'I know . . . I look like a scarecrow,' she said, starting to climb the stairs. 'I'm going to change.'

His voice followed her. 'Like to go out for a meal?'

I must be hearing things, she thought, stopping and slowly turning round. 'I'm not sure,' she said slowly, frowning a little.

His expression darkened. 'You mean you've made other arrangements?'

She shook her tangled head. 'I mean it's dangerous out there right now.'

Anyone else, she thought, biting her lip, would have impatiently told her that it was only wind. Kingsley just said, with unusual mildness, 'Might calm down later.'

'If it does,' she said seriously, 'I'll take you up on that invitation. Er . . . thanks.' She brushed strands of hair from her face and flew up the stairs to her room.

The noise in the thick-walled cottage almost drowned the wind, what with happily running bath water and the gurgles of plumbing from Kingsley's room – not to mention Danielle's voice raised in song as she soaked and drew happy faces in orange-scented foam.

She switched on the radio in her bedroom and sang along with 'Bridge Over Troubled Water', pulling from the wardrobe something her best friend Jane had persuaded her to buy last year at the sales and which she had not yet worn.

Posturing before the mirror, she wasn't displeased. She ran her hand over the clinging blue crêpe dress, which fell just to her knees. The off-the-shoulder collar, original enough to catch the fussy Jane's eye, was blue satin and plunged to the waist. Not bad, she decided. She curved, yes, but her stomach was flat, and while her thighs were on the heavy side her ankles were slim. She slipped on her only decent pair of black, high-heeled shoes. *After the harvest, I really must go shopping* . . .

With her hair up and her slanting eyes emphasized by kohl pencil, the girl in the mirror was not her at all. And outside the wind had lulled slightly.

From the landing, she heard Kingsley moving about in his room, and, hurrying downstairs into the sitting room, she switched on lamps and the electric fire and swished the curtains shut, making the room cosy.

Then she sat down at the piano and began to play, to drown the little bit of wind that was still gusting about.

From her fingers trickled the haunting 'Days of Wine and Roses', and she smiled to herself, thinking of Francesca and her 'go out and enjoy life' philosophy. Tonight, Danielle reflected happily, that was just what she was going to do. She couldn't believe how much she was looking forward to the evening.

When the song ended, she dropped her hands into her lap, turned round and there he was, watching her.

Pulling in a deep breath, she jumped up. Self-conscious, she laugh nevertheless, knowing her eyes were shining. She held up her arms and her voice was husky as she asked, 'Will I do?'

His eyes swept over her and narrowed in a way that made her breath catch in her throat.

I don't believe it.

But it was there again . . . skin-shrinking, blue-grey hate. Her hands fluttered down to her sides, and she never knew whether her cry was uttered or whether it remained inside. For she felt stripped – cruelly stripped.

His words lashed at her. 'Why do you have to be what you are?'

She flinched as if he had hit her; with hurt, shocked eyes she watched him turn and sweep out through the door and then, with stunned disbelief, she heard the front door slam, his footsteps hammering down the path. Her legs gave way then, and she slumped onto the piano stool, her arm striking a low, mournful chord, its solemn vibrations shivering in her head with the question . . . *Why?*

His car started up. Headlamps swept through the curtains, washed around the walls of the room and disappeared. The world went dark.

'Right,' she said shakily out loud. 'You have a choice. You either go out or stay in. Simple.'

With the wind still sneaking around, she decided to stay in, cook herself a chop, catch up on some paperwork.

All dressed up and nowhere to go. She sighed as she ate with a magazine propped in front of her, feeling more than a little sorry for herself. What was wrong with the man? Why had he run out on her? She would never forget the shock and disgust on his face. What had she done? she puzzled, pushing away her half-eaten meal and pouring another glass of wine.

She scarcely read the magazine, and fared little better with her paperwork. Restlessly she rose from her seat in front of the bureau and returned to the piano, finding herself playing music that stirred her heart.

She was playing the 'Moonlight Sonata' when the hall clock struck ten. Soon after came the sound she had been waiting for. The front door opening and closing.

Her fingers ran so softly over the keys during the slow movement that his words on the telephone came clearly out of the kitchen and down the passage, through the open sitting room door.

'Hello, darling. Thought I'd ring before you go to

bed. One more day, then . . . You've nothing to fear . . . I promise.'

Concern and love and a younger voice made him sound like someone else – certainly not the Kingsley she had come to know – and she felt a deep surge of resentment. Who was on the end of the line? What would she be like? Glamorous, obviously.

She changed to a rousing Chopin march. *Who cares who he's speaking to*? she simmered, thumping the keys.

When the music ended she felt the skin prickle on the nape of her neck; resting her hands in her lap, she slowly turned.

Kingsley was propped in the doorway, the glass in his hand obviously containing the remains of her wine.

'I've left money on the kitchen table for the telephone call, and for my board and lodging,' he told her, with that icy, blood-chilling contempt.

'I don't want it.'

He strode across the room, thumped his glass onto the piano top and pulled her to her feet. She saw the look in his eyes. There was challenge, and a glint of excitement that left her in no doubt as to his intention.

Her brief movement away was stopped as hands and arms caught her up. She might have been whirled into a tornado. A shaft of feeling shot through her body like an electric shock. His hand on the back of her head forced her mouth to his face – a face twisted with a

128

darkness that brought her back to earth with something lost and lonely. Her resentful hands, pushing against him, made not the slightest impression. All that moved beneath her fingers were packs of muscle.

Their lips crashed together like steel crushing velvet. The answer to everything in a man's book . . . Now she was flooded with red-hot, heart-exploding anger. She hated the punishing hardness of his mouth pressing her own clamped, stubborn lips against her gritted teeth. Hated it so much she raised her foot and stabbed her heel into his leather shoe. He jerked back, and as she aimed a kick for good measure she enjoyed feeling the shock vibrate through him. Released, she fell back against the stool.

They were both breathing heavily as they glared at each other. His face was flooded an unbecoming red. 'Why others and not me? Am I so repulsive?'

'Your behaviour is,' she choked. What about the telephone call? The cheek of him! To phone his lover and try to embrace her afterwards! Assault, not embrace. She could barely control her fury.

'You're unspeakable and unjust. Isn't the contract enough? Isn't that a powerful enough weapon for you? Must you bring sex into it?'

'What about Piers?' he demanded.

She was confused. 'Piers has been good to me . . .'

He turned away. 'The last thing I want to know about is all the sordid detail of your affair.'

'Why are you so morally indignant?' she asked scathingly. 'Are you so perfect?'

Without waiting for his answer, she flung herself past him, sweeping from the seething room, across the hall and along the passage into the kitchen. Taking milk from the fridge, she slammed the door until everything inside rattled. She pulled a saucepan from its hook and slammed it down on the Aga; she took a jar of Horlicks from the cupboard and smashed it down on the kitchen top.

He had followed her. 'The money's on the table.'

She glared round. Sure enough there it was. And beside it, a large brown envelope.

'Keep it.' Childish, she knew, but didn't care.

'Not much of a business woman,' he sneered.

She spun round, pointing a shaky spoon at him. 'You've been trying to break me down – it's weird – why? You've twisted my conversation, watched me – in fact you've haunted me. What, for Chrissake, are you up to?'

'I wanted to find out what makes a girl who's attractive enough to get her own man take my mother's husband.'

CHAPTER 10

Swish . . .

The milk boiled over, sizzling onto the cooker –
top, as white as their faces.

Everything happened quickly after that. Without
thinking, she moved the saucepan from the heat,
grasped a handful of paper towel and mopped up
the milk.

Hearing her gasp of pain, he was beside her in an
instant, thrusting her fingers beneath running water.

'It's nothing,' she gasped, eyes watering. It was
true. Against everything else, it *was* nothing. He let
go of her hand, she noticed, as if it burned him.

Moving to the nearest chair, she sat rigid, trembling, nursing her burnt fingers, shocked eyes following his every move as he dried his hands on a
towel.

'Kingsley . . . what do you mean . . . your
mother's husband?' she said agitatedly. 'I don't
know . . .'

'Piers is my stepfather.' He fired the words from
grim lips.

131

'Oh, God.' Her laugh held hysteria.

Hearing her laugh, he threw his hands in the air in a gesture of despair and sat down.

Moistening her lips, she said, 'Kingsley, let me explain something to you . . .'

He slowly shook his head. 'Uh – uh! Let me explain to *you*. It's obvious – ' his eyes flickered over her body ' – that you're not expecting a baby.' Ignoring her gasp, he held up his hand. 'Your letter was a lie, and it nearly destroyed my mother.'

Feeling she was in a nightmare, she pleaded, 'What letter? I don't know about any letter.'

'Let me finish,' he barked.

Her hand went to her mouth. She sat frozen, as his cold voice went on. 'My first plan was to come here and plead, if necessary, for you to leave Piers alone – even if it cost me money.'

'Stop!' she shouted. 'Stop, stop, stop! I wish you *had* done that,' she rushed on. 'I would have told you that I've never, ever been out with Piers or had any relationship with him. Apart from a few lunches, that is . . .' Her voice died away.

They were both transfixed, eyes holding eyes, and she saw disbelief and scorn written clearly on his face.

Because she felt so distraught, she flared up. 'You've obviously got the wrong girl, Mr Detective.'

He inspected her with narrowed eyes. 'Mother found a letter, on your headed notepaper, signed 'Danny.'

'Sorry, Kingsley, but I didn't send it.'

She saw that his eyes had never left her, and shivered as he told her, 'I checked his diary; why was he here so often?'

'Piers and Grandy were good friends.' She shrugged.

Watching her closely, he saw a shadow cross her face as she went on, 'Since Grandy died Piers only stayed about half an hour. And another thing: Piers got into the habit of calling me by Grandy's pet name – Nell.' She looked away. 'I would have signed a letter to Piers "Nell" – not Danny,' she added, with a break in her voice.

Looking at him to check his reaction, she surprised herself by feeling a pang of compassion. He seemed suddenly young and torn, as he struggled to turn over all the facts in his mind. The fight appeared to have gone out of him. She saw him loosen his tie and undo his top button, exposing the hollow at his throat.

Seeing the lump there when he swallowed she felt so sorry for him that she put out her hand and touched his arm. 'Kingsley, I'm telling the truth. Honestly.'

His arm felt like a lump of wood as she waited anxiously for him to say he believed her.

Instead he said, 'In his diary, Piers had scribbled against INTOXICATING LADY "red roses". I thought . . . She must like red roses. So if it wasn't you, who was it?'

Unable to provide an answer, Danielle stood up, saying, 'Let's have a cup of tea.'

She filled the electric kettle and stood it on the hotplate before realising what she had done and, feeling a fool, moving it onto the counter and plugging it in. She took a tin of coffee from the cupboard, changed it for the tea-caddy with a picture of Prince Charles and Lady Diana on the front, and spooned tea into the teapot. She carefully took two mugs from the hook. Her mug and his mug. For a moment they blurred before her eyes.

'Watch that kettle,' he warned, as steam spurted out. 'How are your hands?'

'No problem. Maybe I'm too shocked to feel physical pain.' Boiling water sizzled into the pot and she clinked the lid on the fragrant steam, laid a pinewood tray and carried it in shaking hands to the table.

'You don't take sugar, do you?'

He shook his head.

'Strange.' She sipped her tea and a fleeting smile crossed her face. 'Must have been like this during the War the olduns in the pub talk about.'

He pulled the mug towards him. 'What?' he said, as if he hated her.

'I don't know . . . I mean . . . bombs falling all around, and people getting on with ordinary, everyday things because . . . what else is there to do?'

Her smiling-through-pain smile drew a begrudging response, and he shook his head. 'Danielle, what am I going to do without my clown?'

134

He didn't hate her. 'Oh, you'll forget me when you return to your models or showgirls or . . .'

He choked, put down his mug. She passed him a piece of kitchen roll and he wiped his mouth. He actually laughed! 'You're a nutcase,' he said.

'So they tell me. You sounded very loveydovey on the telephone,' she said drily, studying her tea like a fortune-teller.

'That was Mother, to whom I'm trying to show my love and support.'

When her head snapped up, she couldn't doubt the sincerity in his eyes, and she felt colour flood her cheeks. 'Sorry, it's none of my business.'

'It's her birthday today,' he told her.

Danielle shook her head. 'What's happening, Kingsley? What's she going to do – and who is it Piers . . .?'

'All I can think is that the woman lives around here,' he said heavily.

She pulled in a relieved breath. He believed her.

'Mother was pretty devastated – I was afraid she'd do something silly. She's rather emotional, you know. She opened the letter, but said nothing to Piers. She figures that a wife has two options: she lets the husband know she's found out about his affair and risks breaking up the home, or she pretends it hasn't happened.'

Danielle lifted her chin. 'I couldn't do that.'

'What?'

'Oh . . . pretend. I'd need to have it out.'

'She'd do anything to save her marriage,' he said quietly. 'And, while I admit I wanted to face Piers with it, I had to respect her wishes. She's so hurt.'

'Of course,' Danielle said warmly, understanding.

Kingsley went on, 'Mother felt that if they could go away together . . . you know . . .' He shrugged.

'A second honeymoon?' said Danielle doubtfully.

'I offered her a cruise for her birthday, got the tickets and told Piers afterwards.'

'Wow! You took a chance.' Her brain totted up what she guessed a long cruise would cost.

'Quite. But I rather bludgeoned Piers into it.'

'I can believe that.' She grimaced.

'You can?'

She nodded. 'You're good at the bludgeoning.'

'I gave Piers no opportunity to wriggle out; his work was covered and he'd had no holiday for two years. He couldn't offer an excuse without owning up.'

'Maybe he didn't want to,' she said, with some irony.

He gave her a quick look. 'You mean, I think, that a man in his position might have wanted an escape route.'

She nodded, getting up to wash the mugs.

'Danielle?'

'Mmm?'

'Why did you let me think you and Piers . . .?'

She felt her hands sting as she turned off the tap and stood the mugs upside-down on the draining board. Drying her hands carefully on a towel, she crossed to the table and leaned on the chair-back, looking at him with, he saw, bruised and tired eyes.

'I considered my private life had nothing to do with you,' she said, after a long pause. 'I didn't feel I had to explain myself – that's all. Piers was my friend, I must admit. He was good to me when Grandy died.'

'I just wish you'd told me earlier,' he said sharply. 'It would have saved . . .'

Her bottom lip jutted out. 'What about you? Why didn't you tell me who Piers was?'

'I thought you were my stepfather's mistress, don't forget.' Running fingers through his hair, he looked worried as he added, 'If I'd told you, I dare say you'd have got in touch with Piers somehow, in a panic, and that would have been the end of Mother's plan. One of her points of view was why should she let this other woman have the satisfaction of breaking up her marriage?'

'I still think the deceit was on your side,' she argued. 'Let's face it, you pushed yourself in here and I still can't understand why. What could you have gained if I *had* been this woman?'

'Mother spoke of coming here to face you,' he told her. Seeing the shock on Danielle's face, he nodded and went on, 'I was afraid of her being hurt by . . .' He paused. 'By the hard, calculating person I supposed you to be. So I advised her to leave things to me. I intended to make damn sure that you didn't contact Piers, or he you, until the ship sailed. That,' he said cuttingly, 'is the reason why I had to stay here.'

137

'Not because of the contract?'

His answer was to reach for the brown envelope on the table and pass it to her.

Throwing him a puzzled look, she opened it and drew out the contract. 'I see. Right. Thank you.' The contract was safely in her hands. She felt nothing.

'Don't thank me,' he snapped. 'Thank Piers.'

'What do you mean?' A glance at his face had her quickly studying the papers, slipping them through her hands until she reached the last page.

Her voice seemed to rattle in her throat. 'This is the contract that Piers prepared. It's dated the week before you came.' Her eyes blazed. 'The terms and conditions that Piers and I discussed are all here . . . you devious . . . ' *The worry he's put me through*, she remembered; *the fear of losing the vineyard, the pain of it all*.

He stood up. 'All for nothing,' he said, with an ease and unconcern that made her want to hit him. 'This woman, whoever she is, could quite well have contacted Piers without my knowing.'

Heart sinking, she echoed, 'All for nothing,' followed by a hollow laugh.

Already at the door, he paused. 'And I'll tell you something; I wish like hell I'd never come here.'

She tossed the contract onto the table, grasped his money and threw it at him. 'So do I.'

'I came to the office tonight,' he said, bending to pick up the notes, 'to tell you I was leaving.'

Had it only been this evening? It seemed like days

138

ago, and, remembering what had happened there, she pulled in a shaky breath. 'Why so soon?' She asked, watching him thrust the notes into his pocket.

He shrugged. 'I'll pack my things,' was all he said, looking away, hesitating, as if searching for words. But in the end he turned abruptly and left the room. She swiftly followed him, clutching the banister-rail, watching him hurry up stairs that gave panicky creaks. 'Surely you're not driving to London to-night?'

She was left staring upwards, listening to squealing drawers, the squeaky old wardrobe, the creaking floor, crashing hangers and, at last, the thank-God-for-that-type slam of the door as he came out.

He paused briefly beside the landing table and then almost hurtled down the stairs, passing her with his slow smile and saying 'Bye, love. Thanks for having me.'

No apology for disrupting her life, she thought angrily, following him. Not once had he apologized.

He pulled the front door open and strode away down the path. The black night surged inside and dry leaves came in with the wind, pattering along the stone floor like brown mice. She heard the trees moaning before she closed the door and bolted it. She felt most peculiar.

The leaves rustled over to Kingsley's abandoned wellington boots and lay still. To her own surprise, she picked up a boot and held it to her heart, because, believe it or not, she wanted him back.

CHAPTER 11

Danielle was driving back from Canterbury. Beside her, on the seat, sat a carrier bag half-full of indifferent shopping. Food, and the preparation of it, was decidedly and dismally unimportant this week.

She was alone again. *Well, I wanted to be, didn't I?* Yet she felt quite strange. Her mind a frozen pond. Everyday life slipped across the surface.

She missed the usual wraparound welcome from her beloved cottage when she returned from the slopes. And even out there, she thought resentfully, her army of vines gave her no thrill. She couldn't believe how her harvest of bouncing fruit left her cold.

For so long now the vineyard had been her joy and consolation, her reason for living. She was Daniel Summerfield's granddaughter. For as long as she could remember, her main motivation had been to impress him. She had no intention of letting him down, even if her uninvited guest – who had merely requested lodgings for a week – she thought bitterly, appeared to have taken up residence in her mind.

140

Beneath the ice, he – or the image of him – refused to leave her in peace. As a result, she found herself going over and over everything that had happened between them until her life was like a series of television repeats. Uppermost was the question – Who had sent the letter? In other words, who was Piers's mistress? *I would give anything*, she sighed, *to solve that mystery*.

There was something else her convoluted thoughts had thrown up. Jealousy. Did she really feel, very deep down, something like jealousy?

Yes, she admitted, during her silent inner dialogue. She had probably had a crush on Piers at one time. *Come on*, she told herself, *admit it*. She had. His interested, caring eyes had arrowed straight into her plump little teenage lonely heart. He had been too remote from her life to be a danger. He was safe to idolize. And she had.

On impulse, when she turned off the motorway, she headed away from the vineyard.

By-passing the village, she entered a recently widened lane which sliced straight through the Kent of picture books. She passed a country park and a golf course and suddenly – so brake-screamingly suddenly that if you didn't know, you would drive right past it – she came to the tree-screened entrance of a mobile home park. Camouflaged so as not to spoil the picture book.

Each boxlike home stood poised in its own small garden, upon which dying leaves were steadfastly falling as if they, too, were in league with the plan to obliterate the site.

Jo's motorbike, she was relieved to see, was parked outside number three. Pulling up, she climbed from the truck, slammed the door and hurried around the back of the truck just in time to see the front door open.

Tom came out. With a surprised smile, she crunched through leaves along the path, air fresh against her cheeks, smelling damp earth and decay. He carried a canvas bag and seemed to jump when he saw her.

He held up the bag. 'Collecting my ironing.'

Nothing to look so embarrassed about, Danielle thought. With an eye-avoiding, 'See you later,' he made for his car, which she had only just noticed he had parked further up.

She didn't return his wave as he drove past the truck. She was busy wondering why, lately, he kept turning up at unexpected times – fussing, bringing her little gifts. It was very kind, and she should feel grateful, but instead she felt irritated, and then guilty, and then cross because he had changed.

She was careful to be nice, knowing that he had what she called his 'deep blue sea moods'. You could sense sombre undercurrents on occasions. He never lost his temper, although there was a tightness about him at times which suggested firm control.

She turned her head and her face broke into a smile. Jo was waiting at the door with raised brows and her own particular smile. A polite smile, an uncertain-whether-to-stay-or-go smile, Jo's was.

Something reassuring and capable moved like perfume within the older woman, maybe to do with her don't-give-a-damn attitude, her obvious strength.

Jo led her indoors, through the kitchen-diner into the sitting room. 'We haven't had a chat for ages,' she said, in a voice you could grate parmesan on. 'You've been tied up with that Mr Whatsisname. Has he gone?'

'Kingsley. Kingsley Hunter. Yes,' Danielle said more cheerfully than she felt, 'he's gone.'

'Get what he wanted, did he?'

Danielle, with her flash of insight, felt an atmosphere thick enough to carpet a room with. Maybe Jo and Tom had had a row. They were both abrasive people, often had spats. Which would account for Tom's dismissive attitude and . . . did she imagine the resentful look Jo took with her into the kitchen?

Water pelted into the kettle, a plug was jabbed into the electric point; when the tap was jerked off, the pipes gave a good imitation of a cock being strangled in mid-crow.

Have I chosen a bad time? Danielle wondered.

With no door between them, conversation wandered backwards and forwards, punctuated by far from silent preparations.

Answering Jo's question, Danielle made much of the business factor. 'Kingsley was quite satisfied; it was to do with next year's contract.'

'He's a bit of all right. Suppose he's married?'

'Not him. To quote him . . . he likes women who don't rely upon him, who want a good time with no ties.'

'I'm his girl.'

Conversation was interrupted by the steaming kettle, enabling Danielle to ignore the joke.

Instead, in the comforting, china-crashing lull, she concentrated on looking around. She loved this room; it was busy, like its owner, full to bursting with curios and collectables, from contented china dogs and elegant porcelain figures to glowing brass and jewel-coloured glassware in swirling shapes. All displayed like scrubbed, cosseted children.

The furniture was good quality – solid secondhand rather than antique – and comfortably unmatched. Crowded in with everything else in the room was an upright electric organ and a set of drums, and a trumpet in its case – Jo gave private music lessons – stood beside the unyielding, discouraging settee where Danielle had seated herself.

There were no family photographs, no pets, no plants.

Jo came in with a tin tray which she set down on a coffee-table before dropping onto an armchair with the unnatural and uncomfortable look of one who was seldom still. She sat as erect as a garden fence, one strong, jean-clad leg laid across her other knee. As if she was declaring, Private, no trespassing.

Danielle smilingly accepted this, along with a mug

of tea, and curbed her tongue and began cautiously. 'The ironing's going well, then?'

'Mmm. Have a biscuit.' Indicating a plate of chocolate biscuits, Jo sipped her own tea and wondered why Danny had come. The girl looked more subdued than usual. They were fond of each other, but neither was the sort to exchange confidences. Yet something uncertain in Danny's manner said she was reaching out.

Joanna felt herself withdraw. She had enough problems of her own. But who else did Danny have? She was so warm and kind to everyone that even Jo, who had reason to resent her, couldn't. She wondered if she was the only one to see the young, vulnerable girl instead of the businesslike young woman Danny was at work.

Covering her impatience, she smiled encouragingly. 'Bachelors are my best customers,' she winked.

Danielle helped herself to a biscuit. 'You set the tongues wagging, you know,' she said humorously. 'Before you put your card in the shop window.' Shrilly, she mimicked, ' "That Joanna's always in Robin's place." '

Jo couldn't help laughing. 'Love it. I get a kick out of leading the gossips astray. What I'm supposed to be getting up to is a darn sight more exciting than what I'm really doing, I always say.'

With an amused shake of her head, Danielle asked,

'What made you start the ironing? Cherie accused me of not paying you enough.'

'She would. No.' Brushing the question aside, Jo clicked her mug down on the table, reached for a cigarette packet and removed a cigarette. Lighting up with a green onyx lighter, she tossed her head of short, springy, no-nonsense hair and inhaled; a blue-grey screen of smoke soon moved between them.

Danielle crunched a biscuit and waited. After too long a silence, she attempted to make conversation by commenting. 'Cherie's acting as if she has a secret.'

'I know. She's got this cow-like expression that says, Ask me, but I won't tell. Makes her feel important,' Joanna ended dismissively.

'I know what you think of gossip,' Danielle said earnestly, 'but it's based upon interest in each other.'

'Rubbish,' Joanna returned, blowing out smoke. 'Goes back to the days before television and radio, when news was passed around via the inns and at village pumps or church. It's entertainment. At least some is. And, there are people like Cherie, who don't just pass gossip on, they create it. Believe me, she's a torpedo-mouth. A self-propelled, underwater missile.'

'Not your favourite person,' Danielle joked. Nevertheless, she sat back, stretched one arm along the settee back and insisted firmly, 'We're all very concerned for each other. If you're in trouble there are none kinder than the people here. Talking of which . . . is everything all right with you, Jo?'

She saw Jo freeze . . . fear and helplessness stared back at her so briefly that Danielle felt her skin tingle with shock, and then she wondered – or hoped – perhaps I'm imagining it.

For Jo beat her cigarette stub to death in a brass ashtry, saying firmly, 'Can't complain.'

Danielle persevered. 'We're friends, I hope. If you have any problems . . .' She shrugged. 'You know.'

'Problems? My life's been one long problem, my love.' Jo glared around the room, as if searching for something nasty among the beautiful, lifeless objects which aroused no emotion, made no demands.

Seeing Jo's broad shoulders rise and fall, Danielle was tempted, and asked, 'Are you happy here? Country life, I mean, after the city.'

The reply was unexpectedly emotional. 'Coming out to Kent was like a light going on.' This was followed by a sheepish laugh that seemed to say, How did that slip out?

Silenced for a moment, Danielle went on, 'What did you do before – in London?'

Joanna hesitated. She never spoke of it. That East London street the sun never found – merely a grain of dust beneath the giant feet of steaming, bad-egg-smelling factories.

The two-up two-down terraces, squatting like a

row of rotting teeth, had long been bulldozed and anaesthetised by reach-for-the-sky flats. Her memories too. Nothing left.

No mother leaving home and four children when Jo, the eldest, was fourteen. No violent, layabout father or his molesting, drink-sodden friend who had seemed, at the time, to be someone who cared. No baby, mercifully stillborn.

Escape via night-school, various dogsbody jobs in the music business, dreams built and bulldozed, and . . .

No. Joanna began here.

Danielle watched a cynical smile twist the mouth of the woman who seemed to be thinking hard before she made up her mind.

'I was a typist among other things,' Jo began. 'I arrived here with a successful City husband and a beauty-parlour dog to build a house beside the village green – against local opposition.' Her voice softened. 'I loved that house. It was like something out of *Ideal Homes*. As was the man and the dog.'

Danielle helped herself to another biscuit. 'That was your first husband, Tony?' She often saw him out jogging, or walking the great, shaggy white carpet of a dog called Polo.

'Yes. Tony married a model-cum-typist-cum-musician and found himself living with a housewife-cum-hod-carrier, brickie and plumber, who had totally embraced country living.'

148

There was no bitterness in her matter-of-fact voice. 'If men want Barbie dolls for wives they should employ housekeepers, gardeners and builders. He did at least pay someone to decorate the house. Five years on, I fell in love with the decorator. Or maybe it was revenge. Tony was by then having it off with a Barbie lookalike.'

Danielle crunched and swallowed. 'Then you married the decorator?'

'Reg seemed to care. He had this nice house in Maidstone.' Her dark unplucked brows rose. 'You wouldn't think that someone living in such a little palace would be a tyrant. I didn't have to stand for that – not like my mum and grandmother did. Life's too short. I stayed as long as I could for the sake of his two kids. He was a widower. But he knocked hell out of me . . . once too often.'

Silently, as she talked, the gut-tearing guilt sneaked up on her. Those motherless kids. She had informed Social Services before she left, as she had with her own brothers and sisters, afraid for their safety, and it was up to the authorities after that, she told herself often – particularly after her recurring nightmares.

Danielle was listening in that way she had, with her head tilted, her dark brown eyes large but not so brilliant today, pain-filled instead, and concerned.

'I always choose rotters,' Jo admitted, with a smile like toughened glass. 'I don't basically like men, but I fall in love with them so terribly.' Looking down at her clenched fists, she deliberately uncurled them and said, 'I suppose we're all looking for someone to walk in the sun with.' She laughed, hating herself. 'What a twit!'

'Is there anyone special now?' Danielle asked, moved, rubbing damp chocolate and emotion against her jeans.

Jumping up, Jo padded barefoot across to the organ and struck a few low, sad notes. 'According to gossip, the school might be closed down. Have you heard?'

After a taut moment, Danielle said that no, she hadn't heard. And she got up to go, always sensitive about outstaying her welcome wherever she was.

'That's another reason why I want to get this ironing business going.' Jo turned to face Danielle with the remains of a high flush. 'I'll miss the kids in my music classes. There aren't enough children, they say. I'd like a kid,' she added unexpectedly, as if her mind was half on something else. 'Even if he . . . the father . . . didn't love me or marry me, I'd have a baby.'

While Danielle looked at her, stunned and suddenly chilled, Jo seemed eager to talk. 'With Tony, we were too busy making money. Then he was too busy making it with other women. It was hardly a good time to be fat and unattractive. As for Reg, he'd have killed me if I'd become pregnant – no danger.'

Danielle went white, then found her voice and

said, 'Time's the thing. Don't know how you fit everything in now.'

'Life,' Jo said seriously, 'is do or . . . or die. Some live by accident, others by design.' Her eyes became steely. 'I prefer design.'

'Jo?'

'Yes, love?'

'How have you coped with it all?' Danielle shuddered. 'The violence, the deceit?'

She sounds so young, thought Jo, feeling old. What would she know, in her protected world, about violence?

'Listen, Danny. What we don't like, we can change. Discovering that, and the fact that being a victim isn't the only way of life, gives you a certain amount of power, you know? And remember this,' she said ominously, 'if you let someone hurt you once, you're giving them permission to do it again. Right?'

Danielle stared at her, nodded and glanced at her watch, 'Hey, I must go. See you this afternoon?'

'Right.' Jo frowned. 'Wait!' she called with sudden anguish, following Danielle through to the kitchen.

At the front door, Danielle stopped and turned with an enquiring smile, and Jo, looking away, studying a pine dresser loaded with china, said brusquely, 'I'll be late on Monday. Doctor's appointment. It's nothing,' she added, seeing Danielle's shocked stare. She rested her hand on a nearby Formica table and forced a smile. 'Just a check-up.'

151

Their eyes met and held. Appalled, tossing up whether to say anything or not, Danielle was the first to look away. Swallowing, she merely ordered, 'Don't rush.'

She walked, crushing leaves, down the path, lonely somehow, with Jo's voice following her. – 'Thanks for coming. Nice to have a natter, Danny. Bye, now.'

Unconvinced, Danielle waved without turning.

Going indoors, Jo picked up the tea things and carried them into the kitchen. Looking down at the china, she half smiled at the crumby, empty biscuit plate and remembered. Danny hadn't said why she had come.

Then she slipped her boots on, went outside and swept and raked until not a dead leaf remained.

CHAPTER 12

Kingsley blamed it upon Angie.

'What are you doing with your life now, little brother?' she asked, kneeling at his feet.

'Thought you asked me round for dinner,' he said with a fond smile, 'not an inquisition.'

'You know what they say about free dinners,' she said cheerfully, scooping toys from the floor.

He looked down at her calm face and blonde gamine haircut with affection. Curling her long denimed legs under her, she tossed soldiers into a fort without taking her eyes from him. Her uptilted, inquisitive nose pointed straight at him, and her attitude said that she could stick it out as long as he could.

Kingsley knew his brother-in-law was working late, and couldn't believe that he hadn't seen through Angie's invitation. Lonely, indeed!

With a wry smile, Kingsley raised his arms. 'I give in. What do you want to know?'

That's better, her stern, judge-like expression said as she folded her arms. 'First of all, what was going on the week before Mother and Piers went away? I couldn't get hold of you, even late at night, and Mother sounded evasive when I asked about you. She said you were staying at a vineyard somewhere and then she clammed up – when usually you can't stop her talking about her blue-eyed boy. I know,' she added menacingly, 'when people are not telling the truth. I'm a mother.'

'You should know better than to try and track down a bachelor,' he parried, trying to make a joke of it.

She looked worried. 'I wouldn't normally. But Mother didn't seem herself, and I thought . . .'

'If I know my sister, you've been imagining a terminal disease which she had made me promise not to reveal,' he said gently.

Without speaking, Angie picked up a cannon, tossed it into the fort, uncurled her legs and got to her feet with the lightness of one trained in ballet.

'Mother's health is fine,' he reassured her as she perched beside him on the squashy settee, 'and I'm sorry to disappoint you about my disappearance, but it was business.' He told her about it, leaving out anything to do with Piers or their mother.

She visibly relaxed. 'So what is she like, this girl, Danielle?'

He pretended to think hard. 'I would describe her as . . . comedy, heartache and compassion, muddle-headed trust and bright-eyed common sense – always churning out ideas. When she's not sorting out her own problems, she's helping friends.' As an after-thought, he added to his amazed sister, 'And she never stops laughing.'

'Well!' Audrey Hepburn-type eyes goggled at him. 'Sounds an improvement on your usual conquests.'

'She's not a conquest at all,' he said huffily. 'Can I help lay the table?' He jumped up and walked into the kitchen, pulling open the cutlery drawer.

'That,' she said in a menacing voice from behind him, 'says it all. Don't tell me that this time you have to make an effort, little brother?'

She disappeared into the adjoining dining room, and when he followed she was flapping a white cloth across the table with a triumphant smile. He caught the other end and dropped his handful of cutlery in the process.

The knives and forks crashed onto the wooden floor. 'I don't know what you mean,' he said in a hurt voice, bending down to pick them up. 'But I do know that sisters are a pain in the rear.'

'I try to be, I try to be,' she said gaily, as his head popped up above the table. 'Annoying you is my life's work.'

He threw a raffia tablemat at her and, laughing, she ducked. A cross yell echoed from the nursery. 'Serves you right,' he grinned, seeing her face fall.

A shaft of sunlight broke through cloud and fell across the slopes, touching Danielle as she worked. Her brown hands were swift but careful as she clipped, palmed and gently lay down the fruits of her labour.

Work, she thought. Work is the answer. And there was certainly plenty of work. Quite enough to take her mind off other things.

She closed her eyes and he was there, pinned against her eyelids. She opened them and saw him striding towards her through the juicy corridors . . . but it was a mirage . . . that sexy walk, the animal-like stalking . . .

'Hello,' he drawled, in a lazy way which seemed to say that he had to make no effort, that women always did the running.

She felt a sudden stomach flush. The cutters in her hand trembled dangerously.

'I learned something from you,' Kingsley told her, hand raised to shield his face from the sun. 'You said one can choose to be happy or miserable. Today I choose happy. Will you join me? A picnic . . . What do you think?'

Today she chose aloof. She found her voice and kept it cool. 'No chance.'

He held her with a steady gaze. He was dressed, she saw, in jeans and sweater, hair glinting in the sun like new coins, a picnic hamper at his feet, a new look on his face. Younger, more boyish. Still used to getting his own way.

Her fingers gripping the cutters were suddenly as clumsy as a bunch of bananas.

'You've got to eat some time, Danielle. I've

brought something special, all the way from Har-rods. By the way – ' there was a rueful near-smile ' – have you missed me?'

She gripped a stem, clipped, placed the grapes in the bin, glanced along the row at the other pickers.

Looking amused, he said, 'I'll ask you another! Where's the best place to go?'

She raised her hands palms up, and shrugged. 'You know, I have so much to *do* . . .'

'Nonsense. It's Saturday. Besides, you must eat to keep up your strength.'

'You're so *bossy*,' she hissed, wiping her hand across her brow. It was one of those unexpectedly warm late September days – too warm for a sweater, really.

She saw him cross his arms, looking mutinous, and, conscious that the girls' grapes weren't drop-ping quite so frequently into the bins at the moment, she tucked the cutters into a pocket of her dungarees. She was tired and hot, and he'd obviously gone to a lot of trouble . . .

'Okay! Okay! I give in. Just to please you. I admit I did go on a picnic once.' She dimpled. 'I took someone rather special with me. That's where we'll go.'

A memory fell like a cloud over the sun. The smile faded and her face was suddenly one of indecision, until, with the air of one going into battle, she wiped her sticky hands down her dungarees and ordered, 'Follow me.'

He followed her springy, purposeful walk down towards the bottom of the slope. Over in the west corner, just before the orchard, there was a thicket of tree which had seemed a forest to her as a child . . .

In the silence, their feet crunched leaves. Startled birds flapped off screeching, a squirrel, collecting nuts for winter, bounded away up a tree. A train whistled in the distance on its way to London.

And here memories lurked. Once, this place had excited her with a glorious sense of freedom at the start of every holiday. Here she had learned to live for the day, a devil-may-care Tarzan, building camps and swinging from tree to tree.

And here it had ended . . . her childhood. Along with her trust, her innocence, her dreams and her unreserved adoration. They were buried in this lost playground of her youth.

Today she could hardly believe she was walking here with a smile on her lips. She was free from worrying about the contract, free from Kingsley's power, and . . . somehow . . . this place was free from ghosts. And this wasn't a forest; it was so sparse you could see right through the trees. Unimportant. How wonderful.

Once through the copse, pushing through a gap in the hedge that ran alongside the poplars, she explained, 'Old Hutchinson doesn't mind me coming through.'

She was gratified to hear him exclaim with pleasure as they swished through long grasses, clover, the remains of buttercups and daisies. When they reached the river, he climbed onto *her* tree, which, rooted in the riverbank, grew horizontally, forming a bridge across the water.

She smiled, watching him. With arms outspread he sidestepped along the trunk almost out to the branches at the centre. Poised against hills and skyline, he seemed entranced by the river which ran shining through the meadow, tripping over boulders and sliding between trees, singing and chuckling to itself as it went.

How many times had she stretched out on that tree, watched the fish and riverbank life, dreamed her dreams?

Humming, she spread a red-checked tablecloth over the grass and waited to see what the hamper contained.

Throwing himself down beside her, his eyes lingered on the play of excitement on her face, on her eyes, like the river, shining, on the way her hands were clasped as she sat back on her heels, and he wondered who this girl-woman was, and what the truth of it all was.

Reaching out, he whipped off the cap so that her hair tumbled down her back and dropped over her shoulders. 'Your face is streaked with sunlight.' He brushed a gentle finger across her brow. 'And dirt.'

She shrugged, mouth splitting into the good-natured grin he had come to know so well, and he shook his head.

'I can't make you out. You're not what I expected.'

'So you keep saying. What's for lunch?'

He ran an eye down her figure: the bib of the dungarees pushed out by her full breasts, the curve of her hips as she crouched on the grass, waiting, the soft spread of her thighs. He felt his smile die. 'Is that all you think about, your stomach?' he teased soberly, opening the creaking lid of the hamper. 'This is a gourmet feast you'll never forget. *Voilà!*'

Playfully refusing to allow her to peep inside the hamper, he began to lift things out. 'Cutlery, cups, condiments, and, in the freezer bag, tiny dishes of . . .'

Her face shone. 'Pâté de foie gras?' She opened the pot and peered inside, then put it down to take from him the napkins and plates on which she arranged crunchy French bread, butter pats and . . . she peeped inside another bowl. 'Russian salad!'

'And other different salads.' He handed her two more bowls. 'Flask of coffee inside,' he added, 'and grapes and cheese – Brie I think.'

She licked her lips, closed her eyes. 'I'm dreaming.'

'Stay like that,' he ordered. 'Dream some more. Promise you won't look?'

'Mmm.' Light exploded behind her closed eyes, the sun was slanting warmly across her face, and she heard him say, 'Open your mouth.'

After a brief hesitation, she did.

160

She felt the smooth, metallic touch of a spoon, cool against her tongue, and round, slippery things surged into her mouth. There was a whisper and warm breath in her ear. 'Crush them between your tongue and your palate – gently, now.'

The spoon withdrew, leaving . . . bubbles. They were bubbles, and, to her astonishment, she felt a miniature, savoury explosion on her tongue. Her eyes flew open.

He was holding the spoon, blue eyes teasing, smiling at her. 'Such rapture.' His other hand held a jar.

'Caviare,' she breathed, after a delicious pause.

'Your turn.' He put down her spoon and picked up another, holding it out to her with the jar. Taking them, her hands trembled. Watching his sleepy eyes close, his lion-like face tilt, his broad cheeks etched against the sky, her heart turned over. Hadn't she come to know this face so well? She might have known him always.

His lips parted for her to insert the spoon gently inside, filling his mouth with moist black pearls. Her own tongue tingled, aroused in anticipation as she relived the sensation of that blissful explosion, and saliva poured into her mouth . . . a sort of climax with him.

Fascinated, she watched his lips move, the tremble in his throat. His eyes opened, he smiled a lazy smile, they sighed together and, at the same moment, laughed.

Rediscovered laughter for Danielle. Light-hearted laughter – so new between them that she felt a singing-in-the-bones type happiness – quite fragile, but she didn't care.

Twisting round, he reached into the hamper, pulling out champagne and two crystal flutes. Enjoying the delight on her face, he announced seriously, 'Bubbles to wash down the bubbles. We will eat bubbles and drink bubbles.' He uncorked. Birds rose, squawking, from the trees, and the cork flew away too.

She held the flutes steady, or almost steady, while Kingsley, very professionally, cupped the bottle from below, with his thumb probing the dimple, and poured from above. The champagne ran exuberantly and joyfully, but remained below the rim, just as it should.

Placing the flutes on the tray provided, she clapped and laughed. *'Bravo!'*

He covered the bottle with a red-checked cloth and picked up his flute. 'This is by way of saying sorry.'

Picking up her own, she sipped and gurgled with laughter. 'An ordinary, "I'm sorry", would have been cheaper.' She held up the flute and through lacy crystal watched the play of light through the bubbles rising from the bottom. 'It's so emotional, champagne.'

He squinted at her through the sun. 'Champagne is suppressed passion, don't you think? Opening a bottle is almost making love . . . tenderness, the right pressure, position, handling, release . . . an explosion of joy.'

His voice floated around her, lulling her, so that though he waited for a response, none was forthcoming.

Watching her wistful half-smile he went on more prosaically, 'There's a bottle of peach wine as well.'

She took a deep breath and bent her curious nose over the hamper. 'But no bottle-opener.'

'Boom! Boom!' With the air of a conjuror, he whisked one from his trouser pocket. 'I was born with a silver corkscrew in my mouth.' He winked.

Her eyes danced at him. 'I believe you.'

'My father owned a wine import company – he was a successful man. Maybe he tried too hard,' Kingsley went on, between sips of champagne. 'He died of a heart-attack when I was twelve.'

'I'm sorry. What happened to the business?'

'Mother sold it to Lamont's.'

She sipped slowly, letting the bubbles bounce on her tongue. 'Oh, I see.'

His voice cooled. 'Piers took me on when I left college. Mother and my sister and I own shares in the company, and some of the money from the sale was put in trust for me until I reach thirty. Which happens in December.'

The champagne really seemed to be clearing her head, and that was what made her ask, 'So you fancy a vineyard for Christmas?'

He sat up on his heels, placed the wine bottle

between his legs and pulled; she saw his muscles clench beneath the black wool sweater and then the cork popped out. 'How did you know?' he asked, spending a long time looking down at the bottle.

'Maybe because . . . sometimes,' she said honestly, 'when you look around the slopes I see a dream in your eyes instead of a chequebook; I sense something more personal . . . I'm not sure, exactly.'

A violet-blue shadow dropped like an ink-blot onto the tablecloth. She looked up at gathering clouds. So he still wants the vineyard, she thought, disturbed.

'Who did you picnic here with?' he asked curiously, as they ate and drank. 'Piers?'

Shaking her head, she smiled, tucking into the food with obvious enjoyment, mouth too full to speak.

When the last drop of champagne had slipped down her throat, she threw herself back on the grass, loving the scent of it, raising her arms and letting them fall wide, pushing everything away except this moment, which could stay as long as it liked.

'I love picnics,' she cried in her sing-song voice.

Turning her head, she found his eyes fixed on her. 'I've never picked grapes sozzled.' She dimpled up at him. 'But soon . . . oh, another ten minutes . . . or fifteen . . . or twenty . . . I must try.'

Her laughing eyes caught the fleeting expressions on his face. There was curiosity, something troubled, and a flicker of tenderness that made her wonder who he was thinking of. A fine sight she must look – nothing like the Victorian ladies in the picture on the calendar. Who was he wishing he was with? For, as he said, he had organized this as a way of saying sorry – a sort of duty.

Why am I always a duty?

Using her feet, she kicked off her wellies and wriggled her toes in the grass, looking over the mound of her breasts at her old navy sweater and, as she raised her knees, even older dungarees.

Her chest rose and fell, and his face hovered above her. 'Why the sigh?'

She turned away, losing herself in heavens the colour of his eyes, which seemed more blue than grey, and she wondered at how even the sky was emotional today, constantly changing, like herself. The clouds were scudding by so fast she felt giddy, but relaxed, free to float. Her thoughts, too, wanted to fly unrestrained.

'Contentment,' she answered. 'I wish it was summer all the time. I don't like winter.'

'That's strange,' he said, putting his weight on the arm stretched across her. 'I can see you in all seasons.'

She gurgled. 'Wait until winter . . .' Then she remembered. In winter he would be gone. She felt the way she might if someone had shoved a snowball down her neck.

'I can see you in winter,' he went on. 'Quite easily.

165

I see you running through snow with cherry cheeks and I see you at Christmas, your eyes shining in the firelight. You remind me of Christmas.'

He hesitated, and she turned her head from the cold distance she had been contemplating to find his eyes just above her, so close she could see the navy blue line around his iris, so dilated they were a mirror for her own face.

She smiled at her reflection. 'So I look like Christmas pudding?'

Seriously, he said, 'Not at all. You smell like one.' Seeing her face fall, he smiled. 'You have this lingering fragrance of oranges and spice around you, and you laugh a lot; Christmas is a warm, lit-up sort of family time.'

'Ho, ho, ho!' she joked in a deep voice, feeling his peach-scented breath gently ebb and flow on her face.

'I enjoy my Christmases,' he said, looking down at her with half-awake eyes. 'It's a feel-good time and you affect people that way. It's a compliment – that's what I'm saying.'

'I'll accept it as such,' she said brightly, to hide sudden embarrassment.

A most un-Kingsley-like shyness crossed his face. 'Odd, talking like this. Do you find that this place is away from the world? Like coming into another room?'

Her eyes glowed. 'That's exactly how I feel. How clever of you to describe it so well. I used to feel, as a child, that once I scrambled through that fence the

166

world was left behind.' Her voice hardened. 'Do you know what this field is called?'

He shook his head, turning to inspect the over-grown field. 'I didn't know fields had names.'

'Oh, they have,' she assured him happily. 'This one is actually called Paradise.'

'Honestly?'

She nodded. 'Hutchinson told me. Could a field have been more aptly named?'

He quoted softly. ' "A Flask of Wine, a Book of Verse – and Thou Beside me singing in the Wild-erness . . ." '

' "And wilderness is Paradise enow", ' she finished for him, flesh-creepingly aware of his nearness. She had become adept at steering men towards friend-ship; she liked their company. Maybe it had become a habit. Not with Kingsley, though. Kingsley created an inner disturbance.

Into her thoughtful silence, he asked, 'Is the field never cultivated?'

She shook her head. 'It's not good for much. It slopes and it's a long way from the farm.'

The shadow of a scudding cloud passed over her face. 'Grandy nearly bought the field from old Hutchinson once. I asked Francesca about it the other day. She said the deal fell through. She men-tioned a row between Grandy and Hutch. I never saw them speak, you know.' Looking around, she said, 'It gets the afternoon sun, it's massed with wild flowers and plants and I think it's perfect.'

Remembering those far-off days of contentment, she stretched like a cat, languorous, devouring the sun's warmth as she softly hummed something happy.

In this, her childhood place, she dreamed . . . Of his mouth on hers, of touching his skin, of pressing against the long line of his body. She had a sense of absorbency, as if she were blotting paper and he ink, about to fall on to her, cover her, soak into her, until she *was* him.

Kingsley's head turned to follow her movements. He reached down towards her feet and ran a feather-light touch around the outside edge of her heel, and she gasped a silent Wow! at the sensations he aroused.

He turned back to her. A long, considering stare hung between them, tense, electrically charged.

It was an anything-might-happen moment.

Reaching out, he pulled her up to a sitting position as if they were about to go, and, disappointed, she went with it, as if all self-will had left her.

Instead of helping her up, he slipped his arms around her. Hardly daring to breathe, she moved into the gentle strength of their embrace, felt his hand running up and down her back, sending shock waves through her body.

This time he was gentle, but his lips didn't hesitate to find her soft, full, waiting mouth, and as she melted she thought how firm his were, how sweet they tasted, and how her own, damp with champagne, seemed to swell, as her body seemed to swell and surge towards him, aching for closeness. She heard her breathing, and his. Smelled aftershave and wine and grass and skin. She fingered his warm, living scalp through the thick hair, thrilled at his answering groan against her mouth.

He pulled away, and his aroused breath fanned her cheek as he said, 'You purr, Danielle. You're purring.'

His hand slipped beneath the bib of her dungarees, easing the straps from her shoulders, reaching for the full mound beneath her sweater, stroking her responding skin; his lips tasted her hot cheeks, her pulsing neck, his tongue probed her ears, leaving sizzling trails; there was noise . . . breath, heartbeats, pounding blood . . . She felt her nipples tingle and yearn and push, her body straining to burst out of her clothes.

As if he knew, he fumbled with the clip of her bra. She felt the shock of his fingers, firm and warm and throbbing against the shimmering skin on her back, the masculine power of his arm holding her, pinning her to him so that exquisite darts of urgency flew to her loins like fingers, opening her up for him.

A dog barked . . . somewhere . . . maybe on the farm.

A steel blade of fear thrust between her shoulder-blades; she brought her hands up to his chest. 'No, please.'

He stopped so suddenly it was like a broken-down

169

movie – all excitement, movement, life and thundering noise . . . and then . . . freeze.

She felt as if she had jumped from a skyscraper. The ground came up fast, hard. *Smash*. Jarring her emotions.

Remembering her skin screaming at the touch of his fingers, the pressing of her body against him, she felt it still and her face was burning like a flame.

Avoiding his questioning eyes, she drew away, aching, shaking, forcing herself to say, 'Time to go.'

'Danielle?' He gripped her arm with one hand and with the other reached out and pulled her chin around, forcing her to meet his puzzled and perturbed silent interrogation. He took a deep breath, pressed his lips together and shook his head pityingly.

Pity? She was dizzy and for some reason cross – whether with herself or Kingsley, she didn't know. Turning her chin away, trying to calm her breathing, she tucked her bulky sweater down, pulled up the dungarees and flicked the straps onto her shoulders. She tried, with little success, to tidy her hair.

With pins in her mouth she said, 'What's the problem? These things happen at picnics, I suppose. As you said, you've been to many.' She thrust her hair behind her ears, jabbed in the pins, and jealousy thrust savagely into her heart.

He frowned. 'When I was a boy, I meant.' He hesitated. 'There's a lot about you I don't understand. You're full of life – bubbly like champagne –

but if I touch you, you respond and then suddenly you go flat,' he said with a trace of annoyance, and for a moment she saw again the arrogant man she had first met.

He seemed to be waiting for her to say something. When she didn't he pulled in another deep breath, turned away and stared moodily across the fields; he took a bar of chocolate from the hamper, snapped it in two, and, without looking at her, passed her some. For a while they munched without speaking.

'Look,' he said, swallowing. 'I know we started badly, but I'd hoped that now we're free to be friends we could start again. I realize there's still a barrier between us, but you're quite safe with me.'

Safe? She shot his gaunt profile a quick glance and turned away. Why was she safe? Because, as he'd said, she wasn't his type? Then in that case why had he . . .?

'It happened because I'm a man, Danielle, and . . .' He shrugged. – 'You know the sort of woman you are.'

She felt hurt. The sort of woman she was?

He turned his head. 'The woman in my arms was warm and passionate; she more than met me halfway. Maybe I was curious. Perhaps I was unfair – for, of course, there is someone else.' There was a question in his eyes.

What he meant was that his pride was hurt, she decided. Kingsley Hunter didn't expect to be turned down. The sweetness in her mouth turned sour; she

171

tried not to think how her body melted, just like this chocolate, when he touched her. Had he been testing her? Had he been expecting her to be easy to seduce? Obviously so. In which case it was just as well her barriers had come up, despite the way he made her feel. Just thinking of his arms around her sent her heart hammering, and she wriggled uncomfortably.

She didn't know for sure that he believed in her innocence where Piers was concerned. That damn letter was a mystery she had to solve, or it would always lie between them. Not only that, neither did she really know whether he was still after her vineyard.

Because he was watching her, she hid her inner turmoil and smiled. 'It was just a kiss. No big deal.'

'Oh! I see. Let's talk. Tell me about yourself,' he said, swallowing the last of the chocolate. 'I know about your parents and so on, but what are you, yourself?'

'My father was French, my mother half-Italian, half-English. So what does that make me?' She licked her fingers and screwed up the silver paper, tossing it into the hamper, more in control of herself now. Leaning back on her arms, she raised her face to the sky.

'It makes you dark, rich chocolate; it makes you vitally alive, volatile, with quicksilver changes of mood, yet with a serene centre; you're chic and loyal and practical, warm and passionate.'

Sitting up, she hid her burning face by gathering

up the remains of their picnic. 'I'm not passionate.'

He smiled knowingly. 'You are when I hold you; you have amber flecks in your eyes that tell me so.'

Her lashes fell. 'And chic? Look at me.'

'I am looking. You're like a grubby little boy, Danielle. Why do you nearly always dress like a boy?'

With her lips pressed together she slammed the lid on the Thermos flask and piled leftovers into the hamper.

He grinned. 'You remind me of a Dickens raga-muffin.'

'Thanks,' she growled, scrambling to her feet.

He stood up slowly, resting his hands on her shoulders, his eyes asking her to listen. 'Chic is not what clothes do to you, but what you do to clothes. It's an aura that's haunting and memor-able. You're chic, but not beautiful. Now, a chic woman in beautiful clothes . . .'

She could hear herself raving at an exasperated grandmother. 'Dressing up's a bore. Women like you,' she used to cry, 'trap yourselves in front of mirrors and under hairdryers. I have too much to do.' A typically clever little teenager who'd thought she knew everything, Danielle recalled now. And somehow she wanted to smile at herself – yet she wanted to cry too. For dressing up, making herself attractive to men, had been so hard to do. If she searched herself, she would find the reason in dark-ness.

Instead, she busied herself searching the nearby

ground to make sure nothing of their picnic remained. Leave nothing behind. The country code. But when . . . if . . . she returned here, there would be so much left behind, wouldn't there?

'You must be bored, talking about me,' she told him, picking up the cutters which had fallen from her pocket. 'It's the vineyard you're really interested in, isn't it?'

Tucking a strand of hair around her ear, he said softly, 'You *are* the vineyard.' A long silence stretched between them, although birds carried on chirping and the river ran with little splashes, and he watched her place the cap on her head.

He had hoped they could start again, but it hadn't worked. Unused to such uncertainty, he looked for something to say. 'Who did you bring with you to your picnic?'

She hurried off, calling over her shoulder, 'My teddy bear.' And with a peal of laughter she began to wriggle through the hedge.

He watched her round bottom disappear. 'You're an unfeeling girl,' he called, but with exasperation rather than venom. To himself, he added, – *And an intoxicating lady. Watch yourself, Kingsley!*

She stood before the mirror, opened a drawer and looked down at the sweaters. Not the great thick-knit ones she usually wore, but figure-hugging, fashionable, unworn gifts, or impulse buys from years back – for she had been too self-conscious about her heavy breasts to wear them then. Teasing from schoolmates had begun early, with the effect of making her feel different – a schoolgirl's nightmare.

From the mound of size thirty-eight sweaters, she pulled one out at random, and there was a sudden explosion of rainbow colours. The one in her hand was a soft lavender angora, with pearls attached to a neat collar; she slipped it over her head, feeling its softness brush her cheek and hearing a whisper in her ear. There was the trapped, raw scent of unworn wool and then her head was out and silky soft waves were caressing her arms and back, reaching for her skin.

He came up behind her, his hands went around her, supporting her breasts. She faced the mirror, and, seeing his reflected face frowning way above her, asked, 'Don't you like me in this?'

'No.'

His fingers slipped beneath the wool, sliding the sweater up and over her head and brushing her skin to a shimmering response at the same time. There was darkness and breathlessness, and suddenly eyes more blue than grey were accosting her from the mirror. 'I prefer you like this.'

He unclipped her bra and threw it with the sweater onto the bed. He let one of her breasts drop into one hand. His other hand slipped down between her thighs and held her there, so she was pressed against him, feeling his passion uncurl into her backbone, feeling his throbbing with her own throbbing cupped in his hand.

It was a most complete sensation, pressure in every part of her – very satisfying, until the contentment flew away and somehow she was on the bed and he was above her, taking her swiftly, but not too swiftly, his urgency an irresistible force, driving her own excitement. His hot mouth was a match, igniting her passion, setting light here and there and everywhere . . . with a roar that engulfed them both.

Afterwards she slipped from the bed, showered and dressed in jeans and the discarded sweater she found on the floor. All the time he still slept, and a wave of tender softness like melted butter drained from her and lingered on his golden-skinned face, his exhausted face, as he slept his fulfilled sleep.

Her body was light, full of energy. It seemed to her that she floated down the stairs, out through the front door and up the track to her vine slope.

Nature went with love. She smiled, blinded by colours, overpowered by scent, deafened by birdsong; her fingers caressed smooth, cool grapes and when she bit into one the juice spurted onto her tongue and washed around her mouth, tasting like champagne.

She plucked a bunch and took them home to him. For grapes went so well with love. But by the time she got back the green grapes had turned black and shrivelled, like shiny black pearls of caviare.

When she awoke she was alone; church bells were ringing. A glance around the room showed her that the drawer where she kept her sweaters was tightly closed. There were no grapes, there was no Kingsley.

Kingsley had merely taken over her dream world as he was beginning to loom larger than life in her busy, busy days. Her head and her body had, it seemed, parted company. Her body wanted to be where he was, her head knew it wasn't to be. For they didn't even like each other.

She fell back on the pillow, for a moment unable to stand the desolation of waking.

Amber-brown eyes looked down at her from the shelf above, and she reached up, pulling the soft brown body into her arms. She raised her knees and perched the bear on them, facing her, and she spoke to him sternly.

'I'm damned if I'll fall in love with him. There are other men. Besides, I intend to live alone – it's nice, the freedom. A quiet house, my work, no one to worry for. In any case, he's playing some sort of game with me and I won't allow him the satisfaction of thinking he's winning. I won't go running like all his other women and end up hurt. I won't confirm his first opinion of me that I'm cheap. No way. Besides,' she finished sadly, 'he would find out in the end that it's impossible.'

She told the bear straight, just in case he hadn't heard the first time. 'I refuse to fall in love with Kingsley Hunter.'

The bear looked back at her knowingly. This particular bear had always had a disbelieving smile.

CHAPTER 13

Danielle parked the truck and jumped out, noticing that Jo's motorbike was standing beside the postbox.

She had only taken a few steps towards the shop when a shrill 'Danny!' brought her to a halt.

Annette's mother, Lorraine, who liked to be called Raine – 'Like in *reign*,' people muttered – was waving and jogging across the green towards the narrow strip of road that fronted the shop, where Danielle waited.

Raine had an everlasting scarlet smile and a pious expression which told everyone that she was a shining example. Her piled-up hair was also a shining example, as pale and good as low-fat spread. Her stick-insect body was warmly wrapped today, in black sweater and leggings. Heavy gold chains bounced like a stethoscope against her high, pointed breasts as she jogged up.

A verbal haemorrhage of a woman, Jo called her.

Danielle's 'How's Tony and Annette?' as they fell in step was dismissed with a breathy, 'Fine.' Followed by, 'Have you heard?'

'I don't know. You tell me.'

'Cherie's sold the shop,' Raine said, triumphant blue slits noting Danielle's obvious shock.

'You're joking! Why?'

'She says business is bad, and she's getting on.' Raine glanced towards the shop, lowered her voice. 'You'll never guess what she's going to do instead.'

Danielle couldn't wait to know. 'What?'

'She's going to train to be a counsellor.' Raine gave a peal of laughter. 'She says no one knows people like her. That everyone talks to her and she can keep things to herself – '

'Did she say who's bought the shop?' Danielle interrupted, not at all sure how she felt about it.

'She's keeping mum on that,' Raine said, leading by the nose and pushing open the clanging door.

Jo, reading MP-and-call-girl-type headlines on a Sunday tabloid, looked up. Dottie Trout, clutching sherry and *The Stage*, answered Danielle's 'How are you?' with grateful seal eyes and a too hearty, 'Wonderful.'

Cherie looked and obviously felt very important. 'What will it be?' she asked, with a secretive smile as the bell jangled behind Dottie.

Raine, her flow of information stopped, gave her order in a loud, reproachful voice. 'Crispbread, cottage cheese and Perrier water. Oh, and have you any of that herb tea?' She glanced around with a saintly expression.

Jo and Danielle chose their papers and righted the world until Raine ran out of things to say to Cherie and with a self-righteous 'Cheerio' hurried away.

Danielle wondered if Jo was bothered by her ex-husband's wife, but her face was inscrutable. All she said, in a dry voice, as the shop door crashed closed behind Raine, was, 'That woman's mouth runs for England.' And, in the voice of one who knows she added 'Fat-free, low-calorie, keep-fit. Don't eat this, eat that. It's like living in Intensive Care these days.'

Glancing round at Cherie, she deliberately lowered her voice and went on, 'She's having problems with Annette.'

'Serious?'

'She won't believe it is. But you know she owns a hairdressing salon?'

'When Danielle nodded, Jo went on, 'She wants Annette to work there with her. Annette doesn't want to.'

'Surely it would be a good start for Annette?'

Jo shook her head. 'Annette can't handle hair.' Seeing Danielle's questioning frown, she explained, 'She can't stand the feel of it.'

'No point in a hairdressing career, then.'

'You and I know that, but try persuading Raine,' Jo pointed out. 'It would all be so tidy, you see. So fitting,' she said, imitating Raine's regal tone. 'She and Tony like life to be perfect in Barbieland.'

'Annette visits you a lot, I gather?' Danielle said curiously, and saw Jo half smile.

'She comes for some proper food. I give her all the things she's not allowed at home.'

Danielle shook her head in mock reproof. 'Trust you.'

Looking pleased with herself, Jo added, 'Even Robin feeds her when she sits for him.'

'She's sitting for Robin?'

'Iris is most upset,' Cherie butted in, coming over to rearrange some of the bread left over from Saturday.

Passing over a stony glare and money for her papers, Jo left, reminding Danielle that she would be late in the morning. Moments later her motorbike roared away.

Cherie sailed back behind the counter and Danielle went to pay for her papers, inspecting Cherie with new eyes.

'It will be strange without you, Cherie. I've known you all my life.'

Cherie sniffed. 'This shop has been in my family for nearly a century. It's the incomers, isn't it? They don't buy from here much. It's only the post office keeps it going.'

'Who's taking over?'

'You'll see,' Cherie said, with a pleased-to-be-asked smirk.

'It's my childhood, this shop, Cherie. You used to spoil me.'

'I know.' Cherie's lips pressed together; she had the look of a child caught doing something wrong. 'Would you come and visit me in my flat at Ashford, if I give you my address?' she asked, and without waiting for a reply began scribbling on a white paper bag.

Danielle took it, but knew she probably wouldn't go. After all, there must be others closer to Cherie.

Anxiously watching her face, Cherie's bottom lip trembled. 'I don't want to lose touch,' she said in a childish voice. God, thought Danielle, embarrassed. I hope she isn't going to cry.

Instead, Cherie suddenly blurted out, 'You're part of Daniel. I loved your grandfather.'

'So did I.' Danielle smiled, pleased.

Cherie stared. 'That's why you were my favourite.'

All those free sweets, Danielle remembered. Fishes in a jar. She saw the satin blouse – Cherie always wore satin blouses – in a sick pink sway towards her across the counter. 'It was a secret,' Cherie told her importantly. 'Between him and me. He was saving for *her* to go to Italy so that we could be together.'

There was a startled silence.

Hang on, Danielle said to herself. *Something's odd here*. 'What about your husband?' she said aloud.

'Ah! Daniel was special, wasn't he? A real man.'

Wondering if she was dreaming, Danielle inhaled the usual mixture of strong cheese, newsprint, soap. And she had to laugh.

'What's funny?' Cherie asked suspiciously.

'My grandfather wouldn't have had an affair with you. He was twice your age. Besides, he and his wife adored each other – I do know that.' Oh, yes. Their closeness had made her feel lonely.

Cherie's hands folded over her stomach. Her gloating smile said, I'm going to shock you now. 'Ask your grandmother about her affair with Hutchinson, then. And I might have been fifteen when I met him, but I did grow up. At least I was there to love him when she was unfaithful,' she said pointedly. 'He needed me then.' She nodded, as if to say So there!

Danielle, with sudden anger, would have liked to tell her to shut up. It was a ridiculous story.

Beneath her glare, Cherie's eyes slipped away, and she changed the subject, becoming coy. 'Talking of love, who's the handsome stranger? I was telling Tom he'd better pull his socks up or he'll be losing you.'

Tom, Danielle thought, rather unfairly, is beginning to get on my nerves. 'He hasn't *got* me,' she snapped.

Treating this remark as unimportant information, Cherie moved around the counter and made her way, with that odd, slow glide, to the door, where she flipped the 'OPEN' sign round. It was one o'clock. 'You'll be on the shelf so long you'll go stale.'

Danielle eyed the Bath buns. 'You should know, Cherie. Kingsley, his name is. He was here on business. Nothing exciting. He's gone.'

A jar caught her eye. The fish jellies inside were smiling. They had been bait. She bought some.

'Did you know our Iris has lost two stone?' Cherie asked, eyeing Danielle's figure and scooping out the fish from the jar. 'And talk about dolling herself up. Of course, she spends half her time taking her home-made pies over to Robin. It's like meals on wheels! I think someone should tell poor Ron . . .'

'I dare say *someone* will.' Danielle took her fish jellies, her newspapers and her curiosity, and left.

'Get your *News of the World* here' read the sign outside.

'Did you know Cherie's sold the shop, Francesca?'

'No. Never use the shop,' Francesca answered, settling into her chair. 'And I'm not at all inter-ested.' Dismissively, she glanced at the table beside her, which held the things she *was* interested in. Newspapers, gardening magazines, crosswords, tra-vel books. Pavarotti sang Italian love songs in the background.

Calling her attention back, Danielle asked, 'You don't like Cherie, do you?'

She watched Francesca's head turn, heard an almost imperceptible sigh. 'No.'

'Any particular reason?'

'Could be.'

'What does that mean?'

Francesca went quiet. Danielle, curled in the opposite armchair stroking the smoke-blue cat, watching her, was surprised by a sinking feeling. *How fragile Francesca suddenly looks. Or have I only just noticed?*

The thought stabbed her, and her strong hands

moved rhythmically down the furry, responsive body. The heavy, rumbling warmth in her lap comforted her. The cassette finished, leaving the room almost silent, yet Francesca seemed to be listening, as if she heard more than the clock ticking and the cat purring.

Hearing Francesca's rasping breathing, Danielle's heart turned over. She was suddenly hurting. Suddenly afraid. You had to feel protective and softer towards the old, she realized painfully. No matter how much you might have been irritated by them in the past. Their fragility, the wistful expressions and sparrow-like bones, the knowledge that they had nowhere to go from here, no more chances . . . Danielle felt the prick of tears.

She understood, all at once, Kingsley's concern towards his mother. Not that his mother was old, but she was fragile at the moment.

The elderly became so heart-breakingly delicate you feared for them. Children again. Positions reversed. When you had been helpless yourself, they had given so much.

Danielle forced back the tears. No need to mention what Cherie had said. No truth in it. Why upset Francesca? Instead she remarked, 'You're pale. We didn't have a great summer; you need some sun.'

Francesca gave her a sharp look, as if reminded of something, then thought for a bit and made up her mind.

'Anna made it all right again, you know.'

Danielle frowned. 'Who are you talking about?'

'My friend. My only friend.'

Danielle's hand stilled. She looked down at it. Francesca had never rambled before.

'In a way I was to blame,' Francesca said, after a bit. 'I can see myself now – like a puppy, too friendly, wanting to join in. My nature,' she said dramatically, 'was to love too much. By the time you came along I'd learned to be less loving.'

Danielle glanced up, wondering where this conversation was leading. 'You shouldn't have had to.'

Francesca looked the way she did when the cat brought her a dead mouse. 'People's minds in those days were as narrow as sewers.'

There was sadness in her face as she added quietly, 'Some say that Cherie started the gossip, but I don't know. I mean, she doesn't talk to herself, does she? The shop has always been a meeting place for wagging tongues.'

What about Cherie and your husband? Danielle wanted to ask. But Francesca told her something else.

Francesca sat straight-backed in her chintz armchair, arms rigid on the dark-oak armrests. Occasionally she would flick her wrists, flap her hands in disbelief or tap her swollen fingers with irritated piano-playing movements as her musical voice rose and fell. Her speech was punctuated with the tense drumbeat of fingers on oak, or the angry click of wedding and engagement rings.

'They wouldn't accept me here, you know, when I

186

arrived from Italy. Some still called Italians the enemy. Being young, I took it personally. I was different – too busy to mix much. Too close to Daniel because I was homesick and lonely. Any friends I made I took to my heart, but people here didn't understand.'

'Do you want to tell me?'

'Your mother was about eleven, and we were working desperately hard. We were upset because I was unable to have another child.' Francesca gave a guilty grimace. 'Your grandfather had so wanted a son to pass the vineyard to.' Her hands flapped. 'Always the vineyard. Looking back, I over-compensated, I think. With the work, I mean. Then the rumours began about me and Hutch.'

'Hutch?' Beautiful Francesca with old Hutchinson? Danielle couldn't believe it. And who was Anna?

Francesca laughed. 'Danny, if you knew how tired I was! I wouldn't have had the energy for sex with Cary Grant, let alone Hutch. It was a muddle – until Anna went away and eventually ended up in Australia. Then things returned to normal. Except for poor Hutch?

'You haven't told me what happened.'

'About the affair?'

'You had an affair?'

The old hands rose as if Danielle had pointed a gun at her. 'No. No one did at first.'

Danielle could have strangled her! 'What about Hutchinson?'

'Gossip said that he and I were lovers.'

'But you weren't?'

Francesca shook her head. 'Daniel and Hutch's wife, Anna, believed it. They ended up consoling each other. In Paradise field, apparently.' Rings clicked on oak. 'After Anna and Hutch had a bust-up, Anna went away.'

'So you and Grandfather got back together again?' Danielle said, trying to muddle through the story. 'Must have been hard.'

'It seemed oddly natural. Because of Anna. I tried hard to make up for it all. My imaginary affair was a catalyst – made me see I'd neglected him. From then on he came first, the yard second.'

Danielle snorted. 'What an old-fashioned view. You took the blame and spent your life trying to make up to him for something you didn't do? Honestly!'

Francesca raised her hands. 'He was what I wanted.' Seeing Danielle's scornful face, she said patiently, 'Look, during the War we learned what it was to lose loved ones for ever. You have to forgive someone you love or live without them. If you know that living without him will be harder than forgiving him, then – ' she slapped her hands on the oak ' – end of story. You close the book and start again. The secret is not to try to be the same people. You're starting a new book – learning about each other over again.'

Danielle was shocked, but deeply interested too.

'So gossip sent a woman away to the other side of the world!'

'And broke up a wonderful friendship.' Francesca glanced at the clock which sliced up her remaining days into mealtimes and bed-times. 'Time for tea.' She levered herself from her chair. The greedy-eyed cat sprang from Danielle's lap.

Francesca looked rueful. 'There's innocent gossip, my dear, but evil gossip's something else. A whirl-wind. It can blow the lid off people's lives and destroy them. Or . . .' she paused '. . . change them for ever.'

Danielle felt the cat's warmth leave her. She leaned over, switched on the gas fire and sat thinking for five minutes, feeling its warmth on her legs.

Rousing herself to take the tray from Francesca, she laid it on the coffee-table. 'This Anna,' she said, pulling a face. 'She sounds deceitful and selfish to me.'

Francesca concentrated upon pouring steaming tea from a bone-china pot into bone-china cups that Danielle called egg-cups. Adding lemon for herself and milk and sugar for Danielle, she indicated a plate of fairy cakes, which Danielle had already noted, and finally said, 'No, no. She wasn't at all. She was my friend, and a good one.'

It sounded like a reprimand.

Danielle bit into a cake and shrugged. Swallowing, she asked, 'What did she look like?'

Putting down her cup, Francesca glanced trancelike around the room, at the sideboard, bureau, bookcase, television, display unit, finally admitting, 'We didn't take so many photos in those days. But I can tell you what she was like.'

She gave a pleased, remembering smile. 'Hutch used to say she was like a bottle of Guinness. Dark, cool, with a long, beautiful body and a frothy head, and just as mouthwatering and as good for him. She didn't seem the type to be a nurse. To look at her you wouldn't have believed she knew how to tie a bandage. She loved clothes, but why not? In the War she spent a lot of time in uniform in some appalling places. She was dreamy, but active too, and outgoing.'

There was fun in Francesca's eyes as she said, 'I can see her now, swinging along my garden path, with that graceful sort of man's stride, calling out in her fluty voice.' There was a pause, and then she added, 'Wonder what she looks like now?'

Danielle helped herself to more tea. 'You were obviously fond of her.'

She offered tea to Francesca, who shook her head and recalled, 'I was. I might have taught her to laugh again, but in return she gave me that special love one woman can feel for another – you know?'

Thinking of Jo, Danielle nodded.

'I grew up among loving women. I was missing it and very homesick.' Francesca sat back in her chair with a grin. 'Your grandfather and Hutch went through it between the two of us. We teased them unmercifully. Yes, there was a lot of fun and laughter here.' Her smile faded. 'But Anna had her moody side too. She couldn't stand being bored.'

Clattering the used crockery onto the tray, pretending not to notice Francesca wince, Danielle said firmly, 'I still see no reason why she did what she did.'

'You have to understand her. She saw a lot of tragedy, you know. Oh . . .' Francesca said, face falling. 'Are you going?'

Bending down to give her a hasty kiss, Danielle said, 'It's been interesting, all this. But I've things to do. You know . . .'

'Yes,' grimaced Francesca. 'I know.'

Later that evening, Danielle left her account books and made a telephone call.

'Grandmother? Are you okay?'

'Fine,' came a surprised voice. 'There's an old war-time film on television, filmed in Rome.'

'Remember our talk this afternoon? You never got around to telling me about Cherie.'

'She was a schoolgirl when we first came to the village. Her mother had a lovely voice – she wanted to be a singer, I believe, but her husband put a stop to it. Didn't see a lot of him, but we heard him – he was always shouting about something. I thought Cherie was a pathetic little thing. She wasn't intelligent enough to please her father or musically talented enough for her mother. She seemed good at nothing except reading, which made her forget things and get into trouble.'

'I only realized today, Francesca, that I've never seen her outside the shop.'

'No. By the time her parents died her husband wasn't well. Dead opposite to her father, Alf was. Bit meek and not very robust, if you remember. Dead by fifty.'

'I was curious,' Danielle admitted, without saying why. 'Sorry to interrupt your film. Goodnight.'

Danielle couldn't help feeling sorry for Cherie, who had obviously been spinning dreams. On the other hand, could she have been spiteful enough, or desperate enough, to make trouble deliberately between Daniel and his wife for her own purposes?

Clicking on the television, Danielle curled at one end of the settee and watched the rest of the film, trying to put Daniel and Francesca in place of the lovers in war-time Italy. She rested her cheek on one hand, moving the light of her mind to the young Daniel, somewhere amongst the photographs on her grandmother's sideboard, but she couldn't find him. What had he looked like?

Francesca she could imagine easily – in fact their talk this afternoon had, if anything, brought Danielle closer to the old lady, as if her vivid words had brought the young Italian girl into the room.

Danielle felt an inner stirring as she watched the black and white screen. Rome and its surrounding countryside flickered across her absorbed face, oddly familiar, although she had never been there. She could feel herself as a beautiful Italian bride; warm, fun-loving, full of sunshine and hope and love, and tears too, steaming away from Rome to start a new life with her vibrant English soldier husband.

Francesca would have arrived in a grey, drizzly London; it would have been a steam train in those days, hissing up to the platform. Had Grandfather met her there? He must have done, or she would have felt so lost. Together, then, they would have boarded the slower train into Greenwich. And not many years later they would have arrived at the village of Hidden to start a new and successful life. Among people who wouldn't welcome her.

'*The End*' came up on the screen.

The odd thing was that hard as Danielle tried to visualize Grandy, Kingsley kept getting in the way.

She fixed her thoughts on Francesca instead. There had been something different about her today. Puzzled, Danielle thought back over their conversation, for she couldn't help feeling that Francesca had wanted to bring up the past, had somehow turned the conversation the way she had wanted it to go. Why?

Picturing her grandmother, Danielle suddenly saw what the difference was. The impish glow had returned to her eyes. There had still been sadness, but laughter too. The natural laughter of Daniel Summerfield's 'Intoxicating Lady'.

Rising and yawning, Danielle clicked the television off. Somehow she felt a nagging, uneasy sensation as she switched off the lamp, plunging the room into darkness.

CHAPTER 14

The telephone rang. Danielle snatched it up. Her heart leapt and then slid miserably down to her wellies.

'It's almost the middle of October,' came Jane's hearty boom. 'Harvest is nearly over, what about it?'

'What about what?' Danielle tugged on her hair and tried to sound pleased to hear from her friend.

'Oh, come *on*. Our get together in Tunbridge Wells after the harvest.' Jane might have been speaking to one of her children. 'You know – lunch, shopping, that sort of thing, then you come to this madhouse. The kids are dying to see you, by the way.'

Danielle glanced from the window; her ghost-like reflection floated there, eyes enormous in her exhausted face. 'Well . . .'

There was a yell in her ear. 'Put that down, you little . . . Turn the telly down . . .' Jane's voice returned to normal. 'Sorry about that. We were about to fix up a day. You've your harvest dance coming up, Danny; we'll get you a nice dress – and shall I book with Simon for your hair? It'll be great seeing you, I need cheering up . . .'

Danielle smiled to herself as Jane rambled on, and when she paused for breath, suggested, just to please her, 'Let's make it this Thursday.' The thought of seeing the children *was* appealing . . . their exuberance and wet kisses, their unconditional love.

'Smashing! Has that nasty man gone, by the way?'

'Who do you mean?'

'The one from Lamont's you called the Towering Inferno; he had his eye on you.'

'Not me . . . the vineyard. He went three weeks ago. His name is Kingsley. Kingsley Hunter.'

'He didn't take your vineyard, then?' Jane laughed.

'No, no, he . . . just wanted to clear up a few things.'

'You don't sound your usual bubbly self. He didn't bully you, did he? I'd have come and sorted him out.'

'Honestly, Jane. I can look after myself, you know.'

'I know, love – only joking. What's he like?'

'Like?' Danielle glanced at the door, remembering the way it had flown open. 'Well, he's tall . . .'

A long time later, she replaced the receiver and sat without moving, staring at it, daring it to ring again. She smiled ruefully. Jane must have a vivid image of Kingsley now, for, once started, she had – Danielle grimaced – gone on a bit. It was as if talking about him brought him here. For how long was it now since the picnic? Exactly fourteen days.

If she could only remove him from her head as well, she brooded, getting up from the squeaky chair and going over to the window. But the thought of him was like a demented bluebottle in a closed room; it was extremely wearing, and yet when she awoke he was there, and when she lay down to sleep he was there. And she was so tired.

Had Jane felt like this with Timothy? And her mother with her father? Grandmother with Grandy?

She took a Kit Kat from the top of the filing cabinet and peeled back the wrapper. What did one do about it if it was someone . . . impossible?

As she munched the crisp chocolate biscuit she wondered about the woman who had written the letter, Piers's mistress; did she feel like this too? Was it Jo? Jo seemed too independent and straight, you'd expect her to cope alone. She, Danielle smiled fondly, would shout the news from the treetops, if only to shock everyone.

Although love changed people.

Finishing the chocolate, Danielle perched her cap on her head and went out smiling into the wine- and smoke-scented day. Then she reached the pickers – Jo and six casual girls – and her smile abruptly died, for she couldn't resist scanning their jeans and bulky jumpers, wondering . . . Is it her? Or maybe the letter was a lie, or a nasty joke.

Danielle drove into the car park, jumped from the truck and slammed the door. She didn't need her gut-clutching response to tell her who owned the silver Mercedes.

Her eyes fled across to the slopes, back past the winery, and paused at the cottage. Where was Kingsley? Why had he come back?

She made her way down the garden path and let herself into the cottage, half wondering if he had gone inside to wait for her, as she often forgot to lock the door.

'You shouldn't leave the place unlocked,' he had nagged her once.

'Why on earth not?' She had laughed. 'Who's going to harm me here?'

The cottage was empty, she could tell, for an empty house seemed to stop breathing.

She was pouring boiling water into the teapot when there was a bang on the front door and she heard it squeak open; footsteps made irritable thuds along the passage. The kitchen doorhandle rattled.

Putting down the kettle and stirring the tea, she clanked the lid down on the pot before she glanced round.

He was watching her, lounging in the doorway as he had that first night. But the difference, she saw, carrying the teapot to the table, was the smile of approval on his face.

'Well, well!'

She raised her eyebrows and hid her flaming cheeks by turning to the cupboard to fetch out, with fingers like thumbs, two mugs.

'Just in time for tea,' she said, with something like anger. She knew it was ridiculous, but he hadn't been near since the picnic and, illogically, she resented it. The mugs thudded down onto the table next to the teapot and she stalked over to the fridge. And the way he just walked in – like . . . like someone coming home!

He slowly crossed to the table and pulled out a chair. 'I like the new sweater; tan suits you. Brings out the amber in your eyes.'

She slosh milk from the bottle into a jug, slammed the fridge door. Going to the table, she saw the look in his eyes, and to her dismay her breasts surged with life, straining against the soft wool.

'It's an old sweater,' she said shortly. 'I've been to see Francesca – you know what she's like.'

'Thought that's where you were, being Sunday. I had a stroll around while I was waiting.'

'And what brings you here?' She poured milk into the mugs with an unsteady hand, followed by tea. The rising steam made her face feel moist and shimmery and warm.

Watching her, seeing the soft wool curve into the mounds of her breasts, he knew that he had somehow made her angry again. Because he had complimented her on her appearance? With an effort, he kept his voice light. 'My car's on a piece of elastic; it automatically turns this way.'

'Idiot!' She pushed his mug towards him, her face breaking into that lovely smile.

Relieved, he held his mug in both hands, as if warming them. 'No, it's true. Since my sojourn here I find I miss driving home to Kent after work, away from the never-ending rumble of the City. So today I gave in to my inclinations, and here I am. I had a busy Saturday night.' He grinned. 'I need some of your peace.'

You could have sharpened a knife on her voice. 'What is there here, compared to your exciting life in London?'

He leaned back in the chair, regarding her with half-closed eyes. 'Waking to silent, scented mornings – just the cock crowing, Hutch's tractor chugging; the gentle breathing of growing things; being part of the landscape – a big sky; the changes – even day to day; the sense that what lies beneath my feet throbs with life instead of being dead. I miss the breeze on my face at night. In London few sleep with bedroom windows open.'

'You're joking! Why?'

He shrugged. 'Burglaries,' he explained, gulping down his tea.

'Even in hot weather?' she asked, aghast.

He nodded. 'I haven't slept with a summer night breeze on my face for years. But it's more than that – ' He stopped, seeing her shudder. 'What's up?'

'I was just thinking I couldn't bear to live in London – or any city for that matter. I wouldn't . . . not for anything or anyone.'

His eyes lingered on her mouth; he was thinking

how full it was, how sweet and moist. 'You wouldn't?'

'Never.' She closed her lips firmly.

After a thoughtful silence, he cleared his throat and said, 'I've been puzzling about your problems here. If there's anything I can do to help . . .'

'Help?' She laughed. *So that's why he's here; I'm not that daft. All this polite conversation, even flattery, and now offering to help . . . He wants the vineyard, of course.* Out loud, she asked coldly, 'Why should you want to help me? I mean, you don't even like me.'

With surprise in his voice, he shook his head. 'It's impossible to dislike you. As I said to you that day of the picnic, you're the sort of woman no man could hate, the sort a man wants to hold in his arms. You're . . . well . . . quite an intoxicating lady, you know.'

That was what he had meant about the sort of woman she was. Her face split into a dimpled smile.

Returning her smile as if he couldn't help himself, he added, 'You're a warm bundle of fun, like a puppy.'

Her smile died. How would he describe the women he went out with? Racehorses? She wasn't sure about that remark at all, and she disliked the way her emotions were plummeting up and down like a yo-yo.

'I thought we could have a brainstorming session,' he told her.

She felt her face fall. 'A what?'

'Turn over a few ideas for getting more business.'

'I've plenty of ideas,' she said, firmly and dismissively. 'Not much money,' she added, with an accusing glare. Before Grandy died she had been enthusiastic about her ideas. It was only after he'd died that she'd realized why he had not been. When she, too, was faced with money problems, her plans had had to be shelved.

'What ideas do you have?' he asked, a wary smile showing he felt the chill.

Finding herself completely uninterested in her beloved vineyard, or its problems, was a bit of a shock. *I'm tired*, she told herself.

Seeing the soulful look she gave him, he said gently, 'Come on, don't be shy.'

She gritted her teeth. What a man. One minute he was the big, bad wolf, the next a lamb.

'I had an idea about turning the shed into a shop, and opening the vineyard for tours.'

'You should have done that before.'

'Grandy didn't want the place turned into a circus,' she told him, and put on a gruff impersonation. ' "This is a workplace." '

'Not if it makes no money, it isn't. It's a dead loss,' he told her unsmilingly.

She moved uncomfortably, aware that she wanted to return to the subject of themselves. She wanted to be closer to him than she was; there were longings inside her that she didn't quite know what to do with.

When the longing became too strong, patience not

being her good point, she stood up. 'Why are we sitting in the kitchen? The sitting room's more comfortable.' She felt ridiculously flustered, as if she was some *femme fatale*; had she sounded artificial? He gave no sign, and she felt it necessary to cover her confusion with a joke.

'Come into the parlour, said the spider to the fly.' She laughed, beckoning.

At least he smiled before he followed her into the other room.

'Sit yourself down,' she said, indicating the settee which was pulled up in front of the great stone hearth she never used. Bending to switch on the electric fire, she saw him, from the corner of her eye, choose a well-worn chintz-covered armchair to one side of the fireplace in front of the window. Curling up on the settee, almost within reach, she felt her heart began to beat an anxious tattoo. She felt herself on the edge of an abyss, in a state of high tension, whereas Kingsley seemed annoyingly relaxed.

'You could give wine-tastings,' he was saying. 'Send out invitations to hoteliers, restaurateurs, wine merchants,' he said helpfully. 'Serve wine and cheese.'

She ran her eyes over him. He was sitting forward, hands gripped together, face full of saintly concern, while behind him the day was hurrying disconcertingly fast towards evening. She could have hit him. Besides, wasn't there a selfish interest behind all his ideas?

More important, would he, in the cosy ambience of the room . . .?

'Red!' he exclaimed.

She frowned. 'What about her?'

'You need to direct sell. In the winter she isn't fully employed.' A gleam in his eyes made her pull in a breath of annoyance as he went on, 'She'd make a charming salesperson. All she'd need is a car; her natural attributes would do the rest. Who could resist her?'

'Who indeed?' she said, stony-faced. She combed casual fingers through her hair and lifted it with two hands high off her face, holding it there. 'So you've seen Red a lot, then?'

'We have chats occasionally. I wanted to see her today, actually – forgot she wouldn't be in the lab on a Sunday. Where does she live? I owe her some money.'

She let her hair flop. So he hadn't come just to see her, then. That talk about his car being on elastic . . . honestly! Mere flattery. Aloud, she said sharply, 'You could leave the money with me if you like.'

He stood up, reaching into the back pocket of his jeans, pulling out a wallet. While he removed three notes, she found herself looking him over, as her eyes were so often drawn to do.

The expensive jeans were tight-fitting.

'It's for my harvest dance ticket,' he explained as she reached out for the money.

She stood up suddenly. 'A village hop? After what

204

you're used to?' Crossing the room, she put the money in the bureau, next to the white paper bag with Cherie's new address on, and snapped the drawer closed. He must think a lot of Red to take her to a village dance.

Watching her return to her seat, he grinned. 'You should have been with me last night.'

She sat back with her face in shadows. 'Should I?'

'The Dorchester . . . you know?'

'I *have* heard of it.'

He seemed determined to remain in a good humour. 'It was a charity do – boring, but all in a good cause. Like your dance . . . church roof, I believe . . . And I promised Red.'

'Death watch beetle, *actually*.'

Suddenly he clicked his fingers. 'A bottling plant.'

'What?'

'A good sideline, that.'

'I'll think about it.' She felt her insides flush red-hot and curled her legs beneath her, trying to relax.

It's Red he's taking to the dance.

'You know,' he said into an awkward silence, 'your voice reminds me of bubbling toffee. Do you make toffee?'

'Never.'

'Mother used to; she loved being a housewife – not like you. You don't need anyone, do you, Danielle?'

'I enjoy living alone,' she said, a mite reluctantly, and, not bothering to hide the sarcasm, added,

'Shows you have a nice side . . . loving your mother so much, I mean.'

Recognizing the familiar glint in her eyes, he laughed and shook his head, admitting, 'We're not that close. I just have an over-protective instinct where women are concerned. Mother's so timid she worries me.'

Danielle uncurled her legs and stretched her arms above her head, seeing his eyes slip down her body in a way that stirred her to a certain excitement. When he sat back and studied the ceiling as if it were the seventh wonder of the world, she went on coldly, 'As I said, family loyalty isn't something with which I'm familiar. I'm independent. I mean, in your mother's position, I'd rather sort *myself* out, thank you very much.'

She saw his eyes narrow. 'You mean, I think, that you would want everything out in the open.'

Why did she feel a frisson of dislike for Kingsley's mother, whom she had never met? She was irritated by the attention he gave the silly, helpless woman. Some people, Danielle thought bitterly, have to handle life without all that attention.

She shrugged her shoulders, pouting. 'I just mean that we're not all alike.' Trying to be nice, she asked, 'How *do* you cope with her?'

'I find the best way is to just sit down with her and listen. I admit she gets on my nerves sometimes. The trouble is, a single mother tends to make friends of her children – out of loneliness probably. Her dependence can take away a youngster's childhood. My sister's older than me and she escaped . . . well, married young.'

His smile was rueful, honest and heart-catchingly tender, causing a strange tug at her heart. She became aware of a melting sensation, yearnings that were strange to her, and an ache, an intense ache to be picked up and petted; the woman she was walked away . . . leaving behind a soft and gentle and clinging stranger.

'One of the things I like about you, Danielle, is that you're not soft and clinging – you're your own woman. We had quite a few spats, didn't we?'

The flickering coal effect fire picked out a reminiscent glow in his eyes as he sat forward. Watching him, she felt as if she had dived off a high cliff and discovered halfway down that there was no water at the bottom.

While she sat stunned, he rubbed the side of his nose thoughtfully. 'When Mother remarried, I felt more free to enjoy life, but I'm not as good as you at doing it. Too many years worrying, I suppose.'

He sounded so sincere; she leaned towards him, studying his face as he said, 'Perhaps I need some lessons in fun, Danielle.'

This was better. She pretended to pout. 'You came along and spoiled *my* fun.'

His face, hovering quite close, wore a small smile. 'I hated you passionately,' he said.

'I know,' she said, almost feeling his clear brown

207

skin beneath her fingers. 'It showed.'

'I wanted to hurt you as Mother had been hurt . . . take away what you loved most . . . Because she was scared; the thought of losing love terrified her. She didn't know what Piers would do, you see – leave her for this woman, or what.'

Danielle felt a wave of pity. She suddenly ached for all women who had lost the men they loved, because she was aware now that love was feeling that life without him would be desolate.

She felt an urgent kick of longing to run her fingers over the moving muscles in his unusual face, the hard cheekbones and hollows, the smile lines and worry lines, the ridge between his nose and lips.

'And then,' he went on, 'I found you weren't the person I'd expected you to be. I started to make excuses for you: Piers had taken advantage . . . you were lonely . . . vulnerable . . . so eager to please.' His thick brows rose like question marks.

'Not that eager,' she said shakily, sitting back. 'In any case, I've known Piers for years.' She went quiet then, not knowing how to explain that Piers was special to her. Uncomfortably, she remembered how he had changed; it was in the way he'd looked at her.

'Maybe,' she said slowly, 'the girl lied, or made a mistake about the baby.'

Kingsley's face darkened. 'Loyalty is all very well unless it's blind,' he said, in his dictatorial manner.

208

Defensively, she snapped, 'Mistakes about pregnancy are quite common.'

He became still. With a skin-ripping stare, he asked, 'Do you think that's what happened?'

Confused, she played with a strand of hair, winding it around her finger. 'I really don't know. All I know is that I must take Piers as I find him. He's a friend.'

Throwing his hands in the air, Kingsley said, 'I give up. If you push the truth away, you're in danger of burying other things with it. Yourself, for instance. The person you are. As for Piers – ' his eyes smouldered ' – that man has a degree in handling women.'

Although she felt she was on the losing side, she retorted stubbornly, 'After Grandy died, Piers was very protective and helpful.'

He was watching her closely. 'Apart from the letter, there's something else.'

She sighed. Not another serious discussion. She wasn't in the mood, somehow, but he obviously was.

'I found two contracts for last year,' he told her.

'So?'

'One,' he went on patiently, 'was dated the fifteenth of November, and it had "cancelled" written across both of its two copies. The other was the file copy of a contract dated the twentieth of November – I assume you have the other copy. The first lot of prices were lower than the year before, yet on the second contract they were higher.'

She shrugged. 'I only saw one contract.'

'I was suspicious,' Kingsley admitted, 'as to why there was a sudden change in prices. I guessed Piers had some devious reason, and assumed you had charmed him. I was determined to push them back down this year.'

'I supposed that Piers was being kind . . .'

'Piers is a businessman, not Father Christmas. Could be he had another reason for coming here every week.'

'He said he wanted to keep a fatherly eye on me,' Danielle retorted. She felt it was a lame excuse, and knew the doubt showed in her eyes. Swallowing painfully, she said, 'The fifteenth of November was the date Grandy died. He was talking to Piers when he had his heart attack; Piers took us to the hospital, in fact. He was so kind. I remember him saying he would help me . . .'

'I'm sure,' came the sarcastic comment.

Danielle went white. 'Do you suppose Grandy and Piers argued about the prices? Grandy had been worried about losing a supermarket contract – a price-cut from Lamont's could have been the last straw.'

Seeing her stricken face, he warned her, 'Don't you dare feel responsible. There's only one guilty person here – that creep who's married to my mother.'

After an angry silence, he went on, 'Was there an office diary?' An appointments book?

She nodded miserably.

'Would you still have it?'

'In the office. Do you . . .?'

He stood up. 'Let's go and see. I'm curious.'

Dreading what was to come, she went into the winery first, walked around checking, ensuring that everything was working well. And then she could put off going to the office no longer.

The old office diary was in an unused drawer in the filing cabinet. With shaking fingers, she pulled it out and carried it to the desk, switching on the Anglepoise lamp.

With a concerned look at her face, Kingsley took it and flicked through to find the page for November the fifteenth. She made herself look down.

The familiar impatient writing wavered in the golden pool of light. It was the last appointment he had made.

She pulled in a deep breath and read aloud. '"Piers".' She swallowed. '"Discuss new contract."'

'I've a suspicion you're right,' Kingsley told her, adding doubtfully, 'Even Piers might have felt guilty afterwards – thus the higher prices to you.'

Seeing the dubious look he gave her, Danielle wondered painfully if he really believed she hadn't had an affair with Piers.

Tiredness fell over her in waves; she rubbed her eyes and her face, resting her palms on her cheeks. 'What difference does all this make anyway?'

'There's still the mystery of the letter,' he mused, watching her.

Dropping her hands, she stared at him, trying to read his expression. She saw concern mixed with curiosity, and surely a glimpse of distaste?

'It's natural,' he said gently, 'that after losing your grandfather you would feel lost and need someone.

You were afraid, perhaps, of running the vineyard alone, and Piers was there, with a reassuring new contract . . .'

Her heart sank like a stone in an icy pond. She just couldn't forget what Kingsley had first thought of her, no matter how friendly they were now on occasion, and it was obvious from what he was saying that he couldn't forget either.

He was insinuating that she had lied to Piers in the letter, saying she was expecting his baby. Maybe he even thought that she'd been trying to get money from Piers because of her financial situation. Stunned, she could see that this would make sense to someone like Kingsley, who thought money was everything.

She rose and crossed the room to the window, feeling bitterly hurt. The black sky threw back her own reflection, cuddling her body as if she were cold.

Turning, she saw him watching her, elbow resting on the desk, hand gripping his chin, as if planning a chess move. How like Grandy he was, in a way. Something to do with the poised head, the air of dignity.

She felt a knife-like thrust of pain and a longing to have him back.

Her voice, however, was calm, but husky. 'You still don't trust me, Kingsley, do you?'

He paused just a moment too long. He pushed the diary away and sat back in the chair. 'It's that letter, Danielle. Look, I just want the truth.'

Clasping her hands tightly in front of her, she asked, 'Why do you need to know? Why is it so important?'

'Don't you know, Danielle?'

She watched him push the chair away from the desk, stand up and walk purposefully across the room towards her, with a light in his eyes that made her back away. She could never welcome him while he thought she had tried to trick Piers in such a sordid way.

She was afraid – afraid of his strength, his power over her, which had altered to encompass not only her business but her body and mind. As he came up to her she raised her hands against his chest.

He gripped her hands and, despite her struggles, held them tight. His grip was warm and hard. She couldn't trust her body not to give her away, but there was no way she was having anything to do with someone who mistrusted her, was perhaps playing with her or using her.

He searched her stormy eyes. 'You know there's something powerful between us. But you fight yourself all the time. Okay, I know why. I can see that you're still afraid of me. It's because of the way I barged in – and I don't deny I was unpleasant to you.

But I want you.' His eyes ran over her, arousing her body as they always did. 'I see in your eyes that you want me, and that's why I need the truth . . . to start again with no barriers.'

She could have wept and screamed and hurled something. The very words she had longed to hear, and it was too late and for the wrong reasons.

'You want me?' she cried hotly. 'You want sex, you mean. It's a man's way of proving his power – the typical masculine way of using sex as a weapon.'

He stepped back, dropping her hands, his eyes slits. 'If that's your opinion of men, then you won't want me around, will you?'

'You're so right,' she said with an aching throat. 'I just want you to go. Just go.'

His hard stare nearly knocked her sideways, as it was meant to. Then he was striding across the room to open the door, and slamming it behind him with a vengeance. She heard his footsteps on gravel, and then . . . silence.

What sort of a mental state was she in, she asked herself bitterly, that she could order him to go and yet hope all the time that he would refuse to do so? Hope he would take her in his arms and hold her there, make her give in and admit the fact, against her will, of course, that she wanted him?

She heard an engine growl, and even that sounded angry. It seemed to say, as it roared up the track, that it wouldn't be coming back. She had cut the elastic, well and truly. Never had she felt so cold.

CHAPTER 15

Danielle wandered in Paradise field.

The harvest was almost over, except for the Chasselas, and although there was still much to be done there was time to spare. Too much. Too much time to expose the silly, immature side of her that she hadn't known existed.

How silly, for example, to go into his room and sit on the bed, even look inside the wardrobe where he had hung his suit. How ridiculous to linger close to the overall behind the kitchen door and sometimes reach out and touch it.

Today she wandered the meadow, alone with her thoughts and the memory of the picnic. It seemed to her that she saw him balancing on the tree, and she scrambled across to join the ghost of him. Lying on her stomach, gazing down into the slipping, sliding water, her rippled face looked up at her with unaccustomed sadness. A different sadness from last year. That had been a sadness deadened by grief. This was alive and kicking.

Curled in the crook of a bough, she heard the

lonely, harsh call of crows and, turning onto her back, saw them gathering like witches in the trees. The heavens were an angry threshing of clouds, a grey frown with no open blue eyes, no silver-headed young clouds.

Trudging through the long grass, she noticed what a dull, dark green it seemed – almost, she thought, as though someone had turned out the lights in the world.

She sat down, feeling the chill soak through her jeans, seeing in her mind's eye the red tablecloth, tasting the champagne, the caviare.

If she were honest, there had been a spark between them right from the beginning. But it had been born of a desire for revenge on his part and merely of the force of his personality on hers, she supposed. His anger had been brutal, almost a rape of her mind; he had swept into her life and tried to take over. Nothing to do with love on either side. Whatever love was. Rolling over onto her stomach, she pushed herself up and gazed down at what lay in the palm of her hand.

A champagne cork.

She curled her damp fingers around it, forcing back the lump in her throat, daring the tears that sprang to her eyes to fall. Tears solved nothing.

Hurrying back through the hedge, she smiled and spoke to the pickers, who had reached the bottom of the slope now, and from there she made her way into the winery.

An hour later she stood in the dank cellar, dwarfed by the great tanks, while a cold shawl of air fell like ghostly hands on her shoulders.

She took a tissue from her pocket, blew her nose and wiped her eyes. Because of the chill.

'Hi, Danny.'

Locking the cellar door, she turned round. 'Everything's okay, Tom.' She thrust the keys into one of her pockets. Her fingers touched the cork and she reacted as if the whole of her was an exposed, open wound.

Tom smiled his brief smile, and she smiled back, and their footsteps tapped across the stone floor accompanied by the usual hum of machinery, the men clattering about, calling out, someone whistling 'Raining In My Heart'.

'I'll pick you up about eight?' Tom suggested.

She shook her head. 'I might not go to the dance.'

'You always go.'

Glancing sideways, she saw his face was dark with disappointment; irritated, she looked away. 'So?'

At the shed entrance she probed the autumn mist, seeking her beloved hills, feeling mean. 'I probably shall go . . . It's just . . .'

Fussing, he said, 'You're tired – a holiday would do you good.'

'Fat chance.' She grinned kindly, moving away. 'If I do go . . . to the dance, I mean . . . I'll walk. It's only in the village.'

His eyes narrowed. 'I'll see you there,' he promised. A forced smile chased away the scowl as he assured her, 'You'll forget all your worries.'

Fat chance of that too. She groaned to herself, hurrying off. Poor Tom. It wasn't fair to take it out on him. He couldn't do a thing right lately as far as she was concerned.

'Face it,' she addressed her reflection in the mirror.

'You're afraid Kingsley will come and afraid he won't.'

The teddy bear on her dressing table gave her a disapproving stare. Picking him up, cuddling his soft body, the colour of demerara sugar, she was reminded of Jane's children the day before yesterday.

It had been difficult to behave naturally, particularly beneath Jane's scrutiny, but the company of people brought out her sense of fun, and she thought she had managed quite well.

She shook her head and smiled at the warming thought of those kids, and the way they had chuckled. She could hear them now . . .

'Do it again, Auntie Dannel. Do it again!' Her heart turned over with love.

Setting the bear back in his place, she decided she should get ready. No way could she let people down. As Grandy always said . . . 'A promise is a promise'.

Brushing her hair into obedience – easier now Simon had trimmed it and given her a light perm – she tugged at the tangles and when it was smooth fixed it in a cluster of curls, as Simon had shown her, on top of her head.

'It changes you completely,' he had cried dramatically. 'The gypsy has gone. See. You are now Sophia Loren's daughter.'

She'd had to laugh at him: outspoken, known to upset clients, yet so endearingly enthralled by his own genius. He'd pulled her hair up, showing her the slant of her eyes and dark, winged brows, her straight nose, her longer neck, as if they were new.

Danielle had been quite unimpressed. She had seen them before, hadn't she? *A new you*, she thought now, cynically. *Isn't that what these salons have on offer? A new you?* What a pity Simon couldn't do a job on her heart too! But then, the heart was merely an organ which pumped blood; it was her brain that needed seeing to!

The new eyeshadow was as pale as cream, making her eyes darker than usual, like black coffee; another shadow, in a shade called 'Nutmeg', was brushed along the eyelid crease. A steamy vapour scented with ginger and orange drifted into the bedroom from the bathroom.

A room being used in preparation for an evening out always seemed to shiver with excitement. She felt it fall around her like a fragrant whisper of new silk . . . the promising air. It was a pulse-racing time – a crisp new you, adrenalin-flushed, in the mirror, and an evening ahead in which anything could happen.

Or nothing.

Standing up, she reached into the wardrobe for the dress she had chosen, although Jane had been uncertain about the colour.

'A really romantic dress,' the sales assistant had insisted, when a self-conscious Danielle had edged out of the cramped cubicle. 'The fichu neckline shows up your lovely shoulders and bustline.'

Seeing Danielle's dubious eyes, the woman had laughed. 'Must accentuate your best assets!'

Jane had cut in, 'I'm not sure about the colour – perhaps something brighter?'

'I like the colour,' Danielle had told her, looking at the jacquard fabric with its pattern of amber on cream. The curved V waistline made her torso look longer than it was, and a full, gathered skirt over net petticoats came barely to what Jane called her 'nice round knees'. The neckline was trimmed with amber lace.

She had been unable to find any shoes she liked, or maybe she'd lost interest. In any event, later in the day, when they'd trooped back, exhausted, to Jane's home, her friend had produced a pair of cream court shoes which were perfect.

'We're the same size, luckily.'

'They look unworn,' Danielle had noted, slipping her feet into the soft leather.

'Worn once.' Jane had grinned. 'At my wedding.'

'But I can't . . .'

'Don't be daft. When will I wear anything as delicate? And look . . . I picked this up at an antique fair one Sunday.'

'Oh, Jane.' Looking down at the amber necklace, Danielle had given her soft, plump blonde friend a hug.

Jane, looking surprised, had hugged back. For a brief moment, Danielle had hung on.

Rising out of the dark, the church hall reminded Danielle of one of those children's humming tops, with its intertwining colours and movement, music, high-voiced conversations and laughter . . . Drawn into the clammy, perfumed welcome of it, caught up with knots of people, most known to her, she threw herself into the absorbing thick of it.

There was no sign of Red or Kingsley, and Danielle, who took it upon herself to ensure the happiness of those around her, was soon laughing and joking with the best of them. Hearing people laugh, seeing pleasure brighten their faces was fulfilment enough.

Tom it was who came to claim her first, second and third dance, and he didn't hide the fact that he was loth to give her up. There was something stalwart and dear about him that she normally found comforting, but tonight was an exception.

She recognized a disturbing intensity about his way of holding her. The casual-looking arm around her shoulders weighed as heavy as iron when they stood talking to friends; he held her hand longer than necessary when they came off the dance floor, and her fingers felt crushed. Was she wrong in thinking

221

he was deliberately passing on a message of posses-
sion? One thing she wasn't imagining was the bad
grace with which he gave her up to other partners.

She sighed, exasperated, at the ripples Kingsley's
arrival at the vineyard had caused, relieved when
Griff claimed her while Tom was in the men's room.

'Is Suzie all right?' she asked as they circled the
floor.

'Top of the world. Why?'

'I thought she seemed out of sorts lately.' This was
true; the girl seemed miles away. 'Maybe she has
boyfriend trouble?' she suggested, trying to sound
casual.

'Boyfriends? She's only a kid.' Griff always looked
intent when he was dancing. He gripped her firmly
and steered with ferocious concentration.

'She's sixteen, Griff,' she said breathlessly, as he
spun her around.

He didn't seem to hear, just grinned at her, singing
loudly with the music.

She watched Suzie dancing. She had the air of a
child who had borrowed her mother's make-up. She
was blonde, like her mother, but there the resem-
blance ended.

Griff's wife, Paula, was her usual well-dressed and
groomed self, smiling kindly when Danielle joined
her after the dance.

As they talked, Danielle mentioned to her that
Suzie had looked tired and worried lately. But Paula
just crossed one finger over the other. 'Suzie and I

are like this. I'd know if there was anything wrong.'

She was an anxious little woman, who looked as if she had a season ticket for Worryville. The subject of her own tiredness and chores laced every sentence.

'*I'm* the one who's tired,' she complained now – although she only worked part-time and just had a small terraced house to look after. Suzie was their only child.

With her long-suffering smile, she told Danielle, 'This is my sister, Molly, from Walthamstow. Visiting.' Turning to a hard-faced, sharp-nosed woman, she indicated Danielle to her, saying, 'This is the boss; she owns the vineyard.'

Molly's 'see all' eyes stared Danielle up and down. Her smile was cracked concrete, her voice like paint-stripper. 'You've got a bargain, miss,' she shot back, after Danielle had smiled hello. 'The money you pay my sister's peanuts. She passed exams, y'know. And the price of your wine! Wouldn't catch *me* buying any.'

At first Danielle held back her stinging retort, feeling sorry for Paula, who was, indeed, a good clerk. *Don't say I'm going to get staff problems on top of everything else*, she groaned silently.

And then she snapped.

Still standing, she rested one hand on the table amongst empty froth-smeared glasses and looked down with dislike into the raised, vindictive face.

'Would you like a tour of the vineyard? I could show you the interesting sight of the bills on my desk? Red ones,' she added through a furious mouth. She saw the woman flinch but wouldn't let go. 'The bills run into thousands of pounds. If your sister would prefer it, she could run the business herself and pay me a wage to do her job – which pays a darn sight more than the amount I pay myself for three times the hours.'

Swinging round, she marched off, hot and uncomfortable, aware that all her life she had been afraid of not being liked.

She felt defiant.

Until she saw Tom thrusting towards her, and then she felt a desperate need to escape. But at that moment Jo walked on to the stage to join the band, trumpet glittering beneath her arm, and Danielle, with Tom close by, went over to a table near the stage and joined a group of friends.

There was a lot of hilarity at their table, until Jo put the trumpet to her lips and the first silver tears began to fall. Danielle forgot everything else but the toe-curling, lonely-voiced trumpet . . . a cry in the night . . . as echo of lonely footsteps along dark, city streets . . .

It was shivery. And between numbers Danielle watched Jo with admiration. There was hardly an instrument she couldn't play. And she looked smart tonight, in black velvet trousers with a white lacy, ruffled blouse.

After three numbers, Jo came down the steps and joined them, brushing aside the well-earned applause. But her high flush and shining eyes told their own story.

And then Paula came up to congratulate her, and in a commiserating voice said, 'Saw you when I was in town. You were going into the hospital.'

'My, what big eyes you've got!' Jo exclaimed in amazement. 'Actually, I just dropped in for a heart transplant.' She turned away, her happy expression changed. She caught sight of Tom. His arm went around Danielle's waist and Jo noted Danielle's instinctive movement away.

'When are you two going to make an announcement?' giggled Paula, waving her empty wine glass.

Jo, who liked to get horrid things over with, put the trumpet to her lips.

Tom couldn't believe his luck. 'Shall we?' he teased, with all the charm he could muster.

Danielle pulled herself from him and stalked off.

Paula stared after her. 'Some people can't take a joke.

'Got no feelings, that girl,' she told Molly, returning to her seat. 'Last year, at her grandfather's funeral . . .'

An hour later, when she had been shunted around the floor by a hot and bothered farmer giving a good impression of Thomas the Tank Engine, Danielle excused herself.

She pushed through the door, her hot body meeting the cool air in the foyer.

Griff looked up guiltily and slipped his cigarette into a potted fern. Danielle, however, had her attention elsewhere.

Her heart looped the loop!

There was no mistaking the tall, distinguished figure sweeping in from the clinging dark at the entrance. It was Kingsley. He was alone. Maybe Red was in the cloakroom. Remembering how they had parted, Danielle hesitated, wondering if she could slip away unseen.

But he immediately came towards her, and she found herself wishing she had freshened herself up earlier. Instead of greeting him with a smile, she was offhand, wanting to get away, and her voice was more abrupt than she had intended. 'Where's Red?'

He frowned. 'How should I know? Thought she'd be here after practically forcing me to buy a ticket.' He smiled briefly. 'As I like good causes . . .'

So he hadn't invited Red. He looked displeased, though, that she wasn't here. 'You didn't have to slum it by coming here; buying the ticket would have been enough,' she told him, edging away.

'My dear girl . . .' Kingsley, absolutely ravishing, she noted, in a dark suit and pale green shirt, stepped back too, the better to see her. 'Apart from the fact that I never break promises, how can you say a man is slumming when he's greeted by such a sight?'

Her body responded to his blue approval with a lightning flush. It seemed that he intended to ignore their last meeting, so in that case she would too.

Oblivious to curious glances, she asked, with her head held high, 'What do you think, then?' Opening out her arms, she was unashamedly fishing.

His voice, after a long pause, was husky. 'I can't think.' He made a conscious effort to pull himself together. 'I've never seen anything lovelier.'

She was dumbstruck, aware not only of the intensity of his voice but of the sincerity in it. She was face to face with the real man, with the world shut out behind those doors, differences forgotten. A serious old church hall . . . illuminated like a bubble . . . could make moments dance.

After excusing herself, she was soon peering in the ladies' room mirror. Through brown-spotted glass she saw herself lying on a bed, her carefully prepared hair loose, her clothes removed; he was leaning over her . . .

'Oh, hello, Vicar.' Back in the foyer, she smiled and nodded, all the time telling herself that it was just her luck to be hijacked by the smiling, frugal-eyed vicar. He was sweet, but she was in a hurry. Nevertheless, she made herself calm down and listen, until he said, with a toothy grin, 'You must be anxious to get in there with the young ones . . . off you go.'

And off Danielle went.

She saw Kingsley immediately, because he stood out; she also saw him accosted by the precocious Suzie.

Fuming, Danielle danced off with Tom, and then Griff. Paula wouldn't dance. She was too tired, he told her.

I seem to be popular tonight, Danielle sighed, following Kingsley with her eyes, as most of the women in the room were doing. *Will I ever get to dance with him? Will he even ask me after the way I told him to go last week?* Chilled, she decided, *In that case, I'll ask him . . . even if I have to queue up. Not Suzie, again!*

Danielle noted how devastatingly attractive Suzie was, despite the fact that she was dressed in her usual boots, trousers and floppy shirt, standing out against the silks and satins whirling around her.

The dance was fifty-fifty, disco and ballroom, and Kingsley was no mean disco dancer – serious-faced opposite the cavorting girl, his movements fluid and graceful for such a big man. And, Danielle noticed grimly, Suzie was openly flirting with him.

The tempo changed, and to her dismay she lost sight of him. And then, 'At last,' he growled, grabbing her arm in a possessive way that restored her good temper. She glimpsed Tom's scowling face, and then forgot him.

She knew that she had never experienced anything as wonderful as the first time she slipped into Kingsley's arms to dance.

It was easy and all-encompassing. A little like the time he had comforted her during the storm, but better . . . much, much better. There had been fear then, but this was like joined up writing . . . smoothly flowing.

Her pounding diaphragm was welded to his sto-

228

mach, held there by his firmly pressed hand, warm on the small of her back. Her hand rested on his shoulder and sometimes she let her fingers lightly touch his neck, so that it might have been accidental. His skin was so tender, and so mouthwateringly scented. She felt the movements of his firm, muscular thighs, and the bones of his pelvis rocking against her sometimes.

She was no fox-trotter, preferring disco or the odd jive or barn dance, but with Kingsley, she was fluid motion, at one with skin, muscle, bone.

When the band played 'Autumn Leaves', with Jo's trumpet almost bleeding, Danielle sang in her low, sweet voice until she felt his grip on her hand tighten and her throat dried up. Tilting her head, she met a blue gaze so tender that a wave of longing flooded her body, flowed into her own eyes, quickened her heartbeat, burned her skin damply – and stunned her.

It was like a knock-out blow.

She stumbled a bit. He dealt with it. With a sigh, she used his chest as a pillow and closed her eyes. Her fingers stroked his warm nape and her head moved up and down with his own sigh.

They were moving more and more slowly. The rhythm had gone on ahead, leaving them floating somewhere behind. His breath lightly blew her hair; the response in her body was electric. They were swaying now, more than moving. From his breathing, he might have been running, and she could feel his skin burning through her dress, clinging to her own excited flesh with a 'to hell with tomorrow' abandon.

For some reason she thought of hot, buttered spaghetti, twined around a fork.

He bent his head. 'Do you want to stay for supper?'

She opened her eyes, startled to find his mouth so close. His warm breath fanned the soft down on her cheeks. 'I'm not hungry,' she said.

CHAPTER 16

She fumbled with the resisting cottage door, her hands clumsy. Kingsley reached over her shoulder, pushed until the door squeaked open, and they stepped into the dark hall.

Orange and ginger fragrance breathed warmly down the stairs to meet them. The clock ticked like a heartbeat. It was so familiar, this place, that she could walk in the dark. Her first footsteps had been taken here; she had stumbled up the mountainous stairs and tumbled down them.

The polished banister flowed smoothly beneath her hand . . . she remembered the slippery wood between her legs in her tomboyish moments. She had received some, if not all of her hurts in this place; the bumps and bruises, the soap in her eyes, the earache, measles and heartache . . . and the pleasures . . . the surprise gifts . . . Grandy's rare, approving smile . . .

But not love.

The brass knob of her bedroom door, cold and hard beneath her hand, grated as she turned it. The room smelled powdery when she walked inside with Kingsley behind her. The promising air still vibrated.

The glass of her uncurtained window glistened like coal. Outside, the skeletal outline of the beech tree sieved the moonlight so that it trickled down and lay along the branches like newly fallen snow.

She heard a click; a pool of light softly spread over the pillow, and as she stood in the centre of the room he passed her by and the flowered curtains rattled along the pole, but they still trembled slightly.

There was a wind coming up.

She felt odd. Cold and trembly. She felt him lift her, arms hard against her legs and waist. He laid her on the bed, saying, 'Don't let the wind bother you.'

She allowed him to misunderstand.

The bed creaked as he sat beside her, reached out and removed her shoes, leaving her feet throbbing with relief. 'Did you get into your grandparents' bed when you were frightened of the wind?' he asked.

She shook her head. She had never been in their bed. She felt his finger-pads skimming the skin on the side of her heels, and her toes wriggled as if they laughed.

Her insides, it seemed, were still dancing.

'Good?' he asked.

'Wonderful.'

'All women have aching feet after dancing,' he said, almost absent-mindedly, sliding his fingers up her ankles to her calves; his touch behind her knees sent spasms of delight rocketing upwards to gather in her loins.

In the midst of her pleasure, she thought, *How well he knows women.*

His breathing quickened. The bed caved in like a collapsed sponge cake beneath the wall-like rigidity of her back . . . and something was about to begin.

A new you, indeed.

Sensations were running and leaping around her body. His touch brought her nerve-endings alive, aroused them to a fever-pitch of excitement. She was conscious that her heart was pounding and that her limbs were jelly, yet she felt beautifully cosseted at the same time.

He sat up a little, removed his tie and jacket, began to undo his shirt buttons, his eyes holding her there against the pillow, making love to her.

He pulled off his shirt, speaking softly. 'I tried to stay away. But thoughts of what it must be like to make love to you almost drove me out of my mind.'

She had never thought of him that way. He was cool and efficient and strong-willed. Now the desire in his voice and glowing eyes made him a stranger. She was both excited and terrified.

His wide, wide shoulders gleamed like coffee when he leaned forward; she felt him pulling at her panties and tights with one hand, caressing her face, ears, forehead and hair with the other, whispering to her as she stared up at him. 'I want you, Danielle. I have since I first saw you, and I was so angry with myself.'

The passion in his eyes told her it was too late to have doubts. His warm fingers pushed aside her petticoats and he bent to kiss the place where the fire burnt the strongest, his lips hot, the feeling they aroused so utterly rapturous she started to throb.

He laughed and raised himself so that he was above her, his legs hard on her legs. He pulled at the pins in her hair, letting the curls spill like chocolate across the white pillow.

He laughed again, and said, in a possessive voice that made her quiver. 'My intoxicating lady.' His fingers ran firmly through her hair, caressing her scalp, sending her dizzy. He smiled. 'You're not meant to live alone, my love. You're warm and passionate, made for loving.'

He lowered his head and his lips closed on her mouth, his tongue flicking her teeth until she let him inside to slip around the soft, sensitive, womb-like warmth and arouse her tongue to a spasm of delight that put caviare to shame.

Enveloped by the spicy heat radiating from his body, she heard his breathing roughen, felt his control leaving him as his big body moved higher, and when the parts of their bodies which were screaming out to be together met . . . they both gasped.

His tongue became frantic; his fingers imprisoned her face. He was hard and ready for her; she was pinned down; she couldn't move . . . She struggled to free herself, panicking . . . gasping for air . . . almost choking.

When he released her mouth, she cried out, 'Kingsley . . . no . . . please.'

Moving sideways, he slipped down beside her and pulled her to him, so that she felt herself jammed against his body, felt the hot skin of his hand on her buttocks, pressing her into the heat and the hardness of him, felt her zip being eased down her back, his fingertips brushing her spine; her dress fell away from her shoulders.

'Did I hurt you? I'm sorry, darling. Like this, then . . . Undress me too, darling, when you're ready . . .'

One part of her mind felt her body's ecstatic response, the other feared his strength. Trapped, she pushed against him, her hands fluttering uselessly against his rigid arms, her legs pulling away from him.

He released her.

Pulling herself up into a sitting position, she dropped her head in her hands, hating herself.

'What is it?' he demanded, breathing heavily. 'A game? What do you want?'

She shook her head. Unable to speak.

He was hating her, she could tell. *Must get away*, she thought. Slipping from the bed, she unsteadily padded to the door, holding her dress against her chest, seeing from the corner of her eye that his face was grim.

Her heart thudded so loudly she thought she would burst. Her hand reached for the doorknob, her spine tingling as she imagined his hands on her, pulling her back.

She found herself outside the door, pulling it closed, walking unsteadily into the bathroom. The air still held traces of bath oil and soap, a sad reminder of her preparations. She locked the door behind her.

Her face swung tipsily into line with the open bathroom cabinet mirror. Her hair was tangled, a smear of 'Nutmeg' bruised her upper cheek. What was it he'd once called her? A ragamuffin? What was he calling her now? Did he think she had been devious, had teased him?

If only she knew how he felt. This was, of course, one of the differences. In the past, if she had rejected a pass, she hadn't given a damn how the man felt, concerned only about her own feelings, or lack of them.

With Kingsley, though, she cared about the man beneath the skin, muscle and bone; she wanted to know about his past, his future, his thoughts . . . his women. With other men – well, boys really – she had feigned interest, and when she had left them she had shrugged them off.

Kingsley was a garment that she wore all the time.

Perched on a cork-topped stool, she rested her chin in her hands. That great, restless beast of a man with a gentle touch . . . Impossible to love. Impossible not to.

Torn with misery, she couldn't believe that after

all her days of longing she had thrown him away. Although if they had made love, would he have ever come back? He had admitted he was curious, and that would have been followed by indifference. Because they moved in different worlds. Maybe the fact that they had been enemies had added spice to the situation.

Her mouth curled. What would he want with her? The one thing they had in common was that they both preferred to live alone; neither wanted the responsibility of love. The difference was that Kingsley was quite happy with one-night stands whilst she couldn't bear the thought of them. Her instinct told her that if they had made love she would have been left loving him even more than she did now. No good. No good at all. Better this way.

Hearing the stairs creak, she tensed. A door opened and closed. Over. All for the best.

Standing up, she turned on the tap and rinsed her face and hands. A new you, she told her strained face in the mirror. Tomorrow . . . or rather today . . . you start again.

A rapping on the door sent her heart to her throat.

'If you're not out of there by the time I count to ten,' she heard him call, 'I'll break down this door. One . . .'

237

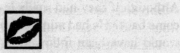

CHAPTER 17

'Tea,' he said grimly, marching her into the kitchen. 'I believe in times of war you like a cup of tea.'

She pulled away, rubbing her arm. 'No need to hurt me, for God's sake.'

Reaching the table, she threw herself onto a chair beside the tray of tea things, suddenly realizing she was thirsty. Not liking herself very much, she said, 'I *am* sorry for what happened, but something wouldn't let me go through with it. I know how it must have looked to you, but honestly I wasn't teasing you. I just . . .'

As she faltered he poured milk into the mugs and reached for the pot. 'I'll survive,' he said grimly. 'No man has died yet from being spurned. It's that *just*, I'm interested in.'

She kept her eyes on the stream of tea pouring into the mugs, jumping when he thumped the pot down.

She picked up her mug. 'You're angry.' The mug was shaking.

'Angry?' He gulped down tea impatiently. 'Oh . . . drink your tea,' he snapped, meeting her miserable

238

eyes. 'It's none too warm in here.'

She was too amazed to do anything other than what he told her, thinking, *He's a strange man.*

'Right,' he said, fixing her with a hard stare. 'Am I annoying you by coming here?'

'No,' she answered, flustered. 'Not now.'

'I left before the week was up,' he reminded her, 'because I found myself wanting to get to know you; I was becoming too involved. I didn't like the fear on your face either.' He slapped the table with his hand. 'But you're still afraid of me, and I'm blowed if I understand it.'

'It's not you,' she insisted. It's . . .'

Seeing the misery on her face, he leaned across the table. 'It's what?'

'Many things.' She shrugged. Her mug clicked carefully down onto the table. 'Look, there are so many obstacles between us.'

'Listen to me, Danielle. I have no need to chase a woman who doesn't want me. And to be honest . . .' He paused, eying her bedraggled hair and shiny face. 'I don't know why I bother.'

'Neither do I,' she snapped, pushing hair from a pair of bewildered eyes.

Watching her, he felt the urge he had known since their first meeting – to kiss the bewilderment, the worry, the tiredness and even the laughter from her. It was a feeling new to him and he wasn't sure he liked it.

'I don't know,' he added seriously, 'what I'm

doing sitting here, when in similar circumstances – if there had ever been any – I'd have gone.'

'Why don't you go, then?'

'Because I want to get to the bottom of you. If I'd thought you were not interested – ' he shook his head ' – I wouldn't have attempted to make love to you, but that isn't the case, is it? I wouldn't push myself onto any woman, but you want me – you always have done.'

She studied her hands. 'I don't know about that.'

'It's true, Danielle. So these obstacles you talk about – what are they?'

She stared at him. 'You know . . . There's the letter, for a start – I feel you're still suspicious that I was Piers's mistress. And . . .'

He held up his hand. 'Even if I am, I might be prepared to forget it.'

Stony-faced, she said coldly, '*Might* be prepared to? I'm afraid that's not good enough for me.'

A sneer crossed his face. 'What do you want, Danielle? Perfection?'

She rubbed the back of her neck, irritated by his attitude. 'I suppose I do. So what? I'm not like you. Whatever you may think about me, you're wrong. I don't want one-night stands, I don't want to be one of your harem and I don't want to be made love to by a man who thinks I'm his stepfather's mistress. Besides . . . I intend to remain alone.'

He laughed.

How dared he? She opened her mouth to tell him what an insensitive pig he was.

'Sorry I laughed,' he said, before she could speak. 'But you reminded me of my first evening here, when you stood up to me, in this room, and spoke just that way.' He heaved a sigh. 'Can I ask you something?'

'You've never needed permission before to delve into my life.'

'I deserved that. What I want to ask you is . . . were you his mistress?'

She looked at him steadily. 'No way.'

'Why did you let me think you were?'

'There were reasons; maybe I thought being Piers's mistress would protect me from you? And afterwards maybe I thought you wouldn't believe me. And lately – well, it didn't seem to matter.'

'Ah, but it does.' He inspected her closely. 'I know it's not that you don't fancy me – that would be simpler. There's something else,' he probed. 'Something dark and ugly, I think.'

When she remained silent, he sat back and sighed in a way that struck her as helpless.

Avoiding his thoughtful gaze, she poured out more tea and they drank in silence.

He heard the ticking of the grandfather clock quite clearly. It seemed to be a countdown, and he was shaken by the knowledge that he might never be here again. You couldn't keep pushing someone who didn't want to know.

Looking around, he said slowly, 'I've spent a lot of time in this room. I've grown very fond of it.'

'It's my favourite room too,' she said, with a small smile that left a shadow in her eyes.

'There were our breakfasts,' he said, watching her expressive face, 'when I felt eyes of hate boring through my back. And there was the night I sat you on the table.'

A ghost of the familiar impish grin crossed her face. 'The night you cooked spaghetti Bolognese.'

He pouted. 'Thought I was onto a good thing there. You do love your food. But even my cooking didn't charm you.' His face softened. 'In this fat-free, sugar-free, low-calorie world, you were delicious. No simpering, giggling . . . "I shouldn't eat this." No guilty, furtive movements. Shameless with food, you were. How lovely.'

She coloured and studied her empty mug. It was as if they were talking in the past. He knew he wouldn't be back.

He picked up a photograph from the table. 'Who are these children?'

'My friend, Jane's,' she told him, looking up. 'My godchildren.'

Letting his eyes slide over her softened face, he asked thoughtfully, 'Don't you want children of your own?'

'I can't see myself marrying, so I doubt that I will. But if I did, I wouldn't send them away to school.'

'Why?'

'Having Matron to talk to isn't the same as family; you miss out on love and contact with one person. You have to make it up and work it out for yourself later. Boarding-schools don't make your inner self independent or self-sufficient as they say they do.'

'You appear very independent to me,' he said with irony.

She shrugged. 'I was pushed in at the deep end, don't forget. It was sink or swim last year.'

'You have a thing about this sending away to school business,' he observed shrewdly. 'But your childhood is in another country; it's time to leave it there.'

Her head snapped up. 'What?'

'I sense you live in the past, Danielle.'

Her heart hammered. 'You're wrong!' she cried. 'There are things there that are firmly locked away.'

He pointed a finger. 'That's it. And what happened there that had to be locked up?' he asked suddenly. 'What happened to put you off men and marriage?'

They stared at each other.

Danielle's eyes were the first to fall, and as her fingers began to play with the old red dressing gown she had thrown on she reflected upon how she had felt when he'd danced with Suzie and when he'd spoken of Red. Jealous. Wanting him for herself. These feelings were new to her, making her very much aware that, although nothing could come of it, she loved him very deeply. Part of her longing to go to bed with him had been a strong urge to make him happy. She might have known it wouldn't work.

All she could give him was the truth. She owed it to him to tell him the story she had told no one before. For no one would have believed her.

She rested her head on her hands, only glancing up once. The compassion in his eyes would have made her cry if she had been able to. But any tears she had shed over the incident had been long spent.

It was as if a cupboard in her head had opened up and they all tumbled out – the memories she had suppressed until tonight . . .

CHAPTER 18

'What now?' he demanded, cocky, scrawny as a bird.

'Don't know. I've shown you the vineyard.' *But not my special place, Paradise field*, she added silently, leading him out of the woods, eyes narrowed. *Just leave him here*, the nasty side of her said. *He gives me the creeps.*

'The contract is important to us, Nell,' Grandy had told her that morning. She'd felt important, grown up, as he'd gone on, 'The boy's on holiday, like you. while his father and I discuss business show him around. Be nice to him, eh? Talk to him. You know . . .'

His worried face had cautioned her. *Don't let me down.*

'What a dump!' The Boy scoffed.

That hurt. Marching off, she whistled. 'Kit! Come on boy, leave those rabbits alone.' The dog paused from his digging and looked round, a tail-wagging, doting-eyed, smiler. 'We could walk to the village if you like,' she said, kicking dead leaves viciously, spraying earth.

'What's there?'

She stopped, turned. 'Well, there's the shop.' She smiled nicely. 'I'll buy you some sweets.'

He moved closer. His nearness was as welcome to her as acne, but, remembering Grandy, she stood her ground and he leered in her face. 'What else?' he asked excitedly.

Kit, bottom in the air, returned to his digging, pushing the earth away with determined floppy paws. Floundering, Danielle admitted, 'Nothing.'

'Isn't there?' He was grabbing her, laughing, thrusting a hand between her thighs. 'Come on.'

Danielle was fourteen. She froze. He moved quickly.

The ground hit her spine, twigs cracking like bones beneath her. She glimpsed leaves pinned to the sky and wanted to scream, to cry *Stop . . . don't*. But Grandy had said . . .

There was Kit . . . looking round, ears dangling, eyes an anxious, loving brown . . . but she was speared to the ground . . . straining against iron. His mouth was pushing up her sweater, snuffling, reaching her breasts. *Kit! Kit! Help me*. He jerked her breast out of the bra and clamped her arm back. His face was smooth-skinned, burning. Deaf to her pleading, he saw nothing, heard nothing. He was uncontrollable, forceful, determined and quivering.

He tore down her trousers and her knickers. She was struggling now, twigs stabbing her skin, exposed roots like iron fists punching her back. Rolling off, holding her down with a bony hand, he was undoing his trousers, pushing down his underpants, laughing. He was on her, pushing, almost crying in his frustration. Skin and bone, sharp knees, smooth chin, an unclean smell. *Kit!*

Kit came. Nudging Danielle's face. Cold nose, whining, anxious sounds. The Boy was jerking, the leaves beneath her were wet. When he released his hold she pushed him away, sobbing, but he was back on top of her.

Kit barked, whined, pawed. A train whistled in the distance and her guilty cries rode away on the wind with the dying smell of crumpled old leaves.

Kit's bark was possessive, his growls hating and threatening. He grasped The Boy's foot, making him roll over, kick out, struggle to his feet, afraid, scrabbling with his clothes. Angry teeth sank firmly through the material, piercing The Boy's flesh, only letting go when she was on her feet.

He ran. 'Who wants you anyway? You're fat.'

She was shivering, different, unreal, going into another life. She wanted yesterday back. *Please bring back yesterday – before it happened!*

So pretend it hadn't happened.

Grandy. What had she done? Would everything be ruined because of her? She leaned against a tree and sobbed as if her heart would break. Kit jumped up. She knelt, stiff and sore, letting him lick her face. Her thighs felt bruised from the boy's bony knees; there were leaves in her groin and her breast was half out of her bra.

She found herself automatically replacing her clothes, but she was not herself. She was putting bits of her body back in place as if she had been ransacked.

At the cottage she sent Kit into the kitchen, slipped upstairs and ran a bath. No one must know.

Bits of leaves floated on the surface of the water. And dirt. And shame. The leaves wouldn't go down the plughole and remained on the bottom of the bath like scabs when the water ran away. Along with the grains of dirt. She grasped a canister of Vim, took up the scrubbing brush and scrubbed the bath until the leaves were shredded, the porcelain left without stain. Her hands were red raw.

Then she started on her body, tearing at her skin, rubbing in the floury Vim, smelling the ammonia, hurting so terribly. And then she ran another bath.

At the end of it, shivering, she jumped from the bath and ran to the toilet to be violently sick.

'There you are, Nell. Don't you look pretty in a dress?' Daniel Summerfield looked proud and delighted in an over-dramatized way. 'You see, Mr Sinclair, I do have a granddaughter.' Nervous, making-conversation words.

Outside, a dog squealed and whimpered as if hurt. A car door banged. From a distant world somewhere.

'I got Sam to take Kit away,' Grandfather said comfortingly to the red-faced Mr Sinclair. 'A dog that turns vicious must be put down. Can't apologize enough.' He turned to The Boy. 'All right, son? Sorry about your clothes.' Daniel Summerfield watched the boy's father open a briefcase. 'Lucky man, having a son.'

Danielle heard, from that other, faraway world, sounds like barking . . . high-pitched, terrified . . . an engine roared. Her eyes went to The Boy's father as his podgy hand gathered up his papers, then to Daniel, who blurted, 'Send me a bill for the new trousers.'

'Too right I will.' The briefcase snapped closed.

Danielle jumped. Kit was howling somewhere outside. She was running from the room and out through the front door. When she'd needed him, he had come. Racing after the van, eyes bulging with effort, heart pounding . . . Kit's face at the window, the van disappearing down the track and in the end nothing. Just Danielle sitting on the ground beneath the sign 'INTOXICATING LADY'. The sound of crows squawking overhead and sobbing . . . helpless sobbing.

'It was instinct to bathe and change,' she told Kingsley. 'I arrived downstairs spotless. Customers were kings – I learned that from an early age. It would have been my word against The Boy's.'

Her face twisted. 'The Boy forced his way in; he stole. My schoolmates laughed and joked about sex – how do you think I felt? I wanted to laugh about sex

249

too. It's a part of it, the mystery, the giggling. He stole romance; he took my dreams. There was no romantic meeting and happy ever after. *That* came first. It had nothing whatever to do with love. It defiled not only me, but all the beauty there was in the world for a while.

'And there was Kit . . .' And the last view of his great, wistful eyes would haunt her always.

When Claude had arrived, he'd told her, 'Danny, it's too late for me to be your father, but let's be friends.'

'I wasn't very Christian,' she told a stern-faced Kingsley. 'I wanted my father to find The Boy and beat him, but . . . my father was ill, so I said nothing.'

All was silent, except for the ticking of the clock, the faint hum of the fridge, odd creaks and groans.

Danielle found herself thinking that the woods had not been a forest after all, that The Boy had been young and foolish, trying to be grown up. Things that happen when you're a child, she was suddenly aware, appear to be much bigger than they really are. Something moved in her.

And if The Boy hadn't known that she and Grandy were in his father's power, he wouldn't have raped her. It all come back to power. Never be in anyone's power, Danielle had learned. *Easier said than done*, she thought bleakly.

She could, though, strangely enough, find it within herself to be glad that she hadn't told her father and urged him to go after The Boy, as she had felt like doing.

She had found joy again; she had been determined to put the incident behind her. She had found real woods to walk in – woods that smiled with open arms and sweet breath, jovial trees she could rest her head against.

She hadn't done badly.

'What I remember most,' she ended up, 'is his strength. How shocked I was to find myself powerless. 'I think any woman who has been attacked will say the same thing – that the first shock is feeling so helplessly pinned down by superior strength.'

Kingsley didn't embarrass her by speaking; he merely stood up, smashed the mugs and teapot onto the tray and carried the lot to the sink. The room seemed filled with silent thunder.

She looked wistfully at his erect back with an overpowering longing to press her face there. Flinching a little at the noise he made, she let her eyes trace his wide shoulders, narrow waist, taut legs. As usual her body flashed messages . . . *Throw yourself at him, hold him tight, don't let him go.* But somehow – she sighed – there was a wall between them which she just couldn't climb.

Not only had she confirmed what she had suspected, that she would be unable to carry it through and therefore must never again encourage him, she didn't want what he wanted. A casual affair. She didn't want to wake in the morning and find him

251

gone, knowing he might not return. What could she give him that more adventurous, sexy women couldn't give him better?

So best to tell him now not to return. Maybe he had the same idea. There was a sort of inevitable goodbye in the way they had talked and cleared the air.

He dried his hands on a towel, stood for a moment looking around the room, and with an aching heart she saw that it was a goodbye look.

'I wish there was something I could say or do, Danielle,' he said, rubbing the side of his nose.

She saw him frown, recognized uncertainty in his eyes and helplessness in his shrug. 'You listened,' she told him through a clotted throat. 'Thanks for that.'

'I know what it must have cost to tell me.'

Polite. So polite. Why should he want a woman with hang-ups? He probably couldn't wait to get away.

She rose. Sick at heart, she loved his dear face for the last time with her eyes, and said, 'I'll come to the door with you.' *I mustn't cry.*

They met in the middle of the room. 'Don't get cold,' he told her. Suddenly he reached out, picked her up and sat her on the table. 'You have no slippers on. Stay there – don't see me out.' He took her face in his strong brown hands and kissed her. Just kissed her.

And then he was gone . . . like the wind.

CHAPTER 19

Danielle escaped from the shop, blowing out a breath of relief. 'Shut your face,' she muttered to the clamouring bell as the door slammed behind her. She was pink-faced and furious. Gossip, they said, could only bother you if there was truth in it. Huh!

They also said not to protest your innocence. But you always did, didn't you?

Cherie had worn what Danielle called her mucky smirk. 'Someone told me you went home early from the dance.'

Cherie herself never went to dances.

Danielle had come over warm. 'I had work to do.'

'Ah,' she'd said, quickly and knowingly, 'but they say that Mr Hunter left with you.'

This is all I need, Danielle had fumed silently, *after this morning's problem*. 'They're wrong, then,' she had answered, with admirable control, 'We certainly didn't leave together.' They had made sure of it. The memory shot back like a painful injection.

'That's not what they say . . . You walked out on

253

Tom, apparently . . . disappeared . . . he was looking for you . . .' And so it had gone on.

Forcing Cherie from her mind, Danielle crossed the spongy, sodden village green, passing the pub resting behind soaked and glistening ivy, not at all sure that what she was about to do was right. Even the ducks sheltering beneath the willow tree beside the pond didn't, for once, raise a smile.

Suzie's visit that morning had left her feeling drained and worried – not to mention, for some reason, old.

Reaching the other side of the green, she came to a road and glanced left and right. Not that there were any cars about. Nothing much happened here on a weekday afternoon. The village might have been sleeping, except for the chanting she could hear from the school just to her left. Further on from there, drenched cottages cuddled up to the grey stone skirts of the church.

She turned away from the village centre, the leaves beneath her rubber boots making depressing squelches.

The angry rain, which had been slashing down all morning, had at last stopped, but sullen-looking clouds still scudded overhead. The wine magazine and newspaper in her basket suddenly flapped like live things, and she pulled a heavy packet of spaghetti on top to weigh them down. She should have borrowed Tom's car while he was looking at the starter motor of her truck. But the rain had eased and she

254

had decided a walk would do her good. Not least to escape from Tom's concern.

'Let me help you more, Danny,' had been his answer to her explanation of why she'd left the dance. Why she should have to keep explaining her movements, she didn't know.

Pushing strands of hair from her eyes, she looked daggers at the threatening sky as she went over in her mind that morning's violent meeting.

Suzie must have waited until Griff had been and gone with the mail. It was her mother's day off and Danielle knew Paula had gone to the doctor for a check-up, which would be followed by shopping in town and a visit to the chiropodist. Griff's van had scarcely disappeared along the track before Suzie arrived in the office.

She looked flushed and petulant. 'What have you been saying to Mum and Dad?'

Danielle, looking up from slitting open an envelope, frowned; the girl was standing with her arms crossed over her chest and was obviously about to blow her top.

'About what?'

'Me. They've done nothing but question me. Mum said it was something you said at the dance. Telling tales about the pub, I bet. Why don't you mind your own business? What I do outside this dump has nothing to do with you.'

'I . . .'

Before Danielle could gather her wits, the girl sneered, 'You're jealous.'

'Oh, come on.'

'Yes, you are. Because I'm living and you aren't.'

Danielle hated arguments. She felt her skin begin to crawl. 'I really . . .'

'You should get out and live, learn what it's all about.'

Aroused, Danielle retorted, 'If I envy you anything, it's your lovely parents.'

Ignoring this, Suzie snapped, 'You owe me some wages. I want them now because I'm leaving.'

'What about your work here?' Danielle asked, aghast. 'With Red out sick . . .'

'Typical. All you care about's this place. I can't put my life on hold just because Red's skiving. There's a world outside. I'm off to London.'

Danielle blurted, without thinking, 'Why London?'

'It's where life's at, right? And I've contacts there.'

'How do you know someone in London?'

'Through Annette. Anything else?'

'Any other reason, Suzie?' Danielle persisted, worried for her. 'Man problems, for example?'

'I should be so lucky,' she snapped. 'Some chance of that, here. Tell you what, though, I'm fed up with you staring at me as if I *am* up to something.'

'Rubbish!'

'You do. Now they're doing the same at home. I'm up to here.' She raised a hand to her high, pale

256

forehead. 'It's bad enough living in a village, anyway. You went away to school; you don't know what
it's like to have eyes watching you when you walk
home with your mates after school, whenever you go
to the shop or get together on the green for a giggle.
Eyes everywhere. The whole village knows where
you are, what you've been doing and who you've
been with. It's no different now I've left school.'

Danielle had never looked at it that way. 'Suzie,
you've such a comfortable home, everything you
want . . .'

'It's boring,' came the reply. 'Boring, boring,
boring. And what does it all mean?'

'That your parents love you and work hard for
you.'

Suzie raised her eyes to the ceiling. 'Very original!
Work for *me*? For themselves, you mean. Money's
not everything, you know. House values are not the
only meaning of life. There are,' she said scathingly,
'more important things.'

Danielle sought desperately for the right way to
handle this. 'Where will you stay? What about
money?'

'Social Services will get me a flat and pay the rent,'
was the triumphant reply. With a don't-you-know-
anything expression, she quoted slickly, 'I just have
to claim I'm estranged from my parents, see, and the
Benefits Agency will give me Housing Benefit and
Income Support. Parents don't have to know where
you are either,' she bragged. 'The Data Protection

Act and Official Secrets Act makes it confidential. So there. I'll tell them life with Mum and Dad's unbearable.'

'That's not true.'

'So? They never check. Annette told me all about it, see. Lay it on thick, she said. I'll tell them this job's seasonal, and I've been laid off.'

'That's not true either.'

'So what? How would you like to work with your Mum? Christ! Talk about round-the-clock protection!'

'I never had the chance,' Danielle said quietly, trying to keep cool. 'Look, give yourself a day or two to think it over, eh?'

Suzie's eyes scorned her. She held out her hand. 'Money, please. And can I have cash?'

Reluctantly, Danielle pulled a cash book towards her, opened it and checked figures. She, who had been so homesick in her time, couldn't understand Suzie at all.

Taking money from a cash box, she handed it over and Suzie said, more quietly, 'Mum and Dad, they treat me as if I'm soap-on-a-rope. I can dip my toes into life but can't get right in, you know? It's time to cut the rope. Do or die, as Jo says.'

Jo, Danielle thought, *I could kill you.* But she said only, 'Do your parents know you're going?'

Suzie's hand went to her mouth. 'I left a note,' she said, nibbling a nail.

Griff and Paula are going to be frantic, Danielle

thought with a sinking heart. *But what can I do?*

Feeling helpless and, if she were honest, a little boring, she said, 'Take care of yourself, Suzie.'

"Course. No danger, as Jo would say.' She hesitated. Her voice sounded less sure. 'Annette was coming until she met Roger; she fancies him a lot. If things don't work out she'll come on later.' With a touch of pathos, she added, 'Her parents don't bother her much. She can come and go as she likes, you know?'

She's brave, Danielle thought, frightened for her. Torn between this fear, and affection for the girl's parents, she said gently, 'Will you do something for me?'

'What?' Suspicious eyes . . . a movement away.

Danielle reached into the cash box. 'Take this twenty pounds; use it for emergency money. And if things go wrong, come home. Ring me first, if you like, if you're in trouble, any kind of trouble,' she emphasized, feeling the salt sting of tears. 'I wouldn't hesitate to help you – confidentially, if necessary.'

Suzie stared at her; her face looked as if it might crumple for a moment, but she took the money, mumbled her thanks, gave a bit of a smile that went to Danielle's heart and hurried away. 'Get a life, Danny,' was her parting shot, before slamming the door behind her.

Danielle, watching her go, suddenly remembered that there were only four years between them.

★ ★ ★

259

Now, walking to see Red, Danielle was arguing with herself. Should she visit a sick employee and ask when she was coming back? It seemed a bit like harassment. On the other hand, Red was a friend too. Nothing wrong with visiting a sick friend whose parents lived abroad.

Leaves, driven by the contemptuous wind, suddenly rose up and hissed like snakes around her ankles. Danielle, aroused from her thoughts, noticed the approaching Dottie Trout make a grab for her hat. Too late. The wind tore it from her head and threw it to the ground.

Danielle's body jolted, as if she had been kicked in the shin.

Dottie's head was a pink, hairless dome.

After a second's stunned reaction, Danielle hurried forward, reached the black turban hat first and handed it over, trying to think of something to say.

Dottie took the hat, looked down at the ground and said nothing.

The wind whipped Danielle's hair across her face. She thrust the hair away as if wishing it was invisible and said, with an effort, 'You're lucky, I can never do anything with my hair.'

Dottie looked up with the sheepish expression of a child caught out. A shy smile crossed her face. 'I know I'm lucky. I got over cancer.'

Danielle had guessed and also sensed the unspoken demand . . . *Don't make a fuss.*

'Well done,' she said briskly. 'You're very brave.'

Dottie had a way of throwing her head and shoulders back in a dramatic way and moving her hands as she spoke, as if conducting. 'Life,' she said, 'is an incurable disease for all of us. You just have to get on with it and fight . . . with all flags flying.'

Clearing her throat of emotion, Danielle said, 'After the harvest . . . we've been so busy, you know . . . we must get together. I mean it,' she said with a smile, noting Dottie's surprise, which made her guiltily wonder if any other invitations had come her way. 'Put your hat on. It's a bit muddy, but you'll get cold otherwise.'

Recognizing Dottie's reluctance to go, Danielle made herself stand and listen to an account of the operation and the chemotherapy. Dottie spoke like one who had been bottled up – and no doubt she had, Danielle thought, with compassion. Nobody, it seemed to her, had bothered to get to know her. Why? Because she was odd, not like the rest? No one had bothered to find out why she was different. Danielle felt ashamed. After the harvest she would put things right.

Dottie had a wide, mobile mouth, and the sweetest smile which, despite her lined skin, made her look girlish. 'When I get up in the morning and put on my make-up I know I'm alive. I'm used to living behind a mask, you see, in the theatre.'

'Will you return to the theatre?'

'If a part comes along . . . My agent is hopeful . . . but I'm not fussing. One step at a time.'

Danielle's willing ear then received a potted life history.

'My father was a miner. I acted my way out of the dump where I grew up by pretending I was meant for better things. I acted so well I made myself believe it.'

Dottie ended with a rich-sounding laugh, and Danielle suddenly understood what Dottie was trying to say. She was apologizing for being different.

Warmly, though she could have cried, Danielle observed, 'Over the last few months you've played your biggest part, I reckon.'

Dottie's limpid eyes were smiling. 'I suppose I have,' she said, sounding surprised. Changing the subject, she asked, 'By the way, have you heard about the new people at the shop?'

Danielle smiled. 'Yes. Bit of a surprise, aren't they? Not what we expected.'

'Not what some like either,' Dottie said with satisfaction.

Danielle had enough problems on her mind for one day, and dismissed Dottie's ominous words with, 'Oh, the villagers will come round.'

'Hope you're right.' With one hand pressing her hat firmly on her head, Dottie smiled goodbye and trotted off, glaring up at the sky as if to tell the wind. Do your worst. As she crossed the green her brightly coloured clothes reminded Danielle of a tropical bird; as she drew further away she was more like a flag, waving in the wind.

By the time Lane's End Cottage loomed up, Danielle was feeling quite unreal. The day had been too full of shocks.

Pushing open the gate, she plodded up the path and rapped on the door. It wasn't like Red to stay away without phoning. Receiving no answer, she listened . . . No sound of a radio, no movement – except for Red's belligerent goose, Gus, honking away in the back garden.

Puzzled, she turned away. Red could have gone out . . . but Gus . . . didn't he sound different, sort of resentful? His honking rose to something like screaming mad, and in between there was something else, a faint cry. Chicken? Cat?

'Red . . . are you there?' She could have sworn she heard an answer, and an icy prickling down her spine told her something was wrong.

She tried the front door. Locked. Stepping onto the lawn, she stared upwards. 'Red?'

'Danny, help me.' The words came indistinctly through the partly open bedroom window, and with her heart in her mouth Danielle called back.

'Hang on. I'm coming.'

Easier said than done. She panicked, trying the downstairs windows and looking round helplessly; she remembered Red had mentioned that her neighbours were at work all day. No help there.

Dumping her basket, she ran out of the gate and back down the lane. Red must have fallen over or something.

Rapping on the back door of the pub brought no answer. She glanced at her wristwatch. Ron was probably collecting the kids from school and Iris was at her art classes. Now what?

On impulse, she hurried into the beer garden, making for the shed.

Bless you, Ron Standing, she thought; *just like you to be careless enough to leave your shed unlocked*. Gritting her teeth, she dragged his new aluminium ladder out, back past the row of blank-eyed cottages and in at Red's gate.

Danielle had taken her first baby steps in an orchard; it was nothing for her to clamber up to the lattice window, which only someone as tiny as she could have climbed through.

A worried glance as she perched on the ladder at the open window showed Red in bed, face pale as mashed potato, watching her with terrified eyes.

After an ungainly clamber over the sill, only a foot above the floor, Danielle hurried the few steps to the bed. 'What happened?'

The despair and grief in Red's face was enough to turn Danielle's heart over.

God, something dreadful's happened here.

'Come on, love.' She took Red's clammy hands. 'You'll be okay, I'll ring Dr Stanley.'

264

'I felt ill, I started bleeding . . . I wouldn't get up,' Red whispered. 'I might save it.'

'What?'

'They say if you don't move . . . Danny, I'm losing the baby . . .'

It took a moment for the truth to sink in, a moment during which Danielle felt the blood drain from her own face. 'Now calm down,' she said, making her voice firm. 'I'll ring the doctor; give me two minutes.'

After making the phone call, she unlocked the front door, left it ajar, and hurried back up the spiral staircase. Should she do anything? Hurrying into the room, she saw Red's face was glistening like candlegrease. Frightened to death, Danielle asked, 'Do you want a drink or anything?'

Red shook her head. 'Danny,' she whispered, after a fraught silence.

'What is it, love?'

'Why hasn't Piers been here lately?'

Danielle's stomach lurched. 'Piers?' She had to clear her throat before she could say, 'He's on holiday.'

'With his wife?'

'I suppose so . . . yes. Why?'

'No reason.' Red's eyes closed tightly, but still the tears trickled down into the hollows in her cheeks and soaked the pillow.

With Red gripping her hand in a trusting way that brought a lump to her throat, Danielle sat transfixed.

Daisy, Danny – so similar; hadn't she often teased Red about her bad writing? She gazed around the room.

An empty wine bottle, two dusty glasses on the dressing table. Red was so clean at work. There was a cassette player, a handful of cassettes, perfume – lots of it. A blood-stained negligee lay crumpled like a dead body from a detective story on the pink carpet. There were body lotions and bath oils. Thornless roses stood in a vase of smoky grey glass. The water smelled like a stagnant ditch. The creamy buds had died without opening.

As Danielle looked at garish postcards from Spain Red murmured, 'Don't tell the parents. Can you give Gus some food?'

Downstairs, Danielle yanked open the back door and tossed Gus corn, which he gobbled up after throwing her a dirty look. The rooms down here had an unused air. As if Red's life was lived in the bedroom.

Back upstairs, in the lonely atmosphere of a waiting room, she shivered, thinking, *Come back to earth, Red*.

Looking at the girl, Danielle saw that something listened in her, something hoped. Something was alive and loving and hurting.

'You don't choose the man you love,' Red whispered, as if Danielle had spoken her thoughts aloud.

'I'm not judging,' Danielle said brusquely, nodding towards the cigarette stubs spilling from an ashtray. 'Thought you were giving up.'

'I was.'

'You should now.'

'Don't.'

Danielle spent three restless hours in the ward waiting room before she was allowed to slip behind the screens surrounding the bed. She found herself looking down at a most pitifully haggard, unhappy face.

'Sorry, Danny. I kept it to myself for so long. I needed the job, unless . . . I hoped something might happen to change things.' Red turned her head away. 'Piers stopped coming. I wished like hell I could get rid of the baby, and then, somehow . . . it became baby and me.' She turned back to Danielle, green eyes brimming with tears.

'The doctor said you and the baby will be fine,' Danielle said firmly. 'Don't worry about the job, for goodness' sake. We're into our slack period now and . . .' She had been going to say, We've got Suzie.

'Besides, by the time you have the baby it will be nearly spring. Don't you dare leave; I'm looking forward to having a baby around. I grew up in a vineyard – didn't do me any harm,' she said, forcing a smile. 'At least I got used to climbing ladders.'

The blaze of hope in Red's eyes went to Danielle's heart, and she found herself bending to place a kiss on the girl's hollowed face, achingly aware of cheekbones bony as elbows and freckles glistening like golden tears. *I can't bring up the subject of the letter*

267

now, she thought. It had either been a desperate attempt to get Piers back or spite – revenge, even.

Downstairs, in Reception, she phoned Tom and asked him to come and collect her from the hospital. *Dear Tom*, she thought, as she searched for the refreshment machines. He'd nearly had a heart attack. She smiled to herself, sipping something similar to coffee from a plastic cup. *He's so kind. He's always there when I need him.* She tore the wrapper from a bar of chocolate. *He's so uncomplicated.* Biting the chocolate, she found it hard, dark and bitter. The sweeter, crispy Lion bar would have been better, only the machine had said 'Sold out'.

CHAPTER 20

The cemetery looked as bleak as cemeteries should. Bony trees were hunched over the rows of silent stones. Today no birds sang; they had fled before the wind to seek shelter.

Daniel Summerfield's remains lay beneath a sad sycamore tree, over in the far corner where the plots were new and dutifully flower-decked. His was the only grave without flowers, unless you counted a small, sodden bunch of maroon chrysanthemums in a jar that had once held coffee.

Three people stood beside the grave. A tall, pleasant-looking man of thirty-something, with straight hair the toasted wheat colour of wholemeal bread and thrust back, lets-get-on-with-life shoulders; and a woman of maybe seventy, her short stocky body hidden beneath serviceable trousers and navy parka, hands thrust into pockets. You knew by looking at her that she was blunt, tough and didn't suffer fools.

And there was Francesca.

No one spoke.

Francesca had not been there since the funeral.

Today was a similar type of day, reminding her of how the merciless wind had torn at her then, trying to break her. She remembered thinking, *I will not cry. I will smile, instead, for him.*

People had been frozen in silence then, as expected of them. Men with dandruff on their dark suits. Female red lips, unmoving for once, afraid to smile, like bloody gashes against black hats and best, self-righteous coats.

Francesca couldn't believe that she had cried as much as she had done since he died. That anyone could have. But not here.

Here, she had stood smiling until it was time to go, when she had turned away and her thoughts . . . *I've lost my love* . . . were tossed in the howling wind. The wild nature of her grief, though, she had refused to let them see. Because they'd expected it. But she was different.

They had been good when she'd lost her daughter. They had brought gifts, made tea, sat with her even though she'd spoken to them through furious lips.

And the same after Daniel died. They had come silently and graciously and properly into the cottage, with their condolences, their cakes, their forgiving eyes. Forgive and you shall receive. She had turned them away.

She had walked away from the graveside without a word, leaving Danielle talking to the vicar. But before she could climb into the car people had come over like a flutter of black crows, to say the proper things.

Francesca allowed herself a little smile as she remembered the shock on their faces as they'd walked off.

Danielle had come over quickly, worried. 'What did you say to them, Francesca?'

'Something the nuns wouldn't have taught you.'

Danielle, so calm and controlled for her age, eyes full of pain, lips smiling, had said, 'Good job I kept the vicar back, then.'

Francesca had laughed. Loudly enough for all to hear.

Even Daniel, maybe.

The windscreen wipers sliced backwards and forwards. Sitting beside Tom as he drove her home, Danielle saw the wind prowling the sky, bullying the clouds.

Her hands were a damp clutch of fingers in her lap, and she waited in dread for Tom's shining, much-loved little old Austin to be picked up and tossed aside or a tree to crash down in front of them.

'Don't worry, Danny. All we can do now is to batten down the hatches. At least the harvest is over.'

'Except for the Chasselas.' She grimaced, trying not to show how she was trembling.

'Nothing we can do,' he repeated as they rattled across the cattle grid. 'I'll come in with you.'

Ignoring her knotted stomach, she shook her head. 'No need. As you said, there's nothing we can do.'

She didn't see his face turn to thunder as they pulled up outside the cottage.

He climbed from the car, gently closed the door and, with a mulish twist to his face, in a voice stubborn and deliberate, insisted, 'I want to talk to you.'

She tried to hide her irritation as she slipped from the seat. She let the slammed door complain for her and made for the cottage, hearing his wellington boots thud and squish-squash behind her.

The rain had stopped again; everything was still. Paths, walls, roofs were glistening from the soaking they had received, and the light was a strange silver-grey.

Her boots thudded and crunched along the wet path. She opened the door and let herself in, glad to turn her back on the weird sense of desolation out there. But it came in with her, the sense of looming disaster.

She made for the kitchen, her mind replaying the day. A piece of jigsaw had slotted into place. She should feel relieved. Instead she felt shattered. She thought of Kingsley in her kitchen, of Tom in there. *No.* She argued with herself about how immature this was. *Excuse me, but this is tiredness – nothing more.*

To hell with it.

Before she reached the uninviting kitchen door, she knew she had to say something. 'I've had one hell of a day,' she said, turning round. 'I'd rather talk tomorrow.'

In the dim light, she met eyes glittering with intent, as a cat's might when crouching to pounce on a bird. He spoke through resentful, gripped teeth. 'What's good enough for him isn't good enough for me, then?'

Wearily, she slumped against the wall. 'What are you on about? I'm tired, okay?' But it wasn't only that. Fear was light and quivery inside her, and she didn't know why. Tom was her friend. Moody, but her friend. She said as much, adding, 'Don't be like this.'

'Is that what you say to Mr Hunter? Don't touch? I bet you don't. We've a lot going for us, Danny. Don't throw it away for some flash-in-the-pan Romeo. Have you seen the way he hangs around Red? He – '

'Shut up!'

But there was no way. 'We're good together,' Tom said stubbornly. 'It was always on the cards we'd marry. Once you got over your grandfather dying . . . I didn't want to rush you, darling.'

It was the way he said darling. It was like being given a nasty dose of medicine. She pushed him away.

His mood changed. Despite the push, he was suddenly too close. She felt his urgency, his hot, anxious breath as he said, 'Danny, kiss me. I'm tired of waiting. Let me . . .' He was persistent, hard, powerful. She felt pinned down, hating his movements, as if he were a python intent on crushing her to death.

273

Tom. A cruel-mouthed, sneering stranger.

How could she feel panicky with Tom? Her friend.
She tried to insert authority into her voice . . . failed
dismally. Past affection didn't help. How could she
knee or kick Tom?

She tried to reason with him. 'Jo would be good for
you. I know you row, but I think she's fond of you,
Tom.'

'What's Jo been saying?'

His heavy hands pressed her shoulders; his mouth
sought hers. And she never knew where she found
the strength to shove him as she did. All she knew
was that she was able to tear herself away from his
grasp and head for the front door.

'Out!' she yelled as he hurried after her. She
tugged the door open. 'Out, for God's sake.'

'Danny . . .'

'The lady said go.'

Neither had seen the man standing at the door,
hand raised to the knocker.

Tom's body jerked, startled, he hesitated, recov-
ered himself. Sidling past Danielle, dwarfed by the
stranger, he slipped out through the door.

The stranger stood back.

Addressing Danielle, Tom sneered, – 'Another
playmate?' He plodded heavily along the path, showing that he wasn't rushing, wasn't afraid.

Danielle watched him go before turning pained
and embarrassed eyes upon the newcomer.

She put both hands to her temples, pushed back

her hair slowly, trying to still everything that was racing inside her. She felt as if she had been put through a shredder. Pulling in a shaky breath, she asked, 'What can I do for you, Mr . . .?'

Kind, concerned eyes in a healthy-looking face looked down at her. 'Paul,' he said, holding out his hand. 'Paul Fairchild.' He watched her keenly, as if he expected her to recognize the name.

She placed her damp, panicky hand into his. His handshake was confident, and longer than necessary. He spoke with an Australian accent.

'Can I talk to you for a moment?'

Danielle was tired, fed up, confused – not in the mood for business. 'What about?' she asked shortly, hating herself for sounding rude. He was a salesman, obviously.

'I'd rather talk inside, if that's okay.'

Nice blue eyes, she thought. 'Why?'

He spoke gently but firmly. 'What I have to say might come as a bit of a shock.'

'Nothing more could shock me after today,' she told him, with feeling.

He hesitated again. Then, as she obviously wasn't going to ask him in, he seemed to make up his mind.

'I've come to have a look at my father's place and meet his folks,' he said softly.

Danielle frowned. He had obviously come to the wrong address. Relieved that she could get rid of him quickly, she said, 'Tell me who your father is and I'll . . .'

'Daniel Summerfield,' he said.

It's strange how you react. Danielle laughed. Nodded. 'Oh, right,' she said, clasping her hands together, as if delighted at a joke. 'Daniel Summerfield. Right.'

CHAPTER 21

In an old-fashioned novel Danielle would have swooned. As it was, after her first strange reaction, her legs died. She heard herself cry out.

He sat her down on the stairs. 'Holy cow,' he said, looking worriedly at her white face. 'Didn't mean to do that to you. You okay?'

She nodded, tried to pull herself together. After a bit, she shook the hair from her face, stood up and let her shaky legs somehow lead the way along the passage to the kitchen. Her safe, normal kitchen.

Chair legs shrieked on the flagstones like chalk on a blackboard. Wincing, she sat at the table and with dark, shocked eyes asked, 'I suppose this isn't a joke?'

He sat down facing her, his face apologetic and gentle – the face of someone you would instinctively trust. Shaking his fair head, he told her, 'I'm Anna's son. You know about my mother?'

Danielle moistened her dry throat and nodded. 'Anna's son,' she repeated awkwardly. 'And my grandfather's. Right?'

'Right.' He watched her digest something bitter,

not liking the pain he saw on her face. It was as if the girl before him was disintegrating in some way.

Grandy's son, she was thinking painfully. *The son he always wanted*. If this man had come back while Grandy was alive . . . She felt shattered, and – worse – she felt nobody.

'We're staying with your grandmother,' Paul was saying from a distance. 'I kind of spoilt her surprise.'

'So she's behind it.' Danielle raised her eyes heavenwards. 'Her surprises have always turned out to be shocks,' she told him, trying to act normally.

Watching the colour creep back to her cheeks, Paul grinned. 'She didn't know who my real father was either, until recently. She tried to telephone you earlier and ask you over to meet the skeleton in your family cupboard.'

Danielle's eyes checked the broad, muscle-packed body. 'Some skeleton,' she remarked, with a rueful attempt at humour.

Curiously, she examined his comfortable rather than good-looking face, one that glowed from a life lived in the open. Something about him said that he was at ease with himself. He was nothing like Grandy to look at, except for his height and the way he held himself – erect and strong as an oak tree.

His eyes, fanned by lines, were shrewd but kind, the same colour as the new jeans he was wearing. Deeper lines ran from his nose to his mouth. He had a habit of running a hand over his face, like someone brushing the sun from his eyes.

As he relaxed, Danielle found his informal manner and take-life-as-it-comes smile hard to resist, and the deathly sense of unreality began to recede. Common sense came to her aid, reminding her that this man had played no part in Grandy's life, but *she* had. Being human, she was selfishly glad they had missed each other, but was also generous enough to acknowledge that it was sad that they had.

She gave an inner shiver, feeling again that ominous, warning sensation prickling her skin. More was to come. Trouble hadn't finished with her yet, it seemed to say.

Although she liked Paul, she felt unsettled by it all. What would the consequences be? Anna couldn't expect to return with her son and not cause ripples. Had she wanted to cause a stir? Did she feel she had scores to settle?

Overwhelmed by all the implications, Danielle felt she was being sucked up into a vacuum cleaner bag of old, forgotten, dusty things and, her mind in a whirl, she heard him speaking to her gently.

'We're quite nice, you know – your family.'

Briefly she caught it: the look of her grandfather in Paul's face. But more self-assured, more contented, with no strain. He looked as if he had never worried or suffered in his life.

Irritated, her voice was sharp as she asked, 'What do you want from me?'

He ran a hand over his face. 'Jesus – nothing!' Then, with a frown at her suspicious tone, he admitted, 'There is something, actually.'

'I thought there might be. Well?'

His answer was unexpected. 'Some tips on wine-growing and my father's personal diary.'

'Diary? I know nothing about a diary.'

'Mother told me he kept a diary about the vineyard from the beginning. It would be real fascinating.'

Danielle said testily, 'We went through everything. My grandmother never mentioned it, so how come your mother knows?' *He has noticed my jealousy*, she realized. *But he understands.*

'Who knows what goes on between people? Look,' he explained, 'I'm thinking of starting my own vineyard with some spare land on my dairy farm.'

She shrugged. Why should she care what happened on the other side of the world? 'I still know nothing about a diary.'

Softly, Paul said, 'You never really knew your own father, did you?'

'You know about me?'

He nodded, eyes sympathetic. 'That's something we share, you and I. If you knew *your* father had written a diary, wouldn't you long to have it?'

The calm, sincere gaze of this man affected her deeply. She had to be fair. He had done nothing against her; he was a victim of circumstances just as she was. Despite the fence she had placed around herself, and being determined that he would take nothing away from her, she understood what he was trying to say.

'If I find this diary,' she said kindly, 'then I'll let you have it. Of course I will.'

She received a grateful smile and a contented, 'Good on ya.'

As they talked long into the night, over wine and coffee, it began to seem to Danielle that they had known each other always. She still inwardly admitted to a touch of jealousy for who he was, yet she realized that she had found a new friend.

She wanted to know why Anna had returned after all this time, and listened with some anxiety for his reply.

'It was my idea,' he told her, easing her mind somewhat. 'I'm writing a book on our family history,' he explained, 'and I need to trace the family tree. Part of it,' he added, 'will interest you, of course.'

Danielle felt like snapping that she had no interest in the past, but she was concerned to see strain on his face as he said, 'The death of two people I loved, my father and my wife, started it off – the wanting to know about those who had been and gone.'

Sensing that he wanted her to ask no questions, she made no comment. And he went on, 'Parents are the first step, so I approached Mother, who told me the story.'

Seeing Danielle's brows fly up, he nodded. 'I've only just learned about myself too. I knew Ralph

281

wasn't my real dad, but I assumed my mother's first husband was. And as she didn't talk about her life in England, I never pushed it. So,' he said, with a self-confident smile which spoke of a happy childhood, 'the next step was England – church records, the records office in London, that sort of thing. And then Mother,' he said a trifle wryly, 'became enthusiastic about joining me on my trip.'

When at last Danielle said, 'Goodnight, see you tomorrow,' she wasn't at all sure she would like Anna as much as she liked her son. She felt a distinct lack of enthusiasm for their meeting. Whatever Francesca said, Anna still seemed a hard, callous sort.

'I wanted to see England once more before I die,' Anna said, holding court in Francesca's sitting room.

'You're two years younger than I am, and I've got a lot of living to do yet,' retorted Francesca with an impish wait-and-see grin that Danielle recognized.

Anna's reply was a hearty laugh. She stood with her feet apart – warming her bum, as she described it – before the gas fire. Her body was sturdy, and somehow made amorphous by the shapeless check trousers and black sweater she wore. She had a slap-you-on-the-back manner and no pretensions, and gave the impression that she could handle most things life threw at her.

She looked out on a world she was quite satisfied with from clear blue eyes set in a strong, calm, square face; her skin was tough-looking, with its fair share of seventy-year-old lines, and was unexpectedly pale. Her springy bush of hair was more white than black, and cut short. Her voice was abrupt, dry – you felt you wanted to give her a drink of water. There was no small talk.

When Danielle asked the obvious, 'How do you find England?' Anna was cursory.

'I forgot how small it is, and crowded. So many more streets and houses. More corners. At home I can see for miles. No corners.'

Danielle, puzzled, saw Francesca give a smiling half-nod, as if she understood. There was no sign of strain. The two women might have been best friends meeting after many years.

Which indeed, they were.

Except for the circumstances.

Glancing across the room, she saw Paul sprawled in an armchair watching her. He seemed to sense her bewilderment and gave her an understanding wink.

Take it as it comes, he seemed to be saying.

Danielle couldn't resist a little dig. 'You're a wicked lady,' she told her grandmother, arousing laughter.

Anna observed Danielle with a kind half-smile. 'The only thing I never liked about your grandmother was her love of surprises,' she said.

Francesca chuckled and gave an apologetic shrug. 'Anna and I usually only exchange notes at Christmas, and then she wrote to me out of the blue saying she and her son were planning to come to England to visit relatives and sort out Paul's . . . er . . .'

'Family tree,' he prompted. 'Mother has relatives at Ramsgate and Canterbury,' he said, addressing Danielle.

'Brother, sister and their various offspring,' put in Anna.

Francesca raised her arms dramatically and said, although Danielle couldn't understand how calm she was being about it, 'I had no idea that Paul was Daniel's son.' Just as if, Danielle thought, astounded, this sort of thing happened every day.

'I thought we might be chucked out,' Anna admitted. 'But you had to know the truth.'

Danielle wondered why. What good would it do?

Francesca seemed to understand, saying with an enigmatic smile, 'Years stretch one's tolerance. And secrets get heavier. What's done – ' she sighed ' – is done.'

Her eyes were suddenly bright with unshed tears. 'And who, meeting Paul, could begrudge his existence?'

Yuk, Danielle groaned inwardly. *If we're going to get all sentimental* . . .

Taking advantage of the sudden silence, she got up to go. 'I've a lot to do today,' she apologized.

It was true, but nevertheless she was glad of an excuse. Her love for Kingsley was still an open wound. She couldn't describe the awfulness of the pain she felt at being cut off from him. And the

284

thought of him with another woman made her feel physically ill. How, therefore, could she understand what was happening today?

As she drove away from Francesca's bungalow, the sky framed in the truck window looked as confused as she felt. Ribbons of blue streaked across the sky, scattering mean-looking clouds. She was conscious of an apprehensive twist in her stomach, the way you felt when something fearsome was approaching. Forces seemed to be gathering, clouding her judgement, making her emotional.

Heading for the village, she thought about the phone call she had made earlier to Kingsley's office. It hadn't been an excuse to speak to him. No. He'd needed to know about Red.

A female voice had answered in a dutiful, over-my-dead-body voice. 'Mr Hunter is away at the moment. Can I take a message?'

Danielle had found herself hating the cool-voiced secretary, who was most probably in love with him.

'Just tell him Danielle Summerfield rang.'

'From?'

'From?' Danielle had repeated, with hatred.

A sigh had come down the line. 'Which company?'

'Intoxicating Lady,' Danielle had told her. 'He knows the number.' And rung off.

'My Suzie was a good kid until that little trollop turned up in the village.' Griff paced the neat, modern living room, hands waving, his taut, uptight expression, tight-lipped manner and injured air more in evidence than usual.

'You mean Annette?' asked Danielle gently.

''Course I mean Annette. And the . . . the other one, Joanna. Bringing their London ways here. Changing everything.' He stopped his pacing and Danielle shrank at the accusation and reproach in his eyes.

She felt she had a foot in both camps. She understood the parents' concern, yet she herself hadn't known what it was like to be treated like a child. As long as she'd caused no trouble, she had been as free as the wind during the holidays. Before she could say anything, he snarled, 'We have rules in our house. What's wrong with that?'

To Danielle's alarm he pushed his face into hers in a threatening way, and even while she started back she firmly said what she was thinking. 'Don't you think that perhaps rules have to change as children get older?'

'Are you saying this is my fault?'

'Of course not. But maybe Suzie's just crying out to be treated like an adult, and going away is a sort of cry for help.'

'Cry for help? She'll get cry for help if she comes back here. There's her mother upstairs ill, under sedation, and all I've ever done for Suzanne has been thrown in my face. She's ruined our lives, changed everything. I'll not forgive her in a hurry.'

He looked at Danielle warily. 'By the way, as far as

anyone in the village is concerned, she's staying with Paula's sister in Walthamstow, looking for work. Right?'

Staring into his cold, rejected face, not knowing whether her sympathies were with father or daughter, but feeling sure that she was doing no good, Danielle left, not liking to ask when Paula would be back at work.

She didn't mean to be selfish, but she couldn't help worrying about her depleted staff and the sense that events were spinning out of control.

Her only consolation was that it wasn't the busiest time of year, and she still had dear, reliable Jo.

And Tom. Well, Tom with a question mark, she thought grimly, driving past the church to his cottage. She didn't in the least relish another scene.

'I don't want to lose you, Tom. I need you, honestly,' she appealed.

When he didn't answer, she wanted to shake him, but tried not to let her irritation show. He sat in his leather armchair and she sat on the edge of another in the cheerless, austere but spotless living room into which he had, through sulky lips, invited her.

He wouldn't look her in the face, but gazed at a spot above her head with an aggrieved, 'persuade me' air that made her heart sink.

'Let's forget what happened the other night,' she said, worrying about her machines. 'I'd like us to be friends again.'

He looked at her then. Ignoring his what's-in-it-for-me look, she smiled encouragingly. 'Come on, Tom.'

He took his time. 'Worse things 'appen at sea,' he said at last, rubbing his strong hands together and giving her the sort of look he might give a recalcitrant machine which was at last playing his sort of music.

'Thanks, Tom,' she said, dimpling and grateful. 'You're a love. Don't know what I'd do without you.'

With no office or laboratory staff, Danielle had a hell of a lot of work to do, and she couldn't help wishing she hadn't promised to call at the shop to say goodbye to Cherie.

A small awkward crowd hovered between the shop and the green, where an important-looking Cherie was shaking hands, kissing and fussing over wriggling children. 'School out is the worst time of day', she had once complained.

Her hair looked stiff and nervous, standing back from an expressionless face. 'The furniture went this morning. I'm waiting for Griff,' she told Danielle, thumbs restlessly dancing on her stomach over the best coat no one had ever seen before. 'He's taking me to my new flat.' Her eyes were riveted on the lane on the other side of the green, along which Griff would come to take her away from the shop she had devoted her life to.

If he came. Danielle felt awkward. 'Er, Paula's not too well.'

288

'Makes a change,' Cherie sniffed, without sympathy.

Danielle had wondered whether to say anything, but couldn't keep it to herself. 'Did you know Anna's back?'

Curious cold eyes turned on her. 'Anna who?'

Danielle said smartly, 'Hutch's ex-wife.'

'Well, I never. After all this time. What's she back for, then?'

Danielle told her, omitting to mention who Paul's father was. She would have loved to tell Cherie, just to see the look on her face, but decided it would make Paul an object of curiosity in the village, and he was too nice for that – besides which, Grandy should be left in peace.

Reluctantly she left that bit out. 'Actually,' she ended, 'it's a strange coincidence, isn't it? I mean, you leaving the village just as she comes back.'

'She's nothing to do with me. Never had time for her. Thought she was too good for us – some farmer's wife, with her posh clothes and everything.' Cherie's knowing expression added that she was no better than she should be.

'I'm sure she'd like to see you,' Danielle said, tongue in cheek. 'You could always come back and see her while she's in England. You're only half an hour away.'

Cherie looked tempted. 'Where's she staying?'

'At my grandmother's.'

Cherie tossed her head. 'I've nothing in common

with either of them. They're hardly my type, are they? Here comes Griff.'

Sure enough it was. His smart red hatchback swooshed importantly into the kerb, and he climbed out and grasped Cherie's suitcases. While he put them in the car Cherie glanced back at the shop. Watching, Danielle thought it was as if she was listening for something.

On impulse, she pecked Cherie's cheek and asked, 'Why did you decide to leave now, after all this time?'

'Come on, girl,' called Griff, holding open the door.

'It's the only time,' Cherie answered simply.

What did she mean by that? Danielle wondered. She saw Cherie reach the car, pause, and stare long and hard across the green towards the church and the cemetery.

And Danielle knew. One man died and lives changed. She felt one of those inner shivers, thinking of how death changed things. If Daniel Summerfield hadn't died . . .

Griff settled Cherie in the passenger seat and climbed into the car, slamming the door with an attitude that said he'd done his bit. As if it was just another day.

He drove off with Cherie waving like a queen as she left the village for the first time in her life. It was surprising how sad everyone looked. Or maybe a better description would have been put out. Disturbed.

The shop seemed a different place already, Danielle felt as she went in.

'We have removed the bossy bell,' smiled the woman who was taking over. 'I'm Mrs Khan.'

Danielle smiled back warmly. 'Welcome to Hidden.' As she introduced herself she decided she liked the look of Mrs Khan. She was a plump, pretty forty-something, wearing loose trousers and a tunic in flowered pink silk with a pink gauze scarf which brought into relief the duskiness of her skin and her wise and compassionate brown eyes.

Somehow soothed, Danielle watched in amusement as the energetic Mr Khan scuttled in and out, accompanied by the taciturn local builder, enthusiastically discussing shelves and mirrors.

'Self-service?' exclaimed Danielle. 'Great idea.'

Mrs Khan smiled. 'I think so. But the people here, they do not like change, I think.'

Danielle had to admit this was true.

'We have had a problem with our caravan.' Mrs Khan nodded. 'The side entrance to the yard is not wide enough to let it in so it must stay in the road until this problem is fixed, eh? People say it looks an eyesore.' Her eyes laughed, nevertheless, especially when her two children slipped silently in through the door.

'This is Hassan,' Mrs Khan said, resting a proud hand, heavy with rings, on the boy's narrow shoulder. He politely shook hands with Danielle, a darkly handsome boy, about fourteen, neatly dressed

291

in navy trousers with a red jersey over a white-collared shirt.

The girl came forward then, a little older than her brother and beautiful, with the same dark eyes, wearing blue tunic trousers and top with a blue gauze scarf. 'I am Shireen,' she said, smiling gently.

The serenity, the dignity, the soothing colours lapped at Danielle like a warm, musk-scented bath after a day in the fields. She told them about the vineyard, ending with a suggestion.

Addressing Shireen, she asked, 'Would you be interested in helping in the office on Saturdays and after school? You could collect figures for Red, the girl who runs the laboratory too.'

Mrs Khan gave her friendly but cautious blessing. 'It must not interfere with her homework. Her education comes first.'

'Red could teach your daughter a lot,' Danielle explained, pleased with her idea.

'That is good.' Mrs Khan smiled again, lowering her head graciously. 'One can never learn too much.'

Danielle, whose education had been of little interest to her grandparents and who had got away with murder at the convent, was surprised. Choosing her shopping, she wondered what was going on behind the girl's gentle eyes. She couldn't imagine her getting up to the pranks she herself had.

On the other hand, she was learning lately that people had hidden depths. She paid for her shopping and left the shop.

Sometimes her heart raced for no reason at all. She seemed to be possessed by a tear-edged anxiety. But there was no time for tears, there was work to be done – especially if she wanted to leave time to see something of Paul.

She tried to push away her nagging worry . . . would Kingsley telephone?

The telephone rang.

Danielle was at her desk, sorting through the post Griff had wordlessly delivered. Remembering the first time she had spoken to Kingsley on the phone, she snatched the receiver, pulse racing.

'It's me,' said Jo.

Danielle's heart plunged. 'You're usually in by now. Something wrong?'

'Everything.' Sounding upset, Jo rushed on, 'Annette . . . she's in hospital. The police have been here.'

Danielle went cold. 'What's happened?'

'Sorry, I can't think. I'll be late in . . .'

Danielle spoke firmly. She had never known Jo to panic before. 'Don't try to explain on the phone. I'll come over, shall I?'

'Would you? It's just that this, on top of everything else . . .'

What 'everything else'? Danielle puzzled, hurrying to tell Tom that she was going out for a while and flinging herself into the truck.

She was driving past the green when she saw Paul,

striding along, obviously on his way to the vineyard. She suddenly remembered that he was going to call in today and spend some time with her out on the slopes.

Screeching to a halt, she pushed open the passenger door, leaned across the seat and explained. 'Want to come with me?' she asked, not knowing what else to do with him. He had already walked the four miles from Francesca's house – which he assured her was nothing to him.

'If this Jo won't mind,' he said, swinging into the truck and slamming the door.

'You met her at the pub the other night,' Danielle reminded him, releasing the handbrake.

'She played the trumpet,' he said thoughtfully, as they rattled off. 'With the jazz band.'

Danielle had too much on her mind to wonder why he sounded so distracted, and ten minutes later she pulled up with an anxious squeal of brakes outside Jo's home. A very pale and drawn Jo flung open the door before Danielle knocked and looked in a startled way at Paul.

'If it's personal,' he said kindly, 'I'll wait in the truck.'

'God, no. Come in,' Jo said, cigarette in one hand, mug of tea in the other, sounding a little less emotional. Without wasting time, she had them listening in horror as she explained what had happened.

It had been about one in the morning when Jo had been awakened by a banging on the door. When she'd gone to answer it she'd heard a car skid away, but had been mainly concerned about the sick-looking girl propping herself up in the porch.

Without saying anything, Annette had collapsed at Jo's feet. 'Her face was blue,' shuddered Jo.

'Jesus,' Paul breathed.

Seeing Jo's face contort, Danielle went to sit beside her on the settee, cuddling her as if she were a child.

With a grateful look, Jo carried on. 'It only took a second for me to realize that her heart had stopped. I gave her the kiss of life and brought her round, but I had to leave her to phone for an ambulance. I was terrified. But she carried on breathing, just about.'

Jo tried with shaking hands to light another cigarette. Paul, who had been silently listening, leaned forward to help. When she had puffed for a moment, Danielle asked, 'Annette, she . . .?'

Jo shuddered. 'She's on a life support machine. It was drugs.'

Paul snapped the lighter down on a side-table, Danielle saw he was looking as sick as she felt. 'Why were you involved, Jo?' he asked in his frank, open way.

'I assume Annette felt ill and asked her so-called friends to drop her at my place instead of taking her home. I suppose she was ashamed for her parents to see her like that. She didn't know she . . . she was possibly dying, did she? None of them do, do they? Think it will happen to them, I mean.'

'Will she recover?' Danielle asked, fighting to keep her voice steady.

'I don't know, love.' Jo sounded tired. 'The police came and interviewed me.'

Paul moved over to the settee, sitting on Jo's other side, taking her hand. 'Why you?'

'You tell me.' Jo shrugged. 'Someone said Annette spent a lot of time here. It might have been her mother.'

'Raine?' Danielle gasped. 'She must be out of her mind with worry.'

'Badly. I saw her at the hospital. They're there now, Raine and Tony.' Jo turned pointedly to Paul. 'He's my ex-husband.'

He said nothing and Jo turned to Danielle, saying, 'The police interviewed Robin too. Someone said that Annette was seeing him, but she was only modelling for him. For Christ's sake! This place . . .!'

Angrily stubbing out her cigarette, Jo put the overflowing ashtray back on the table, rubbed her eyes and said, in a way that went to Danielle's heart, 'Raine blames me.'

Paul patted Jo's hand. 'When people are upset they say things they don't mean.' Wisely, he added, 'And they need someone to blame other than themselves.'

Jo turned grateful eyes on him. 'Yes, that's probably it.'

Thank God, Danielle silently thought, for Paul's support. His common sense, easy manner was very calming. She saw Jo pass him a strained smile. And they were still holding hands.

'Is there anything I can do, Jo?' she asked, glancing at her watch. 'I don't want to rush away, but . . .'

'I'm okay. You go, Danny. There's nothing any of us can do.' A weary hand pushed through her hair. 'I'll be coming to work later.'

'You don't have to.'

Jo nodded. 'Yes, I do, actually. But give me just an hour or two to pull myself together first.'

Danielle understood absolutely. 'Take your time. Coming, Paul?'

Paul rose with her, leaving Jo sitting on the settee looking up at them with vulnerable, heart-tearing, what-have-I-done? pain on her face.

To Danielle's surprise, Paul bent down, placed a featherlight kiss on Jo's ruffled hair and said, 'You're true blue – do you know that?'

'Not me,' Jo answered, her hand going up to skim the top of her head lightly.

'Straight up,' he assured her. And followed a shocked and also bemused Danielle out of the house, folding his sturdy legs into the truck without a word.

They were each busy with their own thoughts until Danielle, turning the truck into the vineyard, suddenly groaned, 'Life can't possibly hold any more shocks, Paul.'

Raising his eyes to the 'INTOXICATING LADY' sign, he rested an arm across her shoulders. 'Smile at the bogey man, my love, and it will frighten him away. Mother always told me that.'

Danielle smiled obediently. 'Do you know, I love you, Paul?' she said through tears. 'And Jo too.'

'I know,' he said softly, giving her a hug.

CHAPTER 22

There was an ominous feel about the day. The light was strange, eerie, as if a menacing, inhuman voice was saying, 'Something's coming . . .'

Paula was standing at an upstairs window, looking out. Beyond their neat, rectangular garden she saw tombs, sword-like dark green cypresses and the bones of other trees, clouds scudding past the spire of St Nicholas's church and wet, fluttering washing she had forgotten to bring in.

This was the view Suzie had grown up with.

Turning away from the window, her eyes were drawn to the clock radio, with its leering red numbers, telling her that about now Suzie would bounce in, her whole body shouting, Go! Go! Go! And everything would.

Paula went over and sat on the bed, stroking the virginal white duvet. A shaft of mournful light fell across the room and the scent of stale hairspray rose from the pillow. Her hand looked bony, she thought. Today she felt like a skeleton, as if her flesh had shrunk. Yet once she had been like Suzie, over-filled with womanhood.

Suzie. She felt a stomach-ripping sensation, as if the flesh were being peeled from her body and her insides with it. She knew now why she had escaped upstairs into this Suzie-filled room. She was in search of a new reason for living, a reason for getting out of bed in the morning.

Her mouth trembled; she knew full well that no doctor could cure her of being a mother. If she could only bring Suzie back from wherever she was . . . It was the silent space in between that she couldn't stand and which was driving her mad. She rested her head in her hands.

How? How? How? From a bundle of cells to a cocky teenage hormone cocktail?

'Who cares?' Griff kept saying.

I care, she wanted to scream.

Paula stood up, bent down and started to pick clothes from the floor and shoes from under the bed. She began to cry . . . it was the old toy box that did it.

Sindy dolls with breasts. Paula's childhood dolls had been babies, and then dolls grew up. Realism, they called it. So why not dolls with acne? Society was to blame. She gulped, finger-wiping her eyes. Society was a child-molester . . . *'Grow up quickly, my dears. There's a whole market waiting for you.'*

The dressing table held a dirty cosmetic bag and lipstick stubs, discarded knickers and tights, an empty hairspray can. She turned away, returning books from the floor to the bookshelf. James Herriot went in beside old fairy stories and nursery rhymes. Clean, new-looking baby books, only ten years old or so. How was it possible?

Little Bo Peep has lost her sheep
And doesn't know where to find them;
Leave them alone, and they will come home . . .
He was watching her from the doorway.

'She'll come home, Griff,' she told him, stemming the tears. 'Look – radio, stereo, telly. Everything a girl could want. She'll miss it.'

'She'll get no welcome from me,' he said through tight lips.

Paula silently picked a hairbrush from the floor and pulled golden strands from it. Even if she did come back, nothing would be the same again. That was what she sensed behind his words.

Clicking the brush down on the dressing table, she made her way to the door. Suzie had committed the ultimate sin. She had changed. Altered things. Moved on leaving Griff behind, rejecting him.

She went downstairs, into the sitting room, trying to take her mind from her child to her husband. Griff's father had died in the mines and his mother – not having been brought up hardened in a mining community – had killed herself. To be with him. Leaving Griff and his brother to be raised by grandparents. Their stern faces looked back at her from a black and white photograph standing on the mantelpiece beside the clock which had belonged to them.

The clock crouched with a white and anxious face.

In the evenings, the ticking clock was a time-bomb. When he got up to wind it, he wound himself up as well. Paula remembered how her heart had raced for Suzie's sake. Not that Griff was violent, but a cold temper could be worse.

'We've got each other,' Griff said, having followed her downstairs. He waited. Paula said nothing.

He was a good, devoted husband, a caring, religious man. But his devotion, which expected complete devotion in return, could become a problem – as if the lover and his passion went beyond the normal way of things.

She went across to her chair, removed from its seat the medical encyclopaedia she had been reading and sat down, the book heavy as a baby in her lap.

He sat down, too, in his chair. They considered each other across the space. Finally she answered him. 'Of course we have each other. That hasn't changed.' She was mentally reaching out for him, but the gap had widened.

Married to a good man, a man who needed you, what could you do? *I'm due for one of my heads.*

'Life goes on,' he said, as he had when Suzie's hamster died.

He followed her into the kitchen. He did his duty as he saw it, she thought to herself. Theirs was the best-tended of The Cottages. He was only guarding his patch. 'All safe and sound,' he would say, locking the front door each night after Suzie came in.

'Children come second,' he often said. But she

was wife *and* mother. Why couldn't he understand that?

She loaded Suzie's clothes into the washing machine, with a dollop of stain-removing powder, and switched on. The kitchen was filled with a comforting hum, the air fragrant, familiar, reassuring.

'Suzie said in the note she was staying with friends of Annette's until the council get her a flat, Griff.'

A noise came from his throat.

Is she cold? What about hunger, muggers, rapists, drugs? 'You've only got to read the papers, Griff.'

'She made her choice. Couldn't care less.'

'Oh, Griff . . .'

'She let me down.'

Paula put a hand to her churning head. The machine turned Suzie's clothes over and over, removing her smell. A belt or something knocked against the glass door. With the onset of an empty, nagging pain in her stomach, she returned to the sitting room. Griff followed.

Fiddling with pill bottles on the mantelpiece, she glimpsed her reflection in the mirror. Like overboiled smoked haddock.

'I've done my best,' Griff said, settling into his chair. 'Can't do more.'

There was a sorrowing, frozen silence.

'We've got each other, Paula.'

'Yes.'

'That's the important thing.'

'Yes.'

Suzie, Suzie, where are you? Is it over? Me as a mother? Where do you sleep? If only she could be left alone to cry. Griff's eyes were fixed accusingly on the clock. For three days it had been silent. No amount of shaking or winding up would get it going again.

That clock was a part of Suzie's childhood, to Paula's mind. The four-hourly feeds, the school runs, the club nights, *Top of the Pops*, curfew times.

She returned to the kitchen to check the washing. Griff followed with the clock. Without looking at her, he pressed his foot on the pedal of the bin. The lid swung open like a pelican's beak and he threw the clock inside. It lay on the mass of rubbish, ticked for a bit like a fluttering heart. Then gave up.

'No good to us if it's stopped,' he said, pushing down the lid, which always stuck. And then, in the tone of one satisfied with the order of things, 'Dustbin day tomorrow.'

Tom's cottage, called The Smithy, sat glowering on a corner opposite the church. It was an uncomfortable-looking place, the old forge having been turned into two cottages many years ago. Consequently, Tom's was tall and narrow, with three floors, a room on each, and a spiral staircase between them. The adjoining cottage, where Dottie lived, was one storey only.

Tom was brushing his shoes until he could see his surly dark face in them. The shoes clanged on the stairs as he climbed to the spartan bedroom on the top floor. He rented the place furnished, carried no baggage in his life.

When Dottie had come in once, to borrow matches, he had shown her around and she had turned to him, saying, 'It looks as if you're not staying. You're riding at anchor,' she had said, delighted at her cleverness.

Silly, dramatic woman. He was full of unspeakable hatred this evening. Likewise, rain hammered on the window and wind caught the churchyard trees and shook them like angry fists.

Standing before the mirror, combing his hair, his neck quivered. When Danny had tried to push him on to Jo, he had felt as if a fist had delivered a blow.

Throwing down the comb, he turned and saw the freshly ironed shirt lying on the bed, arms open like a submissive woman. Jo's work. She reminded him of his mother.

If his mother could see him, successful in business, she wouldn't believe it – never having hidden the fact that she would be most surprised if he did much with himself. Not that he saw her often – went back on Mother's Day for some reason.

He didn't love her. As a kid, he might have loved her; he certainly hadn't liked seeing his father hit her. Only when he was sober . . . when he was drunk he had been kind and child-like. So Mother had fed him beer bought with her hard-earned money from the biscuit factory, and she had fed Tom custard creams. Broken ones.

Picking up the cold white shirt, he slipped it on and began to do up the buttons. He scowled as he thought what a nuisance Jo was becoming – couldn't keep her mouth shut lately about underwear. What was she trying to prove? Was she trying to shock the village? Wouldn't put it past her. What else was she going to start on about? If she did anything to come between him and Danny he would . . .

Jo had had a visitor that afternoon.

Her steamy kitchen had been filled with the home-ly smell of freshly ironed linen as she'd crashed about, opening two cans of beer, singing to herself because she felt happy.

She hadn't felt happy when she'd awoken that morning. Apart from Annette, and the sort of grey misery outside that the Swedish called 'suicide day', she had been through one of her nightmares.

The nightmare was always the same. She heard screaming, slaps and the blows of someone being beaten. It was herself.

But the nightmare was over and the weather didn't matter, because . . .

She carried a tin tray holding beer and two pint glasses into the living room, placing it on the coffee table and glancing questioningly at the man warming himself before the gas fire.

He was openly appraising her with narrowed blue 'I-could-eat-you' eyes that made her heart lurch.

She went over to him. 'Paul?' she queried, with wild agitation and some irritation.

She had never experienced a look like it. It was as keen as the blustering wind outside, and tore through her body until she had the odd sensation that she was fluttering uselessly like one of those dolls cut from newspaper.

His face was different, for her only, like a crumpled bed, and his voice moved her insides as he said, 'You're like a can of iced beer on a sweltering day – d'you know that?'

She quivered, ran her tongue around dry lips. 'No. I'm too old for this weak-kneed experience.'

He rested a cautious hand on each of her shoulders. 'I don't want to sweep you off your feet . . .?' His voice was a question; his hands were burning through her sweater where he had held them near the fire.

'No danger of that,' she said, forcing a laugh.

He saw his own reflection in affectionate eyes. He saw a warm patch of colour and a faint, apricot-like layer of down rippled at his breath as he said, 'Isn't there?'

'Paul. You devil.' She closed her eyes. Her feet left the ground.

A long time afterwards, they lay together listening to the contented sound of rain gurgling down the gutter and chuckling into the drain, feeling the warmth from the fire against their glistening, twined limbs and drinking beer that was very flat indeed.

*　*　*

Dusk came quickly that day.

It was a moonless, cheerless, October night.

Kingsley was standing at the window thinking about his previously uncomplicated life.

Down below, in the street, commuters, heads bent against the wind and pelting rain, were hurrying towards the entrance to the underground station. Scraps of agitated paper skittered in after them.

There was shock on his sharply drawn face. In his hand he held a letter. The letter was the cause of his shock, but his mind wasn't on it; his mind was forty miles away. A frown crossed his face and anxiety clouded his half-closed, considering eyes.

He had been to Oxford on business that afternoon and, driving back through a curtain of angry rain, he had heard the weather forecast on the car radio. A depression in France, which was enduring heavy winds, was heading towards the channel. In the South East of England rivers were high and in some places, particularly Kent, there was a flood alert.

Seeing cyclists struggling, great trees bending over, lorries shuddering, he hadn't needed to be told.

Back in the office, knowing that in these solid old City buildings he was safe from the elements, with nothing to worry about except whether to eat dinner in or out, alone or with company, Kingsley reviewed his easy life.

Then he began to pace the floor.

When Big Ben boomed five times, Kingsley stopped his pacing and pressed a button on his

intercom, asking his temporary secretary – his usual
one was on maternity leave – if she would be so good,
before she went home, as to get four telephone
numbers. Two of his callers he only just caught
before they left their desks. The third was out,
and the fourth said she might have just what he
wanted.

Danielle was driving back from the hospital, keeping
her mind on her conversation with Red rather than
the threshing sky and tossing, drenched trees.

Red was improving every day. She had asked
Danielle to pass on the word about her condition.
'I'd rather have it out in the open; let them do their
worst,' she'd said.

The result was that she was never short of visitors,
fruit, home-made cakes, books, magazines or flowers.
There was just a hurt longing in her eyes sometimes
that curled Danielle's stomach in an understanding
way.

'Piers?' this independent, career conscious girl had
said. 'If he came back, I'd take him – even if I had to
share him with another woman.' She'd sounded
apologetic as she explained, 'When I'm with him I
feel like warm, thick honey. My skin shimmers, I
seem to float in a vast ocean of pleasantness somehow.' Her transparent cheeks had flooded with
colour. 'Does that sound silly?'

'No,' Danielle had said huskily. 'Have you let him
know about the baby? Written or anything?'

Red's face had hardened; she'd given a defiant toss of her head and Danielle had seen shining love freeze to green ice as she'd said, 'I wrote, yes.'

'Did you get a reply?'

'No. I don't want to talk about it.'

So Danielle had had to change the subject. 'Have you heard from your parents?'

Red made a speedy recovery. 'You won't believe this – ' she'd smirked ' – but they're selling up in Spain and coming home.'

Danielle had uttered an astonished, 'Really?' Red's parents, she recalled, had been most enthusiastic about their Spanish retirement home. 'Red's got her own life to lead,' her mother had said. 'She doesn't need us now.'

Red had explained. 'Mum said in her letter she was just looking for an excuse to come back, and that a grandchild is the best one ever. Never know people, do you?'

You can say that again, thought Danielle now, turning into the vineyard with a sigh, wishing she didn't have to go out again. But there was a do at the pub. Organized – surprisingly – by the village, and – ominously – Francesca.

310

CHAPTER 23

On this sinister, threshing night, the pub seemed more welcoming than usual. A rosy glow spilled outside and mingled with coal-black dancing shadows so that as people drove up, or staggered on foot across the green, they had the impression of approaching a flickering fire.

Every now and then the door burst open and a buzz of conversation and laughter drifted out as a howling wind blew in.

'I'm fed up with hearing that door slamming,' Iris snapped.

Ron, panicky-eyed, murmured something about bread and butter and turned away, hurrying to serve someone in the other, larger bar, which tonight had been given over to the celebrations. The circular counter, with its island of mirrored shelves, served the two bars.

Pulling on the pump with damp, plump hands, he glanced across to where the woman all the way from Australia sat in the middle of a crowd, looking, to his mind, a little bemused.

As well she might.

Above her head hung a banner. The message painstakingly sewn onto it wished her 'Happy Seventieth Birthday, Anna'.

It had been obvious when she'd come in, accompanied by a triumphant-looking Francesca, that she had expected nothing, tonight, other than a quiet drink with friends.

More bedraggled, windblown people staggered in, and by the shouts of welcome he deduced that they were Anna's relatives, crying out about high seas at Ramsgate where the waves had apparently stood up and walked across the road, and about Canterbury's clergy, flying across the cathedral's peaceful, soaked lawns like giant bats.

Turning to glance through into the lounge bar, he saw Hutch, in his usual corner, sipping his Guinness in a world of his own.

Poor old sod, Ron thought. *Hasn't anyone invited him? I'm beginning to know how he feels.* He glanced at Iris. Her back was to him and he had a good view of her figure, curving beneath her second new dress this month. It was a sort of glistening toffee-colour and short enough to show off her shiny, bulging Lycra-clad calves and a lot more besides. She was giving instructions to Sally, the casual waitress, and serving Robin at the same time. Showing off, as usual.

The mirrors were unkind to him. He was pale-eyed with pale curly hair – quite babyish – really and a round, flushed and worried face.

He was frightened too, although he preferred to call it anger. He had made love to her more often, in a desperate way. Until that, too, had failed him.

Turning back to the pump, he drew himself a beer.

Iris could tell Robin anything. All about how she and Ron had to have separate holidays with the children, how she organized everything, how, when they did have a chance of an earlyish night, Ron watched videos instead of going up to bed. How he drank too much, didn't appreciate her.

Robin always listened. Not only that, he had introduced her to good music and literature. She enjoyed the sensation of change within herself as she went from lowbrow to highbrow. Ron, of course, was lowbrow.

She ran her hands down her flat stomach, admiring her reflection as she turned round to take glasses and bottles from a shelf. Looked good, the new dress.

Robin drained his glass. As she drew his next pint he grinned, saying, 'You look like sticky toffee pudding.'

'Really!' she objected with a coy smile. 'I don't know whether that's a compliment or not.'

'Isn't it my favourite?'

Mollified, she knew it was true. He loved her puddings and her puff pastry.

She sighed, noticing that Ron, who could be so slow, had a queue. Trust him. She went to join him.

'Funny smell around here,' he muttered, pushing past her to get to the till.

'Maybe you should wash more often,' she retorted. Turning away, her scarlet smile widened. 'What's it to be, love?'

That nice Australian man gave a large order with a very pleasant smile, and she set to.

From where she sat, Francesca could see through into the lounge bar.

'Anna and Hutch were complete opposites,' she said to Danielle, adding enigmatically, 'He took life from her.'

They glanced two tables along to where Anna, who was trying to circulate and thank the villagers for such a surprise, had at last found a moment to join her relatives.

'Hutch used to call me his ray of sunshine.' Seeing Danielle's raised brows, Francesca added, 'It was never more than friendship. Daniel was my love, from the moment I saw him.'

Not knowing what to say, Danielle looked down at her wine. Tom had obtained it for her the moment she'd walked into the bar. He had taken it for granted they would sit together, and, poor man, whatever he said and did lately made her hackles rise. She had escaped by joining Francesca, and was relieved to see that as the room began to fill the empty chairs at Tom's table were taken by some of the villagers.

Where's Jo? she wondered, watching members of

the jazz band drift in and make their way to the small stage at the end of the room.

Absent-mindedly, she asked, 'How did you meet Grandy? Rome, wasn't it?'

Francesca ran fingers up and down her tall, damp glass of Dubonnet and lemonade. Her rings clicked against the side. 'Yes, Rome.' She made the word sound round and warm. 'An English soldier was trying to have his way with me,' Francesca said delicately. 'Your grandfather came along and sorted him out. I took him home.'

Her eyes danced at Danielle as she went on, 'He found himself surrounded by this voluble, excitable family and he looked as if he was wishing he had never stopped to help.' She laughed. 'They loved him, of course. Took him to their great warm hearts,' she said, with sudden sadness.

Danielle, her curiosity aroused, asked, 'What about Hutch?'

'Oh, it was like warming myself against a fire, that's all. It was as welcoming . . .' her eyes misted '. . . as welcoming as a warm Italian evening. You don't understand. Hutch had a bad time in the war – Anna too. They wanted to forget, have fun. Fun? Here? Not allowed. Stupid people.

'They took our fun,' she said, voice shaking, 'our pleasure in each other's company and ate it up for breakfast. Scandal is like food to them. Secrets multiply like cancers here.'

She paused. Danielle called out greetings to villa-

315

gers, who with kind-hearted concern were trying to give Anna a welcome and a birthday she would never forget.

Francesca glanced into the other bar. 'Hutch was a serious young man.'

Following her eyes, Danielle drank some of her dry wine and said, 'I believe you.'

Francesca gulped her own drink as if she were thirsty. Putting down the glass, she said, 'Anna and I had a wonderful relationship. I loved my friends. I could see nothing wrong in loving people. You're the same, Danny. Though you've had little time for friends, poor darling.'

Recognizing something lonely in Francesca's eyes, Danielle was moved to say, 'It's not too late for you.'

Francesca smiled, picked up her glass again and agreed. Before the glass reached her lips, Danielle saw that secret smile.

Tom was breathing down her neck, taking her empty glass and crossing over to the bar with his determined walk and dutiful expression.

At that moment she saw Jo walk in, face flushed, hair wild, smiling and smart in red, of all things. A red one-piece trouser suit in jersey, with a cowl neckline which hid her short neck and accentuated her broad, square shoulders, leaving her strong arms bare. She wore a gold chain belt and black pumps.

Danielle stood up and made her way towards her. But someone else reached her first.

As Danielle came up to them Paul was greeting Jo

with a greedy expression, his body leaning towards
her in a protective or maybe possessive way. Something about the two gave Danielle a chilling sense of
loneliness.

'You look great, Jo.' She smiled, making them
jump.

Jo's eyes glittered at her. 'Thanks. You too. I like
you in that dress.'

It was the amber dress Danielle had worn to the
dance – a ghost of a dress, which had appeared from
the wardrobe with a leer as she'd flung herself
together in a hurry and with little interest earlier.

Tom came up with her drink, nodded at Jo and
Paul, but didn't, she was relieved to see, seem eager
to stay.

A 'hurry up' roll of drums, a piano chord, a long,
drawn-out moan from a trombone and a cry of 'Why
are we waiting?' made Jo hurry off, amid laughter, to
the stage.

Danielle watched Paul watching Jo go.

'Is your mother enjoying herself?' she asked.

He grinned. 'You should have seen her face when
she walked in. She couldn't believe it.'

As if on cue, Anna rose, walked past them with a
kind smile and made her way into the lounge bar.
Shamelessly spying through the gap between shelves,
Danielle saw her approach Hutch. Placing a motherly
arm across his shoulders, she looked right into his
seamed face.

Whatever she said moved him not at all, for she

317

came back minutes later, passing them and approaching Francesca with a shrug.

'About Jo . . .' Paul said.

Danielle turned to him. 'Jo?'

He ran fingers through his hair; puzzled blue eyes swung from her to the stage 'I think a lot of her, you know? I've invited her over home for a holiday.'

'That's great,' Danielle responded warmly.

'Trouble is, she won't say yes. Says it's not on.'

As he watched her anxiously Danielle thought about Jo, who had confided in her recently that she was saving up for a holiday; she had never had one, nor been out of the country. Mulling over the sort of person Jo was, Danielle said cautiously, 'Maybe she thinks you mean more than a holiday, Paul.'

'Like what?'

'Like life.'

'You make it sound like a prison sentence.'

Her heart turned over. 'I didn't mean to. But you see, maybe . . . it's possible . . . well, that Jo thinks of it like that.'

He considered this, his kind face troubled. 'We get on so well,' he said at last. But she says, – "Just these two weeks and no more." ' A little shyly he admitted, almost with surprise, 'That sounds like a death sentence to me.'

He gripped her arm for a moment and left her. She saw him go to the bar and order a beer from Ron. His shoulders had a dejected slope. He and Hutch make a fine pair at the moment, she thought, with a tight throat.

'Does anyone know how Annette is?' someone called out. No one did.

Tom appeared at her side and only half listening to him – he never said much anyway – Danielle took her mind back to her visit to Annette's house that morning.

Raine had been alone, although not for long. 'The neighbours have been . . .' Her shoulders had been shaking. 'I'm hardly ever left alone when I *am* here.'

Danielle knew that she spent most of her days beside Annette's bed. Today Tony had found it necessary to go into the City for the morning; he would go straight to the hospital later.

The neglected house had smelled of nicotine, wet dog and fear. Raine's movements had been stiff, awkward, out on a limb, her hair lank and unattended. She'd cried careful, tidy tears which you felt were never going to stop and had taken to smoking when, before, anyone who'd smoked had been sent into the garden.

'Why?' she had asked of Danielle.

'I don't know.' Danielle had felt as if Raine's long, chipped red nails were clawing painfully into the heart of her. *If only I could make things better for Raine and all of them.*

Haunted, sleepless eyes had challenged her. 'This is a palace. Annette had everything . . . *has* everything she wants. What more is there?'

What can I say? Danielle had swallowed and finally said, 'Suzie was the same. You know she's left?'

Raine had shrugged. 'I heard. Staying with Auntie. Right area that is too.' Her face had crumpled. 'I thought Annette would be safe here. Both she and Suzie lacked nothing. Why?'

Danielle, who had always had her work, had said nothing.

A harassed woman had returned then, with the woebegone, wet carpet dog – a dog-walking rota had been set up by the neighbours – and Danielle had slipped away.

'I'm not sorry Annette's ill,' he muttered.

Paula threw him a look of appeal. 'Don't, Griff.'

They sat alone, isolated, because away from work Griff was shy and pubs were not really his cup of tea.

'Haven't seen you for ages,' Iris had commented as they'd come in. Her expression had said that they were only there because the food at the party was free. 'Suzie all right is she?' she'd asked, with knowing eyes.

Paula went off to the Ladies'. She was stopped by concerned enquiries. Some said, 'You don't look well.'

She perked up. 'Don't I? Well, with Suzie going off – to stay with her auntie,' she stressed, 'in London . . .

It's a bit of a shock, you know, when children leave

320

home,' she said weakly, over the clink of glasses and music.

Reaching the Ladies', tears held at bay, she checked her reflection in the mirror. The skin of her face was almost transparent, stretched tightly over unusually prominent bones. Dark half-moons lay beneath her eyes too. If only she could have told everyone the truth about Suzie. They would have felt so sorry.

Children didn't make any vows or promises. They were, really, born free. *Does any of it make sense?* she asked herself, flushing the loo. You longed to leave home, to be free, then you couldn't wait to get married and tie yourself once more to the watching, the explanations, the reasons . . . the What-time-will-you-be-back type questions.

Lucky Suzie. A glandular orchestra, loud and out of tune. Paula remembered the feeling. You didn't know you were out of tune at sixteen. You felt you were loud and clear and right, and that those who didn't want to listen to you had left the world behind and should be shoved in boxes and buried with hamsters so that life could go on.

How long will it be before I don't cry when I think of her? Will life ever be the same again? Now I'm getting like Griff.

She wandered back, passing a group of youngsters with their loud, hormonal, baying forced laughter, who had taken over a corner and who gave her guarded looks. Empty glasses waiting to be filled,

321

she thought as she walked into the party bar.

Her eyes fell on a figure alone, posture hunched, eating a sausage roll with wide, staring eyes and a dark flush. It took her a moment to realize it was Griff.

He wanted life perfect, that was all. He wounded and was wounded himself. He cut out of his life anyone he felt had let him down. He couldn't bear rejection; there could be no half measures. Which wouldn't have been so bad if he hadn't expected everyone else to be the same . . .

Just as the band had stopped for a break there was a commotion at the door – agitated voices, screams that shivered down your back like a cold steel knife.

There was Raine and her husband, pushing their way inside, and people looking round, hurrying across to them, and there was Raine crying over and over again, 'She's off the life support. She's breathing on her own.'

Tony added, his drawn face smiling. 'She's talking to us; she's going to be all right.'

Everyone went mad – cheering, back-slapping.

'Champagne,' someone ordered.

'It's on the house,' said Ron, and collected his cellar keys, hoping he had remembered to get some.

'Aren't these people wonderful?' Raine cried as Jo came up smiling, hugging her, suspiciously bright-eyed.

'They have their moments,' she answered.

322

Later, when things had calmed down, Raine, in answer to Jo's query, said that the police had not yet found the person responsible for supplying drugs at the club that night. 'I thought you might have,' she told Jo honestly.

Flushed and annoyed, Jo countered, 'Did you tell the police that?' When Annette didn't answer, Jo glared down at the bent head and told her, 'They searched my house.'

Facing a raised pair of strained, apologetic eyes, Jo softened. 'Annette came to me because she needed a loving stranger. I had an older woman friend when I was her age. There's a bond formed. It's someone who doesn't judge or watch you, who you are not responsible to, who can't be hard on you, who will listen, whose happiness doesn't depend upon you. Get me?'

She stopped. Raine looked guilty. After a bit, she said, 'I might have made her feel that I couldn't be happy in life unless she joined me at my salon. But I wasn't strict; she did more or less what she liked.'

'I know,' Jo said critically.

Annette sipped her champagne and said defensively, 'You *have* to let kids do what they like.'

'Why?'

'Because if you don't, they go away. They're given flats and money by the government. They know this and they blackmail us. You try keeping them in today,' she accused emotionally, turning to an agitated-looking Danielle, who had arrived at the end of the conversation. 'Kids are wise today. So you think of the danger out there. You think you would do *anything*,' she stressed, 'to keep them happy and have them come home each night.' Her voice was ragged as her hair.

Puzzled, wondering what had happened to her own teenage years, worrying about her godchildren, Danielle asked, 'What's the answer, then?'

Raine finished her drink with a brave flourish. Looking down into the empty glass, she shrugged and said, 'Don't pay them, I suppose. Build more hostels for the genuine homeless, perhaps. I don't honestly know.'

Danielle and Jo were alone for a moment.

Jo said, 'Can I have a couple of days of my holiday next week?'

Disturbed and irritated, Danielle felt she had to say yes, but added, 'I'm a bit pushed for staff, though.'

Feeling guilty, Jo pulled a face, explaining apologetically, 'Paul and his mother are going straight to Ramsgate tonight, to spend time with their family.'

'Yes, I know.' Danielle felt a pang, knowing she would miss Paul.

Jo, who would obviously miss him more, said, 'We've talked about me biking over to see him, show him around a bit. He seems to like the idea.'

Danielle observed her steadily. 'Of course he does. Jo . . .?

Before she could voice her question, Jo rushed in. 'Did he tell you about his wife?'

'Just that she died.'

With a crinkled forehead, Jo said, 'Her name was Peggy; she was a beauty queen. She got skin cancer.'

Seeing Danielle's appalled reaction, Jo went on, with feeling, 'He nursed her through her last illness.'

'How sad. But I don't see . . .'

'His two sons are being looked after by their grandparents,' Jo said.

Danielle changed the subject, pushing away her hurt at the thought of Paul's sons – How her grandfather would have . . .

She had noticed that whenever she was with Jo, Tom left her alone. 'Jo, can I ask you something?'

Jo glanced at the stage. 'Ask away.'

'What do you feel for Tom?'

Jo looked thoughtful. 'Lonely,' she said, then added, 'But I've only just found out. Anyway, what about Kingsley Hunter?'

'What about him?'

'Couldn't keep your eyes off each other at the dance.'

Danielle studied her empty glass. 'He only came because of the death watch beetle.'

'Sure,' Jo retorted, 'Hidden's death watch beetle is a national concern.'

Danielle's raised colour made Jo feel rotten, and she said more gently, 'It's none of my business unless you want to talk. Don't get hurt, that's all. Have fun, not pain – that's my motto.'

Danielle watched her hurry off and turned to smile at Paul as he came up beside her. They watched Jo pick up her trumpet and begin to play her cool, clear, searching-out-pain notes. 'It's like a silver-bladed knife,' Paul remarked softly.

Danielle turned to regard him thoughtfully and he said, in a low voice, 'I mean the way she plays that trumpet. It's like a surgeon's knife – cuts through to the core of you and pulls your heart out.'

'I'll go along with that,' Danielle said with a shiver.

'It's funny,' he said, brushing a hand across his face, 'you meet all sorts of people and then one day you hold out your hand and you touch love. Sometimes you don't know, sometimes you do.'

Jo was playing 'Autumn Leaves'. Heart aching, Danielle saw the lump that blocked Paul's throat, saw his shoulders heave and felt, rather than saw, the pain in his eyes.

Paul and Anna left with their family, after promising to come back and see everyone before they spent their last few days in London prior to flying home.

'I'll send you details of your forebears,' Paul told Danielle. She shrugged.

Saying goodbye to Anna, Danielle asked, 'Have you enjoyed your holiday so far?'

Anna thought about it before she answered, with a calm smile, 'I didn't come to enjoy myself. It was because I felt I should.' Shrugging into her jacket, she went on, 'My husband died, you see. Death is a catalyst,' she declared, winding a scarf around her neck. 'When someone dies, changes happen. They say death rides in on the back of the wind. Have I said something?'

White-faced, Danielle shook her head. Anna touched her arm, 'See you,' she called out, and, waving to everyone, she strode out into the stormy night.

Tingling with that awful feeling of premonition, Danielle watched her go.

'Lift home, Danny?'

'No, Tom – thanks.' Seeing his face darken, she said quickly, 'I'm taking Francesca home.'

'Right you are. See you tomorrow.'

She smiled, relieved.

'I think Anna enjoyed her surprise,' Francesca said. 'I hate this old truck.'

'You used to drive it yourself once,' Danielle reminded her, waiting as her grandmother settled herself and pulled the door closed.

'Don't remind me,' came her over-dramatic moan.

It was a relief when they were indoors; driving through the dark, tossing lanes had been a nightmare. 'I'm having a whisky and soda,' Francesca said, going to the sideboard and pulling the heavy doors open. 'You, darling?'

'I'm driving – no, thanks,' Danielle said, settling in

the armchair and wishing she didn't have to go out again.

Sitting down opposite her, Francesca sensed her mood and said hopefully, 'You could stay the night.'

'I've got things to do.'

'It's gone eleven.'

'So?' Tugging on her hair, Danielle asked, as if trying to make conversation, 'So, did you enjoy your visitors, then?'

Francesca dimpled. 'Very much.' Then with sharp, questioning eyes, she said, 'You look surprised.'

'The situation's not quite normal, is it?' Danielle shrugged.

'What did you want me to do?' Francesca asked, with a touch of amusement. 'Scratch Anna's eyes out?'

Danielle felt tired, sulky and difficult. She said nothing.

Sipping her drink, Francesca watched her for a moment before she said calmly, 'You don't understand Anna. There has been a lot of sadness in her life.'

'So you keep saying. Mind if I get an orange juice?'

When she came back from the kitchen, Francesca was staring reflectively into the fire, and Danielle had barely sat down when she turned and said, 'Anna grew up in the East End of London. She lost her parents and a young brother while she was nursing in France during the war. She came home on leave, turned the corner of the street where she lived and saw a smoking hole where her home had been. She was nineteen.'

Danielle slaked her dry throat with the orange juice. 'She must have gone out of her mind.' She frowned, feeling sick at the thought.

Francesca nodded, mollified. 'She met Hutch soon after; he was shattered by his wartime experiences too. Looking after him took her mind off her own problems, I think. The tragedy affected her, though. She could be hard, even intolerant. "I've seen worse," she would say. And Hutch used to joke, "Never marry a nurse; you get no sympathy." But maybe her way was better for him.'

The cat Danielle had let in from the garden when she went into the kitchen walked into the room, gave a yellow glare around and seemed relieved to find the room almost empty. Seeming to make a decision, she jumped upon Francesca's lap. 'Ugh! Bella, you're wet,' she complained, but began to stroke her never-theless.

'Anna wanted peace out here in Kent,' she went on. 'Peace. She loved her home and she needed to keep busy. Whether it was work or fun, her mind had to be occupied. She said she didn't want babies because of the world problems – which surprised me, for I got the impression she'd wanted to build something again. She had Hutch, though, and the farm – she encouraged Hutch to expand.

'You see things clearly from a distance, Danny.

She wanted to rebuild a shattered life, fill up that ghastly hole, mend a broken man. She needed to feel safe, to know she could turn the corner and not get any shocks. Then Hutch blew a hole in it. He accused her and she had no defence. So she fired back – turned away from the hole.'

Putting her empty glass on the coffee-table, Danielle said softly, 'She left to build again.'

'Yes, and the fire went out of the situation. One day I received a Christmas card from Australia. It was about two years later. It said she had married again and had a little boy. I wrote asking for photos, but she didn't send any.'

The silence was broken by the hall clock chiming midnight.

'You see,' said Francesca sadly, 'Anna had to be hard on herself and on Hutch. It was her way, and it worked usually. But not with Cherie. Cherie never forgave her.'

Danielle urged Francesca on curiously, feeling as if a piece of jigsaw was about to be put in place. 'What about Cherie?'

'Cherie worshipped Anna when she was a teenager; she was like a puppy dog with her – told her she would like to look like her when she grew up. Well – ' Francesca broke off to laugh ' – you don't know Anna. She used to say to Cherie, "You'll have to do something with yourself, then. I can't do with people moaning if they do nothing to change things. Either do it or shut up, is my motto." '

Seeing Danielle pull a face, Francesca said, 'Oh, Anna was kind to her too. She offered to take her up to London once, to see the Coronation procession and on to a theatre afterwards. It was almost as if she looked upon Cherie as a daughter. She felt sorry for her, slaving away in the shop, with no life outside it and those hectoring parents. But her parents, who didn't approve of Anna, forbade her to go. Cherie was twenty then.

'Anna faced her before a shop full of customers, her parents and all, and told her, in this icy way she had, that she was a mouse, among other things. She told her to pull herself together or she would never get a life, insinuating she would be left on the shelf. She did it for the best, but to my knowledge they never spoke again, and Anna washed her hands of her. Pity. She could have been Cherie's salvation. Anna had so much go in her.'

Danielle watched Bella stand and march up and down, trying to find a new place to rest. 'Ouch!' exclaimed Francesca, returning the indignant creature to the floor.

Danielle smiled as Bella gave a considering glance in her direction, sidled across and made a dive for what she hoped was a friendlier lap. Watching her settle down, Danielle stroked her fur and said, having made up her mind, 'Cherie was in love with Grandfather, you know.' She went on to outline her conversation with Cherie in the shop.

Wise-eyed and thoughtful, Francesca spoke as if

thinking aloud. 'Maybe Cherie tried to live her dream.'

'You mean, she tried to cause trouble between the four of you, hoping to get Grandy for herself? Mmm. Could be. She might have got her thrills from talking about it.'

Danielle stood up, cleverly transferring the sleepy cat into her place on the chair. 'Or it might have just been envy,' she added, stretching and yawning.

Francesca hauled herself up and bent to switch off the gas fire.

'Poor Cherie,' said Danielle, halfway to the door.

'That's what we all called her in those days,' recalled Francesca, following her into the hall and shivering as Danielle opened the door and let in a blast of wind.

'You know,' observed Danielle, with a smile, 'there's something satisfying about hearing someone's story. It's a sort of fullness – rather like tucking into a tasty sandwich. I see Anna differently now.'

Francesca, looking pleased, gave her a little push. 'You and your food. Night, night. Take care.'

And Danielle, thankful that the truck stood right outside the door, felt the wind slap her face only for a moment before she scrambled into the driver's seat and, as fast as she dared, and the truck was able, made for the safety of home.

She had plenty to mull over – enough to help keep her mind off the fact that she had always believed terrible things happened on nights like this.

CHAPTER 24

It must have been around one o'clock when, having only just fallen into a restless sleep, Danielle heard someone call. Grandy? She could have sworn it was.

Sleep fell away, and as she jerked upright, heart hammering, she heard an angry growl followed by a spine-chilling express-train roar. The hairs rose on the back of her neck as windows began to shake, doors rattled. A great animal might have been hurling itself at the walls.

She shivered, huddled in bed. At least she was out of the merciless beast's reach. How wonderful home was at times like this; she let out her breath with an attempted smile. Weren't the walls three feet thick, and hadn't they withstood centuries of storms?

Outside, something ripped and tore and crashed and bellowed! Oceans boomed and wolves howled.

And the urgent voice inside her gave her no rest.

She tried to fight its demand, but in the end she knew she had to find out what was happening to her vineyard beneath the onslaught of this devil.

Grandy would have. It was his voice in her head.

Dry-mouthed, she clumsily dressed and padded downstairs. In the hall, she pulled on cold wellies and a musty-smelling waterproof jacket; with an air of bravado, she jammed her cap on her head and grabbed a torch.

Everything in her shrank from opening the door; her throat was clotted with dread. Staying inside was a strong temptation. Except for that voice. With a deep breath and a rueful half-smile at her shivering cowardice, she reached out and shot back the stiff bolts, and the great, protecting door swung open.

A dark, agitated scene met Danielle's horrified eyes as she was caught by the wind's full force. Everything trembled and bowed down before it; young trees were on their knees and a chestnut fell, its branches flung out in a gesture of despair. There was an inhuman scream. From the orchard came a whistling and a spinning-top hum. The branches of cherry trees stood on end.

Struggling along, she pulled in terrified, choking breaths as boughs and branches flew into the air. The torchlight was feeble and she felt pitifully alone, as if no one remained in the world and she was balanced on the brink of disaster.

All at once, distant flashes illuminated the darkness as trees toppled onto furious power cables and a thousand volts made the scene into a science fiction film.

Battling up the slope, she saw God playing skittles with the stilt-man trees in the copse.

And the vines? The stinging wind was tugging at the leaves, whipping through the skinny, shivering trunks. *The fruit's safe*, she cried silently. *But what about the Chasselas, further up the slope?* She struggled on, and it was as if a cold tongue were trying to molest her; she was fighting a body as hard as iron.

No wind had ever been like this. It slapped, punched, came in waves, almost lifting her from her feet.

She heard a ripping, tearing, sickening creaking, and saw, straight ahead, the dark shadow of an elm topple and begin, so slowly, to fall towards her.

Involuntarily, she flung out her arms.

Suddenly an iron grip from behind lifted her off her feet and, almost squeezed to death, she flew backwards, out of the path of the elm, which crashed down and lay like a fallen soldier, its bedraggled branches not a foot away.

'You fool!' Kingsley shouted in her ear. 'You're a nutcase! What did you expect to do?' he yelled. 'Catch a falling tree with your bare hands? God almighty . . .'

She twisted round. 'My Chasselas —' But the words were muffled as his hand pressed her head, forcing her face into his chest.

She could scarcely breathe, and around her the raging wind roared like a jet plane, but she heard him say, 'You bloody stupid, lovely girl.'

He stood back, cupped her face in his hands and

planted a cold kiss on her lips. Her eyes were suddenly swimming; what a wonderful sight he was. She could hardly believe the relief of him being there, when she had, a moment ago, felt so terribly alone.

'No good crying,' he shouted, placing an arm around her shoulders and hugging her. 'Let's go.'

She stood firm, although shaking, looking around her like one who had come to the end of a cliff. 'Grandy planted the Chasselas . . . he never saw them harvested . . .' The wind tore the words from her mouth, tossed them away.

'Oh, come on,' he ordered, strain showing in his face, but his voice was stern and hard, with no fear.

When she remained still, he put his hands on her shoulders and glared into her face. 'He's dead!'

The rain came then.

Seeing her stricken look, he stood with the rain soaking his hair and lashing down his cheeks, troubled blue eyes trying to get through to her. Reaching out, he tore the cap from her head, and before she could stop him he had tossed it into the mouth of the devouring wind.

'He's dead!' he shouted. 'Accept it! Let him go! Give someone else a chance to love you.'

Her heart seemed to wrench itself from her body. Pulling her arm away, she threw him a glance of such hurt that, stunned, he let her go.

'You're living in the past,' he shouted, hurrying after her. 'You try to please because you're afraid of

336

being sent away. I won't send you away . . .'

The wind shrieked, hurling his words away. He didn't know if the tiny, doubled-over figure ahead had heard him. But he had something terrible to tell her.

In a minute he was gasping beside her, reaching out to stop her. She turned, and the stricken look on his face nailed her to the spot.

'Do you know what I've been bloody well doing?' he yelled above the screeching wind.

With horror in his eyes, he went on. 'I've been searching for your dead body.'

'What?' she screamed.

'The cottage . . .' Intense anguish lined his face as he told her. 'The tree outside your room . . . it's down.'

The drenched shadows on her face deepened, and from her lips came a moan of despair as he went on, 'The tree went through the roof onto your bedroom and bathroom. The rest of the cottage is okay. If you had been there . . .'

He opened his arms and she went back into them. Just for a moment. Then, with a brief searching of each other's faces, they stumbled on towards the winery.

The rain was blowing in all directions, as if it didn't know where to go, spinning first one way, then another until she felt giddy. The wind was like a powerful hand, pulling her by the hair with such force that she felt scalped. Never had she known such fear, yet there was also anger . . . anger at the destruction around her, and the wind's threshing temper vied with her own. She was fighting another bully, that was all.

The buildings had just loomed up when there was the hideous creak of splintering wood. They started to run, a difficult, staggering run, their breath coming in great painful gulps, the wind behind them now, urging them on.

'The office!' she screamed. 'My God, the roof . . .'

'Hang on.' He pulled her back. 'Don't – '

But she had wrenched herself free from his hard grip and he could only lunge after her across the yard. She was tugging at the door. 'I haven't got the keys . . .'

'Sorry, love . . .' Kingsley put his shoulder against the door, forced it open.

She was frozen in the doorway, the blood draining from her face. Her torch probed the darkness, taking in the smashed pictures lying on the floor with papers, bottles, files, the soaked papers still clinging to the noticeboard, tossing angrily. And when she raised her stricken eyes to the roof, the sky raced by, laughing.

She looked frail and frightened. Kingsley gathered her to him and then put her away, knowing that she needed his help; he had no intention of letting her down, the way every man in her life had so far done. He had to show her that he could be depended upon.

Clinging to him, she seemed not to want to let go, and then she took a shuddering breath, as if she battled for air, and raised her head, smiling through her fear – one of her quick smiles, that was suddenly so brave and illuminated more than her grubby face and shadowed eyes.

The smile pierced the fog in his mind and he saw clearly that her cheerfulness was a wonderfully endearing charade, her smile an emblem of her bravery. He smiled reassuringly, even though he thought he might be about to be crushed, grabbed the keys from the desk drawer and hurried away.

Just as he opened up the shed where the fork-lifts were kept Tom drove up, anxious because all the telephone lines were down.

There was an eager, triumphant look on his face. Until he saw Kingsley, when he sobered immediately and asked, 'What are you doing here?'

'The same as you,' Kingsley snapped. 'Trying to batten everything down.'

They glared into each other's eyes.

'Tom,' shrieked Danielle, hurrying up. 'Thank God you came. Quick . . .'

Kingsley had somehow managed to remove the filing cabinets and other vital equipment from Danielle's office into the great shed. Now the two men and Danielle moved the desk, then cleared the laboratory, where the windows had been blown out, and anything important in the other wooden office and stores. In the end, with the wind showing no signs of abating, there was nothing else they could do.

The shed doors were duly locked and Danielle

climbed painfully slowly down from a fork-lift, stumbling, exhausted, rubbing her eyes, the skin on her face aching and stinging as if she had been slapped.

'That's it,' a soiled and perspiring Kingsley said firmly. 'Enough's enough.' Calling out goodnight, they trudged along to the cottage.

Tom watched them disappear into the darkness; the wind roared around him and he thought of his dream, torn to pieces. His hands curled into fists. Anger leapt inside him as if it wanted to be released, to join the howling monster of the night.

Moments later, the Austin's headlamps raced like raging eyes towards Danielle and Kingsley as they staggered up the track, the engine's roar joining the wild wind. Danielle turned, saw Tom coming, and flung her hand over her eyes, blinded . . .

Stepping back, she pulled Kingsley with her, waving, flagging Tom down. 'Do me a favour – call in and see Jo. I'm worried about her.' She had a horrifying mental picture of the mobile homes being picked up like Dinky toys and thrown in the air. And all those trees . . .

His face, peering from the open window, was grey and sullen as she asked, 'Please, Tom.'

His eyes flicked from her to Kingsley. He nodded. 'Why not?' Rolling up the window, he drove away.

Danielle was dead weary, and her red-rimmed eyes

were anxiously fixed upon her home as it came towards her. For the first time that night the moon sent down just enough glow for her to see the slain body of her friendly beech lying across one end of the cottage, roots spanning twenty feet. Lifeless, with severed limbs and hands outstretched, its fingers clawed the sky like a dead man.

They went in and closed the door behind them.

'Grandfather's rule,' Danielle told him, pushing the wet hair from her face, having automatically tried clicking the light switches. 'Candles and oil lamps in every room.'

Soon the thick walls of the lower part of the house were flickering with shadows. The tree had not penetrated the room beneath her bedroom which had once been a dairy and was now a utility room with a door leading through to the kitchen, which was also untouched.

'Upstairs,' Kingsley ordered, giving her a gentle push. 'Out of those clothes and see if the shower's working.'

'And you?' She gave him a slow smile which didn't show in her shocked eyes. 'I think there's a bathrobe in one of the drawers in your . . . in the other bedroom.'

They climbed the stairs together.

'Don't . . .' he began, but with an anguished look at him she carried her lamp along the passage to her room.

Grotesque shadows of the great tree danced on the passage walls; the carpet squelched beneath her bare feet. She glimpsed sky as she pushed her head around what was left of the door. The furniture was invisible beneath masonry, jagged branches, plaster, rubble, broken glass and tiles. Her bed was a resting place for the beech.

Kingsley watched her reach out, pull a teddy from the floor and shake him free of rubble. She had the appearance of a sleepwalker. He bent down. 'Don't forget your slippers.' He shook the rubble from them. They were, amazingly, dry.

Her great shocked eyes looked up at him and, as if remembering something, she sighed and the corners of her mouth lifted.

By the time she came downstairs, Kingsley was heating milk on the Aga and making hot chocolate, adding a generous dollop of brandy. She saw his eyes flicker over the blue satin negligee she was wearing and explained, 'I use the chest in your room to store clothes I never wear. Bit of luck, as I can't get at my own. Francesca bought me this.' She smiled guiltily. 'The chest is full of her gifts.'

They sat together in the dim kitchen, with nothing, it seemed now, but the table between them, the fridge silenced and the wind moaning beyond the walls.

'Why did you come?' she asked, warming her chilled fingers on the cup.

He spoke with detached honesty. 'Because of the elastic. Because you called me. Because, although I first came here to hurt you, now I don't want you to be hurt – in fact . . . I can't bear it. And . . .'

'And?'

'To hell with Piers. I wanted you from the first time I saw you . . . what went before is of no account.'

The chocolate slid down her throat like silk.

He seemed to want to talk, and Danielle, feeling unreal, was too stunned to do anything but listen.

'I walked into your office hating you, and saw before me – most unexpectedly – a warm, vibrant little thing, with the friendliest face and eyes I've ever seen, who obviously wouldn't have hurt a fly. I was thrown.'

'You were a beast,' she said, tears pricking her eyelids though she didn't know why.

'I was pompous,' he admitted, noting by her glinting eyes that she was starting to come round. 'The idea of visiting my Stepfather's mistress was intriguing. The idea of falling in love with her was shattering. It was a wholly unsuitable liaison and could bring nothing but trouble to all concerned. That's why I left so abruptly.'

He gulped his drink and sat back, sleepy eyes fixed on her face. 'I felt it all . . . self-disgust, desire . . . But somehow there was more than that. I couldn't sever my connections with you. Oh, I tried. I kept going away in order to protect my uncomplicated life. But the truth was I wanted all the things you are . . . your warmth, laughter, trials and tribulations . . . for myself.'

'You certainly got your money's worth tonight.' She smiled, wondering what he meant by 'falling in love'.

He laughed. 'Nice to see you looking more cheerful.'

He's so . . . conversational . . . she thought restlessly. *As if he's talking in the past tense.* In a matching tone, she told him, 'I found out something.' She went on to explain about Red. 'That's why I left a message with your secretary to ring me.'

He shook his head. 'She must have forgotten to pass it on. But look . . . That note in Piers's diary – so obvious now – roses for Red, not red roses.'

She stood up and carried the mugs to the sink. While she was washing them he said, 'By the way, I got some news today too.'

'What's that?' she asked curiously, turning and meeting shocked eyes.

'I received a letter from Mother.'

Danielle dried her hands. 'And?'

'She's jumped ship.'

'What!' Returning to her seat, she exploded with laughter at the comical disbelief on his face.

He looked a little aggrieved. 'She left the ship at Naples, and,' he went on indignantly, 'she said she'll send me a card from Capri. She said it's time she was her own person, not an extension of someone else. She said she married because she wanted someone to make her happy after Father died; she said that's the wrong reason to marry.'

There was silence, until Danielle said softly, 'Good luck to her.'

They exchanged a long, searching look, and she grinned at him, conscious of the wind still prowling outside, conscious that she had fought it and come through, conscious that at this moment she felt utterly safe and glad to be home – the way she had felt as a child during the holidays. And Kingsley had said . . . she was sure he had . . . that he loved her . . .

Seeing the smile, he bit his lip. 'You won't be smiling when I confess what I've done.'

Her face fell. 'What?'

He rose, towering over her, and she looked up in awe at the sheer masculinity of him, somehow even more pronounced in his bedraggled state.

Looking down at the amber flecks in her widened eyes, tormented by the thought of the big white bed upstairs, Kingsley clenched his hands and took a calming breath. She had more than enough problems tonight.

Abruptly he spun round, strode out through the door and into the sitting room, leaving her gazing after him in bewilderment. Turning back, she rested her elbows on the table and supported her head in her hands.

Behind her, the door swung open. 'Danielle.'

Tensing, she remained where she was.

'Danielle, close your eyes – don't look.'

She did as he said.

'You can look now,' he called softly.

She slowly rose to her feet, gazing down at the hamper he had placed on the table. She turned to him. 'A midnight picnic, is it?' She dimpled.

He watched her with an intent expression. 'Open it.'

Gingerly, she reached out, pulled up the lid. It fell back . . . there was a familiar musky smell . . . Her heart turned over and began to thud.

Eyes like melting chocolate gazed hopefully up at her; she saw floppy brown ears and a plump little brown and white body, a damp, chocolate-coloured nose.

'Oh . . . Oh, Kingsley, what have you done?'

Tears pricked her eyelids, and before she could stop them began to fall. She reached out and bunched up the soft, warm body, pulled it to her face. A fast-beating heart pattered against her hand; he was so frightened.

She stroked him, whispering, fur like silk beneath her hands, a warm tongue licking her cheek, a whimper. He went straight to her heart, which couldn't seem to stand the strain of so much love and burst like a balloon.

A tiny pink tongue licked her salty tears, which were streaming now, and then Kingsley reached out and replaced the puppy, protesting, in the hamper.

'I can return him. He's on approval.'

'Oh . . . I can't speak . . . I can't . . .'

His hand went to the back of her head and pushed

346

her face into his great chest, where she nestled, crying as if her heart had broken. As if she was never going to stop.

'Cry, my love,' he whispered. 'You deserve time to cry.' His hand gently ran up and down her spine and his fingers caressed her damp hair. He took a deep breath of orange shampoo. 'By the way, he's a she.'

'Don't take her back,' she sobbed.

'Shh. She's yours. Did you see she has eyes just like yours? What will you call her?'

Her voice was muffled. 'You choose.'

His chest moved up and down. 'What about . . .?' He moved backwards, the better to see her tear-streaked face. 'What about . . . Amber?'

She smiled through her tears. 'That's nice.'

'And after we've fed and watered her, we're going to bed, my love.'

Her insides contracted. 'What?'

He gave his lop-sided smile. 'You wouldn't turn me out on a night like this, would you?'

Mutely, she shook her head.

He tilted her chin. 'And, as it's windy, you're coming into my bed.' At the change in her expression, he added, 'To sleep. You see, my darling, I don't just want to know you carnally. I want your warmth, your companionship, your laughter.'

'Oh!'

Danielle lay for the first time in the four-poster bed.

Self-consciously, she had put on black silk pyja-

347

mas, from the trunk while Kingsley washed in the kitchen and shaved after going out to retrieve an emergency toilet bag he kept in his car. She turned her back when he slid into bed wearing just his . . . Well, she hadn't looked.

She lay tautly beside him, wishing that things were different, and yet not discontented. How could she be? The wind had ebbed, but still shook the windows; the bed was a warm cocoon and he radiated heat.

He kissed her goodnight, turned his wide back on her, put out his arm and pulled her to him. 'Cuddle up to me,' he ordered. And, tentatively at first, she did, finding, to her surprise, an almost divine sense of security and peace, lying against his big body, enjoying the contrast with the fury outside.

Yet, sleepless, she wondered too much about what it would be like to be made love to by him. Unused to a sleeping partner, she lay rigid, afraid to move in case she woke him. His rhythmic breathing told her that he was sound asleep and hadn't found her at all . . . well, disturbing. Would he have just fallen asleep with his other women? She began to feel irritated. Oh, so many things. She was so mixed up.

Yes, friends were important to her; it was wonderful that he had come back. He obviously intended them to be loving friends. But there were friends and friends.

Listening to his breathing, it came to her that most people were background music, but that a special person was a singing inside – which she thought very profound for that time of the morning.

When she heard the hall clock strike four, she carefully slipped out of bed and crept downstairs.

She was greeted with enthusiastic kisses, a spinning tail and anxious, loving eyes, and, singing to herself, she lit the lamp and reached into the dark fridge for milk. There, on the shelf, stood a bottle of champagne. She looked at it. Then she removed it and opened it. The cork flew out; the drink exploded.

She was staring down at her froth-soaked pyjamas in dismay when the door opened. She looked up guiltily.

Kingsley leaned against the door, sleepy blue eyes amused. 'Your secret vice. You're a midnight drinker.'

While she stared at him he went to the pine dresser, removed two glasses, placed them on the table and took the bottle from her hands. Then he picked her up and perched her beside them. 'Where are your slippers?'

Their faces were level and she grinned. 'Did you bring the champagne?'

'Yep.' He filled the glasses. 'Thought it might come in handy for a celebration.'

Raising the glass to her mouth, she smiled. 'Don't we do daft things?'

His eyes smiled back. 'Daft and wonderful things; things I've never done before.'

'Really?'

Nodding, he raised his glass. 'To Amber. Welcome home.'

'To Amber.' Glasses touched and sang.

Her lips were wet with champagne when he leaned forward and kissed her. His soft mouth then moved down and planted a damp, shivery kiss on the side of her neck.

Caught in a flurry of delight, she raised her glass and finished her drink.

When she jumped down from the table, he threw back his drink, put down his glass and caught her arm.

'Not so fast, young lady . . .'

Pulling away, she moved around the table, afraid that he might see how her flesh quivered at his touch.

He prowled after her. 'Look, I've not been unfair – '

'Not unfair?' she cried. 'I'd have said blackmail is unfair. You forced yourself into my home . . .'

He pounced; she darted away. The puppy, ears pricked, head on one side, looked from one to the other.

Kingsley followed Danielle round the table. 'But while I was here I was no trouble. I'm house-trained.'

She backed away, heart pounding at the determination in his eyes. 'You burned the toast.'

'I'm not used to your grill; I have gas.' He was an animal stalking its prey, padding on bare feet, the gaping towelling robe exposing long, muscled, tanned limbs.

Avoiding his reaching hand, she smiled weakly. 'You know what they say about getting out of hot kitchens!'

He stood with his hands on his hips. 'Maybe I'd rather put up with the heat.'

On the other side of the table she turned away, rinsed the glasses under the tap, picked up a teatowel.

He darted up to her, grabbed the towel and threw it aside as, laughing, she struggled to evade his enfolding arms, trying hard to avoid those mocking eyes and his seeking, laughing mouth. But not too hard, for the laughter got in the way.

It was the laughter that made it easy.

They laughed as he struggled up the stairs with her in his arms. They laughed when he dumped her on the bed and she bounced.

And then the laughter died.

He said solemnly, 'I love you.'

She held up her arms, and, while the wind raged outside, their bodies, almost with relief, came together to spend their own store of passion.

Kingsley had waited so long, he was like a bee guzzling honey; slipping the silk pyjamas from her body, he lovingly explored, his lips and hands so gentle that he aroused in her exquisite responses and a surge of love that devoured her fear. Her body could do no more than open as naturally as a flower, stretching and waiting.

Looking down at her dark eyes, swimming with amber flecks, the trust he saw there tempered his sense of victory and power with care, and he handled her with love.

So it was a long time later – too long – when his hands and mouth had brought her to an agony of longing, when her body had thrilled to a thousand light, rhythmical touches, that her flesh responded with joy and shrieked relief with a sudden explosion as she welcomed him inside the most private of places with an impatience that delighted him.

The heat of their skin flashed and burned and they pulsed together to the highest climax, remaining in a deeper than deep relaxation through the rest of that tempestuous night of the winds.

CHAPTER 25

Kent awoke to an uncanny silence.

Griff drove with the stern yet alert look of one who thrives upon getting stuck in and helping.

For mile upon mile he drove past and around trees which had fallen like skittles and telephone lines in snakes of twisted coils. The air coming through the open window was thick with the mournful scent of crushed pine and beech leaves, and he began to hear the rasping of the first chain saws, which was soon to become a familiar tune.

He stopped and talked to men already at work; they answered him with exhausted, drawn faces and voices thick and dry with sawdust. Already diggers, army vehicles, bulldozers and Jeeps were out in force, along with the Red Cross, delivering tarpaulins and blankets.

Griff swerved the van around a monster JCB, which was gobbling up tree trunks and tossing them aside to clear the road, and at last arrived back in the village.

It's a miracle, he thought, face etched with pain,

353

catching a glimpse of his own cottage standing undamaged. But other poor devils were going through it.

A tree was spreadeagled across Ron's car, fortunately having missed the pub itself – but why Ron had left the car out in the car park anyway, he didn't know. Trees had punched holes in two cottage roofs, outbuildings were smashed, trees uprooted, chimney-pots down, walls collapsed. It went on.

Thanking God for his escape, Griff pressed buttons on the radio. The local radio station had returned to the air, gravely describing Kent as 'the closest to a nuclear disaster area we may ever see'. At the height of the storm the National Grid had failed, apparently, blacking out London and the south east. The winds had blown at speeds of more than one hundred miles an hour, tearing at townscape and landscape 'like a savage beast'.

Griff manoeuvred around the massive limbs of a cedar tree and drove past the church. The sixty-foot spire lay on the ground in a tangle of twisted timbers. He heard the woman beside him gasp.

Gravestones had been lifted up in the cemetery, headstones smashed and crosses cracked.

'Do you want me to stop?' he asked solemnly.

'No. The wind would not have dared,' Francesca told him stoutly, averting her eyes.

A little later, Danielle's grandmother said in a stunned voice, 'The landscape has slipped back years.'

354

The funereal voice on the radio continued. 'At Biggin Hill airfield, light aircraft have been overturned . . . phone cables look like spaghetti . . . woods have vanished.'

A sudden cry burst from Francesca's throat, and Griff went cold as he turned the van into the vineyard and rattled across the cattle grid.

The sign, 'INTOXICATING LADY', lay on the ground beside what was left of the wall. And the cottage . . .

The sun looked white-faced and seasick in a storm-tossed sea of cloud in a sky much bigger than before.

For Danielle, it was one shocked, indrawn breath after another. Surveying her tattered vines, she saw that the Chasselas area was destroyed, crushed by two fallen elms, and she pushed her face into Amber's warm, quivering body for a moment. If this had happened before the harvest . . . Her blood froze. It could have been the end; she wouldn't have had the reserves. *Don't think of it.*

After bending to put the wriggling Amber down, she stood up and found herself, with a sense of unreality, looking straight across to Paradise meadow. For the trees in the copse lay like matchsticks.

In the distance she saw woodlands, like her orchard, littered with broken limbs, and neighbours' houses she had never seen before. She shuddered, frightened by the unfamiliarity of a landscape which had changed overnight.

The poplars, though, were standing like sentinels,

as, with Amber on her new lead, Danielle slipped through the hedge.

No need to avoid the copse. Nothing, now, stood in the way of Paradise.

Long grass whispered against her wellies, and her hurt eyes flew here and there, checking. Two trees were down and the water was running high, almost touching the boughs of her leaning tree. Heaving a pained sigh, she surveyed a scene which resembled the aftermath of a battle.

As she sat there, with her chin in her hands, she saw the sun suddenly burst through, like a smile, which made things seem even more unreal. She watched it until her eyes ached and black spots danced in front of them.

One spot grew, filling her vision, and Amber yelped, hurled herself forward, stopped by the lead which Danielle had tied to a tree.

Danielle's insides contracted. She remained where she was, but her eyes ran to meet him . . . That wonderful head of hair, inherited from his father, who had gone white as a teenager, his thrusting body, the muscle-rippling legs, the grey trousers stained dark to the knees, the posh, mud-soaked shoes.

Coming up to her, champagne bottle swinging in his hand, he smiled easily and, seeing the sudden warm colour flood her face, said, with the teasing familiarity of a new lover, 'Just how I always picture you, my little ragamuffin. My, what you hide under those dungarees.'

356

She felt her body burst into life, wanting nothing more than to make love again. The thought delighted her – her body delighted her – and Kingsley, also, by the way he was inspecting her, was not displeased.

'I woke up and there you were gone,' he accused her, standing the bottle on the grass. Taking a glass from each jacket pocket, he perched beside her on the trunk, brown hands fondling the ears of the ecstatic puppy.

Danielle thrust back her hair, her face breaking into a warm, loving smile. 'You've come prepared for a celebration, I see.'

'That's right,' he said, folding his arm around her and pulling her close. 'And I've something to tell you,' he added as she snuggled up. 'Your grandmother just arrived. Griff is delivering tarpaulins and stoves, and he brought her with him. I said I'd come and get you.'

Worried, Danielle twisted her head to look up at him. 'She's okay, I take it?'

'Fine.' He nodded, dropping a kiss on her forehead. 'In fact, she's also jumping ship.'

Studying her from beneath sleepy eyelids, he ran his little finger lightly down the sudden crease between her questioning eyes, telling her, 'She's flying to Italy next week. Spending a few weeks with relatives. She says you can go if you like – meet your family.'

With something like accusation, she said, 'I'm staying here; maybe another time.'

He accepted her statement without surprise. His arm about her tightened. 'Not too upset about the damage, darling, are you?'

Of course she was. Tears were pricking her eyes like pepper, but she just said, 'I have a pain here,' indicating her chest. 'But it will take more than tears to repair the cottage. Besides, it's insured, and . . .' She grimaced. 'I might not even have been here now, and somehow,' she said, with a break in her voice, 'that lets you know exactly where your priorities in life lie. As for the yard – the main harvest is over.' She smiled, looking on the bright side. 'Where's that champagne?'

Francesca, who hadn't seemed at all surprised at Kingsley's presence, said, 'On the way here we stopped at the shop. I wanted to welcome the new people.'

Danielle looked at her in surprise. 'You did?'

'Of course. I wanted them to feel they were among friends.'

'What did you think of them?'

'Lovely. A great asset to the village. They were supplying hot drinks and soup for free from their caravan. People were queuing up. They sent a message . . . their children will come by later to see if they can help.'

In the sitting room, Kingsley pulled the electric fire out of the grate and, with great concentration, lit a coal fire while Francesca perched on the settee and told him all about Paul and Anna. Danielle bustled about in unironed jeans and sweater, making drinks and talking to Griff, trying not to think of the damage over her head.

While Griff went out to the shed to bring in logs Francesca wandered back into the kitchen, saying, 'I met the most odd person.'

'Oh, who was that?' asked Danielle, turning from the Aga with an opened can of tomato soup in her hand.

'Her name is Dorothea Trutt,' Francesca said with relish. 'We got talking, and when I return from Italy she's going to teach me how to play Bridge.'

When Francesca and Griff had gone, and Danielle was sitting with Kingsley in the kitchen drinking yet more tea, and Amber was chasing sunbeams, she said, 'I've suddenly got all this family. I don't know what to do with them. Italy, Australia . . .'

'And France,' Kingsley reminded her. His face looked troubled. 'You just love them. There's a whole new world of love waiting for you out there, darling.'

Silence.

Danielle kept her eyes averted. With her body sending panicky, fluttering signals, she wanted to ask, What about us? Don't you care if I go away? But she couldn't. It was too like Francesca.

He was looking at her quizzically. 'You're so young. You have a lot of living to do yet.' With a touch of guilt in his voice, he added, 'There's nearly ten years' difference between us.'

She jumped up and carried their mugs to the sink. Why should it be 'between' them? What was he trying to say in that schoolmaster's voice?

With her back to him, she said accusingly, 'You've had your way, now you're off. Don't make silly excuses.' Reaching up for the teatowel, she tugged so hard that the hook fell off the wall and she swore.

'Don't be cheap,' he said sharply, pushing back his chair and coming over to her. 'I'm thinking of you.'

'Then . . .' She swung round, her voice breaking. She cleared it and started again. 'Then be with me; don't leave me.' She had never said that to anyone before; she was voicing a silent and old plea.

With a quick, indrawn breath, he pulled her to him, sudsy mug and all, and held her with her face tucked into his chest, as he had done on a windy night weeks ago.

Kingsley remained for a blissful day and night, after which he returned to work and to check on his own home and his mother's house. He had only just left when the excited children from the pub, Samantha and Timothy, cycled along to the vineyard.

'Our phone's been reconnected,' they told her importantly, handing her two notes. When she read them she found one had Paul's number on it and the other Jo's.

'You've got to ring them,' Samantha said bossily.

'Mum said Jo's number is the hospital,' Timothy pointed out importantly.

The pub was busy with workmen as well as with local people, for the countryside was filled with rasping saws and screeching, dentist-drill-type sounds. Ron and Iris were able to heat soup and ready-cooked meals from the dead freezer and, with no shortage of logs, each bar danced and crackled with blazing fires.

Iris looked up from polishing the counter as Danielle hurried in. With an automatic smile, she questioned and sprayed comforting words, which she felt was part of her job, ending, 'You know where the phone is.'

Hutch was there, surprisingly, with a group of farmers who were sitting around the fire toasting muffins, mulling over their misfortunes with burning intensity. Hutch, with his Guinness in one hand, toasting fork jabbing like a sword in the other, looked almost animated.

The door opened. Iris knew it was Robin because she had seen him approaching through the window, and had wondered who his friend was.

'This is Ben,' smiled Robin, coming up to the bar. 'He works for the BBC.'

Iris put down her cloth and held out her hand. Ben's handshake was warm and moist. He was the same height as Robin, brown-haired, with a sensitive mouth and kind, gentle eyes. 'Oh, really?' she gushed, brows shooting up, 'The BBC?' Iris *was* surprised.

'He came to report on the storm,' Robin added, with a fond, embracing smile at his friend.

'Funny old life,' Ben said happily. 'When I heard about this assignment I thought, That's where Robin lives.' With a grin, he went on, 'I hear you look after him well. He told me about your cooking. Actually – he winked ' – that's why I'm staying for a while.' He glanced at Robin, sure of himself, adding, 'Or even longer.'

Iris was speechless.

Ben took a small tape recorder from a briefcase she hadn't even noticed before.

'An emergency,' one of the farmers was saying, 'brings people together, see.'

'The storm,' Iris told the machine importantly, 'was like a raging beast. Uncontrollable.' She shivered. 'Made you feel that big,' she said, holding up thumb and forefinger. Voice taking on the happy relief of a survivor, she added, 'But my family are safe and, selfish as it sounds,' she said firmly, 'that's all I care about.'

Ron came up behind her as the machine clicked off. 'I've had enough. I'm putting my foot down.'

She spun round. 'You're what?' she asked, as if he had suggested climbing Everest.

'You need a holiday, my girl,' he said, giving her an awkward hug. 'You look tired.'

Annoyed, Iris released herself and glanced in the mirror. Surely not! He had to say the wrong thing.

* * *

Seeing Danny hurry into the ward, anxiously searching and then beaming recognition, Jo wondered what she was going to tell her. About Tom and about the other thing.

'Jo,' Danielle said, coming up to the bed. 'What's happened?' For a second the dark eyes were brimming with something happy, and then they clouded over. 'What are you doing here?' she asked in a loud whisper. 'I knew it would be dangerous where you live.'

'I did have a brush with a tree,' Jo admitted. But didn't add that the tree had done her a favour.

'Are you hurt?' Danielle wanted to know, anxiously eyeing the bits she could see.

'Er . . . a few bruises . . . but it's not only that.'

'What, then?'

Jo looked down at her hands, nails like clots of blood on the white sheet. 'Tell me how things are with you first,' she prevaricated. 'Much damage?'

Danielle looked mulish, but, not being one to talk about herself either, obediently explained about the damage at the vineyard and how the villagers were coping.

She paused then, as if there was more and she wasn't sure whether to speak. Jo was surprised to see the secret smile, and her movements as she pulled a chair out to sit down were more fluid, calmer. Having ascertained that Jo wasn't in danger, she sat there with a smug, feline look, as if someone were stroking her tummy. But who?

Jo panicked. *Not Tom. Please not Tom.* But Danielle's next words dispelled her fear, for, pushing the hair from a suddenly solemn face, she said, 'I'm worried about Tom. He didn't turn up for work this morning and he isn't at home.'

Jo shifted painfully in the bed, flinching. How much did Danielle care for Tom? He had been in a vile mood that night; he'd said he had come to check that she was okay, but she hadn't let him in.

'What will the neighbours say?' she had joked, glancing down at her flannel nightdress. But he couldn't take a joke lately. Like when she'd joked about her intimate knowledge of her ironing customers' underwear.

With wild-eyed determination, he had come in anyway, his belligerent attitude warning her that he meant trouble. She was used to trouble. Soothe first, chat normally, but stay guarded. She even made him tea and supplied biscuits. Custard creams. No beer.

Jo suppressed a shudder, remembering his ranting and raving, equal to anything outside. But one thing she had learned in life: women could fight. Being raised to think they couldn't was their weakness.

Then the tree had crashed through her window.

'Tom will turn up like a bad penny,' she said at last, returning to the present.

Danielle was staring at her rather like a worried child and asking, in an awed voice, 'Jo, why are they keeping you in?'

There was a long silence. Jo pulled herself up so that her back was straight, drew her legs up, clasped her knees, and in a 'let's get this over with' rasp said, 'I've a lump in my breast, okay? They have to operate.' She pressed her lips together, shrugged.

Feeling as if cold hands had grabbed her throat, Danielle stared at her, shattered. She heard her own indrawn breath and knew her eyes were full of fear as she saw Jo, her mouth making ugly contortions, finally give in and cry, with the awkward, reluctant weeping of one who never did, her head bending to her knees.

You mustn't cry, Danielle warned her filled eyes, but immediately they overflowed and tears began to slide down her face, and no way could she stop them. She reached out and for a panic-stricken while they just held hands. When Jo finally spoke tearfully, it was of Paul.

'He's the light at the end of a tunnel. Being with him is like a sore that has healed, you know? And now, just when I have a chance of happiness, my body is taken over by an alien. It isn't fair, is it?' she pleaded, as if she needed an excuse to cry again. 'He's been through this before. I won't – ' she gasped, shaking her head, clutching Danielle's hand ' – put him through it again . . .'

'People get over cancer.' Danielle wept anew, thinking of Dottie.

Jo reached for a tissue. Danielle passed the box over and took one herself, dabbing her eyes, while Jo

365

sniffed and dragged in a loud breath like someone drowning.

After a bit, she said more calmly, 'Raine invited me to stay with them when . . . when I get out of here. Until my windows and so on are repaired. With all the problems they have too. Cherie,' she recalled, with a bit of a smile, 'would have said, "It's like something you read in the papers." But aren't they wonderful, the people here?'

She almost laughed at Danielle's am-I-hearing-things? expression and, in a stronger voice, explained, 'I said thank you, but no, to Raine. Think of it . . . a fat-free zone, squeaky clean fridge, fight the flab, germs dying of malnutrition. Not to mention,' she said with a wink, 'Tony taking "free-range" literally.'

Danielle pulled in a shaky breath, forcing the tears away. If Jo could cheer up, then so could she.

'No,' Jo went on, 'I'm staying with Dottie instead. She came to see me as soon as she heard.'

Danielle asked, 'Why didn't you tell me about . . .?'

'I believe in going into battle alone,' Jo pronounced, with the old toughness in her voice.

Anxious for her, Danielle said stoutly, 'Well, you can't. Who do you think you are? Boadicea? You're my friend, and I love you. And – ' she glanced up ' – if I'm not mistaken, here comes someone else who loves you.'

Danielle, wanting to surprise Jo, had spent the

afternoon driving to Ramsgate and back. Now she stood up. 'I'm going shopping, so I'll say cheerio until tomorrow.' Addressing Paul, who had yet to be told, she tried to keep the sadness from her voice as she said, 'I'll see you downstairs in an hour. By the way, Jo, shall I arrange repairs to your house?'

'Thanks, love, but it's being seen to. The neighbours,' she said proudly.

'I didn't know I was coming in today,' Jo finished gravely. 'The bed suddenly became free and the doctor called round to tell me, as the phone was off. He saw the tree,' she said, forcing a grin, 'and thought I wouldn't need the bed. No – only a scratch,' she added, seeing Paul's face, and decided to say nothing about Tom. For now.

Paul took her hand, played with the fingers for a moment, then looked up, moving his eyes over her face. 'I must go back home. The people looking after the farm have their own holidays booked, and there are my boys . . .'

When she didn't answer, he went on, 'You know I want you with me, don't you?'

Slowly, her hand crept away from his. 'Paul, my love, I can't.'

He looked mulish. 'Come out for a holiday first, and we'll go from there.'

Feeling tired, she let her head fall back against the pillow; a tender, 'let's pretend' look softened her face. 'Where will we go, Paul?' she asked dreamily.

He leaned forward, covering her hands with his big one. 'Wherever you want to go. And however far,' he said, with meaning. 'I'd like a couple of weeks in charge of you.' He smiled bleakly. 'And then we'll see.'

Her hand went up and her fingers slipped across his warm scalp, playing in his hair, touching his face. 'You're taking advantage of my weakness,' she murmured. 'You great Aussie, you.'

'Too right I am.'

She shook her head so vigorously that tears dropped onto her cheeks.'

Worried, he grabbed the lovely hand that caressed him and held it tightly wrapped in his own, as if it were a wounded bird trying to escape. 'If I get too bossy, just play that trumpet of yours. Turns me into a mouse.'

Tracing her face with loving but determined eyes, he said, 'I've told Danny I want to be kept in the picture when I've gone. You'll be okay.'

Her insides writhed like snakes. 'Will I?' she asked, as a child might.

'I'm telling ya.'

Their lips clung. She closed her eyes. When she opened them, he was pushing through the swing doors as if he had a grudge against them.

And her 'someone to walk in the sun with' was gone.

A strip of blue split the clouds apart, letting the sun streak across roofs, towers, factories and cranes, laying a glistening path on the tea-brown Thames and brushing the creamy walls of Greenwich Palace with gold.

Instead of driving straight back to Kent after seeing Paul and Anna off at Heathrow, Kingsley had wanted to show Danielle where he had grown up, and also check on his mother's house.

Unlocking two locks and disconnecting the alarm, Kingsley ushered her into a glowing red-walled hall and up a dark oak, red-carpeted staircase. The house was as tall and narrow as a dignified old lady, and smelled of furniture polish, wood, old books and leather.

In the first floor sitting room, she walked across to the high, wide windows, draped in kingfisher-blue and beige, and looked across at the sad park with its damaged trees. Turning to inspect the room, she saw that it was furnished with both beige leather settees and chintz ones, matching the curtains – like, she thought, his and hers.

While Kingsley checked the mail that the daily woman had placed on an antique desk Danielle wandered around humming, studying the antiques, the brass, the paintings, the photographs and books, telling herself that her edgy mood was caused by seeing Paul and Anna off.

Had Paul opened the parcel?

Danielle paused in front of a marble fireplace. An enormous gilt-framed mirror reflected her big, unstoppable smile which said, If only I could be watching Paul. What a surprise he'll get.

Only yesterday she had been up in the attic with Samantha and Timothy, whom she'd been looking after for the day. Iris and Ron were in Greece and Ron's parents were running the pub in their absence, with the help of Robin.

It had been raining, their planned zoo trip was off, and the men were due to come to repair the roof at any time. Tarpaulin covered one corner of the attic, but rain had got in anyway. It smelled of damp and dust, but it was spooky enough, however, to enthral two children.

It was Samantha who had spotted the old dolls' pram. 'Was this yours?'

'No,' Danielle had said, having to control a sudden stomach wrench. 'It must have belonged to my mother.'

Samantha had slipped searching hands inside the pram and pulled out not a doll, but a heavy cardboard box. There had been moans of disappointment when Danielle blew off the dust, removed the lid and exposed five leather diaries.

Later, downstairs, the children gone, she had pulled the settee up to the electric fire and read Grandy's account of the vineyard's beginning. Step by step. With sketches too. And, most excitingly, with black and white photographs of the slopes, of people working there. She had wondered if Francesca or Anna were among them, but Daniel had rarely taken photos, and those he had taken were seldom perfect. What a pity.

She had phoned Kingsley, who had returned to London and was taking Anna and Paul for a farewell dinner, and excitedly told him of her discovery. She'd warned him not to say anything and had gone to bed in the lonely four-poster, and read through most of the night.

At Heathrow, Paul had been just polite faraway smiles, until Danielle had handed him a parcel, saying, 'Promise you won't open it until you're on the plane.'

Forehead wrinkling, he'd promised, taking the parcel from her with his warm smile, those kind, honest eyes, that tough, nice face that she loved so much.

'I remember when I first left England,' Anna had said over the tinny commands from the loudspeaker. 'Flying over Tower Bridge, I was wondering if I would ever see it again.' Danielle had felt her spine tingle as Anna ended, 'And now I have. It's like completing a circle.'

Danielle's eyes filled now, as she recalled the cool, leathery feel of Paul's cheek beneath her lips, and Anna . . . Anna whose body had suddenly seemed not so sturdy as she had expected as Danielle had held her closely, and lovingly, as if she didn't want to let the surprised woman go.

They both heard it at the same time. Kingsley and Danielle's questioning eyes met across the room. It was the front door opening. Danielle's heart thumped. She had heard Kingsley talk about the burglary problems in London.

Kingsley shook his head and, bracing himself, slunk lion-like across the room as footsteps thudded on the stairs and the doorknob began to turn.

When the heavy door swung open, both Kingsley and Danielle cried out together, 'Piers!'

CHAPTER 26

He held a brandy glass in his hand and raised brows gave way to a charming, lightning smile. 'I wondered why the door wasn't locked.'

Kingsley took a step forward. Recognizing a threatening expression on his face, Danielle crossed the room to his side, steadying him with a touch on his arm.

Kingsley snapped the door closed and followed Piers into the room. 'What are you doing here?'

'End of holiday,' smiled Piers, dropping onto a leather settee. 'You have to come home, don't you?'

Turning those deep-set, hypnotic eyes upon Danielle, his voice was honeyed curiosity. 'This is a surprise, Nell!' He drew his eyes from her and set them on the surly-faced Kingsley. 'You've got to know my Nell, then?'

Seeing Kingsley make a move towards him, he smiled and said, 'Come on, Kingsley. We've both got too much dignity to grovel on the floor.' When Kingsley hesitated, Piers said, 'About your mother. Leave everything to me.'

373

He was so suave; Danielle couldn't believe her ears.

'Like Red, at the vineyard,' Kingsley sneered. 'The poor girl's expecting your baby.'

Piers swallowed some of his drink and clicked the glass down on a coffee-table. 'So I hear. Your mother told me. Maybe Red wanted one – women do. Then she probably panicked about the practicalities. After all, why should she write here, instead of to the office? I'll tell you why,' he said, with indignant eyes. 'She wanted Elizabeth to find the letter, wanted to break up my marriage. Hoping I'd go to her, I suppose.' He flashed a smile at Danielle, who had perched herself on another settee. 'You know the way women's minds work.'

Kingsley's voice was cutting. 'You're turning yourself into the victim.'

'Not at all.'

Kingsley would have none of it. 'I think you guessed Red might get troublesome and was getting serious, he sneered. 'I wondered why you agreed to the holiday.'

Piers looked down at his nails. 'Why should I look a gift horse in the mouth? Besides, Red *had* got a little heavy lately. The trouble is, some people live so passionately, one can tire of it.'

Kingsley saw the way Piers's eyes ran up and down Danielle and couldn't conceal his hatred. 'More than likely you wanted Danielle.'

Danielle felt her face flood an unbecoming red.

Unbelievably, she experienced that old sense of guilt – the sort of guilt it was possible to feel for no reason other than that someone was accusing you. And then she remembered a recent talk with Anna . . .

Kingsley's eyes glittered in a stony face. 'About the time Danny's grandfather died, I believe it was. But, being you, you were not sure about Danny's response, so you kept Red on a string as well. That's why you made up to Danny with the new contract.'

Piers replied in a voice of hurt sincerity. 'Nonsense. I was fond of Daniel.'

'So fond,' put in Kingsley, 'that you forced him to lower his prices.'

'The financial climate,' Piers murmured, pious-eyed. 'Even I must justify my actions to the company, my boy.'

Kingsley began to pace the room. 'This house is still in Mother's name. I want you out.'

Piers sighed. 'Not that simple, I'm afraid. Elizabeth left the ship in Italy with the intention of thinking things through – "finding her feet", whatever that means. Things are by no means final between us.' A silent 'so there' hovered in the brandy-scented air.

'One thing is,' Kingsley snapped. 'I'm leaving the firm and taking my money with me.'

Danielle looked at him in astonishment laced with worry. Whatever Kingsley did, she still needed Lamont's, and the old fear raised its head. *Keep on the right side of Piers.* 'Having a baby changes a woman, somehow,' she told him. 'Red wants security.' It was as if she was trying to draw feeling from him, but it didn't work.

Piers looked around like someone pleased to be home, leaned back and stretched his arms along the back of the settee, crossing his legs. His body, small and neat, still oozed vitality, she noticed. And he was impeccably dressed, as usual, in a grey suit and mauve shirt.

'Nell,' he said with a caressing smile, 'I loved your grandfather. He said I was like a son to him.'

Kingsley and Danielle looked at each other. They had asked themselves what attraction Daniel could have had for man-of-the-world Piers. A father-figure? Had he needed Daniel's admiration, even envy?

He clasped his hands together, leaning forward, eyes latching onto Danielle. Despite everything, she was drawn to him. Women were. She was surprised to recognize that, deep down, her admiration of Piers remained. Hero-worship? Maybe. Years ago. Did you really ever forget it?

'What about you, Nell? How are you keeping?' he asked smoothly. And then said, 'You have to understand something about me.'

She stared at him steadily. 'What's that, Piers?'

'Women have low self-esteem. I like to boost it for them. I only want to help them feel good, but they fall for me.' He spread his ringed hands. 'It isn't my fault.'

Oh, no, Piers, Danielle thought suddenly. *It's you*

376

who needs to be liked, who has low self-esteem. As she had, she realized. 'Piers,' she said, quite kindly, 'if your wife takes you back, it might be on her terms, not yours.'

A look of complete astonishment crossed his face, and he addressed Kingsley, who had stopped his pacing. 'Men aren't made to be faithful – are we?'

'You're right, of course.'

Astonished, Danielle could have hit him.

'Nature intended us to play the field,' Kingsley went on. 'Why not? We're not forced to marry.' Moving towards Piers, he leaned over him. 'Anyone who chooses commitment, however, should stick to it. Deceit is unforgivable.'

Danielle felt a deep-down hurt. But why should she? She didn't want marriage. Although she couldn't for the life of her remember why.

'Absolutely,' she told Kingsley. They would have a glorious affair. No complications, no strings. Her life was definitely the richer for him. So no problem.

'Look, Kingsley, this is between Piers and your mother. She might love him enough to forgive him,' Danielle said, thinking of Francesca.

Feeling Kingsley's eyes chilling her, she kept her face averted. 'You're a rotter, Piers,' she told him. He didn't seem to mind at all. She might have been praising him.

Kingsley walked away. 'Let's get out of here. I can't trust myself much longer.'

* * *

377

They were silent on the way back to Kent, busy with their own thoughts. Danielle could tell that Kingsley wasn't very pleased with her. What sort of man was he? Intelligent, sensitive, passionate about honesty and fairness, protective towards women and those weaker than himself, and yet sometimes she sensed that he was wanting and waiting for something more important to happen.

And me? she wondered. *What am I?*

'I think you're unforgiving, Danny,' Anna had told her startlingly.

It had been when she'd driven Paul back to Ramsgate. She and Anna had strolled along the heaving sea-front for a breath of air. To her surprise, Danielle had found herself talking about the rape.

'I mean,' Anna had gone on calmly, 'that you've so easily blamed yourself. You say that by not making a fuss after the attack, hiding what happened, you felt you condoned it. And that when the attack started, there was a moment when you thought of giving in to it – because of who he was – which again left feelings of guilt.

'My affair with your grandfather didn't start merely because of the trouble over the gossip,' she continued. 'I wanted him. I always had. Although I loved Hutch as well. I was also bored, and wanting to get back at life for throwing death, carnage and suffering at me before I was ready. I just used the gossip as an excuse.'

Danielle had felt the same easing of pressure that she'd felt after talking to Kingsley as Anna, looking out to sea instead of at her, had said, 'I've found that forgiving those you love is easy; forgiving yourself is harder. You must learn to blame others too,' she'd ended, thrusting her hands deeper into her pockets.

I do. Danielle realized now. *I do see myself differently.* She felt more tolerant, more understanding towards people. There was also a sense of self-confidence, as if she didn't have to worry too much about being liked any more; *she* could decide who was important to her. She also loved and was loved. It was brilliant. With a surge of warmth, she pressed one hand on Kingsley's thigh. He took his hand from the wheel for a moment, to press hers. Perhaps he had been thinking too.

He drove her back to her patched-up cottage and used the lateness of the hour as an excuse for staying the night. They made love slowly and beautifully, and she found herself, afterwards, clinging to him as if she was afraid to let him go.

Sliding little kisses over her soft, warm skin, which smelled of orange blossom, he found the feeling one of indescribable lightness. *To make love to the woman you love*, he decided, *goes beyond ecstasy*. And an inner voice kept saying that he had found something important, something he had been waiting for.

It was like discovering a secret.

* * *

Danielle had just arrived home from the hospital when the telephone rang.

'Paul?' she cried into the receiver. The excitement in her voice died. She took a deep breath and told him, 'It *is* cancer, Paul. That's the bad news.'

'And?'

Her voice only wobbled a little. 'Look, Paul, the good news is that it hasn't spread. They won't even remove the breast. They intend to do what they call a lumpectomy. It's just a small lump, Paul. Then she'll have radiotherapy. The doctor told me,' she said belligerently. 'Only one in ten need more surgery. See? Jo will be fine.'

CHAPTER 27

The air from the high downs blew softly down on the village of Hidden. People awoke to a cloudless day, with a calm drift of apologetic blue sky overhead.

Dottie opened her front door and clinked an empty bottle down outside, waving to Griff as he drove past. Her round pink head looked newly washed, her big eyes eager. She had a guest room to prepare, and she was among those planning to clean Red's house before Danielle picked her up from the hospital later and brought her home.

She glanced at the abandoned-looking house next door, remembering how Danielle had been frantic about Tom's disappearing. When Dottie had said she'd seen him load suitcases into his car the day after the storm and drive off, Danielle had just answered sadly, 'That's the way he came. He just walked in from nowhere.'

'You can see for miles.' Danielle pointed as they walked through Paradise. 'The fallen elms made a mess, though.'

'Sue your neighbour,' Kingsley suggested, half seriously. 'They're his elms.'

He stopped walking as she came to an abrupt halt and cried, 'Sue Old Hutchinson?'

'Your neighbour, I said.' With an exaggerated sigh, Kingsley added mournfully, 'Looks as if you and I are about to be involved in another fight.'

Puzzled, she said, 'Stop talking in riddles,' pretending annoyance.

He turned her to face him. 'My darling,' he said, kissing her after every word, 'I . . . am . . . the . . . owner.'

Her breath quickened, but she drew away from his intoxicating lips, laughing. 'Kingsley, stop kidding.'

'Darling, it's true. Since the day of the storm I've been negotiating with Hutchinson to buy his land this side of the lane. That's what the champagne was for. But I couldn't get him on the phone so I said nothing, in case it fell through.' He looked pleased with himself. 'Strange to think that if you hadn't introduced me to Old Hutch . . .'

Ashamed, remembering that night at the pub, Danielle admitted, 'I thought you would be bored with him.'

'Bored? Old Hutch was a bomber pilot – still has nightmares about it, and about the Japanese prison camp. Messed up his health a bit – he couldn't have kids.'

Her wide, brilliant eyes were fixed on him with compassion. 'No one knew that.'

'We'll be friends, I think. He's a perfectionist,' Kingsley explained. 'Can't move with the times, hates what's happening to the country he fought to save.'

She could have wept with joy. 'Then you . . .?'

'I have some ideas for the future, Danny.'

'Oh?'

Straight-faced, he said, 'I'd like to become your partner. I could supply a new bottling plant and machinery . . . we could come to an arrangement.'

'Oh! Great.' She turned away but he tugged her back gently.

'I won't be able to afford caviare in the future, but I can give you Paradise, if you'll let me.'

Recognizing the uncertainty in her face, he responded with a most un-Kingsley-like expression of pleading.

'What I'm trying to say is that I looked into your eyes and fell in love and I couldn't fight it. Big explosion. The only thing to do is to marry you and live with you in Paradise. What man can offer more? Come on, say yes.'

Her face crinkled with amusement. 'Kingsley, you're so bossy.' She deliberately kept him waiting.

He grasped her wrists, pulled her closer, glared sternly. 'Come on, young lady, say yes . . . or . . .'

She pulled away and tried to run. He caught her and swept her, laughing helplessly, down onto the grass. 'Stop it,' she screamed, as Amber barked, frantic to join in the fun, and in the distance the whistle of the London train shrieked across the valley. Laughing up into his face, feeling damp seep through to her spine, she cried breathlessly, 'You're a beast, but I love you . . .'

'Impetuous, just like your mother,' Francesca grumbled when she returned, smiling, from Italy to find herself faced with the prospect of helping to arrange a Christmas wedding.

Fortunately, Kingsley's mother, Elizabeth – smart, charming, tearful – proved not to be helpless at all, but highly competent, and she knew where to obtain the impossible.

'I get on with Elizabeth fine,' Danielle told Jane during a hurried dress-fitting. 'Kingsley was perfectly right, though, when he said that she "acts" her life.'

'What do you mean?' Jane asked, straightening the headdress and standing back as calmly as if she wasn't in the midst of her Christmas shopping.

'There was mother, businessman's wife, scorned woman, and now it's "spread my wings and fly" mode.' Danielle grinned, giving her friend a thank-you hug.

The day of the wedding was pale and calm, as the day after Boxing Day often is. At the church door, waves of scent from freesias, roses, old wood, polish and greenery came to meet Danielle. She was pleased that Hutch was wearing his medals, but his tie . . . She straightened it; he looked sheepish and her laugh rang out, making people inside look round.

As well as Kingsley's relatives and friends, including his lovely sister, Angie, there was Suzie, with attentive boyfriend in tow, and her parents, Annette, with Raine and Tony, and Dottie beneath an Ascot hat. There was Ron, Iris and children, and many others from Hidden.

Elizabeth came alone, blonde and glamorous in silver-grey with red accessories; she would stay overnight with Francesca, who was dressed in rich royal blue. She was a sympathetic ear with whom Elizabeth had discovered much in common and from whom she had learned to laugh.

Hearing Danielle's burst of rich laughter, Kingsley, resplendent in grey morning suit, turned and watched her coming towards him with a proud Hutch.

He felt a quiver of emotion at the vision she made. Her floor-length dress was simple, with no train, just a scooped neck and long sleeves. It was made from shimmering white-on-white metallic brocade, against which her dark hair and eyes flashed mischief as she joined him before the altar and recognized how nervous he was.

On her upswept hair rested a lace-edged short tulle veil; the headdress was decorated with red and white silk flowers and diamanté glittering like dewdrops. She carried two matching bouquets of white freesias and wine-red roses. One silk, to save, and one fresh.

She was followed past greenery-decked pews by Jane's children and Kingsley's niece and nephew: two page boys in green velvet, and two bridesmaids in red velvet with Alice bands and nosegays to match the bride's bouquet.

After the service, Jo passed the bride and bridesmaids white velvet capes for the chilly photo-taking.

'This time tomorrow,' she whispered to Danielle, 'you'll be on your way to Oz.' Her face was softer and thinner, but she looked well, if envious. At the end of January, when her treatment ended, she was to go to Australia too – just for a holiday . . . so she said.

The photos taken, the laughing crowd followed with curious eyes as the bride disappeared with her grandmother somewhere around the back of the church.

Luiza . . . Beloved wife of Claude Dubot . . . Mother of Danielle . . .

Danielle bent and placed her fresh bouquet on the grave. For a moment the two women stood silently, thinking of the young girl who had also been married in this church.

Francesca felt the pain move inside her and realized that grief didn't go, it just came to rest. She saw that she had held back from Danielle, unable to bear the thought of loving a child again, and turned to her, saying, 'Today is for happy things, but one day I want to talk to you about your mother.'

'You don't have to. I know.' Danielle looked into

386

her grandmother's face and was moved to see there things which had never been said. She suddenly felt the pulse of continuity, a surge of happiness and an acknowledgement of the long line of women to whom she was suddenly, heart-poundingly aware that she was joined. She understood, and put her arms around Francesca and held her, before they walked back.

Turning the corner, she saw the bridesmaids, the red velvet as hot as her singing blood. She felt a fierce need, and hurried towards Kingsley, who was waiting for her.

The cottage closed around them, smelling of oranges, cinnamon, spice and pine needles. They went straight to the kitchen. 'I'm exhausted,' Danielle said, resting against him, her dress rustling like whispers as his arms enfolded her. 'What a year it's been – especially autumn.'

'You shouldn't have spent so long fighting me, then,' he answered, a taunting smile crossing the planes and hollows of the face she loved.

'What will you remember most about today?' she asked.

'You coming towards me down the aisle,' he said seriously. 'I wondered if you were wearing your wellies.'

'Kingsley,' she said crossly, and pulled up her skirt, exposing knee-high soft white leather boots.

His expression became tender. 'You looked unforgettably, heart-stoppingly beautiful. And I shall remember your laughter, the way we danced, Jo playing her trumpet, you tucking into dinner.'

When she pretended to hit him, he kissed her mouth, her cheeks, her forehead, the gold band on her left hand, and she thought, *Just when I think I can't feel happier, more happiness bursts out*. She closed her eyes against the unbearable power of love to delight.

Then she felt herself lifted and seated on the table, and when she opened her eyes Kingsley was at the fridge taking out a bottle. She watched him with a lump in her throat, thinking, *This man's like hot chocolate sauce on ice-cream; he can move me without trying*. 'You're like a conjuror with your champagne bottles,' she teased as he took glasses from the cupboard.

'I feel like one,' he said, as the cork popped most satisfyingly and champagne flowed into the glasses. 'You've brought magic into my life, darling. The magic of love and laughter, my intoxicating lady.'

They raised glasses. 'To us,' she said softly. 'To the success of the vineyard, and next year's new vintage.'

Seeing his enquiring look, she dimpled and went on, 'I wanted to talk to you about a new vintage for next year . . .'

His face was a picture.

Kingsley drove, with careful consideration for his two passengers, through lanes sparsely lined with oaks.

'The contract with Lamont's – ' Danielle began.

'Signed, sealed and delivered,' he interrupted. 'I like the new buyer. Piers concentrates on the French side now.'

'Good.' Danielle looked contentedly from the window, seeing the sad gaps beneath a wider sky, but seeing also where new trees had been planted, since the storm just over a year ago – planted with the next generation in mind.

She felt an inner stirring, vividly aware of the life that was lying beneath the wintry earth, being kept safe and warm until it was ready to push out into the world.

Sweet scent rose from the two-day-old bundle in her arms. Her skin prickled with the pleasure of it, and as she gazed down at the tiny pink face of her child she felt her own completeness, a sense of cherishing, like the earth. She was a mother.

Kingsley had just collected them from the hospital to take them home. What a busy harvest it had been, she thought, warm with satisfaction. She smiled. Busy, but successful – particularly the new vintage . . . Melissa.

Kingsley reached out, his hand covering her hand, flat on Melissa's shawl, which Jo had sent from Australia. Feeling his warm skin, her heart contracted and tears filled her eyes. Tears of joy, that was.

But no time for tears, here was the vineyard. Kingsley slowed, glanced round and saw her face break into a lovely smile. The baby smiled too. Or was it wind?

They clattered across the vineyard entrance, beneath the sign, 'INTOXICATING LADY.' Woman of joy. Home.

THE EXCITING NEW NAME
IN WOMEN'S FICTION!

PLEASE HELP ME TO HELP YOU!

Dear *Scarlet* Reader,

As Editor of *Scarlet* Books I want to make sure that the
books I offer you every month are up to the high standards
Scarlet readers expect. And to do that I need to know a
little more about you and your reading likes and dislikes. So
please spare a few minutes to fill in the short questionnaire
on the following pages and send it to me. I'll send *you* a
surprise gift as a thank you!

Looking forward to hearing from you,

Sally Cooper

Editor-in-Chief, *Scarlet*

P.S. Only one offer per household

QUESTIONNAIRE

Please tick the appropriate boxes to indicate your answers

1 Where did you get this Scarlet title?

Bought in Supermarket ☐

Bought at W H Smith ☐

Bought at book exchange or second-hand shop ☐

Borrowed from a friend ☐

Other _____

2 Did you enjoy reading it?

A lot ☐   A little ☐   Not at all ☐

3 What did you particularly like about this book?

Believable characters ☐   Easy to read ☐

Good value for money ☐   Enjoyable locations ☐

Interesting story ☐   Modern setting ☐

Other _____

4 What did you particularly dislike about this book?

_____

5 Would you buy another Scarlet book?

Yes ☐   No ☐

6 What other kinds of book do you enjoy reading?

Horror ☐   Puzzle books ☐   Historical fiction ☐

General fiction ☐   Crime/Detective ☐   Cookery ☐

Other _____

7 Which magazines do you enjoy most?

Bella ☐   Best ☐   Woman's Weekly ☐

Woman and Home ☐   Hello ☐   Cosmopolitan ☐

Good Housekeeping ☐

Other _____

cont.

And now a little about you –

8 How old are you?

Under 25 ☐   25–34 ☐   35–44 ☐
45–54 ☐   55–64 ☐   over 65 ☐

9 What is your marital status?

Single ☐   Married/living with partner ☐
Widowed ☐   Separated/divorced ☐

10 What is your current occupation?

Employed full-time ☐   Employed part-time ☐
Student ☐   Housewife full-time ☐
Unemployed ☐   Retired ☐

11 Do you have children? If so, how many and how old are they?
_____
_____

12 What is your annual household income?

under £10,000 ☐   £10–20,000 ☐   £20–30,000 ☐
£30–40,000 ☐   over £40,000 ☐

Miss/Mrs/Ms _____
Address _____
_____
_____
_____

Thank you for completing this questionnaire. Now tear it out – put
it in an envelope and send it before 31 April, 1997, to:

Sally Cooper, Editor-in-Chief

SCARLET
FREEPOST LON 3335
LONDON W8 4BR
Please use block capitals for address.
No stamp is required!   INLAD/10/96

Scarlet titles coming next month:

THE JEWELLED WEB Maxine Barry
Reece Dexter only has to snap his fingers and women come running! Flame is the exception. She doesn't want Reece to give her his body – she wants him to give her a job!

SECRETS Angela Arney
Louise, Robert, Michael and Veronique all have something to hide. Only Daniel is innocent, though he is the one who binds them all together. It is Louise and Robert who must find the strength to break those invisible ties. Yet their freedom *and* their love carry a dangerous price . . .

THIS TIME FOREVER Vickie Moore
Jocelyn is puzzled: 'Who does Trevan think he is? He seems to know everything about me, yet I'm sure we've never met before . . . well, not in this lifetime. I can't believe he wishes me harm – but someone does! Can I afford to trust Trevan?'

THE SINS OF SARAH Anne Styles
But Sarah doesn't think she's committing any sins – all she's guilty of is wanting the man she loves to be happy. Nick wants to make Sarah happy too – but there's a problem! He already has a wife and Diana won't give him up at any cost. Throw in Nick's best friend Charles, who wants Sarah for himself and the scene is set for a red hot battle of the sexes!